Roger Taylor has also written the four Chronicles of Hawklan (*The Call of the Sword*, *The Fall of Fyorlund*, *The Waking of Orthlund* and *Into Narsindal*) and the epic fantasies *Dream Finder*, *Farnor*, *Valderen*, *Whistler*, *Ibryen*, *Arash-Felloren* and *Caddoran*, also available from Headline Feature.

The Return
Of The Sword

The Last Chronicle of Hawklan

Roger Taylor

HEADLINE
FEATURE

Copyright © 1999 Roger Taylor

The right of Roger Taylor to be identified as the Author of
the Work has been asserted by him in accordance with the
Copyright, Designs and Patents Act 1988.

First published in 1999
by HEADLINE BOOK PUBLISHING

First published in paperback in 2000
by HEADLINE BOOK PUBLISHING

10 9 8 7 6 5 4 3 2 1

ISBN 0 7472 5900 3

Typeset by
Letterpart Limited, Reigate, Surrey

Printed and bound in Great Britain by
Mackays of Chatham PLC, Chatham, Kent

HEADLINE BOOK PUBLISHING
A division of the Hodder Headline Group
338 Euston Road
London NW1 3BH

www.headline.co.uk
www.hodderheadline.com

The Return
Of The Sword

Chapter 1

The water had travelled a long and ancient journey, Andawyr mused as he dipped his hand into the stream and splashed his flushed face: mountain, sea and cloud, over and over, ever changing, ever the same. And though it shaped the land, it ran through his fingers unresisting. He gave a grunt of approval at the coolness it brought, then sat back, closed his eyes, raised his face towards the sun and took a long, slow breath. As it filled his lungs, the mountain air seemed to carry the sunlight through his entire frame. It mingled with the bubbling clatter of the stream and he felt the tension brought on by his too-rapid walking through the hills ease.

'Simple pleasures,' he said to the flickering shapes dancing behind his eyelids. 'Simple pleasures. Being here is enough.'

It was no new thought, but it had as much meaning for Andawyr now as whenever it had first come to him. Not that he could remember when that had been, he reflected. It was as though he had always known the truth of this. But that could not have been so, for such a realization could only be attained after a great struggle. Or could it? Children often had it – that sureness of touch in their lives. Eyes still closed, Andawyr's nose curled. He compromised. Perhaps the realization – the insight of the child – could only be *rediscovered* after a great struggle. Yes, that would do. He chuckled softly – he already knew that, too.

'You're rambling, you old fool,' he said into the warm air. He'd not come here to mull over his own long-learned ways of dealing with his life . . .

He opened his eyes and propped himself up on his elbows. 'Being here is enough,' he said again, testing the words thoughtfully. They were all that could be said, but necessarily they were only a pale reflection of a truth that was, perhaps, inexpressible.

Many things were thus, but not all were so easily accepted. Or so benign.

Andawyr scowled in self-reproach. What he *had* come here for was to do nothing, not continue along the ruts his mind had been ploughing relentlessly for . . .

How long?

Too long . . .

He rolled on to his stomach and, resting his head in his hands, stared down into a small sheltered pool at the edge of the stream. An oval, battered face stared up at him unsteadily through the gently wavering water. A blade of grass floated idly around the image, then drifted back out into the main flow. It was followed by a scuttling insect that left brief dimpled footprints in the water as it pursued some urgent errand.

Andawyr's image looked rueful.

Not the face of a great mage, he thought, tweaking his broken nose, then running a hand through his bushy grey hair, leaving it quite undisturbed. Such a person should have a conspicuous dignity. He should be patriarchal and stern, with a looming presence and a gaze to quell men.

Lips pursed, the image weighed this uncertainly.

Or perhaps he should be beatific, saintly; exuding the inner tranquillity that came from years of devoted study and a deep and profound understanding of the world. The image raised its eyebrows knowingly and, with a self-conscious cough, Andawyr withdrew from the debate.

If only, if only . . .

If only his years of study *had* brought him that kind of knowledge.

The image broke and scattered as Andawyr prodded it with a knowing finger. He supposed they had, in a way. He had learned what was of real value to him and that indeed gave him an ease of mind and a clearness of vision that many would envy. Nor was he disturbed by the fact that his endless searching for knowledge had brought with it a measure of the

2

vastness of what he did not know: it was, after all, in the nature of things that questions bred questions; children soon learned how to destroy their parents with the simple question, 'Why?'

It did not even disturb him too much that, at the limits of his understanding of the inner nature of things to which his searching and his conventional logic had led him, there was apparently paradox – and certainly bewilderment. That was simply another challenge to be met and wrestled with joyously.

Or would have been.

But now, a darkness was tingeing his discoveries: a darkness that possibly might not allow him the luxury of a scholar's leisurely debate; a darkness that could be growing even as he lay here and that might burst forth all too brutally out of the realms of academic consideration and into the world of ordinary men.

He swore softly and sat up. Just beyond the shoulder of the mountain he knew he would be able to see the maw of the great cave that was ostensibly the entrance to the Cadwanen – the Caves that were the home of the Order of the Cadwanol – the Order of which he was the leader – the Order charged originally by Ethriss with opposing Sumeral and, on His destruction, with seeking the knowledge that would guard the world against His coming again.

For come again He must, Ethriss had known, though of how he had known he never spoke. Suffice it that, although Sumeral took mortal form, He was no mere man. He had come in the wake of Ethriss and the other Guardians from the Great Searing that had been the beginning of all things and, with lesser figures that had emerged with Him, had set out to destroy the world that the Guardians had created. Though His mortal body had eventually been destroyed, after a long and terrible war, there were many places within the warp and weft of the fabric that formed all things where His dark and festering spirit could find sanctuary.

And come again He had, for the Cadwanol had failed in their charge as generations of stillness and peace had taken Sumeral from the minds of men and reduced Him to little

3

more than a myth, a tale to make children tingle. Yet some sixteen years or so ago He had again taken form in this world. Silently, His ancient fortress, Derras Ustramel, had been built again in the bleak, mist-shrouded land of Narsindal and it was as much good fortune as courage that had eventually brought Him down before – it was hoped – His corruption had spread too far out into the world. Nevertheless, much harm had been done and many had died.

No special reproach had been offered to the Cadwanol, for others had failed in their vigilance as well, and all had paid a bitter price. But a day did not pass without Andawyr thinking of the events of that time and, whenever a problem taxed him to the point of despair, it was these memories that returned to spur him on. For ignorance and the darkness of the mind and heart that it brought were the greatest of Sumeral's weapons and only knowledge could prevail against it.

But what was Andawyr to do now? At the very heart of his work lay a maelstrom of confusion and illogicality: conclusions which, though reached through modes of thought and observation that were unimpeachably correct, led to consequences that seemingly defied the reality of the world as ordinary men knew it. As *he* knew it, for pity's sake, he mused bleakly, throwing a small pebble into the stream and watching the ripples spread and disperse. No one would claim to understand what this strangeness truly meant, but until now it had not really mattered. It was sufficient that it was consistent and that it worked; it could be used to predict the outcome of experiments and went a considerable way towards explaining many once-mysterious things, not least the powers that the Cadwanwr themselves possessed. But what had once been a vague suspicion had grown of late. It could no longer be dismissed as an inadvertent aberration twisting and curling at the distant edges of their calculations. And it could no longer be ignored.

There was, beyond all doubt now, a flaw deep in the heart of the way the world was made. Something that, even within the terms of the strange nature of the Cadwanol's work, could not be. As an academic exercise it had been speculated upon from time to time for many years, but in the surge of learning

4

that had followed the war it had been confirmed and accepted. Fortunately, though disconcerting, it should have been of no pressing significance. It was something that would manifest itself in the world very rarely and then only fleetingly and in the smallest ways. But now there were signs that for some reason it was growing, signs that it might manifest itself much more conspicuously, that it might bring great destruction. And, too, there were indications that something else was pending, something rare and ominous, though whether the two happenings were associated could not be determined.

Andawyr growled irritably and threw another stone into the stream. He was ploughing the old ruts again after all. He had come out here to clear his mind, to rid himself of its interminable circling arguments and now he was teetering back to them again. He felt as though he were trapped in an hourglass, scrabbling to escape the sand being drawn inexorably to the centre.

Abruptly he let the thoughts go. He was sufficiently aware of his own way of thinking to know that he had reached a stage where pounding incessantly at the problem would merely drive any solution deeper into hiding. Like a shrewd predator, all he could do now was mentally wander off – do something else – anything else – knowing that eventually the prey would quietly reappear, probably quite unexpectedly. He smiled broadly and looked again at the stream. The sunlight sparkling off it in endlessly varying patterns and its clattering progress down the hillside were indeed an antidote for his preoccupations.

As he watched the stream, his gaze was drawn to a ripple piled up over a large stone. It wobbled from side to side as if trying to shake itself loose, but generally it maintained its shape and position. Tongue protruding, Andawyr tossed a pebble towards it. It missed. He closed one eye, put out his tongue a little further and tried again.

This time the pebble landed squarely in the ripple with a satisfying plop. As he had known it would, nothing happened apart from a few bubbles drifting to the surface and floating away. The ripple would only change if the rock that was causing it was moved, and then another would form elsewhere.

Until that happened, the ripple would remain unchanged while changing constantly – indeed, it could not exist without that change – who could shape *still* water thus? From his sunny vantage, Andawyr could see many such ripples in the stream. And other parts, which, though fed by smooth, untroubled waters, were turbulent and disordered, never settling into any single pattern.

This stream's cleverer than I am, he thought. *Without a moment's thought it knows how to form strange and complex shapes that I couldn't predict if I did calculations for a year.* The idea amused him. It was the kind of example he delighted in slapping his students' faces with when they became either too involved in something or too sure of themselves.

Forget it, he reminded himself, putting his hands behind his head and lying back on the soft turf. *Get on with your wandering.*

And wander he did. But though he assiduously avoided the concerns that had sent him out of the Cadwanen for relief, the thoughts that came to him were scarcely lighter as he found himself pondering the Second Coming of Sumeral and all the changes that had happened since His defeat.

The Orthlundyn, for example, were now like a people awakened from a long sleep. They travelled far and wide and had a seemingly insatiable thirst for knowledge. They had become very much the guiding spirit of the Congress that followed the war. The Fyordyn, by contrast, were less steady, less confident than they had been, cruelly hurt by the civil war that had followed Oklar's murder of their king and his near-success in seizing power for his Master. A lesser people might well have descended into a spiral of disintegration, but many things sustained them through their trials, not least their finally having come together to face Sumeral's terrible army in Narsindal. And, too, their almost universal affection for their queen, Sylvriss, and her son Rgoric, named after his ill-fated father. Less emotively, the Geadrol, the Queen's Council of Lords, the actual government of Fyorlund, also played no small part, with the stern, truth-searching discipline of its deliberations. The Riddinvolk, with their fanatical love of horses and riding, seemed to be the least changed, but even they felt the guilt of their failure to note the return of Sumeral.

And what about the Cadwanol? Andawyr thought as the old memories rehearsed themselves again. *Where do we stand in this great analysis?* Like all the others, wiser by far, he supposed. Wiser in their understanding of themselves, and certainly much wiser in the ways of the Power. First there had been the shock of accepting what had happened, and the ordeal of their frantic and futile search for Ethriss. Then, while his fellow Cadwanwr had stood on the battlefield, using their skills to protect the army against the Power used by Sumeral's lieutenants, His Uhriel, Andawyr himself had accompanied Hawklan and his companions to the very edge of Lake Kedrieth in the middle of which Derras Ustramel had arisen again. Despite the sunlight, Andawyr shivered at the memory of Sumeral's presence in that place. For him, it had hung in the air as tangibly as the mist that shrouded that awful lake.

Such experiences brought insights in a way that nothing else could and subsequently, in quieter times, many old, intractable problems had been solved with an almost embarrassing ease.

The memory of Hawklan brought the healer's words back to Andawyr. 'There is no healing for this, any more than there is truly for any hurt. Time will blur and cloud the memory of the pain, but your lives cannot be as they were. Make of it a learning and you will become whole, and worthy teachers of your children. Cherish it as a grievance and you will twist and turn through your lives seeing only your own needs, and burdening all around you.' Wise words, timely uttered. Words that had proved to be a healing salve for many.

'Always the healer, Hawklan,' Andawyr said quietly. 'Always the healer.' Hawklan's touch perhaps more than any other single thing had ensured that killing hands were stayed after the battle. Without doubt it had ensured that the three allied nations determined to learn what they could about the dank land of Narsindal and its wild inhabitants, the Mandrocs, rather than simply crushing them in a war of mindless vengeance.

Andawyr propped himself on his elbows again. It was a

long time since he had thought of Hawklan. He clicked his tongue. Everywhere he looked, paradoxes. In his studies, in the little rock-formed ripple where water flowed upwards, even in what he was doing now – ignoring his questions in order to answer them. And now, Hawklan. Healer, warrior, ancient prince – what was he? How had he come to this place, this time? Andawyr let the questions go. They might well be intriguing, but they were neither new nor answerable. What Hawklan knew of himself he had shared freely, and that had raised more questions than answers. Besides, attempting to analyse a friend thus was somehow distasteful. It had to be sufficient that he had been there. More than sufficient. For what would have happened without him? He had been pivotal. He it was who had appeared out of the mountains years before and opened Anderras Darion, Ethriss's great fortress in Orthlund. And it was the opened Anderras Darion that had disturbed Oklar into the precipitate and reckless actions that had led ultimately to the exposure and downfall of his Master. Hawklan's quiet words had affected so many decisions. And, in the end, it was Hawklan that Sumeral had sought, not to destroy but to turn to His cause.

Pivotal.

The word lodged in Andawyr's mind.

Why would he perceive Hawklan in this way? It was not something that Hawklan would have claimed for himself. He was always a reluctant leader. And, logically, Andawyr knew well enough that any one of the countless actions and decisions made by countless people at that time would have brought about a different outcome. It was rarely possible to trace a single line of cause and effect to any one happening, and least of all in the chaos of armed conflict, where chance ran amok. As someone had once said to him, 'Ifs were strewn everywhere.'

Andawyr's face became unexpectedly resolute. Ifs notwithstanding, Hawklan loomed large in all considerations of those events.

Pivotal.

Andawyr recognized that something in his wiser self was prompting him. The word 'paradox' had come too glibly: it

8

had misled him. The water over the rock was no paradox, he knew. It was simply the outcome of forces within and without the water which, at least in principle, were calculable. His relinquishing of fretful questions in order to reach an answer was a little more mysterious but was at least based on his own tested and quite consistent past observations. And Hawklan? Healer and warrior. No real paradox there – no inherent contradictions. It was the duty of those who had the ability to stand between the less fortunate and harm, be it with poultice or sword. Hawklan was simply skilled at both, and skilled far beyond the average. He was . . .

Pivotal.

The word lurched Andawyr back into his deeper concerns. Although clarity was being denied him in these he had throughout an impression of movement, of turning, of innumerable spiralling ways coming together, joining. He trusted such instincts. Many times, vague though they were, they had pointed him in a direction that had subsequently proved fruitful. They were not enough in themselves to lead to conclusions but he knew that nothing else would be forthcoming. His walk through the hills had been helpful after all.

He would follow this instinct. He would go and see Hawklan. At the least, it would be good to see him again. And good to see Anderras Darion again. The prospect brought him to his feet. There was a considerable interchange of visitors between Anderras Darion and the Cadwanol but somehow there had always been something here that needed his immediate attention whenever he had thought about returning there himself.

'Always allowing the urgent to displace the important,' he said, repeating the reproach he frequently gave to others. Well, not this time. This time he would go and see his old friend – and talk – and talk – and talk. And prowl around that marvellous old citadel.

He nodded to himself, well satisfied.

Then, suddenly, he started, alarmed.

Something had touched him – touched his mind. Something feather-light and cautious . . . but strange . . . and disturbingly feral.

There were no dangers around here, a faint breath of reason

9

whispered to him. Not of any kind. But his older senses gave the assurance the lie. And it was a very alert leader of the Cadwanol who slowly turned round to see silhouetted on an outcrop above him, and watching him intently, a large grey wolf.

Chapter 2

A ndawyr started violently and only just managed to prevent himself from lashing out with the Power to defend
himself. The effort left him breathing heavily but with icy
control.

Too quick, he reproached himself savagely. Too quick to
reach for the easy way. Angrily he forced reason to take
control of his fear. The animal had not menaced him, he told
himself slowly. Nor was it likely to. There was plenty of food
around here so it could not be hungry, and, besides, wolves
were far from being stupid: they rarely attacked people. It was
probably as startled as he was.

Nevertheless, it was still watching him and it had not
moved. And its hackles were raised, albeit only slightly.
Probably in response to his own initial reaction, Andawyr
decided uneasily. Either that, or it was sensing his own anger
at himself. He would have to take the initiative.

He made himself relax. Then, briefly, he met the animal's
gaze and turned his head away slowly and deliberately.

As he did so, he found himself looking into the eyes of
another wolf, crouching low on the ground barely five paces
from him. Despite the fact that he was counselling himself to
move carefully and slowly, Andawyr jumped back. The wolf
did not move.

'Very thoughtful, old man. A nice gesture.'

The voice filled Andawyr's head, further unbalancing him
and making him stagger backwards. Still the watching wolf
did not move, though it continued to stare at him fixedly.

'Don't be alarmed. We didn't mean to startle you.'

There was reassurance in the voice, but it resonated with

11

strange, wild overtones unlike anything Andawyr had ever heard. It took him a moment to realize that he was not actually hearing it, but that it was really in his mind. He had no time to ponder this discovery.

'But you're unusual, aren't you? We felt you some way away, and there was a control, a refinement, in your manner that's rare in humans. We thought we'd see who it was.'

Was there a hint of mockery in the words?

Andawyr's eyes narrowed suspiciously and he cast a quick glance at each of the wolves in turn. What was happening here? Carefully he tested his responses. It was deep in the nature of his training to see things as they were, not as others or perhaps his own errant mind might wish them to appear. It occurred to him that perhaps one of his colleagues was playing a joke on him – they were not above such antics from time to time when life in the Cadwanen became boring or fraught. But how could they be doing this? There was no hint of the Power being used and even he had not known where he was going to walk when he set out. It was not a prank. And he was definitely not hallucinating. The voice in his head was unequivocally real. It left him with a bizarre conclusion. Somehow these creatures were talking to him!

'Creatures, indeed. How churlish.'

Mockery, without a doubt.

'Wh – what are you? Who are you?' Andawyr stammered, his voice sounding harsh and awkward in his own ears.

Surprise washed over him. 'You *are* a Cadwanwr, aren't you?' came the reply, full of sudden realization and no small amount of excitement. 'Just wait there a moment.'

And, in a flurry of grey urgency, both wolves were gone. Andawyr shook his head as if to reassure himself that, notwithstanding his vaunted clarity of vision, what he had just seen and 'heard' had actually happened. It helped him that he could hear occasional barking in the distance.

Wolves that spoke directly into his mind! He wanted to dismiss the idea out of hand. But he had heard what he had heard. Then the memory of Hawklan returned to him again. Hawklan could both hear and speak to most animals. But then, Hawklan was Hawklan and an exception to many rules.

12

Andawyr gave a self-deprecating shrug. He was still who he was, leader of the Cadwanol, much respected counsellor to the wise, learned in the ways of the Power, blah blah – and he couldn't hear or speak to animals. Nor did he have any idea how Hawklan did, despite lengthy discussions with him.

All of which left him no alternative but to investigate the matter.

Straightening his scruffy grey robe Andawyr set off quickly up the steep grassy bank in the direction the second wolf had taken. Briefly it occurred to him that not being unreasonably afraid of wolves was one thing, chasing after them quite another, but the thought was lost amid the curiosity that was now powering him forward. He stood for a moment on the rocky outcrop that the first wolf had chosen for a vantage and looked down at where he had been sitting.

Crafty devils, he thought. Pack hunters. If they had been inclined to attack him he would have had precious little chance. Even though he had sensed the one above him, the other could have seized him effortlessly. *Tactics, tactics*, he mused. And where was your awareness, your sensitivity to the nuances of your surroundings, great leader? As scattered and disordered as that damned stream, he concluded, with a scowl. He stooped down to examine the immediate terrain.

A dark stain of dampness on a small stone showed that it had been turned over recently and some scuffing of the grass bounding the merging rock indicated which way the animals had gone. It was not up the hill but along the contour towards the shoulder of the mountain to his right. Andawyr sniffed thoughtfully and massaged his squat nose. A little caution managed to force its way into his thoughts again.

Chasing wolves across the mountain. *Is this a good idea?*

He rationalized. They'd run away once, they'd probably run away again. Besides, he had the Power if he really needed it, and he wasn't going to be taken unawares again. And why not go this way, anyway? It was still early, the weather promised to be marvellous for the rest of the day, and while this was not the way he had originally intended to go, it was as good as any. He quickly ran mentally through a route back to the Cadwanen to confirm to himself that he was not being recklessly impulsive, then he dismissed the caution completely and strode off towards the distant skyline.

Questions bubbled through him, matching the rhythm of his steps. These animals had touched his mind! How could that be? Had he suddenly, unknowingly acquired Hawklan's gift? Was it some inadvertent consequence of his latest studies into the Power? And if so, would there be others? And would they all be so benign? It was not a particularly welcome idea. He stopped the self-interrogation abruptly. It was going nowhere and it was serving only to cloud his thoughts. He went over what had happened again, capturing his reactions after the strange first touch he had felt. He had sensed nothing new in himself and such a change in his ability could not have happened without some prior indication even if it only became apparent in retrospect. And it did not. There was nothing. The contact – the voice – had come from outside. It had definitely been initiated by the wolves; or at least by one of them.

Then he remembered their parting remark. 'Just wait there a moment.'

What had that meant?

Perhaps they've gone for their friends, declared part of him malevolently. He ignored it. But he stopped. As he did so, he realized he had been walking too quickly, and that a combination of the sun and his excitement had conspired to make him feel unpleasantly warm.

Calm down, he instructed himself, flapping his robe indecorously. *They were running when they left, you're not going to catch them unless they've stopped.*

He took a drink from his water bottle. He had filled it at the stream and the water was still very cold.

'Simple pleasures,' he reminded himself with a chuckle as he wiped some across his face. 'But what about complicated ones – like talking wolves? Just as good!' And he was off again, his pace unchanged.

As he rounded the broad shoulder of the hill a cool breeze greeted him. It was drifting up from the shallow valley now spread out before him. Green and lush, the valley was hemmed protectively by rugged peaks and ridges, bright and clear in the sunlight. Cattle and sheep were reduced to tiny dots by the distance and the small orderliness of a few cultivated fields marked some of the farms that served the Cadwanen.

'You really should get out more often, Andawyr,' he said as he took in the sight.

Then he felt again the soft touch in his mind that had heralded the arrival of the wolves. There was the same wildness about it and, though it carried no menace, it nevertheless startled him. He looked around anxiously, screwing up his eyes to peer through the brightness. Almost immediately, he saw horses in the distance. Three riders and a pack horse, he judged after a moment.

And two dogs . . .?

But that question was set aside by others. From the direction the riders were moving in, it seemed they had dropped down from a col between two all-too-familiar peaks. Andawyr frowned. That meant that at some point they must have travelled along, or at least crossed, the bleak Pass of Elewart. The thought brought a momentary darkness to him. Even on a day like this, the Pass of Elewart was barren and inhospitable. The only people who travelled it were those who had to, and they were mainly Cadwanwr and others who studied the land of Narsindal to the north. And, whatever else they were, these riders did not look like Cadwanwr.

They were heading directly towards him, the dogs, if dogs they were, trotting ahead of them. He half expected to hear the wolf's voice ringing through his head again. But there was nothing other than the soft wind-carried sounds of the valley. He sat down on a rock and waited.

The two 'dogs' were indeed the wolves, he decided as the small group drew nearer. *Strange companions for men*, he thought. So wild, so shy, so free. Not tame, surely? No one could tame a wolf. Train it, perhaps, but never tame.

Other impressions began to displace his thoughts about the wolves and he leaned forward intently as if that might bring the riders closer. Then he stood up and began walking towards them, every now and then breaking into a little run. In their turn the riders urged their horses to the trot.

'It *is* you,' Andawyr cried out as they reined in alongside him. The first two riders dismounted excitedly. 'Yatsu, Jaldaric . . .' Andawyr extended his arms wide as if to encompass the entire group, horses and all. His face was beaming and his mouth for some time was shaping unvoiced greetings as he embraced each of the men in turn.

'It's so good to see you,' he managed eventually. 'Where have you been? What have you been doing? What . . .' His voice fell. 'What in the name of all that's merciful are you doing coming back this way? Did you come through the Pass?'

'We crossed it,' said the elder of the two. 'We didn't mean to return this way, but . . .' He stopped and shrugged. 'It's a long story.'

Andawyr made a gesture that indicated they had all the time in the world, then impatiently seized the hand of the second rider. Taller and younger than his companion, he had fair, curly hair and a round face which, for all it was weather-worn and had lines of strain about it beyond his age, had also an unexpected hint of innocence.

'Jaldaric. You're getting more like your father every day,' Andawyr advised him, as much for want of something to say as anything else. He clapped his hands excitedly, then put his arms around both of them again. Yatsu disentangled himself and indicated the third rider, who was still mounted.

Andawyr looked up at him. In age, he was perhaps between his two companions but, though he sat straight and upright, he had the aura of someone much older. And he had black-irised eyes that returned Andawyr's gaze disconcertingly.

'This is Antyr,' Yatsu said. 'A valued friend. He's been travelling with us and I think, like us, he'd value some simple hospitality – or at least a soft bed.'

Antyr dismounted and offered his hand to Andawyr who clasped it with both of his own. 'Welcome to Riddin, Antyr, valued friend of Yatsu and Jaldaric. Welcome to the Cadwanen and to whatever hospitality we can offer you.'

'Thank you,' Antyr replied, bowing slightly.

'Remarkable.' The voice filled Andawyr's head causing him to look around quickly. The two wolves moved to his side and began sniffing him energetically. He decided to stand very still for a little while. 'This is Tarrian and this is his brother, Grayle,' Antyr said, touching the heads of the wolves gently as if to restrain them. 'Grayle doesn't say much, and Tarrian usually says *too* much. They're my Earth Holders, my Companions. They're also very impolite,' he added sharply, looking down at them. The two wolves ignored the rebuke and continued sniffing.

Questions lit Andawyr's face.

'We'll explain it to you later,' Yatsu said, not without some amusement. 'Or at least Antyr will try. But I have to warn you, he's not managed to make either of us understand so far.'

The wolves finally retreated. Andawyr pointed at them and then lifted his hand to his head vaguely as he looked inquiringly at Antyr. 'Did one of them . . . actually say something?'

'Later,' Yatsu said. 'Antyr's story's even longer than our journey. But he's come with us because he needs help and guidance. He's special – very special – and he needs to speak to you – or Hawklan – or both.'

The village that served most of the daily needs of the Cadwanol nestled untidily against a sheer rock face. Some way to the west of it was a cave entrance which, together with the towering height of the cliff, made the buildings seem little more than children's toys.

'It's enormous,' Antyr said softly, as though the cavernous maw might echo his newcomer's amazement all over the village.

Andawyr momentarily preoccupied, started slightly, then gave the cave a perfunctory glance before agreeing offhandedly, 'Oh . . . yes.'

Antyr caught his companions exchanging a knowing glance.

'You've been telling me what an amazing place the Cadwanen is for long enough,' he said, with a note of challenge in his voice which told Andawyr that, although Antyr was the stranger, the three men were close friends.

'It is, it is,' Yatsu and Jaldaric said, almost simultaneously and with heavy innocence.

'They're having a small joke at your expense,' Andawyr intruded, adding tartly, 'too long alone in the mountains, probably,' before speaking again to Antyr. 'That's not the real entrance to the caves. We just let people – travellers, passing students – think it is.' He wrinkled his nose unhappily. 'We were founded in bad times and secrecy is still important to certain aspects of our work. Regretfully.'

As they drew nearer, Antyr's attention moved from the imposing presence of the cave to the houses and cottages that were scattered seemingly almost at random over the tumbled and rocky terrain that marked the foot of the cliff. Steep pitched roofs, intricately patterned with green and blue slates, swept down almost to ground level.

As they rode along the winding main street, Andawyr acknowledged the occasional greeting but although Tarrian and Grayle attracted some long glances, it seemed to Antyr that he and his companions were being wilfully ignored. Eventually they arrived at a building set hard against the cliff face. A couple of villagers appeared from somewhere and dragged open two large wooden doors. Andawyr nodded his thanks and motioned the others to follow him as he dismounted and walked into the building.

It took Antyr's eyes a few moments to adjust to the comparative darkness as the doors closed behind them, but the characteristic smell, both fresh and musty, told him that it was a barn. It was tall and airy with a depleted haystack occupying one side while down the other were stalls for horses, and a hanging clutter of rakes, pitchforks and other farming paraphernalia.

As the four men unsaddled and tended their horses, Tarrian and Grayle scurried about, examining the place minutely.

'Well, well.' Tarrian's voice filled Antyr's mind. It had that emphasis which told him the wolf was speaking to him alone. 'This *is* an unusual place.'

'It looks like any other barn to me,' Antyr remarked, in like vein. 'And if Andawyr can really hear you, you can speak to him as well if you wish.'

'No, not yet. It unsettles him,' Tarrian replied. 'He's unusual, as well. I think we're going to like it here. It has a distinctly civilized feel to it.'

'Fit place for wolves, eh?'

There was a thoughtful pause. 'I'm not sure I'd go that far, but it's got promise.'

'What's he saying?' Yatsu asked casually, giving Tarrian a suspicious look.

'Are you *sure* you can't hear him?' Antyr said.

'Not a word,' Yatsu replied. 'But I can tell when the two of you are talking.'

It was not the first time they had had this exchange. Antyr gave an apologetic shrug. 'He was just saying this is an interesting place, though what he sees special about an ordinary barn he hasn't bothered to let me know yet.'

Yatsu laughed softly and cast an appreciative glance at the wolf.

'Come on,' Andawyr called out, indicating a small battered door at the back of the barn. 'Cover your eyes,' he said to Antyr. 'We never seem to get round to adjusting the lights and you might have difficulty in seeing. Just walk straight ahead.'

Before Antyr could speak, Andawyr had opened the door and was ushering him forward vigorously. Antyr gasped as a brilliant light flooded into the barn. He had no time to hesitate, however, as Andawyr's firm grip carried him forward a few paces and through a second door. A soft ringing tone greeted him as he emerged, blinking, into a long corridor.

A tall figure rose from a chair to fill his momentarily blurred vision, then it was waving its arms in confusion as Tarrian and Grayle pushed past it and ran off down the corridor.

Antyr shouted after them but to no avail.

'I'm so sorry,' he said, turning to Andawyr. 'I don't know what . . .'

'It's all right,' Andawyr replied reassuringly, though he was staring anxiously after the fleeing animals. 'At least, I think it's all right. They're safe aren't they?'

'Oh yes, *they*'re safe,' Antyr replied. 'But anyone who interferes with them isn't.' He reached out to touch Tarrian's mind, but found only uncontrollable animal curiosity ploughing through innumerable new sensations of sight and scent and hearing. 'They'll be all right,' he added unconvincingly.

'What in the name of Ethriss is going on, Andawyr?' came an angry voice. It belonged to the figure that had risen to meet them as they entered the corridor. Tall and heavily built, he loomed over Andawyr but a hesitant beard fringing his chin accentuated rather than disguised his comparative youth and this, coupled with his nervous manner, served to make him the more subservient figure.

'Ar-Billan, we have guests,' Andawyr said, taking his arm and giving it a discreet but firm shake. The big man was still waving his hands vaguely in the direction the wolves had taken. He gave an incongruous little cry as the two animals abruptly reappeared and hurtled past the watching group in the opposite direction, very much to the amusement of Yatsu and Jaldaric and the discomfiture of Antyr.

'I'm afraid they're just excited,' he said apologetically to Andawyr. He made another attempt to reach Tarrian but again without success.

Andawyr, however, seemed more concerned about his bewildered colleague. 'Guests, Ar-Billan,' he was saying, insistently. 'Guests. Commander Yatsu and Captain Jaldaric of Queen Sylvriss's Goraidin, and their companion Antyr. They've travelled a *long* way and I'm sure they'd all value a bath and a meal before they tell us what they've been doing.' As Andawyr spoke, Ar-Billan's eyes widened and his mouth began to drop open.

'Yatsu and Jaldaric,' he mouthed. 'I've heard about you, of course, but I never thought I'd meet you. It's a great honour.' He shuffled awkwardly, then gave the two men a nervous bow, followed by one to Antyr as a flustered afterthought.

'Bath, food!' Andawyr urged, prompting him to movement with a nudge of his elbow and a significant look. 'We'll deal with the . . . dogs – don't worry.'

He gave a small sigh as the big man lumbered off. 'Nice lad,' he said, shaking his head. 'And very bright, though he does stand in his own light at times.'

Tarrian and Grayle returned, to Antyr's conspicuous relief. They were panting noisily and both of them jumped up to plant their forepaws on Antyr's chest. They were big animals and he staggered under the impact, making them drop to the

20

floor. 'What's got into you two?' he said, laughing. 'You're behaving like pups.'

'This place is amazing.' Grayle's voice burst into both Antyr's and Andawyr's minds, overwhelming his brother's for once. 'Full of the Song and all manner of learning.'

The images that flooded into Andawyr's mind had meaning far beyond the words he was hearing. 'And you're filling me with more and more questions, each time you . . . speak,' he said out loud.

'They're speaking to you?' Yatsu asked in some surprise. He flicked a thumb towards Antyr. 'You can hear them like he does?'

'It would seem so,' Andawyr replied. 'But don't ask me why or how.' He made a dismissive gesture, placed his hands against his temples and announced forcefully, 'One thing at a time. I went out today to have a quiet think about some difficult questions. Now I've got two hundred more, and growing. Let's get you all fed and watered, then we can talk.' He looked at Yatsu and Jaldaric. 'It really is good to see you again. I'm sure you've some rare tales to tell. Where are you going first, Vakloss or Anderras Darion?'

'I'm not sure. I thought we'd stay here and rest a little while,' Yatsu replied pointedly. 'I think *you* need to talk to Antyr first and then advise us. It may be best if he stays here. He's at least as many questions for you as you have for him. And he has a gift – a skill – that you need to know about. Something far more than just being able to talk to these two.'

Andawyr turned to Antyr and smiled reassuringly. 'Yatsu and Jaldaric wouldn't bring you here on any slight matter,' he said. 'If we can help you, we will.'

A little later, bathed and fed, they were sitting in a bright and spacious room. In common with most of the rooms in the Cadwanen it was simple in style and plainly decorated. Along one side, a large window opened on to a sunlit mountain vista.

'We're very high,' Antyr remarked as Andawyr offered him one of the several chairs that were scattered about the room and then dropped heavily into one himself. Like the room, the woodwork of the chairs was plain and undecorated, but the

21

upholstery was ornately embroidered. Antyr found his unexpectedly comfortable and almost immediately felt several months of harsh travelling beginning to ease from him. Tarrian and Grayle flopped down noisily at his feet and apparently went to sleep.

'Actually, we're quite deep here,' Andawyr said.

'Deep?' Antyr's arm encompassed the view questioningly.

Andawyr cast a glance at Yatsu and Jaldaric. 'I don't think they have them where Antyr comes from,' Yatsu said casually. 'Though to be honest we were occupied with other matters than architecture for most of the time we were there.'

Andawyr looked mildly surprised. 'They're mirror stones, Antyr. They bring the outside world into the depths for us. We might live underground, but we're not moles, we need the daylight.'

Antyr looked at him suspiciously, then eyed Yatsu and Jaldaric as if suspecting some elaborate jest.

Andawyr laughed. 'I can see you've been too long in bad company,' he said. 'I can't do it from down here, but, trust me, that view can be changed. We tend to call them windows, but they're not. Not as you'd think of them, anyway. What you can see is coming from high above us.'

Antyr held out his hand. 'I can feel the warmth of the sun.'

Andawyr went over to the window and touched a small panel to one side of it. The soft mountain noises of distant streams, high-peaked winds and low-valleyed breezes drifted into the room. Andawyr touched the panel again and they were gone.

'We can carry many things to where we want them,' he said. Antyr's eyes were full of wonder. 'Nothing magical,' Andawyr went on, returning to his chair. 'Just clear thinking, a little ingenuity, and some determination. I'll show you how they work before you go, if you're interested.'

He clapped his hands. 'Now, tell me what you've all been up to.'

Chapter 3

After Sumeral's second defeat, a great Congress was held. Fyordyn, Orthlundyn, Riddinvolk, the Cadwanol, all debated what had happened and the reasons for it, to determine what should be done to ensure that such a horror might be avoided in the future. The Congress's doors were barred to no one.

There were many bitter cries for vengeance, for much hurt had been done. Wiser counsels eventually prevailed, however, for the victory had been complete: Sumeral and His Uhriel had been destroyed and His army utterly routed. And, too, it was acknowledged that He had returned because there had been neglect. The wisdom enshrined in the various traditions of the different peoples had been long buried under the mere forms of those traditions and their true purpose thus lost.

It was decided, though far from unanimously, that the Mandrocs, the wild and barbarous natives of Narsindal who had formed the bulk of His army and who had suffered grievously in the final battle, were as much the victims of Sumeral as the allies themselves and that nothing was to be gained save further, enduring hatred by seeking to punish them. Thus while Narsindalvak, the tower fortress originally dedicated to the Watch, the observing of Narsindal, was reinvested by the Fyordyn High Guard, it became also a centre of learning about that blighted land and all who lived in it.

The Fyordyn were left with the burden of dealing with those of their own who had sided with Sumeral. There had been many such, drawn to Him through the long and insidious treachery of the Uhriel, Oklar, who, bearing the name Dan-Tor, had come to them initially as physician and seeming saviour to their ailing king, Rgoric. And there were many degrees of guilt to be determined, ranging from refusal to acknowledge what was happening when the truth became apparent, to acquiescence under varying degrees of duress, to enthusiastic and active support. Fortunately, Dan-Tor's quiet depredation of their land had not totally destroyed either the Fyordyn's innate tolerance or their deep sense of justice and though, on his passing, there was much confusion and bitterness, their judicial institutions repaired themselves remarkably quickly.

It was the Fyordyn way to demand an open Accounting of any who were accused of offending, and they were always painstaking affairs, intended not only to find the truth but also a punishment that would both seek to repair any injury and guide the offender away from any future offence. For many they proved to be a benign and healing forum.

However, there were those whose participation had been both wilful and brutal and most of these had fled when Sumeral's army was broken. It was mooted by some of the Fyordyn that, notwithstanding the guilt of these people, they should be allowed to go their ways; that relentlessly hunting them across foreign lands had an aura of vindictiveness over a defeated enemy which could only demean and degrade the hunters. But, again, wiser counsels prevailed. Lord Eldric, Jaldaric's father, spoke in the Geadrol. 'The desire for vengeance is indeed a dark and corrosive emotion which ultimately consumes those who nurture it. But so is neglect and, as a people, we have a duty not only to ourselves but to our children and their children's children. And as a strong and fortunate people, we have a duty to those who are less strong and less fortunate. It is one that cannot be avoided if we are to live at ease with ourselves. We must say to those who choose to yield to the darker forces in their nature that the consequences of such conduct are inexorable. They, *and any who would follow in their steps*, must know that neither time, distance, nor the strength of princes shall protect them from accounting for their deeds.'

Thus it was that the likes of Yatsu and Jaldaric began their journeying. It was their charge not to deliver justice but to discover the fate of those who had fled so that the Geadrol might determine what should be done. To this charge was also added the obligation to learn about other peoples. For just as it was realized that neglect of history had helped to bring about the war, so it was realized that neglect of lands beyond their own might also have been an error. While Sumeral and His Army had been contained and defeated in Narsindal, Dan-Tor had been many years in Fyorlund and it was not known how far Sumeral's influence had spread out into the world. Many others as well as the Fyordyn undertook this last commission, not least the Orthlundyn and the Cadwanol.

Andawyr spoke again before either Yatsu or Jaldaric could begin their tale.

'Did you find the ones you were looking for?' he asked impatiently.

Yatsu did not answer immediately. Then, obviously moved, he said, 'Yes,' very quietly. 'In Antyr's land. They were much changed. True servants to an honourable lord. Many had died for him. Many died while we were fighting by their side. We shall give an Accounting for them when we return to Vakloss. Nothing is to be served by seeking anything further of them.'

'An unexpected development for you,' Andawyr said, responding to Yatsu's subdued tone.

'Indeed,' Yatsu replied. 'But a welcome one. The travelling wasn't easy and it would have been even harder if we'd been pursuing a trail of pain and destruction brought by our own people to strange lands.'

Andawyr looked at him shrewdly. 'But there's something else, isn't there? You don't have the look of a man bringing wholly good news.'

Yatsu's brow furrowed a little and he pushed himself back into his chair. 'We've no definite bad news as such,' he said. 'But things happened over there I think you need to know about. It's just that I'm a little uncertain where to start.'

Andawyr raised his eyebrows theatrically. 'So much for the vaunted Goraidin skill in gathering and reporting information,' he jibed. 'Come on, Yatsu, since when have you been lost for words? Do what I do when I've an intractable problem

– when you don't know where to start, start.'

Ar-Billan entered the room, rescuing Yatsu. He was accompanied by a stern-looking individual, tall and very straight
with a high domed forehead and a long narrow face. Tarrian
opened one eye to watch him as he approached, but did not
otherwise move.

Yatsu and Jaldaric, however, stood up and greeted the man
warmly. His stern expression was dispelled by a bright and
welcoming smile as he returned their greetings.

'Excellent,' Andawyr said when they had finished. 'I'm
glad you're here, Oslang. I thought you wouldn't be back for a
few days yet.' He introduced the newcomer to Antyr as the
Under Leader of the Cadwanol, then motioned him to sit
down with them.

Tarrian closed his eye and gave a soft rumbling sigh as he
rolled onto one side. 'He's all right,' came his judgement to
Antyr. Grayle's unspoken agreement followed.

Oslang took a chair that Ar-Billan was offering with a nod
of thanks. 'Fine . . . dogs . . . you have, Antyr.'

'On the other hand . . .' Tarrian muttered.

'They *are* wolves,' Antyr confirmed to the uncertain
Oslang. 'And they're not mine, they simply travel with me.
They're my friends.' A brief shake of his head arrested
Oslang's hand which was descending tentatively with a view
to stroking the apparently sleeping Tarrian. He withdrew it
nervously. 'It's rather complicated,' Antyr added unhelpfully,
a remark that prompted knowing looks from both Yatsu and
Jaldaric.

'Join us, please, Ar-Billan,' Andawyr said to the considerable surprise of the young Cadwanwr who was quietly retreating from the room. He glanced from side to side hesitantly, as
if the remark might have been addressed to someone else,
before responding to Andawyr's beckoning hand and position-
ing himself on the periphery of the group.

'Continue, Yatsu,' Andawyr said briskly.

Yatsu's telling proved to be equally brisk. His journeying
with Jaldaric in search of those that the Geadrol had named
had taken them south through Riddin and thence, perilously,
across the sea, in the company of one of the few traders who

26

were prepared to risk encountering the Morlider in their fast, marauding ships. A further journey northwards overland had eventually brought them to Antyr's land.

'A strange place. Full of many wonderful things and splendid people, but . . .' He hesitated, searching for a word. Then he gave Antyr an apologetic look. 'No offence to you, Antyr, but they're wilder, less civilized than we are in many ways. More quarrelsome, more easily inclined to violence, more apt to deal out summary justice than true Law.'

'Like the Fyordyn were not all that many generations ago?' Andawyr intervened acidly in defence of their unprotesting guest.

The remark stopped Yatsu and he was thoughtfully silent for a moment before conceding, quite genuinely, 'Yes, you're right. Interesting. That hadn't occurred to me.'

Andawyr gave him a suspicious look but Yatsu continued unabashed.

There was no single government in the land, just self-governing cities and towns that continually vied for power and advantage over one another. Treaties were made and broken with despairing regularity, alliances shifted similarly, treachery abounded, and assassinations and minor wars were not uncommon. Yet, throughout, the various peoples managed to live and, on the whole, improve their lives despite the antics of their leaders. Gradually, war was beginning to be seen as a poor substitute for reasoned debate.

Although the shifting web of loyalties and obligations that plagued the land was tangled beyond measure, there were two cities whose influence tended to dominate affairs: Bethlar, with its disciplined and spartan people, locked into their stern traditions and their gloomy, harsh religion, and Serenstad, a vigorous trading city, bustling and hectic under the relatively relaxed rule of Duke Ibris. At the time of Yatsu's and Jaldaric's arrival events had been set in train that were threatening to bring these two into direct and violent conflict. A war the like of which had not been known for a long time seemed imminent and promised grim consequences for an equally long time to follow, whoever was deemed the victor. Yet, even as this developed, an even darker threat was looming over the two unknowing antagonists and their allies.

It came from the many tribes who roamed the vast and barren plains beyond the mountains to the north. They had been united under a powerful and ruthless leader, Ivaroth, and, fired with his ambition, were preparing to sweep down through the mountains and seize what their legends told them was their old land when the two main protagonists had fought themselves to exhaustion. As they surely would.

'It gets difficult here,' Yatsu told his now enthralled audience. 'There was more to Ivaroth than at first appeared. He had a companion: a man, apparently blind, yet who could see, and who had . . . powers that you need to know about. We only learned of him after everything was over, from Antyr who . . . met him and . . . dealt with him. I think perhaps he should tell you the rest.'

As all eyes turned towards him, Antyr shuffled awkwardly in his chair. Throughout the long journey from his homeland with Yatsu and Jaldaric he had pondered what had happened to him in the weeks before the terrible battle that had destroyed Ivaroth and the blind man and sent the tribesmen, broken and bewildered, back to their old nomadic life.

Though he had prevailed in a vital and mysterious part of that battle, and though he was many times his former self, the man who had spent years slowing sinking into bitterness and drunkenness, he knew only that he felt himself inadequate to deal with the skills that he now possessed. He had left his homeland because he knew that no help would be available to him there, though he had followed little more than instinct – and, he suspected, the silent urging of Tarrian and Grayle – when he had accepted Yatsu's and Jaldaric's offer to take him to the man Hawklan, a healer, who 'might be able to help.' True, at no time since had he been seriously inclined to regret this decision, and during the journey he had learned many things: about his companions, about Hawklan and the Cadwanol and the Second Coming of Sumeral and, not least, yet more about himself. But now he was here, he was at a loss to know where to start his tale, rather like Yatsu just before him. Two other things were not helping him. One was Yatsu's own clear, orderly and uncluttered telling, the other was an element of malicious chuckling coming from Tarrian at his pending discomfiture. He did his best to ignore this as he cleared his throat and turned stiffly towards Andawyr.

'In my land, I'm what's known as a Dream Finder. I enter into the dreams of people and, as circumstances dictate, comfort them, assure them, advise them, whatever's needed.' Immediately he saw questions in Andawyr's eyes but the Cadwanwr remained silent. 'How I do this, I don't know. I'm afraid that's a phrase I have to use a great deal. How any of us do it, I don't know, though it's not an uncommon skill in our land.' He glanced at Yatsu and Jaldaric, 'It's a born skill of some kind, but I understand it's not something you're familiar with here.'

Andawyr still made no comment, other than to give him a nod of encouragement.

'Tarrian and Grayle here are my Companions, my Earth Holders.' He reached down and touched the two animals gently. Tarrian's ear flicked irritably. 'They guide me through the dreams and protect me in some way, though again I don't know how or from what. It's something deep in their wolf natures, too deep for them to explain to me even if they felt inclined to.' He grimaced. 'I'm sorry if this is vague, I'm not used to talking about what I do.'

'It's not vague,' Andawyr said. 'It's strange, that's all. Very strange, I'll admit. But we'll have plenty of time to go into details, if you're willing and if you want to stay. There's a vast store of knowledge here and at Anderras Darion. It could well be there's something about your particular talent just waiting to be found. And if there isn't, we'll learn what we can from you and then there will be. You're doing fine. I'm intrigued, to say the least. Please carry on.' Before Antyr could continue, however, a thought struck Andawyr and, leaning forward, he put a firm hand on Antyr's arm. 'Let me state the obvious, just to ease your mind. Should you have any doubts about speaking to us like this, rest assured that the very fact that Yatsu and Jaldaric have brought you here means we know you have a true need and that you're neither fraud, madman nor charlatan. And that they've called you a valued friend says much more.'

'He's more than just a Dream Finder,' Jaldaric intervened. 'He's a brave man. Someone with considerable resource.' Yatsu nodded in agreement.

Seeing his guest's further embarrassment at this unexpected praise, Andawyr again came to his aid. 'He'd have to be, to put up with you two for any length of time.' Then, with exaggerated sternness, 'And let's have no more interruptions, young Jaldaric. Have you forgotten the Fyordyn ways of Accounting already?' He motioned Antyr to continue.

Encouraged, the Dream Finder plunged on. 'My father – my late father – had been Duke Ibris's Dream Finder once, long ago, and when the Duke began having strange dreams he asked me for help. What I – we – discovered, eventually, was that Ivaroth was himself a Dream Finder, albeit an untrained one, and that he was using his skill to assail the Duke and also the leaders of Bethlar to foment the war between the two cities for his own ends as Yatsu told you. What we also discovered was that his Earth Holder was not an animal, but a man. I didn't even think such a thing was possible. And he was terrifying.' He shuddered as old memories flooded over him. 'He was what we could call a Mynedarion – a person who has the ability to affect physical things, to change them, with a mere gesture – or with a thought – I don't know.' He gesticulated unhappily. 'You must understand that as far as I was concerned – as far as any Dream Finder, any rational person, was concerned – Mynedarion were mythical – part of a quaint tale come down through the ages about how the world was made – not real flesh and blood.' Antyr made a slashing action with his hand to cut through his own confusion. 'But he *was* real and he *did* have powers of some kind. Powers that defied logic but that he used to sustain Ivaroth as ruler of the tribes and that he didn't hesitate to use against either people or things as the whim took him. He was dementedly evil.'

His manner and sudden passion brought a deep stillness into the room and when he spoke again his voice was soft, as though the words themselves might bring some retribution in their wake. He continued speaking directly to Andawyr.

'When we enter a dream, there is a place we know as the

Nexus: a place into which our client's many dreams, past and present, leak, as it were. From there, our Earth Holder, our Companion, guides us to and through the Portal of the dream where our client's need lies. In the dream, we become the dreamer and can sustain or comfort him as needed and quite often learn enough to be of further help on waking. This is what all of us can do. It's our gift and, given the gift and a suitable Companion, there's neither difficulty nor mystery in the *use* of it.'

His black-eyed gaze held Andawyr.

'As you might appreciate, much thought has been given over the years by learned men as to how such a gift could come about – why such a thing should be possible. And while much has been written and conjectured, there's more speculation than hard fact, and the whole business is mingled with storytelling and legend. However, there's a dominant belief that some – we would call them Masters – can move through what are known as Gateways in the dreams themselves and into the Antechambers of the Threshold to the Great Dream itself.'

His hesitation returned.

'You were there, man, tell them! They need to know.' Tarrian's command jolted him but he still found it difficult to continue.

'The Antechambers are . . . other worlds. Places as real and as solid as where we are now, but . . . not here.'

Oslang shifted uncomfortably in his chair. Andawyr's hand came out to still him and his look urged Antyr on.

'The Great Dream itself is the place – though place is hardly an appropriate word – in which all things and all times exist. It's believed that, just as dreams leak into the confusion we call the Nexus, so these worlds are but echoes of the Great Dream.' He shrugged. 'It's said that only the most gifted can find the Inner Portals that lead to the Great Dream. Such individuals are known as Adepts. More fully, Adepts of the White Way. Tradition tells us that there were few Masters and even fewer Adepts, and all of them lived in times long gone. Times at the beginning of time when we were known as Dream Warriors, and charged by Mara Vestriss, the creator of

31

all things, with the duty of protecting Mynedarion – those in whom he had vested his own power – from Marastrumel, the Evil Weaver, whom he had created to be his companion and who turned against him.' He released Andawyr and looked round at the others.

'I did tell you it was difficult,' Yatsu said into the ensuing silence.

Andawyr nodded thoughtfully. 'Yes. But even at first hearing, there are some disconcerting resonances in the tale.' He turned to Antyr. 'Where are you in this ... hierarchy of Dream Finders?' he asked.

The silence returned until, very softly, Antyr said, 'I don't know. I was perhaps better than average at my job when I chose to be, but nothing more. But, as I said, Masters, Adepts, these were just part of our tradition. Not real.'

'Yet?'

'Yet I've been to other worlds – worlds that were not this one. I've walked in them, breathed their air, felt their sun. And I've been somewhere that I believe to be the Great Dream insofar as I could perceive it. There I saw, in ways that are not seeing as we understand it, the myriad worlds of the Threshold – shifting, changing, coming together, drifting apart, flickering in and out of existence, endlessly.' His eyes widened. 'All knowledge was there. Everything was there.'

Andawyr spoke very softly. 'How did you come there?'

'I told you, I don't know. I know so very little about my gift. That's why I'm here, searching.'

'You wish to go there again?'

Antyr did not speak for a long time. 'It's not a place where people belong. It's not a place we can begin to comprehend.'

'Then why are you searching?' There was a penetrating coldness in the question. Both Yatsu and Jaldaric flinched slightly, seeing their travelling companion thus pinioned.

Antyr lowered his eyes for a moment. When he raised them, it was Andawyr who found himself transfixed. 'Because something is wrong. Something is flawed. *He* was there too. Ivaroth's Earth Holder, with his corruption and his awful power. And others. How he had come there I don't know. Perhaps it was through me, perhaps through Ivaroth, perhaps through some unknowable conjunction of the two of us. But it shouldn't have been. Yet he was there, and in search of still more power. He was possessed by a desire to rend and destroy all that he saw and reshape it after his own way.'

Despite the bright sunlight being carried into the room by the mirror stones, Antyr's face was drawn and grim.

'Yatsu said that you "dealt with" this man,' Andawyr said. 'Unusually for a Goraidin, that had a hint of euphemism about it.'

'I dealt with him,' Antyr replied flatly. 'And Ivaroth too. For he was there also.' He frowned. 'I've learned so much about myself. And not all of it's been to my liking.' For a moment it seemed that he was going to break down, but he composed himself. 'Ivaroth I killed in the way men kill. He attacked me and I was lucky. He died on the knife of one of his own victims. The blind man . . .' He shook his head. 'For an instant he was my Earth Holder, he became me, and I him, as is the way. And in that instant I understood him. Saw to the heart of him. Saw the tortured route he had followed, the desires that bound him. And when he attacked me I returned his own power, his own inner knowledge of himself, to him. In pity, you understand, not malice. But it destroyed him. Sent him to places beyond this world.'

Andawyr glanced at Yatsu who answered his question before it was asked.

'Ivaroth's body was found, but there was no sign of the blind man. But he existed all right. Many people saw him. And it seems he knew how to use the Power and use it well.'

'He'd been taught.'

It was Antyr. Andawyr turned to him sharply.

'What I learned from him faded almost immediately. It always does. But some impressions lingered, for what they're worth. Someone, at some time, loomed large in his life – literally – a tall, powerful figure – someone who held him in thrall with the knowledge and the promise of power he offered. And whatever took his sight was . . . a great light, or . . .' He searched for a word. '. . . something that was torn from him, something that was bound to him in the deepest way.' He nodded. 'Yes. It was a loss. A terrible, wrenching loss.'

33

'You sound almost sorry for him,' Yatsu said.

'How could I not be?' Antyr replied without hesitation. 'Who am I to say that I might not have travelled his way in his circumstances? You're a soldier, you understand that. But sorrow for how he came to be as he was gave me no qualms then about what I did to him, nor does it now. I'd have had it otherwise but I'd no choice. He was evil beyond imagining. Removal from this world was all that was left for him, for all our sakes.'

There was a long silence. Attention turned to Andawyr who was looking out at the sunlit valley. 'Twice now you've referred to him as being gone from this world.' He turned and smiled slightly. 'Have you picked up our Goraidin's unexpected flair for euphemism?'

There was enough humour in his tone to lighten the dark atmosphere that had crept over the group. Antyr returned it.

'No. I've picked up their painful insistence on accuracy. I don't know whether the man's dead or not. He was just gone from where we were. And gone from this world. He was no longer a threat. And he was hurt – badly hurt. That I do know.'

Andawyr's eyes narrowed. 'So many, many questions,' he said. 'I can see why you'd feel the need to seek help.' He gave a rueful laugh. 'It would be much easier for us all if we could just declare that you're rambling due to a sickness of the mind, but I fear you're all too sane. And, in any case, I'd have you stay here if only to find out more about your splendid Companions.' He clapped his hands and just managed to restrain himself from reaching down to stroke the two wolves. 'You're welcome to stay here as long as you wish, though I do feel obliged to warn you that while you're sane now, you might well not be after dealing with our incessant questioning.'

'That's true,' Yatsu muttered.

Before Andawyr could respond to the taunt, Antyr said, 'I doubt you can ask as many questions as I've asked myself, but I appreciate your kindness and thank you for it. I'd welcome the opportunity to learn more about who I am and what's happened. Not only because of my ignorance about my own abilities, but because there were others as evil as he bound in that place . . .' He stopped.

'And?' Andawyr prompted.

'As I said, something's wrong. While I was there I "saw" something which has been returning to me constantly, and which disturbs me in a way I can't explain. It's as though I've seen a hurt deep in the heart of the way the world itself is made.'

Chapter 4

Andawyr had been about to rise but he froze as Antyr spoke. The coincidence of Antyr's words with his own recent concerns suddenly made him feel afraid.

'Finish your tale, Antyr,' he said quietly. 'I shouldn't have interrupted you. Tell us about this . . . hurt . . . you found, and the others you saw there.'

Both Grayle and Tarrian opened their eyes and looked at him.

'I saw no one. Only the blind man. The others I heard. Voices ringing around and through me.' Instinctively Antyr wrapped his arms about himself as the memory of their cold presence returned to him. 'They were captive there, they said. Chained by others, long ago. Others like me. For using – misusing – what they called the true power. They called me an Adept – cried the word out in a frenzy. They were waiting for the blind man to bring me to them. They needed me so that they could be free again – free to move amongst the Threshold worlds – to wreak vengeance. Their ambition was the same as the blind man's – to destroy everything and to remake it in a fashion of their own.'

He chuckled humourlessly. 'Somehow, I defied them, or rather I spoke defiantly to them. Threatened them with the name they'd given me and added my own personal menace as best I could. "I am an Adept of the White Way. Heir to those who bound you here." ' He shrugged, then curled his lip in a self-deprecating sneer. 'Whistling in the dark, I suppose. It had as much effect as it would on you. I was less than an apprentice, they told me. As if I didn't realize that for myself. A thing of clay and dross with the merest spark of past

37

greatness in me.' Antyr paused, mulling over the cold dismissal, still vividly with him. Then a flicker of triumph displaced his bitter sneer. 'Still, I defeated them. When the blind man fell, they fell with him. Bound again by their own malevolence.'

He looked at Andawyr. 'But they're still there. Still festering, waiting, until some other innocent stumbles upon them. Someone less fortunate than I was. And they told me there were others, too; that their punishment was but part of a greater ill and that they were only the vanguard for the reshaping that was to come.'

Andawyr waited for a moment, unsettled by this eerie tale, then asked again, as casually as he could. 'And the hurt you thought you saw. The hurt deep within the world.'

'I've no words for that,' Antyr went on. 'I didn't see as we see here. Nothing there was as it is here. This place is a vague shadow by comparison. As am I. I was both part of and separate from everything. All I can tell you is that there are countless worlds, somehow both here and not here, and that they're being disturbed by a wrongness which emanates from here. I'm sorry I can't explain it better, but those are the only words I can find. Though the memory keeps returning to me – disturbing me.'

'Your words are fine,' Andawyr said. 'And your pain needs no explanation.'

He massaged the remains of his nose.

'Ar-Billan, what do you make of all this?' he asked abruptly.

The young man started violently and made several peculiar noises before managing to speak properly. 'It's a strange tale,' he stammered. 'But it seems honest enough.' He flicked a rueful glance towards Antyr as if trying to retrieve the awkward words, and added hastily, 'And, as you said yourself, the trust of the Goraidin in the teller adds much to it. It demands serious study.' Then he was floundering. 'But I don't think *I* can make anything of it. I know that you and the Senior Brothers have conjectured on the idea of other worlds, here but not here, as Antyr put it, but I'm still struggling with what you find to be much less demanding concepts. I'm afraid all I

38

have at the moment are questions.' Then he became youthfully earnest. 'But whatever else it might mean, if someone has trained another in the use of the Power – and it seems they have – and there's been so little discipline in that training that they've run amok with it, then we'll *have* to make something of it. If this ... tall ... man's trained one, he might have trained others and there's no saying what the consequences might be.'

Andawyr nodded appreciatively. 'A good down-to-earth point which, I'll confess, I'd missed, Ar-Billan. What do you think we should do, then?'

Ar-Billan, pleased by this response but all too aware that a lesson was in progress, fumbled with his faint beard anxiously. 'With Antyr's permission, I think we'll have to go through his story again. Slowly, and very carefully, And, too, the Goraidin's. Then we can lay out those things that are known for sure and decide what questions we need to ask to test the reliability of whatever's left. *Then* we'll be able to consider what it all means.'

Andawyr looked round at the others. 'Seems reasonable to me. Does anyone have any problems with that?' he asked generally. No one demurred.

'Good,' he said to Ar-Billan, with a broad smile. 'Well done. Unanimity's such a rare event.'

He turned to Yatsu. 'I was out in the mountains this morning because I wanted to break some rigid patterns of thought that had been encumbering me lately. I'd made a decision when Tarrian chose to "introduce" himself to me and I've just made it again. It also deals with the advice you wanted me to give you. As Ar-Billan has just summarized for us, the first thing we need to do is work through your stories again, slowly, carefully. I suggest we do that as we all go down to Anderras Darion.' He added a hasty reassurance to the two Goraidin. 'Don't worry, I wasn't proposing we dash off immediately. I have a sense of urgency about this, but it's not *that* urgent and I can see you need some time just doing nothing. Take whatever rest you need here, then we'll have a nice leisurely trip down there. The only thing I'd suggest you do now is write a preliminary Accounting for the Geadrol.

And, Jaldaric, you can write to your father as well. Just to let everyone know you're back safely. There are riders to and from Vakloss nearly every day now.'

Only Oslang seemed to be put out by this decision. 'What can we do at Anderras Darion that we can't do here?' he asked.

'I don't know until we get there,' Andawyr answered obtusely, standing up and starting to pace about. 'But a good break from what we're doing won't do us any harm, will it?' Oslang began to frown but Andawyr opened his arms expansively. 'Besides, we'll see all our old friends. And doubtless meet new ones if half of what I hear about the comings and goings in Orthlund is true.' He gripped Oslang's shoulders. 'And who can say what they'll have found in that place? Remember that library? At least the equal of ours. Not to mention just the atmosphere there.'

'We've got plenty to do here,' Oslang countered weakly.

'And what we don't take with us will be here when we get back.' The grip became a hearty slap. 'The fact that you're disputing with me shows it's too long since you've been there.' He became sympathetic. 'I know. What we've been doing is difficult and disturbing and you've got your own patient methodical way of tackling it.' He met Oslang's gaze – old friends. 'But we're stuck, aren't we? We're going round and round – going nowhere.' He indicated Antyr and the Goraidin who were watching the exchange with interest. 'This is just what's needed. A random happening. Something uncalculated, incalculable. Something at right angles to all known directions. A stone under the wheels to shake our weary thoughts loose!' He made to snap his fingers dramatically in front of Oslang's face but failed miserably.

'You never could do that, could you?' Oslang snorted, his expression a mixture of despair and delight as he snapped his own fingers with a crack that made the others jump. 'All right, you've made your point. I can't face being metaphored to death. You're probably right.'

'I *am* right.'

Ar-Billan coughed discreetly to remind his seniors that he was still there.

40

'Have you ever been to Anderras Darion, Ar-Billan?' Andawyr asked.

'No, I haven't. I've heard a great deal about it from those who have, of course. It's a marvellous place by all accounts. I'd love to go.'

'Good, that's settled then. You will. We'll leave in a couple of . . .' He caught Yatsu's eye. 'We'll leave when everyone's ready.'

He whispered to Ar-Billan who nodded and left, then he turned to Antyr and the Goraidin. 'He's just gone to prepare some of the guest rooms for you all.' He became proprietorial. 'We're getting to be quite good at providing hospitality these days – a veritable hostelry. There's every chance you'd be comfortable with us even if you hadn't been travelling for months.'

'I'm sure I would,' Antyr agreed.

'I'll show you round in the meantime. I think you'll find the place unusual. Don't be afraid to ask about anything.' He took Antyr's arm and spoke to him intently. 'You're no longer alone. We may not be able to find answers to everything that's happened to you, but we'll find a lot. And whatever torments you've got, remember that this place is safe – very safe.'

Antyr looked appreciative but doubtful. 'I don't think anything's threatening me now. And I suspect that any difficulties I have I carry with me.'

'Yes,' Andawyr said. 'Quite probably. We all do. But even on our limited acquaintance I can see that you're given to surviving, not self-destruction. I'm fairly certain that anything you've brought here *you* can cope with, quite possibly without our help. Just be assured that nothing can assail you from outside.'

Leaving Yatsu and Jaldaric, Andawyr spent the rest of the day showing Antyr about the Cadwanen – or part of it, for the Cadwanen was a vast and complicated complex of workshops, halls of experiment, teaching rooms, living quarters and recreational areas. And in places, it was very busy as members of the Order went about their tasks.

Tarrian and Grayle necessarily attracted a great deal of attention as they flanked the two men on their journey, but

41

their presence did not protect Andawyr from being constantly accosted.

'I can see why you'd want to be alone in the mountains at times,' Antyr said sympathetically as Andawyr managed eventually to disentangle himself from a particularly persistent, albeit apologetic, individual. Andawyr chuckled good-naturedly.

'It's a strange thing, Antyr. Circumstances have made me the Leader of this Order, and I've no regrets about that. But the only authority I have is what these people give me and when I look at the kind of people they are, and the qualities they bring to this place, I find it very humbling. It sounds portentous, I know, but it's an honour to serve them and I wouldn't have it otherwise.'

'From what Yatsu and Jaldaric told me, it was more than mere circumstances that made you what you are,' Antyr said.

They were walking along a high balcony overlooking an echoing hall. 'They exaggerate,' Andawyr replied.

'I thought the Goraidin were noted for their ability to observe in great detail and to report with great accuracy,' Antyr said, risking some irony.

Andawyr gave him an arch look, but his reply was unexpectedly serious. 'Circumstances placed me where I had to change or die, Antyr,' he said. 'Just like they did with you.' He paused and leaned on the stone balustrade to gaze down at the figures passing below. 'Purposeful movement with no discernible pattern,' he muttered absently, then, 'we each of us found a resource from somewhere. Who we can thank for that I've no idea, save our forebears. I find it helpful to remind myself that maybe I was just lucky and, given that, that I should devote the rest of my time to learning more about everything and passing on my knowledge to others so that if there's a next time, they – or I – won't have to rely on luck.'

There was a coldness in his conclusion that disturbed Antyr: not by its strangeness, but by its familiarity.

Then Andawyr was jovial again. 'But you're right,' he said. 'I'm not above irritability when my halo gets too tight and a little solitude from time to time is very welcome. I just tend to forget that, until something like today happens.'

They left the balcony and went down several flights of stairs to enter the hall itself. 'I do try to remember,' Andawyr said, with a look of bewildered concern. 'I write notes to remind myself. But then I lose them. Tidiness isn't one of my stronger character traits, I'm afraid.'

'I can see that that would present difficulties,' Antyr said with a laugh. He stopped and gazed around the hall. 'This is truly an amazing place,' he said. Sunlight was streaming in through high-arched windows that, vivid with coloured patterns, ran along both sides of the hall. The ceiling too was elaborately decorated, unlike almost everywhere else he had seen so far. 'It feels so open, so fresh, I find it difficult to imagine that we're underground – inside a mountain.' He pointed to the windows. 'Are they mirror stones too?'

'Yes. All the windows you see are mirror stones. Remind me to show you how they work before we leave. You'll appreciate it, I'm sure.'

'I'm sure I will,' Antyr agreed. 'Though I have to say that from what I've seen as we've walked around they're very disorientating.'

'I don't understand.'

'They give views of the mountains and the valleys that are markedly at odds with the stairs we've climbed up and down.'

'That's because you're not paying attention,' Tarrian said impatiently, speaking to both of them before Andawyr could comment. 'Why you don't use your nose more, I don't know. There's a kitchen along here, for example.' He and Grayle began padding off down the corridor.

'Yes,' Andawyr intervened quickly. 'But I doubt the cooking Brothers would be pleased to have you wandering about them. If you'd like something to eat, there's a more suitable place down here.'

'That's very kind of you,' Tarrian replied affably. 'I'm not particularly hungry myself. It's for Antyr, you understand. His concentration wavers if he gets too hungry. But I'll have a little something to be sociable, of course.'

Andawyr took them along a broad corridor into a communal dining hall. Plain wooden tables were flanked by plain wooden benches and at one end there was a large counter on

43

which was arrayed a wide variety of food. There were several people in the room, some of them eating, some of them serving themselves from the counter. Tarrian and Grayle headed straight towards the counter, causing several startled diners in the process of returning to their tables to change direction abruptly.

'Get back here, you two,' Antyr hissed to them, adding out loud to Andawyr, 'I do apologize. They've been too long in the mountains.' The two wolves stopped but did not return, choosing instead to wait for him to reach them.

'Don't concern yourself too much,' Andawyr said. 'We have felcis in and out of the place all the time. It's just that they're not as big as these two.'

'Felcis?' Antyr queried.

'You'll find out soon enough,' Andawyr replied. He indicated a nearby table and spoke authoritatively to the two wolves. 'Would you like to wait over there while I get something for you?'

After a visit to the counter and a negotiation with a red-faced and flustered-looking individual he returned with food for himself and Antyr and two large bones for the wolves. Rather to his surprise, the wolves sniffed them suspiciously before taking them.

As he sat down, a low bell-like tone reverberated through the room.

'I've heard that several times,' Antyr said. 'What is it?'

'It's a warning,' Andawyr replied. 'Or, more correctly, *that* note is a confirmation that all's well throughout the caves.'

Antyr's brow furrowed. 'A warning,' he echoed. 'What do you need to be warned about here?'

'What did Yatsu and Jaldaric tell you about the Cadwanol and these caves?' Andawyr asked.

'That you were an Order of learned men established by Ethriss at the time of the First Coming of Sumeral with the intention of gathering knowledge so that He could be opposed in many different ways. They said the caves were full of strange devices, but they didn't elaborate.' He looked around. 'And they certainly didn't prepare me for anything I've seen today.'

44

Andawyr broke a piece of bread from a loaf and began nibbling at it idly. 'Well, that's all true enough, though pared thinly even for a Goraidin's telling.'

Concerned that he might have inadvertently betrayed his friends, Antyr protested gently. 'No, no. They told me a great deal, but I'm afraid I've not remembered as much of it as I should. The journey was demanding, to say the least. To be honest, I slept whenever I could. I'm no soldier, least of all like they are, and though they were patience itself I'd a great many simple practical things to learn as we went along if I wasn't to be too much of a burden to them. Especially through the mountains. And I don't think it helped that it was winter when we set out,' he added ruefully.

'It's all right,' Andawyr reassured him with a smile. 'I wasn't criticizing. Besides, the three of us have known one another long enough to be quite free in our exchanges of abuse.' The smile became a quiet laugh. 'But, answering your question. Do you see that?' He pointed to a panel by the main doorway to the hall. On it was a symbol. As Antyr looked at it, the symbol gave him the impression that it was suffused with a slowly shifting glow, though if he stared hard at it he could see no actual change.

'I've noticed several like that, though with different symbols on them,' he said. 'They're very strange. I was intending to ask you about them.'

Andawyr became pensive. 'They're part of what I suppose you'd call the darker side of our life here. Yatsu and Jaldaric are quite right, this place *is* full of strange devices. In fact, it's full of very dangerous devices.' He leaned forward and his voice fell as if he did not want to be overheard. 'When Ethriss founded the Order, it was a terrible time. The more I read and learn about it, the more I realize just how terrible it was. Sumeral held great sway then. His armies were powerful and fearsome. It seemed that nothing – nothing – could stand against His ultimate victory.' He tapped the table with his forefinger for emphasis. 'Part of the horror of it was that He had many honourable and very able people fighting for His cause: people deceived by His words, seduced by His promises or just terrified by the lies He spread about His

45

enemies. And it was Ethriss's greatest sorrow that in order to defeat Him, he'd no choice but to use His own weapons against Him. He had to teach his own followers how to make war and every cruel thing that that entails. It was a brutal loss of innocence.' He twitched his hand irritably to stop himself from digressing. 'It was a desperate matter that this place be kept secret. Had Sumeral learned about us then He'd have known the risk we posed and He'd have launched His entire might against us. But it was no slight thing, avoiding His eye: He'd many and different spies roaming the world. At first, Ethriss was able to shelter those who were working here, but he couldn't do that for long as his very presence would eventually have drawn the enemy here. So very soon the first Brothers had to protect *themselves*. They did this by doing what we do yet – learning and practising the skills with the Old Power that Ethriss had taught them.' He sat back and glanced admiringly around the hall, almost as though he were looking at it for the first time. The jarring sound of Tarrian and Grayle massacring their bones rose into the silence. 'And, I have to say, from a purely professional point of view, some of the work they did was staggering. Such minds, Antyr. Such minds. It's difficult to comprehend. In many ways we knew so little. Some of the things we regard as elementary now – things we teach almost casually to our novices – were at the very limits of their knowledge then – brilliant insights. To discover them from nothing, as it were, betokens vision and intellect which humbles us all yet. Some of the discoveries they made actually turned everything that was then accepted upside down.' He gave a guilty shrug. 'I'm sorry, I'm wandering again, aren't I? I'm apt to when I talk about the past. I've always had a keen sense of history and after what happened to us it's keener than ever these days. Anyway, coming to your question again, the symbols that you see and the sounds you hear are part of a vast, intricate web of warning devices and traps developed from those that the first Brothers made to protect themselves. It's altered, refined, adjusted, extended constantly, but at its heart it's still what they made.'

Antyr turned to look at the panel and its symbol, which still seemed to be at once moving and not moving. 'I told you I'm no soldier, but I served my time behind a shield wall when I was younger and had to learn something about sieges and the kind of traps that can be laid within a castle – falling stones, sprung spears, counter-weighted blades and the like – but that doesn't look like any device I've ever heard about.'

'I'd be very surprised if you had,' Andawyr said. 'And more than a little alarmed.'

Antyr raised a questioning eyebrow.

'We search endlessly for knowledge here, but all knowledge can be abused, and all knowledge carries responsibilities,' Andawyr replied. 'And that,' he nodded towards the panel, 'carries responsibilities far beyond the average.' He stood up. 'Come on, I'll tell you more as we go.'

'*We* haven't finished.' Tarrian's indignant voice touched both them.

'Bring your bones with you,' Antyr retorted with heavy patience.

Tarrian muttered something indistinguishable, then he and Grayle loped after the retreating pair.

As they reached the door, Andawyr chuckled and briefly ran an affectionate hand over the panel. Antyr stopped for a moment and looked at it intently. Even so close, he could not decide whether the glowing symbol was moving or not. Nor could he determine where the light was coming from that illuminated it.

As they walked along he began to notice many similar symbols along the walls, though most of them were smaller than the one on the panel.

'*All* these are traps?' he queried, unable to keep some incredulousness out of his voice.

'Oh yes,' Andawyr replied straightforwardly. 'But don't worry, you won't be suddenly sliced in half by a swinging blade. They're not intended to deal with armed assaults as such. We rely on more traditional methods to cope with that. We're protected from enemies coming from the south or along the Pass of Elewart, for example, by the Riddin Muster. We receive training from the Goraidin so that we can guard our own doors if we have to, and for the rest, the mountains themselves are virtually impassable for a large force. Even so, we watch them constantly.' He extended an arm to move Antyr through an open doorway. 'Come in here, I'll show you.'

Chapter 5

The room Andawyr ushered Antyr into was circular. A group of men and women sat at a table in the centre. Some were reading, some were writing, others were talking quietly. One appeared to be asleep, his head cradled on his arms, though a quick nudge from his neighbour brought him suddenly upright, wide awake and diligently applying himself to the study of a large book. As the two men entered, the group turned and made to stand up but a signal from Andawyr sent them back to their tasks. Nevertheless, as had been the case throughout their tour of the Cadwanen, Tarrian and Grayle proved to be a discreet distraction.

Around the walls, set close, side by side, were a great many of what again appeared to be windows. They looked out over the mountains, filling the room with sunlight. Around each of them were yet more of the symbols that had attracted Antyr's attention, though they were much smaller than those he had seen in the corridor. Some of them were glowing.

'More mirror stones, I presume?' Antyr said.

Andawyr nodded. And as Antyr looked round at the views they offered, he could see this confirmed disconcertingly by the fact most of the individual vistas were not continuous with their neighbours.

'*We* think of them as windows as well, if it helps,' Andawyr said with an encouraging smile. But Antyr was staring at a series of views of what he now knew to be the Pass of Elewart. Though part of it was flooded with bright sunlight, this cast jagged threatening shadows and merely served to deepen the darkness of the shade that pervaded the rest. Andawyr shivered. He had not spent long in the Pass but it

49

had had an atmosphere that weighed on him like nothing he had ever known before and that he felt was not due solely to its stark barrenness and the wind whose moaning tones shifted and changed constantly. Even Yatsu and Jaldaric had felt subtly uneasy and they had pressed on at a very steady speed, sombre-faced and unspeaking. The horses too had been noticeably unhappy and Tarrian and Grayle had been unusually silent, drawing away from him utterly, deep into their wolfish selves, as they trotted ahead of the riders, ears flattened and tails between their legs.

'Yes, it's not a happy place, is it?' Andawyr said, easing him away from the bleak view. He gestured towards the group around the table and one of the women stood up and came forward in response. About the same height as Andawyr, she was slightly built with an oval face framed by neatly trimmed black hair. She had brown, challenging eyes and a slightly crooked nose that served to enhance her appearance rather than detract from it. The long hooded robe she wore was similar to that worn by everyone else Antyr had seen in the Cadwanen, though it was particularly neat and clean and had a small golden clasp securing it at her neck.

Tarrian's approval rumbled into Antyr's mind and, dropping his bone noisily, the wolf pushed past Antyr and walked straight over to her.

'Stop that!' Antyr snapped silently. But it was too late: Tarrian was standing with his forelegs on the woman's shoulders, rapturously receiving a brilliant smile and a vigorous caress of his long head. As he dropped down gently, Grayle, leaning against the woman, received the same.

'Aren't you both beautiful?' came the words that Antyr had heard so often when the two wolves chose to act thus. Tarrian replied to Antyr's rebuke with a malevolent chuckle.

The woman's accent was noticeably different from Andawyr's, with an almost musical lilt to it.

'I'm sorry about that,' Antyr said to her, adding, with a glower at the two wolves, 'I'm afraid they're not particularly well disciplined. And usually they don't like to be touched.'

'It's all right,' the woman said, turning the same smile on him. 'They're a delight, aren't they? Are they yours?'

50

'No,' Antyr replied quickly. 'They don't belong to anyone. They're just my companions. They choose to stay with me.' The woman gave him a quizzical look.

'This is Antyr, Usche,' Andawyr said. He nodded towards the mirror stones. 'As you probably saw, he arrived with Yatsu and Jaldaric. He's come a long way and there's much more to him and his . . . than meets the eye.' He glanced significantly towards the wolves who were now prowling around the room, sniffing purposefully at each of its occupants in turn but assiduously avoiding any further contact. 'I'm looking forward to some very interesting discussions with him.'

Usche took Antyr's offered hand. 'Anyone who rides with the Goraidin and travels with wolves must necessarily be interesting,' she said, looking at him keenly. 'Welcome to the Cadwanen, Antyr, traveller from a distant land, friend to the Goraidin, Yatsu and Jaldaric, and companion to . . .?' She looked at the two wolves. 'Do they have names, your companions?'

'Tarrian and Grayle.'

'Companion to Tarrian and Grayle.' Usche completed her greeting and released his hand.

'Usche's a Riddinwr. They can be very fussy about introductions,' Andawyr said. 'Think yourself fortunate she didn't know any of your relations. Meeting someone you know in Riddin can be a very lengthy matter.'

Usche gave him a look of both reproach and threat. 'And our great leader here, unfortunately, isn't a Riddinwr – as you'll realize as soon as you see him on a horse – and thus hasn't been brought up in the ways of civilized courtesy.'

'I was just showing Antyr how we protect ourselves here,' Andawyr said, ignoring the taunt. He swept an arm around the many views being brought into the room. 'From here, as you can see, we can watch every part of the mountains around us for a considerable distance.' Quite abruptly a look of pain passed over his face. 'We always have done, after a fashion,' he went on softly. 'But we allowed the Watch to become a mere ritual; a condescending nod to the past. A dreadful lapse. Such arrogance.' The last words were spoken as though to himself. He straightened up and the mood was gone as

51

quickly as it had come. 'But now we watch and we watch well,' he concluded emphatically.

Antyr looked at the views before him. They were a remarkable sight, and even a cursory glance told him that no army nor, for that matter, any lone rider could approach the Cadwanen without being seen. But his memories of the mountains were very fresh. 'What do you do when the mist comes down?' he blurted out.

His tone provoked some laughter.

'Which is most of the time. Yes, we know,' Andawyr conceded. 'But as with everything else here, there's . . .'

'More to this place than meets the eye? Like me.' Antyr finished the sentence for him.

'Yes,' Andawyr replied with a hint of apology.

'Anything that moves, we have ways of seeing, or hearing,' Usche volunteered. 'Do you know anything about the Power?'

'He knows *of* it, I suspect, to his cost, but not *about* it,' Andawyr replied on Antyr's behalf. 'But we can put that right with a little effort.' Usche gave a slight bow and took a step backwards.

Antyr pointed to the symbols surrounding the Mirror Stones. 'As you seem to be so well protected against assaults by armies and the like, I presume these and all those littered about the place use this Power to protect you against anyone who could use it against you.'

Andawyr gave him an appreciative look. 'Yes, indeed,' he said.

A fleeting recollection of his fateful confrontation with the blind man flitted through Antyr's mind, leaving, as ever, tantalizing hints of all that he had then known and now forgotten. 'A web, you called it. Then the Power pervades this entire place?'

Andawyr's face took on the expression of a parent asked a too-penetrating question that time and circumstance, perhaps even ability, did not allow him to answer as he would have wished.

'The Power pervades everything, Antyr,' he replied, rather hastily. 'It *is* everything. I'll explain what I can later. We both of us have a lot to talk about and there's no urgency.' He became brisk. 'Usche, are you free to come with us now?'

The woman hesitated for a moment. 'Yes, my duty spell here finished a few minutes ago, I was just discussing something.'

'Well, if your discussion can safely be left, would you come with us, please?'

'Of course.'

She picked up a book and some papers from the table and followed them. Tarrian and Grayle recovered their dropped bones and acted as her escort.

A short walk brought them back to the room from which they had set out. Yatsu and Jaldaric were still there. Both of them were writing. Antyr was conspicuously surprised. He greeted them with an exaggerated and apologetic shrug. 'I've been doing my best,' he said. 'Doing what you told me. Taking careful note of where I've been in case I might have to return that way. But this place is so bewildering. I could've sworn we'd been walking away from here all the time. Not to mention, on the whole, moving upwards.'

'No nose at all,' Tarrian muttered disdainfully as he flopped down noisily underneath the large window and began gnawing his bone again. Grayle joined him.

'You're a bitter disappointment to us,' Yatsu said, shaking his head with mock reproach as he returned to his writing.

Andawyr intervened. 'No small part of your confusion is wilfully built into the design of the Cadwanen, Antyr. If you were to study it carefully, you'd find that, amongst other things, it's extremely defensible by conventional means should the need arise. In many ways it has the qualities of an elaborate board game, except that any enemy who managed to gain access would know neither the shape, the layout of the board, nor the number, positions and strengths of any of the pieces. And they certainly wouldn't know the rules. We're protected inside and out against every assault we've been able to envisage.' He rubbed his hands gleefully. Antyr's response, however, was a weak smile.

Though he had known Andawyr for less than a day the man's manner was such that he felt it had been much longer. He had to remind himself that this rather scruffy little individual was the leader of the Cadwanol and presumably

53

responsible for the running of this enormous place. Further, from what he had been told by Yatsu and Jaldaric, Andawyr was highly respected not only by the Cadwanwr themselves but by all those who held authority in neighbouring lands. And, too, it seemed he possessed great personal courage.

Yet as he had walked about the Cadwanen with him, Antyr had had no sense of Andawyr's exalted stature. Indeed, there seemed to be very little sense of hierarchy in the whole place. People had accosted Andawyr as they might a friend in the street, and addressed him directly by name, without any formal salute or title – even Ar-Billan, whom Antyr now took to be a Novice. And Andawyr had answered in like vein, openly and straightforwardly. Antyr himself found that he was treating him as a friend of long standing. The word 'openness' seemed to typify everything he had seen and heard. Not only with Andawyr, but in the place itself. Open and airy, it was like a building in which all the windows and doors had been opened so that sunlight and spring breezes could drift through. And the few people he had met seemed to be as willing to listen as they were to speak. Yet there was a paradox, too. The place was *not* open. It was an intricate network of caves buried deep within and beneath the mountains. The people *must* have their ordered places and responsibilities. And the precautions taken to protect the place far outweighed anything he had ever known in his own apparently much more violent society. They disturbed him.

Andawyr stopped rubbing his hands and looked at him closely. 'You find our concerns for our safety obsessive?' he said shrewdly.

Antyr hesitated for some time before Andawyr's manner again drew a frank, albeit reluctant response from him.

'Intense, certainly. They feel somehow out of place in what I'd taken to be primarily a teaching Order. My admittedly limited dealings with the powerful in my own society showed me how such things can come about, and how they darken people's lives: the constant looking over the shoulder, searching into shadows for fear of ambush. But that was in connection with gaining and keeping political power. People who for various reasons didn't aspire to those heights – or depths – scholars, tradesmen, ordinary people – weren't constantly worrying about enemies.'

Jaldaric caught Yatsu's eye, then cleared his throat conspicuously.

'Well, all right,' Antyr added, flustered. 'I did feel the need to take one or two lessons in swordwork, I'll admit. But that was because . . .'

'Because Serenstad was a violent place,' Jaldaric said with an emphatic jab of his finger, though not without some humour. He addressed Andawyr authoritatively in the same vein. 'It was frightening just walking the streets there. Not like Vakloss or . . .'

Andawyr rescued Antyr. 'Leave him alone,' he said sternly. 'You survived, didn't you? And I suspect he's much further away from his home here than you ever were in his land. Get on with your letter.' He pulled a chair up to the window and, resting his elbows on the broad sill, cupped his head in his hands and stared out at the view.

'I understand what you mean, Antyr,' he said. 'But I think the key to your uncertainty about us lies in the word "worrying". The point is, we don't worry – well, not excessively, anyway. We think, we assess, we act. We adjust our ways of living as needs demand, changing things if we can, coping with them if we can't. And once that's done, there's little else that *can* be done, save be aware. That's what anyone should do if they don't want their life to slip by unnoticed.' He gave Antyr a significant sidelong look but, still seeing that his guest was uneasy, he turned back to the view and pressed on. 'Our history – both ancient and all too recent – tells us quite clearly that there are dark forces in the world: forces that are actively malevolent, that delight in destruction. And, as a Teaching Order,' he gave an amused grunt, 'or perhaps I should say, a Learning Order, we take an interest in the nature of such forces as we do in many other things. What are they, for example? Where do they come from? Are they something inherent in nature itself or just in *our* nature? Are they in some way *necessary* for us if we're to move forward – whatever forward might mean? Have *we* created them, or are they something inflicted on us from outside, something that came from beyond the Great Searing when all things are said to have begun? Or are they some combination of all these?' He shrugged. 'We've plenty of ideas, as you might expect, but no indisputable answers. Indeed, it may well be that they're questions that are unanswerable in principle, but even discovering that for sure will teach us a great deal.' He turned to Antyr and smiled. 'Still, knowing what we know, we'd be foolish souls indeed to ignore the dangers that are offered. And knowing that, the steps we take to protect ourselves no more dominate our lives than do any other simple everyday precautions. It's hardly burdensome to take care walking around the back of a horse, to dowse a camp-fire properly, to put on a warm coat when the weather threatens, is it?'

'I didn't mean to cause offence,' Antyr said almost plaintively.

Andawyr's smile became a laugh and he slapped Antyr's arm. 'You caused no offence, Antyr,' he said. He pushed his chair back alarmingly and swung his feet up on to the sill. 'You spoke honestly and it pleases me more than I can say that you felt you could. We thrive on debate. Nothing is immune from question.' Then he became unexpectedly earnest. 'One thing we *do* know. Whatever they might be, wherever they might come from, the forces of destruction pervade everything and they fester unseen in the darkness of the unspoken thought like a house-rotting fungus.' He opened his arms wide as if to embrace the entire view before him. 'Light, Antyr. Light. Shine it into everything. Bring clarity and reason to everything. You mightn't always like what you find but it's infinitely safer than any other way. And you may even gain some understanding.'

'One of the things you'll soon understand is to be careful what you say to Andawyr, if you don't want a protracted philosophical harangue or an interrogation.' It was Jaldaric who spoke and the remark provoked some general amusement.

'Have you finished that letter to your father yet, young Jaldaric?' Andawyr retorted tartly.

Antyr, however, was intrigued by what Andawyr was saying. 'But don't you ever wish that all these precautions weren't necessary? That this place didn't have to be the . . . fortress . . . it appears to be? That you were free of these endless concerns?'

'Have *you* ever been?'

The question made Antyr start. He stammered out, 'Well . . .' a couple of times and made a few vague gestures before ending with, 'Yes . . . No . . . but . . .'

'But nothing,' Andawyr went on. 'From what little you've already told us you've had many bad things happen to you. Some of them self-inflicted, seemingly, but all of them things against which you had to defend yourself eventually.'

'Yes, but . . .'

'But nothing,' Andawyr repeated. 'Would you say you're a man bowed down by burdens?' He did not wait for an answer. 'No. You're a man doing something about what he perceives to be his burdens. Searching. Far from your home. Looking for a light you can shine into their hearts.' He pushed his chair back precariously near to its point of balance and putting his hands behind his head, cocked it on one side to look at Antyr.

'Why did you choose to fight the blind man?' he asked.

'I didn't choose,' Antyr replied indignantly after a startled pause. 'I was there through no fault of my own. And it was a matter of opposing him or being bound to his will for ever. And who could say what hurt would have come of that? Not least to me.'

Still balancing his chair dangerously, Andawyr turned his attention back to the view. The sky was darkening and the mountains were beginning to throw long shadows across the valley. A skein of birds fluttered urgently over the scene.

'Aha,' he said, with an air of someone reaching a conclusion. 'There you are. You did what you did because you're who you are and because you were where you were. That's something that three of us here understand all too well. And even Usche understands it with her head if not yet with her stomach.'

Another skein of birds flew down into the valley.

Andawyr's voice fell. 'I don't belittle your pain or your needs, Antyr. As I've said, what we can do to help you, we will. But mainly you'll help yourself. And ponder this, for I'm sure you already know it. And I'm certain your two Companions know it. There's only here, now. If we're sensible we learn from what has been, and it's in our nature to plan what is to be, even though we know that almost certainly reality will be different.' He laughed softly. 'What calculation could've told me this morning that you'd be here today, opening up so many fascinating avenues of search for us? What calculation before I met you could've told me I'd decide to go to Anderras Darion and that that would be what you'd need as well? But *still* there's only here, now, and it's only a failure to appreciate that that can truly burden us. If we cloud our minds, our hearts, with the shades of an immutable past and the looming clouds of unknowable futures then we miss the scents, the sounds, the colours of the valley and the flight of the birds heading home. And, too, because we're elsewhere all the time, our enemies catch us unawares and unready. We bring on ourselves the very doom we most fear.'

No one spoke.

He turned back to Antyr. 'Sorry,' he said. 'I'm afraid Jaldaric's right. I can be a little . . . lengthy . . . at times. It's very remiss of me, especially to a welcome guest.'

Jaldaric was about to say something but thought better of it.

'No apology's necessary,' Antyr said. 'You've taken my breath away, that's all. What you've described, I suspect, is what I aspire to, though I'd never thought of it quite like that. It's just difficult at times. The past is so intense it's not easily let go, nor is it always easy to know what you've learned. And the future's *so* uncertain.'

Andawyr swung his feet down from the sill and spun his chair around in a manoeuvre that made Usche draw in a sharp breath and the three men start forward in anticipation of a catastrophic fall.

'Well, it's not so uncertain for the next few days,' he said heartily before Usche could utter the rebuke forming in her expression. 'You can sleep, eat, wander about, ask questions, read, do nothing, whatever you wish. Then we'll set off for Anderras Darion.' He held up a reassuring hand. 'Don't worry, incidentally, the journey's nothing like the one you've just made. And the company will be better. Which reminds me, I'd like you to come as well, Usche. You've been before, haven't you?'

Usche's eyes widened. 'Only once, quite a long time ago, when I was a novice,' she said. 'But I'd love to go again. It's a marvellous place.'

Antyr, however, had some reservations. 'I appreciate your kindness and your hospitality, Andawyr. You've made me so welcome that I'm forgetting my manners and I'm beginning to feel rather awkward about just arriving here uninvited and accepting everything you've offered. I'd feel much easier if there was something I could do to repay you – anything. I doubt there's any need for my Dream Finding skill around here, but I'll sweep, chop wood, whatever you want.'

Andawyr puffed out his cheeks. 'We have guests coming and going constantly,' he said. 'And we stay with others in the same way. It's nothing unusual. The Riddinvolk in particular do it all the time. They're . . .' He floundered for a moment. 'You'll be repaying us just by telling us about your profession. It sounds extremely interesting. I told you, we thrive on learning.' He clapped his hands. 'In fact, perhaps I could impose on you this very night. Do you think it would be possible for you to . . . enter . . . into one of my dreams?'

'Yes, yes!' Tarrian's and Grayle's voices burst into Antyr's mind simultaneously, making him wince.

'I'd be more than happy to,' he said, shaking them away. 'Though I doubt *you* need any help I could offer.' He nudged the two now wide awake wolves with his foot. 'And I have to warn you that these two seem unusually enthusiastic about the prospect.'

'This is bad?' Andawyr asked, eyebrows raised.

'This is suspicious,' Antyr replied. 'They're nothing if not hedonistic.'

Andawyr held out his hands to them. 'Well, so am I. And they won't harm me, will they?'

'No, of course not,' Antyr said. 'It's just that they're very nosy, that's all. They like to wander the dream ways.'

'Which means nothing to me,' Andawyr retorted. 'And if it doesn't hurt I don't mind.'

'It doesn't hurt. You'll probably enjoy it.' It was Yatsu.

Andawyr looked at him askance. 'You did this?' he inquired.

'And me,' said Jaldaric. 'It's interesting. Try it.'

'You're not the exclusive repository of curiosity, you know,' Yatsu said smugly.

'Well, well,' Andawyr muttered. 'What did you find?' he asked Antyr.

'You'll have to ask them about that,' came the reply. 'What passes between a Dream Finder and his client stays between them.'

'I stand corrected,' Andawyr conceded. 'A little thought and a little less excitement would've told me that, wouldn't it? Anyway, what do we have to do?'

'Nothing yet,' Antyr laughed. 'Unless you're particularly anxious to get to bed.'

'Hardly,' Andawyr replied, glancing over the valley as the daylight faded.

'You're due for a long night, Dream Finder, he hardly ever sleeps,' Jaldaric chimed in, standing up and stretching. He waved what appeared to a completed letter in anticipation of any further ripostes by Andawyr. 'And unless you want us for anything special we'll go and eat.'

'Don't get lost,' Andawyr chided caustically as they were leaving.

He stared at the door for some time after it had closed. 'It's so good to see them back safely,' he said reflectively. 'I'm afraid we're none of us totally immune to those looming clouds, Antyr.'

'You've many out searching for those who fled after the war?' Antyr asked.

'Yes. And as many just out rediscovering the world.' His brow furrowed. 'And we've precious little idea where most of them are. All we can do is put the head in charge of the heart and keep telling ourselves they're all more than capable, and doing what they want to do.' He slapped his legs. 'But that's the way it is, so we have to cope with it.'

Usche cleared her throat.

'Ah yes. I'm sorry, Usche. I'm intruding on your time.'

'That doesn't matter,' Usche replied. 'But if you don't need me, I've plenty of things to do.'

Andawyr drew in a breath. 'First corrected now reproached: this is turning into a chastening day for me.' He cast a glance over his shoulder at the darkening valley, then reached out to touch the edge of the sill. With barely a sound the surrounds of the window became alive with movement as a series of small panels began to unfold and move towards the centre. Antyr could see no pattern to the movement but quite suddenly, with a final soft sighing turn, the whole became a seemingly solid shutter, elaborately decorated with intertwined leaves and stems. At the same time lights around the room bloomed into life.

Antyr could do no other than touch the shutter. 'Marvellous,' he said. Then, staring round at the lights, he added, 'And I presume you have no Guild of Lamplighters here.' He looked at Andawyr. 'Doubtless you'll tell me this is all the result of clear thinking, ingenuity and determination, but it *looks* magical.'

'You're showing me the world through your eyes, Antyr, and I suppose it does,' Andawyr replied. 'But to other matters. Matters that look magical even to me. Usche, before you go, explain to Antyr about the Power.'

Chapter 6

'What!'

Usche's manner thus far had been pleasantly and politely attentive. Now she was bolt upright and gaping.

'Tell him about the Power,' Andawyr repeated.

'Just like that?'

'Just like that. There's nothing like teaching to help you get to grips with what you think you know. And you'll be doing a lot more soon.'

There was a flicker of stark panic across Usche's face that left her cheeks coloured slightly as she recovered. She made a strange whimper and, with an apologetic sidelong glance at Antyr, asked in a half whisper, 'What does he know?'

Andawyr seemed to be quietly enjoying himself. 'Listen carefully,' he said.

Then, very quickly and very succinctly, he repeated Antyr's story to her. Both she and Antyr were wide-eyed when he finished. She with the story itself, he with the grasp that Andawyr had shown of everything he had told him.

'Did I miss anything out?' Andawyr asked him.

'No, no,' Antyr stammered. 'It was very accurate . . . very clear. Better than the way I told it.'

'Now you know what I know, Brother Usche, but all questions are for later. Tell him about the Power. Keep it general, no maths.'

Usche was still wide-eyed as she turned her attention back to Antyr. She coughed and swallowed nervously, said 'Yes' meaninglessly and swallowed again before beginning.

'This blind man *attacked* you with the Power?' she asked almost disbelievingly.

'No questions,' Andawyr insisted, but she scowled at him. She was about to speak when Antyr answered her.

'Yes,' he said. 'At least that's what I presume it was.'

'And you . . .' Usche gesticulated vaguely. 'Sent it back to him.'

'Yes.'

Usche shook her head. 'If you could do that then I don't think there's anything I can tell you. *You* should be teaching *me*.'

'I'm afraid not,' Antyr replied. 'Although I remember much of what happened, far more has slipped away from me, rather, as I'm told often enough, dreams often fade on waking. And as for *how* I did what I did, I've no idea. It was almost as if something woke inside me and took charge.' He frowned as memories of the terrifying confrontation returned to him, suddenly vivid. With them came a familiar aching feeling of loss. 'For the briefest of moments I knew . . . everything. Everything that had ever been – that could be – known. But it was *so* short – almost as though it had been trapped between the moments.' He indicated the book on her lap. 'It was like looking at the edge of a page, yet seeing everything that was written on it.' He gave a fatalistic shrug. 'I've no words for it, I'm afraid. Whatever it was, it wasn't to be mine. Perhaps some part of me held enough of it to save my life, I don't know.' Then he smiled to encourage his still reluctant teacher. 'I've heard a lot about this Power and I'd be very interested to know more about it, but I can see you're having the same problem in finding words for it. Just try. I'll ask if there's anything I don't understand but I'm sure the world won't come to an end if I don't grasp the matter fully.'

His manner relaxed Usche a little. She straightened her robe and carefully placed the book and papers she was holding onto a small table standing nearby.

Andawyr was sitting slightly behind Antyr and, though Antyr could not see him, he knew that he was watching her intently. It gave him a welcome sense of familiarity.

There is *a hierarchy here, then,* he thought. *It's just more subtle than I'm used to.*

Conspicuously plucking up courage, Usche began. 'Unfortunately, it doesn't help that we use the term "Power", but it's so rooted into our ways of speaking and writing that any more appropriate term would be unlikely to dislodge it.' Antyr sensed that a point was being made here that was not particularly for his benefit, but Usche continued without a pause. 'It's actually a relic of times long gone when this . . . pervasive phenomenon . . . which we still call the Power – or, rather, the ability to use it – was thought to be magical – something that was beyond rational explanation – something that came from a vague "other place" peopled by gods and spirits and the like.' She took on a schoolteacher's tone. 'Now we're a little more enlightened, and we also know much more about it. *Much* more.' She looked at Andawyr pointedly. 'Largely due to a certain person's considerable courage, the full extent of which I've only recently begun to learn about.'

'You should be concentrating on more important matters, young woman, not tittle-tattling in the recreation rooms.' The comment came from over Antyr's shoulder, though it patently did not impinge on Usche who calmly turned her gaze back to Antyr.

'That's not to say that we understand it fully. Far from it. There are many aspects of it that are deeply strange. At its heart, things happen in ways that are quite contrary to what we would expect in our everyday lives. However, let me show you something.'

She pulled the table between them and moved the book so that it was in front of her. She gave Andawyr an inquiring look and, apparently receiving his consent, opened the book and sat back. She became very still and, as Antyr watched, the pages of the book slowly began to turn, apparently of their own volition.

Antyr frowned and shot a suspicious and rather embarrassed look at Usche. He turned the same expression towards Andawyr, suddenly very uncertain.

'What's the matter?' Andawyr asked, obviously surprised at this response.

Antyr's embarrassment deepened. 'This is just a . . . trick.' The words came out in a half whisper, as though they were

65

reluctant to be heard. It was Andawyr's turn to frown, though in confusion, not anger. The book was still now and Usche was watching the exchange with great concern.

'I don't understand what you mean,' Andawyr said into the awkward silence.

Unhappily, Antyr turned the book around to face him and leaned forward, his head resting on his hand as though deep in thought. As before, the pages of the book began to turn.

'Good grief,' Andawyr exclaimed, leaning forward himself and watching intently. 'How did you do that? You certainly didn't use the Power.'

Antyr put his fingertips to his mouth and splayed them apart rapidly as he puffed out noisily. 'Breath control,' he said. 'Silent, focused. It takes quite a lot of practice to do properly, but I can do it well enough for a party trick. My father taught me when I was a child. He learned it from a friend who was a market trader. He used tricks like that to gather a crowd. He could do the most amazing things. I'm sorry . . . I . . .'

Completely discomfited by what he now realized was an ill-judged and wholly inappropriate intrusion, Antyr stammered to a halt. Andawyr's face contorted alarmingly but when it resolved itself it was not into indignation and anger but into laughter. It proved to be beyond his control though eventually he managed, 'You're right. That's a good trick. But it's not what Usche was doing.' As the laughter threatened to take over again he waved to her to continue.

Usche, however, did not appear to be amused. Jaw set and eyes now grim, she closed the book and turned it so that its spine was towards her. Slowly she lifted its heavy cover a little way, then slammed it shut with a vigorous slap, making Antyr start. Pausing only to shoot a dark look towards the still laughing Andawyr, she sat back in her chair as she had before. Very slowly, the cover swung open until it was vertical. Then, equally slowly, it continued opening until it was resting on the table. A good half of the pages then opened and followed it in the same manner. Throughout, Usche kept her eyes fixed sternly on Antyr.

'Blow *that*!' Andawyr whispered loudly in Antyr's ear.

His laughter escaped his control again and bounced around

the room. It was infectious and, for a moment, it seemed that Usche's glare was going to disintegrate under its onslaught. She crushed the impulse. 'One of our beloved leader's more peculiar traits, Antyr, is that he laughs a lot – and very easily,' she glowered.

Andawyr's hand landed on Antyr's shoulder. 'And one of Brother Usche's many charming traits is that she can be remarkably solemn. A trait which you can see your confusing her with a market pedlar has brought out to its full.' Still chuckling, he spoke to her, kindly. 'Worse than that can happen, Usche. Remind me to have Oslang tell you how a demonstration of the Power he once gave nearly got him his throat cut.'

'I'm awfully sorry,' Antyr began. 'I didn't mean to . . . it's just that you caught me unawares . . . I . . .'

A gentle pressure from Andawyr's hand silenced him. 'You've done no hurt, Antyr. You reacted openly and honestly which, I told you before, I – we – value, and value highly. What Usche's just shown you is a small example of what a trained person can do with the Power. It's a basic exercise to test skill, control, many things. Let me show you.' He laid his hand over Antyr's and nodded to Usche.

As slowly as it had opened, the book closed itself. Andawyr removed his hand and looked at Antyr expectantly. 'Did that help you understand?' he asked.

'Did what?' Antyr asked in return.

'That,' Andawyr said, taking his hand again. 'That feeling when the book was closing.'

'I felt nothing,' Antyr replied.

Andawyr tilted his head on one side as if he had not heard correctly.

'Nothing?'

'Nothing.'

Andawyr looked at his hand with the expression of a man looking at a faulty timepiece.

'Nothing at all?'

'No. Sorry,' Antyr confirmed, beginning to be alarmed that he had made another social blunder amongst his new friends.

'How very odd,' Andawyr said slowly, staring now at Antyr

as though *he* might have been a faulty timepiece. Antyr shifted uncomfortably and Andawyr was suddenly alive with apology.

'I'm so sorry,' he said, words stumbling out in his haste. 'You caught *me* unawares this time. I've never known anything like that. You should have felt *something*. That's one of the most effective teaching aids to get past the difficulties we run into when words alone aren't really sufficient.' He waved his hands vaguely as if trying to still what were obviously many clamouring questions. 'I can see we're going to learn a great deal about one another over the coming days – with your permission, of course,' he added quickly. 'But for now, I'd like Usche to finish her discourse for you.'

He sat back, out of sight of Antyr again, and, playing alternately with his battered nose and his straggly beard, fell silent, except for an occasional soft and tuneless humming.

Usche's face reflected Andawyr's curiosity and excitement and it was a visible effort for her to gather the threads of her explanation before she could continue. She started with an apology of her own. '*I*'m sorry,' she said, mouthing the words rather than speaking them. 'It was rude of me to react the way I did.'

'Everyone's apologized to everyone else now,' Antyr said. 'I think honour's satisfied.'

Usche nearly smiled, then she cleared her throat and patted the book. 'That's what can be done with the Power, if you know how,' she said. 'That and many other things.'

'How did you do it?'

Usche pulled a wry face. 'I don't know. That's to say, I know how I did it, just like I know how to plant a seed to grow a flower. But the deeper reasons for such a thing being possible . . .' She shrugged. 'We search, though. Here we search endlessly.'

'How do you think you did it?'

The humming behind Antyr stopped abruptly.

Usche smiled broadly. 'I can't begin to tell you about that,' she said. 'I'm not trying to avoid your question but it really is very complicated. As, I'm sure, are the details of your own profession, if I understood it correctly from Andawyr.'

Antyr acknowledged the point and the humming started again.

'What I *can* tell you, though, is that while most people have some sensitivity to the Power,' she gave him a brief, curious look, 'not everyone can use it as I just did. A certain ... inborn ... quality has to be present. Without it, no amount of training and dedication will have any effect.'

'It's the same with my own trade – profession – call it what you will. Some can do it, most can't. If the ability is there and if a suitable Earth Holder can be found ...' Unconsciously he reached down and stroked the two wolves now lying at either side of his chair. '... Then it can be developed. But if it isn't there, then ... nothing.'

Usche could not resist. 'Does this ability run in families – father to son, mother to daughter?'

'Sometimes, but there's no logic or pattern to it. For the most part it appears at random. My father was a Dream Finder, but there was no guarantee that I would be one.'

Usche leaned forward. 'So it is with the ability to use the Power,' she said, waving a finger for emphasis. 'Quite arbitrary. As big a mystery as the Power itself, in many ways. It's really very odd.' She became earnest, drawing him into the discussion. 'We know that this inborn quality is similar to those that make us left-or right-handed, tall or short, but to some extent they're calculable traits, while this is extraordinarily elusive. It ...'

Andawyr coughed significantly.

Usche gave Antyr a guilty grimace and sat back in her chair again. 'But, whatever the reason for any of us having this ability, if it's there, then using it, for the most part, is logical, consistent and orderly. Obviously some tasks are harder than others, but when I wished to open the book, for example, I did it, and when I wished to close it, I did that.'

There was another slight cough.

'So, at one level – at the level of ordinary use – of practical applications, here, now – we know a great deal. Going deeper, the picture becomes far less clear. It's always been known that the Power pervades everything. Until quite recently it used to be thought that it came from what we call the Great Searing – the beginning of everything. But we think now – in fact, we're fairly certain, actually – that the Great Searing was something that happened only on this world and that it itself was just an unusual manifestation of the Power. It's becoming apparent now that the Power truly *underlies* everything – me, you, this book, the table, these walls. We're all simply different aspects of it.' She was warming to her explanation. 'And not just us, here, but quite literally everything. The sun, the stars, the great islands of stars far beyond our own.' There was wonder in her face. 'So many things come together to make this highly probable,' she went on excitedly. 'It's . . .'

'It's enough for now,' Andawyr interrupted. 'Well done. That was a good effort under the circumstances. I'll go through it with you tomorrow. Track me down if I look like forgetting. Now, if you'll excuse us, I need to talk to Antyr for a while.'

Usche, a little flushed at this praise, quickly gathered up her book and papers.

'Thank you,' Antyr said, offering his hand. She took it. Then, with a slight bow, she left.

'I don't think it was her fault, but I'm not sure I'm much wiser,' Antyr said when she had gone.

'Don't worry,' Andawyr said. 'It's far from easy to understand but we've plenty of time to talk and I'm sure you'll pick up enough to get a feeling for what it's all about. Then, if you want to study it – where better could you be?' He frowned. 'Though I'm puzzled that you felt no response when I passed Usche's sending through you. Very puzzled.' Then he smiled broadly. 'You see, we're just as mystified by you as you are by us.'

Andawyr glanced towards the door that Usche had left through. 'It was a little unkind, dropping that on her without warning, but she did very well.' He burst out laughing again. 'Though she really didn't like being taken for a market trickster. I think if it had been anyone she knew, she'd have floored them.' It took him some time to recover. 'She's a very capable woman,' he went on eventually, wiping his eyes and then tapping his head. 'Both intellectually and in her methodical use of the Power. But she's reached a stage where she needs to . . .' He made an expansive gesture. '. . . to fly a little – to let go – to trust her intuition – to realize that it's actually the fine invisible edge of her intellect, not something vague and separate and . . . faintly undesirable.' He mimicked her voice and manner with these last words, with an accuracy that made Antyr laugh. 'When she does that, she'll be a tremendous asset to us here.'

The remark brought to the surface a question that had been forming in Antyr's mind for some time. He was hesitant about voicing it even though everything he had seen since he had arrived had shown him that Andawyr encouraged inquiry. He started it carefully.

'I hope you won't think this is an impertinent question, but . . .' He hesitated. '. . . Exactly what is it that your Order does? How does it sustain itself? Even what I've seen of this place is enormous and there must be so many people here.'

'Ah, food, water, clothing, and the like, all the many services that any community needs, eh?'

'Well, yes.'

As ever, Andawyr seemed to be pleased with the question. 'We get by very much the same way as any other community, I suppose,' he said. 'We support ourselves in those things that we can, and trade with our neighbours for those we can't. We offer many services. We're not concerned exclusively with esoteric studies into the nature of being and existence, or with preparing for the return of Sumeral, by any means. We study anything and everything.' He became unexpectedly serious. 'Ethriss himself set us on that way. Always he inveighed against ignorance. "A shadow-dwelling creature" he called it. "A bringer of darkness and superstition and all the horrors that only the arrogance of mindless certainty can create." It was perhaps the only thing he was known to get angry about – even in himself – *especially* in himself. In fact, it's said that the reason for his ultimate injunction to us was that he'd discovered something he knew he himself could never fathom. He told us to "go beyond". Go beyond.' Andawyr mulled over the words silently for some time before continuing in a more matter-of-fact vein. 'Still, return-ing to your question. Some of us are farmers – you may have seen the cultivated fields as you came through the valley. Some go out as teachers, some as healers, some as advisers to those who find themselves obliged to rule, some as arbitrators to smooth out disputes, some as musicians, and, as you might imagine from this place, we know more than a little about building. We've many, many useful trades and skills.' He gave a knowing laugh. 'No Dream Finders, though.'

'Not yet, anyway,' Antyr offered.

Andawyr inclined his head with heavy graciousness.

'And, too, we're fortunate. History, both the old and the terrible recent, has given us the trust and support of those same neighbours, the Riddinvolk especially. They're an unusual people.'

'So Yatsu and Jaldaric told me. It seems they live for their horses and . . . the Muster . . . is it?'

'They do, and it is,' Andawyr chuckled. 'Hence Usche's caustic reference to my own riding ability. They judge everyone by their horsemanship. It's a social code of unbelievable subtlety – quite defeats me, for sure. But they're very tolerant and good-natured – live and let live.' The chuckle became a laugh. 'It's always fun to see them "making allowances" for outlanders like me as we wobble along on horseback – doing their damnedest not to be patronizing – or not to laugh. You watch when we go down to Anderras Darion. I'll be more than surprised if at least once you don't catch Usche looking at you as though you were a particularly awkward child. They'll even do it to the likes of Yatsu and Jaldaric. They can't help themselves.'

'Where did this . . . enthusiasm . . . come from?' Antyr asked.

'Oh, like many things it harks all the way back to the First Coming. It's a military tradition that's become an integral part of their society. The Fyordyn have something similar with the service of their young people in the Lords' High Guards.' He became pensive. 'Though, like us here, in the absence of threat I'm afraid much of the original intention had been allowed to slip away. It's more than fortunate there was enough left to save us all when He returned.' He shrugged off the mood. 'Anyway, happily, the Riddinvolk still have a highly

72

developed sense of neighbourliness and this adds much to our life here in addition to the winning of our basic necessities.'

'It sounds very civilized – very comfortable.'

'It is, though you'd not have thought so sixteen years ago. We were as war-torn and fearful as I suspect any of your peoples have ever been. However,' he clapped his hands. 'Enough of that. This profession of yours. This Dream Finding. My curiosity's burning a hole in something. I feel like a child at the Winter Festival. Are you sure I'm not imposing on you, asking you to do whatever it is you do, for me, tonight?'

'It's no imposition at all,' Antyr replied.

'It might well mean a long night for you. Jaldaric was right, I don't sleep a great deal.'

'Don't worry. That's nothing new for me. Quite often my clients have difficulty sleeping . . .'

'That's why they need someone to help with their dreams, of course.'

'Exactly. But don't concern yourself about me. Just do what you normally do, Tarrian and Grayle are already watching you. They'll tell me when you're asleep.' Antyr's tone became confidential. 'But I'll have to go to bed myself soon, it's been a long day. Yatsu and Jaldaric have a great flair for getting up as soon as the sky begins to lighten and it's not something I've managed to get used to. Nor do I think I'm likely to.'

'Yes, they're very stern with themselves, the Goraidin,' Andawyr said understandingly. 'I'll have Ar-Billan show you to your quarters as soon as you're ready.' He put his hand to his forehead. 'And I'll have to show you where my room is, won't I?'

'That's no problem,' Antyr reassured him, indicating the wolves. 'But there *is* something very important that you need to know about. Or, more particularly, that anyone likely to come into your room needs to know about.'

Andawyr gave him an enigmatic look.

'Does anyone wake you in the morning – a servant, perhaps?'

'Not as a rule. But if I oversleep, Oslang usually takes a malicious delight in playing the Goraidin himself.'

Antyr thought for a moment. 'Everyone's so unfamiliar

with Dream Finding round here,' he said, half to himself. 'We must be careful. I think – no, I know – we should have Jaldaric or Yatsu present. They understand what's involved. And I'd like to speak to Oslang anyway.' He took Andawyr's arm. 'It's very important that he, or anyone else liable to enter your room, does exactly as I tell them.'

'You're beginning to make this sound rather alarming.'

'Yes and no. For us, it's all quite safe – innocuous even – but for any inadvertent intruder, it's more than alarming, it's dangerous – *very* dangerous.' Antyr released Andawyr's arm and his manner became professional. 'Tarrian and Grayle guard us both and they guard us totally and in a manner over which they've no control. Put briefly, if anyone tries to touch us or wake us, they'll be attacked without hesitation. And, Tarrian and Grayle being the animals they are, that person will probably be killed.'

Andawyr looked uneasy. 'You talk to them, don't you?' He touched his temple. 'Can't you tell them in advance who they should and should not attack?'

'No.' Antyr's denial coincided with one from the two wolves resonating in Andawyr's mind. He shook his head and screwed his eyes tight shut. Antyr went on. 'I told you, it's beyond any control – theirs or mine. But there's no danger, providing everyone knows what to do and does it – namely nothing, except sit still and watch.'

Andawyr adopted an expression of qualified reassurance.

'As you've just been saying, the danger lies in ignorance,' Antyr said.

'What can I say to so apt a student of so wise a teacher?' Andawyr retorted. 'If Yatsu or Jaldaric want to spend the night in my pit, they're welcome. And I'll make sure you get a chance to instruct Oslang in the do's and don'ts of Dream Finding. The only other problem I can see after that is where I'm going to put you all. I think I might have mentioned that tidiness isn't my strongest point.'

Some time later a paw gently prodded a sleeping Antyr into wakefulness.

'It's time,' Tarrian whispered.

Chapter 7

A ntyr could not suppress a twinge of regret as he followed the two wolves along the softly lit corridor. It had been a long time since he had lain in a proper bed and though he had reached a stage where sleeping in a tent or in the open air was not without its own satisfaction, even importance, to him in its spartan demands and simplicity, the softness of the bed had been more than alluring.

The corridor was thickly carpeted and their progress was very quiet. There was no hint of sound reaching them to indicate that the rest of the Cadwanen was anything other than completely at rest.

'Come on, hurry up,' Tarrian urged.

'I am hurrying,' Antyr yawned. 'And the pair of you can just control your impatience.'

'Don't know what you mean.'

'Yes, you do.'

'We're here.'

Tarrian nosed open a door that was standing slightly ajar and he and Grayle walked straight in. Antyr entered a little more discreetly, noting as he did so that there was nothing about the door that was materially different from any of the others they had passed. Nothing that said it was the room of the leader of this enormous place and all its inhabitants. And, in marked contrast to his experience in Serenstad, there was no gauntlet of suspicious, hard-eyed and heavily armed guards to run. He found the absence of such restraints strangely disorientating.

The room itself, however, brought him sharply to the present. Two low lights illuminated it sufficiently to confirm

Andawyr's admission that tidiness was not his strongest point.

'This place is a tip,' Tarrian announced bluntly as he and Grayle began arbitrarily searching through the various articles of clothing and bedding scattered about the floor.

'Behave yourselves,' Antyr snapped.

He caught a faint stream of grumbling abuse as the two wolves pulled away from him.

Already inside the room were Oslang and Yatsu. They were sitting by the door in large comfortable chairs that had obviously been imported into the room for the night's vigil.

'Young Jaldaric needed his beauty sleep,' Yatsu whispered mockingly as he stood up and acknowledged Antyr.

'You don't have to whisper,' came a voice from a rumpled bed at the far end of the room. 'I'm not asleep yet. Nor likely to be with all this din. I must say I hadn't bargained on such a crowd gathering.'

'I'll be with you in a moment,' Antyr said professionally. He crouched down in front of Oslang.

'I remember what you told me,' Oslang said before he could speak.

Antyr spoke softly and urgently. 'I'm sure you do,' he said, recalling Andawyr's accurate and perceptive retelling of his own story to Usche. 'But no one here knows anything about Dream Finding and for *my* peace of mind I need to remind you.'

Oslang did not argue.

'Tarrian and Grayle may make some strange noises, possibly quite frightening ones, as perhaps might I or Andawyr, though that's less likely. Whatever happens, remember that there's no danger here to anyone, except you. And only to you if you intervene. You must *not* come near us and still less must you make any attempt to touch either of us. If you do, Tarrian and Grayle *will* attack you and there's every chance they'll kill you. I doubt even Yatsu here could cope with the two of them. Just stay where you are. You're here out of curiosity, I appreciate, but your job is to intercept anyone who might come in unexpectedly. Do you understand this?'

'Yes,' Oslang said, though he was patently taken aback by Antyr's sudden authoritativeness.

Yatsu grinned and patted him on the arm in a fatherly manner as Antyr went over to the bed, carefully trying to avoid Andawyr's scattered clothing.

A chair had been placed by the bed for him. As he sat down in it, Andawyr turned over with a peevish grunt. The two wolves were each circling repeatedly prior to lying down. Antyr smiled. Small, familiar rituals were closing about them all.

His mind reached out to touch Tarrian's and Grayle's. They both looked up at him.

Their eyes were bright burning yellow, penetrating and profoundly wild. He was vaguely aware of Oslang drawing in a long breath.

Then, briefly, he was Tarrian and the wolf was him. As always, countless scents and sensations pervaded him, but he ignored them. He looked up to see himself staring down, a looming figure with eyes that were now entirely black. 'Pits of night,' they had been called. It was a sight that few could look on with ease, but that was as it should be. All was well. And, as suddenly, he was himself again, as was Tarrian, though, as usual, the wolf was momentarily unsettled by its temporary occupation of what it regularly denounced as an ungainly, unresponsive and claustrophobic frame.

Slowly Tarrian and Grayle closed their eyes and lowered their heads. Antyr turned to Andawyr. 'Close your eyes and give me your hand,' he said.

'It's no good. I'm not asleep,' Andawyr protested, though doing as he was asked.

Antyr did not reply, but took the offered hand in his right and gently passed his left over Andawyr's face.

'Sleep easy,' he said, very softly. 'Whatever befalls, nothing can harm. Dreams are but shadows and you are guarded in all places by a great and ancient strength.'

He felt the Cadwanwr drifting into sleep immediately. Then he, too, was drifting after him. The room faded and the night that filled his eyes seemed to spread inwardly through every part of him until there was nothing but darkness and silence. Nothing save his awareness, hard as diamond yet as insubstantial as a summer breeze.

Then there were faint sounds all about him, like distant voices and strange instruments carried on an uncertain wind. Mingling with them came lights, twisting, flitting, swelling and star-bursting through the darkness, iridescent and hued beyond the rainbow, some jagged and lightning-fast, others hovering, drifting, watchful.

And then he was whole again, as solid as the figure sitting by Andawyr's bed and holding the Cadwanwr's hand, but other than he. Tarrian and Grayle were there too, but not to be seen. As he always did, a remnant of his earliest apprentice days with his father, he touched the wolf's soft, unseen fur. It was a mutual reassurance. Here, in this strange other place, surrounded by countless shifting sounds and insistent, luring lights, a Dream Finder was lost. For this was the Dream Nexus of Andawyr, leader of the Cadwanol, and all around were the Portals of his many dreams: dreams forgotten, dreams remembered, dreams waking, dreams sleeping, dreams undreamt. And here only a Dream Finder's Earth Holder could guide.

Yet here there was a newness, still unfamiliar to Antyr, for he had not one, but two Earth Holders. It was one of many changes that had come about since he had been drawn along the way that eventually brought him into his terrible confrontation with the blind man and set him on his long, hard journey from his homeland. Unlike many of those changes, however, this one did not disturb him, for his trust in Tarrian and Grayle, as theirs in him, was absolute. But it still puzzled and intrigued him. It was a commonplace in his profession that a Dream Finder could have only one Earth Holder. But why should that be? How an Earth Holder roamed the dreamways was knowledge far beyond the reach of any human inquirer: it was something hidden deep in the wild nature of such creatures. And, too, though he still felt a need for Tarrian and Grayle to be with him, how had it come about that he no longer truly needed their guidance at the Nexus? He let the questions drift away: he could not answer them, he knew, that was why he was here. And this was neither the time nor the place for them. Now, he had a client to attend to and it was sufficient that all was well.

He could feel Tarrian and Grayle reaching out, testing their surroundings just as they would whether in the city or in the mountains. Once he would also have felt Tarrian resisting a deep desire to roam the dreamways unfettered, but that was gone now. Somehow, between them, the two wolves fulfilled this desire, though in what manner neither of them ever spoke of nor could any interrogation elicit.

'This way. This way.' Tarrian's familiar and expected call billowed into his mind. The sounds and sights of the Nexus moved around and through him and, though there was no sensation of change, Dream Finder and Earth Holder were Andawyr.

They were in the mountains.

'As you see and feel, so shall we,' Antyr said. It was the traditional assurance to a client.

'Aah,' said Andawyr. 'Interesting.'

The same thought was occurring to Antyr. He had entered many dreams and witnessed many fantasies, but even though there was a degree of commonality between many of them, each one had not only been unique but had always contained visions that surprised him, albeit not always pleasantly.

His surprise now was not at the vaulting span of Andawyr's imagination, but at his control. Antyr had known clients who were deeply aware of their dreams and who could, to some extent, manipulate them in order to move within a world where wishes that were perhaps forbidden or impossible in the waking world could be freely fulfilled. But this was very different. Andawyr's control was like nothing he had ever encountered before. Yet . . .

'Where shall we go?'

Antyr did not reply, nor would he. Only at some moment of great terror might he gently touch the dreamer, to give a little reassurance, otherwise he would just watch and listen, and feel. The time for talking was on waking.

'Ah. I see. My dream, my choice,' Andawyr deduced correctly.

He was looking down at his reflection at the edge of a motionless lake. Everything was vividly intense. Snow-covered peaks, bright in the sunlight and sharp against the blue sky, were all around him. They too were reflected in the lake, but so clearly that it was difficult to know which was real and which was image. A giddying ambivalence oozed into the scene but Andawyr forbade it. As he looked up, the mountains were still bright and clear, but the sky was filled with dark and menacing clouds.

'Come along,' he said to Usche and Ar-Billan. 'We must reach Anderras Darion before the storm comes.' Neither spoke, but stood looking at him expectantly.

They were not dressed for hard walking, he thought. He should be more careful with his charges. On the other hand, some things they had to learn the hard way.

The wind was screaming all about him, shaking and battering him. It threw stinging white spears of snow into his face as he struggled along the corridors of the Cadwanen, dimly lit by familiar symbols whose meaning had slipped away from him. They blinked distantly and urgently through the streaked gloom, the touch of their uncertain light turning the flying snow into black, prison bar streaks.

It's very bad this year, Andawyr thought. *I must get this place swept out.*

The snow was deep, and curving drifts piled up against the walls, blocking the doorways and wilfully stifling the symbols. Andawyr's calves were aching with the effort of walking and he was beginning to breathe heavily.

The tall figure by his side turned and looked down at him.

'Hawklan, I didn't know you were here. What a happy surprise. We were coming to see you, but the weather seems to be unseasonable.' He could not go on. The wind was like a solid wall and he was exhausted.

'Let's sit here for a moment.'

He moved into the lee of the figure and rested against him.

'You've found the Sword, I see. That's good.' He looked at the hilt of the black sword with its inner motif of intertwined strands. They seemed to stretch for ever, across a dark void filled with countless stars. There was such mystery in this thing, he had to know . . .

He reached out to search into it . . .

Then a force was tumbling him violently into wakefulness.

80

His heart was pounding so fiercely that it threatened to choke him, his hand was being gripped tightly and he was surrounded by confusion and noise. It took him some time to realize what was happening.

The two wolves were barking frantically and a strident, wavering note was filling the room. It was a chilling sound. One that should never be heard here. It emanated from two symbols by the door, as did a baleful, pulsating red light, though Andawyr did not need to look to know this. Frozen in this masque was Oslang, eyes wide and mouth gaping, while Yatsu was little better, half standing with one powerful hand extended sideways to prevent the Cadwanwr leaving his seat.

An urgent knocking made itself heard above the din, then the door burst open. Yatsu was on his feet and the first person through the door found himself spun around and pushed into others close behind him. Several of them went sprawling.

'Stay where you are, all of you!'

Yatsu's powerful command overrode the mounting confusion in the room. The wolves stopped barking and slithered close to Antyr, their tails low and wagging hesitantly. He let Andawyr's hand fall, then slumped forward and began cradling their heads.

Oslang was grasping the arms of his chair, his gaze oscillating desperately between Yatsu and Andawyr. 'Can I move now?' he demanded of the Goraidin.

'Antyr?' Yatsu called out in his turn.

The Dream Finder straightened up and stared blankly at the two men and the crowded doorway for a moment. Then he released the wolves and held up a pleading hand. 'A moment, a moment,' he said breathlessly. 'Let me get my wits back. There's no danger now.'

'The hell there isn't,' Oslang shouted angrily, pointing towards the symbols. 'What do you think that is?'

Antyr looked at him helplessly.

'Still that and see how many others have been activated, Oslang. See how far it's spread.' It was Andawyr. He had swung out of bed and was unsteadily fastening his robe about him. Oslang hesitated, torn between the instruction and attending on his friend. A gesture from Andawyr brightened

81

the lights. 'See how far it's spread,' he repeated, firmly. 'And for mercy's sake, still the damned thing.'

He acknowledged the small but obviously anxious group being held at bay in the doorway by Yatsu. 'Well done, all of you,' he said. 'It's nothing to worry about. Just a little experiment that went awry, I'm afraid. Help Oslang get the measure of it, then get back to your beds. We'll talk about it tomorrow.'

Oslang, brow furrowed, was peering closely at the symbols. Their pulsing red light lit his face, etching its lines deeply. He looked as though he were staring down into a furnace. Then, apparently satisfied but still fretful, he placed his hand over each in turn. The noise stopped immediately and the redness faded until both symbols were still and pale again. The sudden silence jolted breaths of relief from everyone.

Oslang took Yatsu's arm. 'Well done to you as well. Thanks for not hurting any of them.' Then he disappeared into a babble of voices in the corridor.

'An explanation wouldn't go amiss,' Yatsu said to Antyr and Andawyr as the door closed.

'I couldn't agree with you more,' Andawyr said, dropping back on to his bed.

He looked at Antyr. 'What happened in there? What happened to "Dreams are shadows? Nothing can harm?" ' There was both fear and anger in his voice. His expression softened, however, as he saw the pain of the Dream Finder's face.

'Are you all right?' he asked.

'Yes,' Antyr replied, though his voice was weak. 'Just shaky.'

Andawyr waited.

'I don't know what happened,' Antyr replied after a moment. 'But whatever it was, it came out of nowhere and without any warning.' He put his hand to his head. 'You'll have to excuse me. I dragged you out of there as much by pure reflex as anything else. I'm not thinking clearly yet.' He allowed himself no time to recover, however. 'Maybe it was something to do with your being able to use the Power.' He looked at Andawyr intently. 'Were you about to use it when you reached out for that sword?'

82

'No, of course not, why should I? Besides, I don't think I could. I know I can control my dreams but to use the Power you need control over every faculty.' He raised his eyebrows. 'Though I confess I'd never thought about it.' He became pensive for a moment then frowned. 'It *must* be impossible, surely,' he said, though more to himself than for the information of the others. 'There's no saying *what* the consequences might be if it weren't. Then again, it's an intriguing problem. If I used the Power in a dream would it be the Power or just a dream of it? Fascinating. This will make an excellent project for someone.'

'Before you become too enthralled we need to find out what just happened. Because it was dangerous, and there shouldn't have been even a vestige of danger there.' Antyr's stern interruption ended Andawyr's reverie abruptly. Antyr waved towards the door. 'What was that noise and that red light? And why did those people break in like that?'

Andawyr scratched his head vigorously, then held out his hand. It was shaking. 'Yes, there was a danger, wasn't there?' he said. 'As for the Beacons, that's a good question.'

There was a discreet tapping on the door and Oslang entered. He was more relaxed but he was still obviously concerned. 'It was just in here and immediately outside in the corridor,' he said. 'There's no danger. Everything's stilled now, though I doubt it will be tomorrow when the word gets around.'

Andawyr looked relieved but puzzled. 'Well, it seems that it was confined, so that's one problem the less but several more new ones. As for the gossip, we'll just tell them what happened.'

'What *did* happen?' Oslang demanded.

'One thing at a time,' Andawyr replied. He pointed to the now quiescent symbol and turned to Antyr.

'Something in that dream set off one of the devices you were asking about earlier – one of the Beacons. That did what it did because there'd been a use of the Power in here that didn't come from any of us – any members of the Order, that is.' He looked at Antyr curiously. 'Are you *sure* you've no skill with the Power?'

83

'I know nothing about it, except what I felt from the blind man and what I've learned from Yatsu and Jaldaric and yourself.'

Andawyr pursed his lips. 'Well, that was my judgement, too. And it certainly *should* be the case. The ability of any individual to use the Power is tested automatically when they enter the place.' He glanced at the symbols again. 'Furthermore, if by some highly improbable chance you'd spontaneously acquired such an ability while you were actually here, then the Beacons would not only have detected it, but would've immobilized you, one way or another – up to and including killing you if your intention had been destructive.'

Antyr's eyes widened. His mouth went dry.

'Are you sure you're all right?' Andawyr asked.

'Yes,' Antyr insisted, though his general demeanour gave the lie to this. 'It's just that your dream was dangerous enough without finding out I was in danger here as well.'

'And that's another problem. You weren't. It had no effect on you. Which confirms what I already knew, namely that whatever activated it couldn't have come from you.'

'All of this makes no sense,' Oslang said. 'Beacons don't just go off like that. Nor should it have been confined to such a small area. And at that level of intensity I'd have expected to see one of the Uhriel coming through the door, not a crowd of bewildered Brothers.'

'You always were given to exaggeration,' Andawyr snapped, adding lamely, 'maybe it's faulty.'

Oslang gave him a look verging on disdain. 'Faulty! How could it possibly be faulty? And I'm not exaggerating, you know that. For crying out . . .'

Andawyr raised his hand to accept the rebuff. He blew out a noisy breath. 'Well, I couldn't sleep now even if I wanted to. Let's get started on this while everything's fresh in our minds.' He looked down at the wolves and clicked his tongue reproachfully. 'Are *they* all right?' he asked Antyr softly.

'Yes, thank you.' Tarrian's voice filled Andawyr's head. 'And, for what it's worth, you can thank Antyr for getting us all back safely. Whatever you did in there nearly lost us all.'

'What *I* did?' Andawyr exclaimed out loud, startling both

Oslang and Yatsu. 'What do you mean, what *I* did? I did nothing.'

'Antyr didn't, we didn't, you were the only other one there.'

'But . . .'

He received the canine equivalent of a dismissive shrug, which ended the matter as far as Tarrian was concerned. Faced with silence, Andawyr made a gesture that further brightened the lights, then he beat his pillow vigorously, swung his feet up on to the bed, and lay back, his hands behind his head.

'Can't we go somewhere a little more . . . congenial . . . if you want to talk about this now?' Oslang asked with a pained glance about the disordered room.

'I'm comfortable,' Andawyr said with finality.

Oslang adopted a martyred expression and dragged his chair over to the bed. 'You'd better go through it in detail, then,' he said, flopping into the chair ungraciously.

Andawyr did not reply immediately. He was staring vaguely into the distance. 'It was an odd dream from the start,' he began eventually. 'I felt Antyr there.' He twisted round to look at the Dream Finder. 'Fascinating. We really must go into how . . .'

Oslang cleared his throat noisily. Andawyr gave him a sidelong look and returned to his recollection.

'An odd dream, as I said. I was looking at my reflection in a lake – and the mountains. Usche and Ar-Billan were there, though they didn't say anything – or do anything. They just seemed to be . . . there . . . waiting. Then there were storm clouds, and I was walking through the corridors here, in the middle of a howling blizzard – snow everywhere. All the Beacons were signalling an assault but it didn't matter – it was only a slight one – I knew that even though I didn't know what it was. And Hawklan was there.' He looked at Oslang. 'With the Sword – Ethriss's sword. For some reason I wasn't surprised to see it again. I reached out to touch it, then . . .' He threw his arms up explosively.

'That's what happened,' Antyr confirmed. 'It was a quite ordinary dream. I don't know if the figure was Hawklan but Andawyr certainly thought it was. And, despite what happened, there was no element of nightmare in it: no underlying hint of real terror. The only thing unusual was that the control I suspect he normally has in his dreams wasn't there. He was letting events take their own course.'

'Or they were taking me,' Andawyr said. 'It *is* odd, that, I must admit. Normally, as you say, I'm fully in command of events, but not this time. It wasn't unpleasant, but it certainly wasn't usual. Perhaps it was just because you were there.'

'Possibly, but *you* made no conscious decision about it.'

Andawyr pulled a wry face and fiddled with his nose.

'And you weren't being wholly truthful about the sword,' Antyr went on. He was searching for words. 'Something about it drew you. So many strange feelings. Feelings I've never known myself and couldn't begin to explain. Tarrian?'

'He's a Mynedarion,' came the terse reply.

'It seems they may all be around here,' Antyr said. 'But at least they're benign.'

'Maybe, but that's where your answer lies. And in that sword.'

Antyr let out a noisy breath. He could sense that Tarrian and Grayle were talking to each other beyond his awareness. They invariably did after they had been in the dreamways and he knew from past experience that nothing was to be gained by badgering them. Tarrian would have said all he wanted to say for the moment and he could do no other than follow his suggestion.

'Tell me about this sword,' he said to Andawyr.

Chapter 8

'Yes, the sword,' Andawyr mused. 'Strange I should think of that after all this time.' He smiled ruefully. 'Using my dreams to fulfil my wishes, that's all.'

'It's very special, then?' Antyr asked.

'Oh yes. Very special. I don't have a great many regrets in my life, but one of them is that I didn't take the opportunity to study it further while it was here.' Andawyr shrugged. 'Still, we weren't then what we are now, we'd probably not have learned much from it. Not to mention the fact that we'd a good many other things to occupy us at the time.' He became dismissive. 'It's probably come to mind because I've been thinking about Hawklan so much today. I can't see that it's of any particular relevance to what happened.'

'Tarrian thinks it is, and if you feel at all reluctant to talk about it then that's even more reason why we should.'

A spasm of irritation passed over Andawyr's face, though whether in annoyance at himself or at his interrogator Antyr could not hazard.

'You're right,' he said after an uncomfortable pause which he ended by fiddling with his pillow again. 'It's hard to know what to say about it. It was Hawklan's sword when he fought in one of the great battles of the First Coming.' His hand was reaching out to forestall Antyr's startled question even before he had finished speaking. 'There's no point in asking,' he said. 'We've no idea how Hawklan – or some aspect of him – could be both in that time and here with us now. No idea at all. Nor has he. But it is so. Indisputably so, as far as we can tell. There are many mysteries from that time. Although I'll admit that could well be the greatest.' He

87

stopped abruptly as the difficulties of this long-debated problem threatened to rehearse themselves again, then he pressed on quickly. 'For now, let's concentrate on our own particular mystery. As I said, the sword was, and is again, Hawklan's, though after he was lost in that awful battle Ethriss took it for his own and reforged it. Hawklan found it this time in the Armoury of Anderras Darion. Or rather, *it* found *him*. It literally fell at his feet from a heap of weapons. Drawn to him, almost. No one knew what it was at the time, still less how it came to be there. When we realized what it was, the presumption was that Ethriss had left it there – he went unarmed to the Last Battle, definitely – but no one really knows.'

Antyr's mind was full of questions about Hawklan but Andawyr's manner had indicated unequivocally that he did not wish to pursue that subject. He forced his attention back to the dream.

'So this sword is special because of its association with Ethriss – it's a symbol of former victory?' he posited. 'A rallying point, like a battle flag.'

'No,' Andawyr said simply. 'It's special because it's special. In its own right. It's a very unusual artefact. It's something like . . . a focus . . . a concentration of the Power itself. It's not easy to explain. In fact, it's not *possible* to explain.' He held up two clenched and quivering fists like a petulant schoolboy. 'I just wish I could have hold of it again.'

'What happened to it?'

The clenched fists wilted. Andawyr looked down at them sadly. 'Hawklan dropped it into Lake Kedrieth when Sumeral confronted him. *Dropped* it.' There was reproach in his voice.

'Hardly surprising under the circumstances,' Oslang said sternly, offering a reproach of his own.

Andawyr recanted hastily. 'No, of course not. Still . . .' His face became thoughtful. 'He only ever spoke about that time once, to me, anyway. I remember him saying it fell and it fell, through the darkness, until it landed with a great ringing sound. I've no idea why I didn't ask him what he meant.'

'As I recall you and the others telling me, there were a lot of strange noises at the time, to put it mildly,' Oslang said.

'What with Sumeral's passing and Derras Ustramel being destroyed.'

'True,' Andawyr conceded. 'But this was before all that. And he was quite clear about it. It fell and it fell through the darkness until it landed with a great ringing sound. What a strange statement. It didn't just splash into the Lake as it fell off the causeway. More mysteries. And why have I hardly bothered to think about it since?'

'You have,' Oslang retorted sourly. 'Or have you forgotten *delegating* to me the job of organizing those High Guards to search for it?' He turned to Antyr as though to an ally of long standing. 'Weeks we were there. In the very bowels of Narsindal.' He shivered massively. 'It's a wonder I didn't throw all this up and go back to the family farm afterwards, I can tell you. As for those poor young men, doing their damnedest – dredging, trawling, even diving into that awful lake – diving, for pity's sake. Some of them were so ill. You can't imagine how dreadful it was. Blighted doesn't begin to describe the place. Do you know . . .'

'Yes, yes,' Andawyr intervened heatedly. 'I *do* recall it. And I also recall apologizing for it at great length thereafter. And several times.' The two men eyed one another silently until Andawyr established a truce with a final schoolboy flourish. 'Even so, I still wish I had the sword now. We must make a point of talking to Hawklan about it when we get to Anderras Darion.'

'All of which isn't bringing us any nearer to finding out what happened in your dream,' Antyr said as tactfully as he could, in case Oslang decided to continue the old spat. 'Whatever became of the sword, it is definitely lost?' he inquired of them both.

Cursory nods confirmed his conclusion, though both men seemed to be preoccupied.

'Then I am, too,' Antyr declared. 'Although I have the impression that this weapon's more important to you than you're prepared to concede at the moment, whether you know it or not. That might perhaps account for the unusual sensations I experienced as you made to touch it, though that doesn't feel like an adequate explanation. And it still doesn't account for the sudden danger.'

He glanced towards the symbols glowing softly on the panel by the door. 'If that . . . Beacon thing . . . that machine, whatever it is, truly isn't faulty, then why did it do what it did? And why were you surprised that it had only set off a few others in the corridor?' He addressed this last question to Oslang.

There was a long silence and Oslang's tone was sober when he eventually spoke.

'The Beacons aren't machines, Antyr. At least, not as I imagine you'd normally conceive a machine. In many ways they're more a great store of knowledge – our knowledge, accumulated over the years. They're all linked together, continually testing for . . . inappropriate . . . uses of the Power throughout the Cadwanen. They don't exactly think, but it's almost as if they did, the way they check and double-check each other constantly to provide many overlapping and different layers of defence and protection. You have to understand that they were designed to protect us against an enemy of both great cunning and great ability and that they're very sophisticated devices. More so now than ever before. What that one signalled was a threat of the first order – a serious and unexpected use – abuse – of the Power. For such a thing to happen under normal circumstances, we'd have expected a major incursion of some kind, with Warnings sounding all over the Cadwanen. To just activate spontaneously like that really makes no sense.'

There was another long silence. 'You're trying to tell me that what happened was actually impossible,' Antyr offered tentatively.

'Yes, damn it, he is,' Andawyr said, this time unequivocally angry. He swung off the bed. 'Quite impossible. Let's get out of here, I need to think properly. Oslang, take Antyr to my study. I'll join you there shortly when I've washed and changed.'

'Do you want me?' It was Yatsu.

Andawyr looked at him and his grim expression softened into a smile. 'Ah, the ever-patient, ever-watching Goraidin. Our silent Beacon out in the world. Where would we be

90

without you? I'd forgotten you were here, Yatsu, I'm sorry. Thanks for what you've done tonight. I suspect you saved lives, keeping Oslang in his seat and our vigilant Brothers out of the room. You're welcome to join us if you wish, but it'll just be endless talk. There'll be no more "experiments" tonight, you can rest assured.'

Yatsu bowed. 'You don't think you'll need me to keep you two apart?' He nodded towards Oslang.

'I have the feeling that Antyr can cope with that,' Andawyr replied.

Yatsu smiled. 'Then I'll leave you. It's been a long day.

Andawyr's study was only a little way from his bedroom, but on the way to it Oslang and Antyr passed quite a few people apparently engaged on urgent, if discreet, errands. Though they received nothing but quiet, passing greetings, Antyr gained the distinct impression that they were attracting a great deal of attention.

Oslang gave him a weary look. 'It's going to be pandemonium tomorrow,' he said. 'One of the *dis*advantages of encouraging so many clever and irredeemably curious people to become even cleverer and more curious is that they do.'

His hangdog manner drew a laugh followed by an insincere apology from Antyr.

When they entered Andawyr's study, lights came on to reveal a room that was markedly different from his bedroom. It bristled with quiet efficiency. Two walls were lined with simple, elegant shelves stacked with books and scrolls. All of these were set out in a neat and orderly fashion and were clearly labelled. They complemented several sets of drawers of various sizes that in their turn were also carefully labelled. A series of small tables served as satellites to a large one in the centre of the room, and there were two decorated panels that Antyr now knew to be mirror stone windows.

'Different, isn't it?' Oslang said, correctly interpreting Antyr's hesitation and his surprised expression.

'It is indeed,' Antyr replied.

Tarrian and Grayle pushed past them to make their own detailed examination of the room.

'There *is* a reason for this,' Oslang went on, confidentially. 'When Andawyr says that tidiness isn't his strong point, it really is a gross understatement.' Oslang tapped his temple. 'In here there are thoughts as sharp as crystals, lines of logic straighter than the horizon at sea, a childlike clarity of vision, and leaps of intuition for which the word inspired is also an understatement. But out here . . .' He shook his head. 'He's a disaster. So this place is in the nature of a compromise. It's his and, for the most part, his alone, but *we* . . .' he tapped his own chest '. . . keep it – and the records of his work – tidy and in good order. It causes a little friction from time to time, but on the whole it works.'

'Compromise?' Antyr queried.

'The compromise is that he lets us keep the place – and him – in some semblance of order and, in return, we feed him.'

'Oh, *that* kind of a compromise,' Antyr laughed, taken again by Oslang's quietly acid manner. 'I'm familiar with the idea. It's what I would call doing as I'm told.' This time Oslang laughed, a deep, restrained affair that nevertheless lit up his face. He ushered Antyr to a seat at the large table.

'Speaking of which,' Antyr finally voiced the question that had occurred to him several times since his first meeting with Andawyr. 'Who *does* tell anyone what to do around here?'

Oslang gave him a puzzled look, obliging him to stumble on awkwardly.

'There seems to be an almost total absence of formal authority here. Andawyr is described as the Leader, and you are the Under Leader, yet you wear no special clothes or insignia. Andawyr's living quarters seem to be no different from anyone else's, at least from the outside. He eats in a public refectory. You're both spoken to by the likes of Ar-Billan and Usche – your juniors in every sense – as casually, as openly as . . .' He paused.

'As you and I are talking now?' Oslang prompted. 'As equals.'

'Well, yes,' Antyr agreed.

'Does this disturb you?'

'No,' Antyr said without hesitation, though his tone gave the contrary answer. 'Quite the opposite . . . I think. It's just that I find it very unusual. Where I come from – particularly in the palaces of the rich and powerful – it's quite the reverse. People know their places and everyone else's and have due regard for them. Respect for those in authority is conspicuous.'

Oslang looked at him narrowly. 'I think you mean that a *show* of respect to those with *power* is conspicuous, don't you? That people behave in ways that best serve their own ends – be it survival against the arbitrary abuse of authority by others, or the gaining of that authority for themselves – ambition.'

'I suppose I do,' Antyr agreed reluctantly after some thought. 'That's quite often the case. But not always. There are some in authority who are both feared and quite genuinely respected.'

'But only some.'

Antyr began to flounder. 'Yes . . . but . . . I didn't mean to criticize the way you do things here . . .'

Oslang smiled. 'I'm just teasing you a little,' he said. 'Something of a risk with a guest, but my feeling was that you'd take it in good part.' Before Antyr could in fact respond, Oslang edged his chair a little closer and became instructive. 'I'm at far greater risk of sounding smug when I tell you about us, because it was an interesting question. There *is* authority here, of course. A pecking order's inevitable whenever there's more than one person present – it's the nature of the creatures we are. But, on the whole, it's not a rigid thing and we manage to avoid the worst excesses of the pack.' Tarrian's ears went up. Abruptly, Oslang was earnest. 'We were created by Ethriss to acquire knowledge – and perhaps wisdom – so that it could be brought to bear against a terrible enemy. But he also told us to go beyond – to search forever – because our greatest enemy will always be ignorance – ignorance of ourselves, ignorance of the world around us. So that's what we do – what we've always done, with varying degrees of success. We accumulate knowledge both for its practical value and its own sake – for the beauty and wonder we find there. We set great faith in reason – in open inquiry – truth seeking – testing by both argument and experiment – testing ruthlessly.'

He raised a finger to forestall a question from Antyr. 'And in this search we despise no source of knowledge. Insight comes from the strangest of places. Andawyr will listen to a stablehand as keenly as he would to me or any of the other senior Brothers. Sometimes the least word can change a perspective completely – shine an unexpected light into the darkness – sometimes a darkness you didn't even know was there. And anyone who joins us has to learn that from the outset. We try to minimize the more corrosive effects of our personal vanities with honesty and trust. Not that it's always possible by any means – it's no easy lesson to learn. We're still pack animals at heart and more than a little fallible. But on the whole we aspire to be a community of self-sufficient, co-operating individuals and the authority that any of us holds has strong roots in both ability and general consent. It helps, of course, that it's an exciting time with many new things happening and plenty for everyone to do both here and out in the world. I suppose what you might call the "government" of this place is both structured and unstructured. Structured in that each of us, of course, has specific responsibilities and must account for any failure to fulfil them. Unstructured in that everyone also accepts responsibility for the whole.' He chuckled. 'Andawyr, for example, will do more than just chat to stablehands. If the stable needs cleaning and everyone else is better employed, he'll clean it himself.'

'That's a metaphor, I presume,' Antyr said.

'Absolutely not,' Oslang laughed. 'How do you think his robe gets in such a mess?'

Antyr's eyes widened. 'I can't imagine the Duke of Seren-stad cleaning the stables, still less some of his officers. Then again, when he was younger, he was always at the forefront of the battle. At least in war he wouldn't ask of others what he wasn't prepared to do himself.'

'And they followed him loyally as a result?' Oslang said.

'Many did, for sure,' Antyr replied. 'But his rule of the city was far from the triumph of reason and logic you seem to have here. Conspiracy and plotting were the norm, with endless different factions jostling for power.'

Oslang laughed again. 'That was just because I said it all

very quickly. I wouldn't call it a triumph by any means. It's pretty good, but we're not without a fair amount of downright inefficiency, and some of the petty squabbling and rivalry that goes on between ostensibly rational adults wouldn't be tolerated in a schoolyard, believe me. As for power, there you have it. What is power over others? I order you to do something, you refuse, so by superior strength or the threat of it, I force you to. But then, having set the rules, as it were, I've constantly to be on my guard that someone won't do the same to me. That's how it goes, isn't it?'

Antyr frowned. 'Yes, but it works well enough, especially when your superior strength allows you to kill me with impunity.'

Oslang's face became serious. 'Yes indeed. I apologize. I didn't mean to trivialize what you said. Ethriss knows, we above all understand it's a fundamental mistake to imagine that violence solves nothing. Indeed, it's perhaps because we have such a frightening measure of the power that can be made available for the terrorizing – the destroying – of others that we set such store by our way.'

'Aha. By your solemn faces I see you've been putting the world to rights in my absence.' It was Andawyr. He sat down next to Antyr and clapped his hands jovially.

'And who better to do it?' Oslang said emphatically, relaxing back into his chair. 'We were just coming to defining the purpose of humanity.'

Andawyr made a disparaging face. 'Oh, an easy one, eh? Our purpose – the purpose of humanity – is to discover all the secrets of the universe, and to find out both where we came from and where we're going to. Next question!'

Antyr risked entering into the spirit of their exchange. 'And will we do it?' he asked.

Andawyr's reply was unexpectedly serious. 'Oh yes,' he said with a calm smile. 'Without a doubt. It may take some time, though.'

A scornful sound, not dissimilar to a raspberry, filled the minds of Antyr and Andawyr. It came from the two wolves. Grayle had his head on his paws and was staring at them, Tarrian was scratching himself vigorously.

'Would you like to join in the debate?' Andawyr asked caustically.

'You're not ready for it yet,' Tarrian replied. 'Carry on. We'll join in as soon as you've something interesting to say.'

Antyr gave a disclaiming shrug.

'Well, it's another perspective, I suppose,' Andawyr said, looking at the wolves enigmatically. Then he took Antyr's arm. 'Are you fully recovered?' he asked. 'No after-effects of any kind?'

'No, none at all. And you?'

'Still puzzled, that's all. And concerned.' He leaned his chair perilously backwards and reached out to take some papers from a nearby chest of drawers. Dropping them on the table he rifled into his gown and finally produced a pen. He began doodling idly.

'A first-order Warning set off, Oslang. Highly localized. Your initial thoughts.'

Oslang drummed his fingers on the table. 'First and last thoughts, I'm afraid – none,' he replied. Andawyr continued to look at him expectantly. Apparently cornered by this, Oslang gave a noisy sigh. 'I'd have thought it impossible,' he said. 'But I saw and heard it, therefore it isn't. So I'd have to say that it was a very unlikely event – low probability. But even then, I'm not sure where to start looking.'

'To find an unlikely event, look in an unlikely place, presumably. Your thoughts, Antyr.'

The suddenness of the question startled Antyr. 'I've no idea.' The words blustered out. 'I told you. It was mainly reflexes that brought us back. There was precious little conscious thought. But it makes no more sense to me than it seems to do for you. Nothing was unusual about the dream other than the absence of the control you normally have – hardly a disturbing thing in itself. Tarrian and Grayle have found nothing untoward or they'd have told me by now. Whatever it was, it came out of nowhere and without any warning and my feeling – and that's all it is – is that it was associated with that sword.'

Andawyr nodded, but, as he had with Oslang, kept on looking at Antyr as if expecting more. Antyr dithered. He pointed to the Beacon symbols by the door. 'Just how do those things work? Exactly what is it they detect?' he asked.

Andawyr followed his gaze thoughtfully, then turned back to him. He did not address the question, however. 'You're here, in this strange place, so far from your own land, because you're no ordinary Dream Finder, are you? You told us that somehow you'd been able to move to worlds that were as real as this but different from it.'

'Yes.'

'What control do you have over this ability?'

'None that I'm aware of. I suppose that's one of the reasons I'm here.' He glanced at Oslang. 'My ignorance burdens me.'

'Why?'

Again Andawyr's question startled Antyr, though the Cadwanwr did not wait for an answer. 'Why shouldn't this ability be a source of excitement and liberation to you? An opportunity to explore realms that few others can even dream of, let alone travel to.'

Antyr was shaking his head. 'You don't understand. There's a subtle feeling of wrongness about being in another world.' He stopped. 'No, that's not correct. There was a subtle feeling of wrongness about *me* when *I* was in another world. A feeling of . . . inadequacy . . . inappropriateness. This gift, if gift it is, and however it came to me, was – presumably still is – substantially beyond my control. I didn't know what I was doing. What I did I did by instinct. I was parted from my Earth Holders. They were hunting through a realm that was separate from me – somewhere between the worlds. For all I know I could've been lost in one of those worlds for ever – my body here perhaps neither dead nor alive.' He shuddered as fears he had not experienced for a long time returned to him. 'I'd forgotten how awful it was. And, too, in those worlds there was a deep feeling of intruding, of my presence having consequences that I couldn't see.'

Andawyr's eyes reflected his pain. 'And now my ignorance burdens you,' he said. 'I'm sorry. I've been worse than thoughtless. I was so intrigued by your story that I've behaved appallingly. After such a journey, the least you were entitled to was a little time doing nothing. And there I go, imposing on

97

you. Dragging you into my dreams, of all places. Now questioning you into the deep hours of the night.' He brushed the papers to one side and slapped the table. 'The Beacons are all quiet. Nothing untoward's happening. I can't apologize too abjectly for my disgraceful conduct. Get off to your bed and some rest. Tomorrow you can lounge in it all day or wander about to your heart's content. We can talk about all this some other time, whenever you feel like it.'

He made to stand up, but Antyr stopped. 'No: I *am* tired, but I doubt I'd be able to sleep after what's happened. I'd rather talk for the time being.' He looked at Andawyr shrewdly. 'Why didn't you answer my question about the Beacons? That's the second one you've avoided.'

This time it was Andawyr who was startled. He fidgeted with the papers for a moment and threw a quick glance at the Beacon before replying. 'You're right. I was going to say that I was distracted, but I think that might be a lie – a conversational sop. The truth is, I'm not sure why I didn't answer your question.' He frowned. 'There's nothing about the way the Beacons work that needs to be hidden from common knowledge.'

'Perhaps the other place to look for an unlikely event is under our noses,' Oslang said.

Andawyr nodded. 'Indeed, we should know that by now, shouldn't we?'

He went over to the Beacon, motioning the others to follow him. Humming quietly to himself he touched the panel. Antyr let out an incongruous 'Oh!' as the panel and a section of the wall around it became alive with symbols and numbers. Tarrian and Grayle wandered over to see what was happening.

For several minutes Andawyr and Oslang studied the panel intently. Occasionally one of them would touch one of the symbols, bringing about a cascade of change amongst the others. Finally Antyr could not restrain himself.

'What does all that mean?' he asked.

Andawyr puffed out his cheeks. 'I'm not avoiding your question this time, Antyr, truly, but I can't begin to explain this to you. You just don't know enough.'

'I think I'm in the same position,' Oslang said, resting a finger on a long string of figures and shaking his head in bewilderment. 'These seem to confirm our original conclusion.'

'That what happened was impossible?'

Oslang muttered something under his breath that made Andawyr raise his eyebrows and click his tongue censoriously.

'Oslang's a student of some very interesting old languages,' he said to Antyr by way of explanation. Oslang coloured and cleared his throat.

'We're just going to have to study these at leisure and in great detail,' he said, ignoring Andawyr's amusement. 'There are anomalies – paradoxes – in these figures that simply shouldn't be there. It's almost as if . . .'

Andawyr caught his arm and turned quickly to Antyr. 'Your question,' he said. 'What do the Beacons detect? Oslang touched on it before. They detect uses of the Power that are either from other than one of us, or directed to some divergent – destructive – end. They do nothing that we can't do as individuals, but they do it better, continuously, thoroughly – without flagging and with great sensitivity and accuracy. Under our noses, Oslang. Under our noses. That's where it is, I can smell it.' He jabbed a finger towards the panel. 'For an instant there *must* have been a source of the Power here. A considerable source.'

'But you and I would have felt something that was strong enough to cause such a Warning.'

'Not if that instant was very short.'

'*Very* short,' Oslang confirmed.

'Perhaps even between the moments,' Andawyr said, looking at him significantly.

Oslang straightened up and returned his gaze with a challenging one of his own. He made two attempts at starting before he finally managed to speak. '*That* is highly conjectural, to say the least. But even if I allow it – which I don't – it still leaves us with the problem of where such a manifestation could come from.'

'It's not that conjectural,' Andawyr rebutted. 'It's just that you're reluctant to accept the implications.'

'Who wouldn't be?'

'Maybe, but that's irrelevant, isn't it? It wouldn't be the first time everything we think we know has been upended.'

'Just make your point.'

'My point is that the only explanation – or at least the best so far – is that Antyr, with his strange ability, which he admits he cannot control, reached out and brought into this world, for that moment between the moments, Hawklan's sword.'

Oslang shook his head, not in denial, but as if to clear it. 'Too fast, too fast. Too many unfounded leaps.' He grimaced guiltily and gave Antyr an apologetic glance. 'We don't know what Antyr's ability is. What he's experienced isn't necessarily what he thinks he's experienced. We need to talk with him at length. We . . .'

'We need to take it at face value for the moment,' Andawyr interrupted. 'We already have some interesting hard facts from Yatsu and Jaldaric, and even from this evening's limited exercise, I can tell you that Antyr has an ability that's . . .' He gesticulated wildly. 'At right angles to every direction *we* know.' He became excited. 'Antyr, is it possible . . .'

He stopped.

Antyr, eyes closed, was swaying unsteadily.

Tarrian and Grayle moved menacingly to his side.

Chapter 9

Andawyr stepped forward instinctively towards the swaying figure of Antyr but Oslang, remembering the urgency
of Yatsu's hand as it prevented him from leaving his seat when
Andawyr and Antyr had burst so suddenly from their dream,
seized his arm quickly. He remembered, too, the sight of the
wolves, their eyes bright, yellow and baleful.

'No, don't go near him.'

Briefly Andawyr resisted Oslang's restraint but, even as he
made to pull his arm free, Tarrian's hackles began to rise and
his upper lip curled back to reveal glinting and powerful teeth.
The sight was accompanied by a rumbling growl.

Oslang's grip tightened, as much now to seek protection as
to give it.

Andawyr stopped his struggle and froze as Grayle joined
his brother by Antyr's side.

'What's the matter?' Andawyr said to all three of them,
vainly trying to keep his voice casual. Antyr, still swaying, did
not reply, but violent and disturbing images flooded into
Andawyr's mind that patently came from Tarrian. Among
them was a faint and rapidly fading hint of regret, then
Andawyr sensed the wolf withdrawing into his wilder self.

'I understand,' he said, slowly moving backwards in
response to Oslang's urging. 'This is what you are. You have
no choice. We will guard him also.'

There was no reply other than the continued growling.

Andawyr, his eyes fixed on the wolves, groped behind him
for a chair. He motioned Oslang to sit down also.

'We'll seem to be less of a threat if we look smaller,' he
said.

Despite the fact that it was he who had pulled Andawyr back, Oslang hissed, 'We can't just sit here. Antyr's ill.'

'I don't think we can do anything else under the circumstances,' Andawyr replied.

Oslang grimaced. 'Perhaps we could restrain them,' he suggested, making a discreet gesture with his hand.

'No, no.' Andawyr seized it. 'Not yet, at least. Not unless we're actually threatened with harm or if he's obviously in danger.' He spoke his thoughts as they came to him, a hurried descant to the broken growling of the two wolves. 'We don't know enough about any of them except that they mix uneasily with the Power. There's no saying what might happen if we use it directly against any of them.'

Oslang's eyes flicked towards the Beacon, then back to the two wolves.

'Don't stare directly at them,' Andawyr said urgently.

'I know. But their eyes aren't the same as when . . . oh.'

Even as he spoke, the eyes of the wolves became suddenly and unnaturally bright again. Andawyr drew in a sharp breath at the sight. The growling slowly faded and Antyr, his eyes still closed, sank to his knees and slowly lay down. It was the measured movement of a man still sufficiently in control to protect himself from a fall before he lost consciousness. The wolves lay down beside him. Their appearance now was even more frightening than it had been before and, though they had stopped growling, the ensuing silence increased rather than eased the tension in the room. It did not lessen even when they both closed their eyes.

'That's what happened when Antyr entered your dream,' Oslang whispered. He repeated the stern warnings that Antyr had given about leaving him undisturbed but, with the memory of the touch of the wolves' wild natures fresh in his mind, Andawyr needed little convincing.

The two men looked at one another helplessly.

'I suppose all we can do is wait,' Andawyr said eventually, reluctantly voicing their common thought. Nevertheless, he leaned forward carefully and looked intently at Antyr, seeking for any signs of distress in the motionless body. One of Tarrian's eyelids moved slightly to reveal a sharp, thin yellow line. Unnecessarily, Oslang reached out to prevent his friend from moving any further.

'He just seems to be asleep,' Andawyr said softly as he responded to this restraint.

Oslang nodded, but his attention now was on the Beacon. Though it was making no sound, the symbols and arrays of numbers surrounding it were changing – changing so quickly that they were little more than a blur.

All was darkness. Antyr stood very still. He was whole. And, too, he was aware of his body lying motionless in Andawyr's study, guarded by his Earth Holders. As he was there, so he was here. It had always been thus at such times. For, wherever he might be, he was not in someone's dream. This place was real. That he knew. Somehow, and without any sense of transition or conscious effort on his part, he had been drawn through a Gateway just as he had been in his desperate struggles with Ivaroth and the blind man.

He was afraid. And afraid in many different ways. Primitive fears: what dangers were there here? What knives, what strangling ropes, what malice lay in the darkness? Then more rational ones: how had he come here? Had it been at some unwitting bidding of his own? Had it been at the will of some other agency and, if so, who, or what, and, not least, why? Perhaps most frightening of all, had it been at the whim of mere chance – as a falling roof tile might strike one man and miss his companion? And tumbling in the wake of these, the question, how could he escape this place?

He was trembling.

When he had finally faced the blind man and all his terrible power in that place beyond all places, the voices of the others imprisoned there had rung out in triumph, calling him, Adept. Yet, too, at the same time, they had despised him. He was 'Scarce an apprentice.'

He had little doubt that whatever the former meant, the latter was true. All he knew was that somewhere Tarrian and Grayle would be searching for him, and searching frantically, their predatory natures hunting through the ringing, turbulent spaces between the worlds, through tides of chaos and change, in places beyond his imagining: beyond any imagining.

Tarrian, Grayle, he cried out silently.

Fleetingly, there was a hint of distant howling.

To me! To me!

You are guarded in all places by a great and ancient strength. Silently he mouthed the ritual reassurance that all Dream Finders gave to their clients. Its emptiness heightened his sense of futility. Panic curled into the fringes of his mind but he managed to hold it at bay with a battery of carefully ordered reasons. Had he not always returned from such translations? Had not some inner resource carried him through the direst of threats both in his own world and in the worlds beyond? And was it probable that he would succumb now, after the terrible enemies who had sought to destroy or enslave him had been destroyed? And when he had finally reached the Cadwanen, the goal of his journey? A place that, even with his limited knowledge of it, he could see was full of hope and inquiry and that used the light of the past and the present to illuminate the future. Nothing save hard walking, bad weather and seasickness had threatened him since he had left his home: surely nothing could threaten him now?

Nor did anything . . . that he could sense.

But . . .

His reassurances to himself had a wan and feeble air about them.

The panic threatened to return but again he held it back. Above all, he must maintain control over whatever he could. In the absence of knowing what he should do, he could only await events.

To me! To me!

Nothing.

Where was this place?

The darkness and the silence were so total that surely he could not be outside. There, by now, his eyes must have searched out a hint of lightness in the sky, or his ears would have heard a faint sound – a night insect, a scuttling rodent, the rushing wings of a hunting bird. But there was nothing. Not even the hint of shifting night air on his face.

A thought came to him, almost incongruous in its practicality. Yatsu had given him a small radiant stone lantern with the injunction that, along with many other small, innocuous items, he should always have it with him. Experience and the quiet, moment-by-moment discipline of journeying through the mountains had instilled the rightness of this advice into him, but older habits – a soft bed, a hasty awakening to serve the needs of a client – had taken command and the pouch that should have hung from his belt was, along with the belt itself, draped over a chair in his room.

He denounced himself a fool, though not, somewhat to his surprise, without a degree of dark humour. *Some Adept, you! Some Warrior of the White Way!* To be suddenly carried into an alien place at least had the dignity of being profoundly mysterious. To forget to bring a light was bumbling incompetence of the first order.

A sober resolution formed within him. As much through good fortune as any ability on his part he had survived a great ordeal and discovered within himself a strange, perhaps precious gift. He must bring to the questions that came from these events the utmost dedication and effort at all times. He must strive to become like Yatsu and Jaldaric: to attain that peculiar awareness of the nature and value of the moment, of the extraordinary in the ordinary, that they possessed. A warrior's mind, they had called it, though they laughed at its portentous ring. But they laughed easily and at many things, these most serious of men. And they had the clarity of vision, a quietness of spirit, that he could only aspire to. It was in their every movement.

The resolution was not a new one and he clenched his fists violently, driving his nails into his palms to punish himself for his folly in having to make it again.

He let out a faint breath.

The action was relaxing, the sound reassuring.

But as it drifted away, the darkness around him was suddenly alive with a myriad of such sighs. So soft was it that he was scarcely aware of the sound. Then, with almost imperceptible slowness, it began to wash to and fro. At first it was no more than the sound of the sea lapping against a distant shoreline, but with each retreat and advance it grew louder and stranger.

His concentration wrapped tight about it as he searched for some clue that might tell him where he was, Antyr began to feel the shifting sound reaching deep inside him. As it did so, he felt it touching ancient, unspoken fears – stirring them up to cloud his mind, to obscure his thoughts. They grew and resonated with the sound itself.

Then, not knowing how it had come about, he could no longer tell which clamour was outside him and which within, so awful was the noise – if noise it was by now, for there was a malevolence in it, rising and falling, pounding him from every side.

He felt a scream forming. A scream that the sound had been searching for. A scream that it would feed on. A scream that it would drown and smash him with, until he was at one with this choking darkness.

Yet still a spark of his awareness flickered.

He was who he was. He had faced cruel and powerful enemies before and prevailed.

From deeper even than his fears came a defiance, savage and cruel.

'No!'

Andawyr started violently and Oslang echoed Antyr's cry as the Dream Finder's eyes opened abruptly and his clawed hands reached out as if to seize something. At the same time the two wolves sprang up and, tails wagging, began licking his face. There was an interlude of spluttering confusion as he both fended off and embraced them.

'Is it safe for us to move?' Andawyr asked, already half out of his chair, adding, before Antyr could reply, 'What happened?'

Oslang too did not wait for an answer, but moved to the Beacon and began examining it closely.

'It was to find an answer to that question that I came here,' Antyr said as he finally managed to quieten the two excited animals. 'I was in another place.' He levered himself shakily back into his chair.

There was an awkward silence.

'You were here, lying on the floor, with your Companions guarding you,' Andawyr said carefully.

Antyr leaned forward, his head lowered and his hand extended in an appeal for a brief respite.

'Yes, I know,' he said, sitting up after a moment. 'At one point you bent forward to look at me and Oslang restrained you, didn't he? It was sound advice.'

In spite of himself, Andawyr's eyes became suspicious and uncertain.

'I don't resent your doubts,' Antyr said quietly. 'But I can do no other than tell you the truth as I know it. I was both here and somewhere else. Somewhere dark – very dark. And silent – at first. Then . . .' He told Andawyr what had happened.

The Cadwanwr listened intently but asked no question. His face was unreadable

'It was as real as this place,' Antyr concluded. 'Though where it was, why I was there, or how I came to be there, as ever, I don't know.'

To dispel the images that had returned with this telling he turned to Oslang who was still earnestly studying the Beacon. 'Does that tell you anything?'

Oslang made a peculiar noise. 'Only that Andawyr's comment about something being at right angles to all known directions seems to be singularly appropriate.' Petulantly he touched one of the symbols and the entire array vanished, leaving only the original panel. 'Later,' he said, turning away from it with a scowl and shaking his head. 'I'll think about it later when my wits are either less scattered, or scattered far enough for me to be able to make sense of it.'

'Was there any intrusion?' Andawyr asked him unsympathetically.

'No. *That* I'm sure about,' Oslang replied confidently. 'But what else there was . . .'

He shrugged. 'Well, you can see for yourself whenever you feel like it.'

The three men looked at one another silently.

'He was gone.' Tarrian's voice sounded in Andawyr's mind. 'As has happened before. Through one of the Gateways.

107

Grayle and I can do no more than hunt and call out for him. The ways become . . . very strange. They are . . .' Images, full of visceral need and frantic, driving urgency washed through Andawyr, filling not merely his mind, but his entire body. Though they were so fleeting that they were gone almost before he felt them, their power, at once primitive and immeasurably subtle, made him gasp.

'You've no words for that, human, any more than I have for that part of you which lies beyond the narrow span of this strange sharing we have. But that's all I can give you.'

'Are you all right?' Oslang was asking, his concern now transferred to his momentarily transfixed and gaping friend. Andawyr nodded and indicated Tarrian as he recovered his breath.

'Any chance of me joining in these conversations?' Oslang asked acidly.

'No,' Tarrian said starkly to Andawyr.

'It seems not,' Andawyr told his friend. 'But don't ask me about it, I can't do anything. It's very peculiar.'

'Well, what did he say, then?'

Andawyr told him but it added nothing to their thoughts about what had happened to Antyr.

'Where in the name of sanity can we start on all this?' Oslang asked after a long pause.

'We'll need to think about what Antyr's just told us, then . . .' Andawyr nodded towards the Beacon. '. . . Tomorrow we can analyse whatever's been registered in that and the one in my bedroom and all the others that were joined to them at the time. We'll work on it with Usche and Ar-Billan, they'll . . .'

'Ar-Billan? You're not serious. He's . . .'

'He's a very talented young man,' Andawyr said in a tone that was more an instruction than a comment. 'All he needs is more confidence and he'll get that if he's given the right guidance and responsibility.' Oslang looked set to pursue his objection but Andawyr became insincerely avuncular. 'And I've every confidence in *you* that he'll gain it under your experienced tutelage.'

Oslang's eyes narrowed and his chin came out, but

Andawyr's raised eyebrow reminded him of the presence of Antyr, a guest who should not have family disputes inflicted on him, and he abandoned his protest, albeit with some reluctance.

'Whatever you say,' he said tersely, leaving a loud but unspoken 'but . . .' hanging in the air.

Andawyr left it there but then it was he who was shifting uncomfortably in his chair. He held out both hands in a gesture that encompassed both Antyr and the wolves. 'I believe absolutely that you believe what you're saying, and I can see for myself you've been badly frightened. Without a doubt, something very disconcerting, perhaps dangerous, is happening. I'm not sure how to put this but will you accept it as a measure of the way we are here that I have to be sceptical – open-minded – about your interpretation of what's actually happening?' He hurried on, skidding over his awkwardness. 'It could be exactly as you say, of course. Some of us have considered certain aspects of such a phenomenon theoretically possible for a long time, though we've no idea how it could come about.' Faintly he thought he caught a disparaging, 'Man's a fool!' from the normally silent Grayle, though it vanished immediately under the sound of Antyr coughing. 'But none of that's important at the moment,' he went on quickly. 'What is important is your personal well-being, and that concerns me greatly. Is this kind of thing liable to happen to you any time, any place? Because if so, perhaps it might be better . . . if you stayed . . .'

Tarrian's lip wrinkled menacingly, as did Grayle's. 'He needs no guards,' came two voices, fierce and categorical. The statement was hung about with feelings of near-uncontrollable anger at the prospect of restraint.

Involuntarily, Andawyr edged back in his chair. Antyr reached down to stroke the two wolves and they became quiet, but he too was frowning. 'It would seem it can happen at any time,' he said. 'Though it hasn't since I entered the Great Dream and the three of us have worked normally with several clients since then. Once or twice I've had the feeling that something strange was nearby – perhaps a Gateway – and that if I exerted myself in some way I'd be able to pass through it.

I've even had the feeling that I could create one, but I've had neither the desire nor the insight into how to do such a thing. In any case, at the moment, whatever happens to me there's no one here who can help me – no one. I'll leave if I'm likely to be a burden, but I'd rather stay and work with you towards explaining all this. For myself, I've no desire to be constrained other than by the limits of your hospitality, but Tarrian and Grayle will *not* be constrained by anyone. That's the way *they* are. I think it will be sufficient if everyone here knows that should I be found . . . unconscious . . . with my Companions by me, then I am simply *not* to be approached.'

Andawyr made a concerned gesture, but Antyr did not allow him to speak. 'You *know* you can't help me. Not yet, anyway.' His voice became very soft. 'It's possible that no one anywhere can help me: that I and I alone have to discover what all this means; that my real journey shouldn't have been over the seas and mountains, but into myself. I don't know. But if that's so, and I find myself suddenly both here and in another place, then apart from the hurt that Tarrian and Grayle will do to anyone who intrudes, and the hurt you'll then have to do to them, their need to protect my body here may draw them away from helping me against greater danger.'

Andawyr's thumb and forefinger moved from massaging his nose to squeezing his eyes. His voice was strained when he spoke.

'You're right,' he said, equally softly. 'We can't help you. Not with what we know at the moment. And, too, you may be right – perhaps your journey's going to be for you alone. That's something that many of us here are all too familiar with.'

He affected a heartiness he did not feel. 'We'll do whatever you wish. Everyone here is here freely. You're welcome to stay or go as the whim takes you. If you choose to stay – which I should prefer – if only because I've taken quite a shine to your Companions – and to you,' he added as a conspicuous afterthought. 'Then we'll do as you say. We'll leave you wherever you fall.'

The next day, Antyr slept late, much to the scorn of Yatsu and Jaldaric.

'I'm sure you two have letters to write, or something,' he growled as the two Goraidin finally rousted him from his bed, adding reproachfully to the two wolves, silent witnesses to this atrocity, 'Fine guards you are.'

'I thought we'd resolved to emulate our good friends here,' Tarrian retorted, affecting injured surprise. 'You know, spartan, self-denying, uncluttered by unattainable desires, firmly rooted in the present, looking always . . .'

'Shut up.'

'Oh. I must have misunderstood. Then again, I usually do, whenever you make this particular resolution.'

'We were up at a respectable hour,' Yatsu said, correctly interpreting the half of the exchange he heard. He took on Tarrian's righteous air. 'We've done everything we need to for the time being. We thought you might like to eat.'

'Did I ever tell you that your capacity for doing things with such cheery gusto first thing in the morning is one of your least endearing traits?' Antyr said sourly.

'From memory, every day, I think,' Yatsu replied blandly, looking at Jaldaric for corroboration.

'Not *every* day,' Jaldaric offered in Antyr's defence. 'I'd have to look in my journal but I'm sure he forgot at least twice. When he was seasick, if you remember.' He ignored Antyr's baleful look and touched the panel covering the mirror stone window. It unfurled silently and gracefully and light flooded into the room. It was accompanied by a cool breeze. The two wolves stretched luxuriously, then jumped up to put their forepaws on the sill so that they could examine the view.

'Isn't this place splendid?' Yatsu said, banter replaced by openness. Then, concerned, 'I hear you had a bad time last night.'

Antyr was uncertain how to answer. 'Yes,' he said finally. 'I was whisked into some other place without warning. An awful place. Dark, frightening, full of terrifying sounds.'

'Andawyr told us.'

'Good,' Antyr replied, with genuine relief. 'I don't particularly want to go through it again.'

Yatsu patted him on the shoulder, then gave a soldier's

111

shrug. The gesture told Antyr he had survived and that he had probably learned something, and that was all that mattered. He felt a twinge of injured indignation at this seemingly cavalier dismissal of his ordeal, though even as it came, he found he was able to set it aside. It *was* all that mattered. He had learned more than he had realized in the journey that had taken him to the Great Dream and thence brought him here. And he knew that Yatsu and Jaldaric were stalwart friends to him. Insofar as they could, they would guard and help him at all times, unbidden. They were quite deliberately helping him now, their presence anchoring him to the present so that he could cut away that part of the past which was valueless.

'Everyone knows you're to be left if it happens again unexpectedly,' Yatsu said.

'Everyone?' Antyr echoed, incredulous. 'Already?'

'Everyone,' Yatsu confirmed. 'I told you this was a remarkable place. Get yourself cleaned up and decent, then we can eat.'

They ate where Antyr and Andawyr had eaten the previous day, though it was much busier now. At first Antyr found it difficult to cope with the undisguised attention he was attracting, though he soon learned to meet the looks he was receiving with an open greeting of his own.

'I wondered how long it would take you to pick that up,' Tarrian said patronizingly. 'These aren't the oafish inadequates that used to inhabit your old drinking haunts, you know. All of them are most intelligently curious. Indeed, they're almost civilized.'

'I'm sure they'll set great store by your approval,' Antyr retorted.

'I'm sure they will,' Tarrian agreed.

For much of the rest of the day, Yatsu and Jaldaric being occupied, Tarrian and Grayle chose to go their own way, leaving Antyr to do the same, alone. He set off with great confidence, wandering through busy halls and chambers, large and small, but despite his best efforts, he found the complex maze of twisting, interlinking corridors and divided and subdivided levels deeply bewildering. It did not help that no door he encountered bore any indication of what was behind it, and no junction bore any indication of what lay in what direction.

With the unerring knack of a stranger in a strange place, he sought advice mainly from those who knew little more than he did.

'How do you find your way around this place?' he asked one red-faced individual he found himself walking alongside.

'With great difficulty, Dream Finder,' came the reply. That he was known to this stranger was by then no surprise. However Andawyr had spread the news about him through his domain it had been singularly effective. It was just one of a mounting list of questions that he had about the place. A brief conversation identified the man as a novice of barely a week and the two of them parted firm friends in adversity and still lost.

Eventually his wanderings brought him through a suddenly widening corridor and into a spacious communal area of some kind. For a moment he thought he had stepped outside, as along much of one side was a vista of the mountains and the broad plains beyond. The sight brought him to an abrupt halt.

There were many people there, talking, reading, dozing, though the place was so large that there was no feeling of its being crowded. An abrupt silence greeted him as he became the focus of a collective inspection but it lasted for only a moment as the looks became as many smiles and several hands were raised to attract his attention. A hand on his elbow spared him the difficulty of making a choice about which to accept.

It was Usche.

'I'm sure you'd like to sit down,' she said, her voice full of laughter. 'You have the despairing look of an irredeemably lost novice.'

'I've met one of those,' Antyr replied. 'You're probably right.'

Usche motioned him to a group at the far end of the room. She shooed one of them out of the way and placed Antyr on a low couch. He sagged into it with conspicuous relief and rubbed his ankles. His reaction provoked a response similar to Usche's initial greeting. 'You'll get used to the place,' was the

113

common advice, but Usche shook her head.

'I don't think so,' she said. 'It's never easy, and the Beacons aren't much use to him. Antyr seems to be closed to the Power.'

The group was suddenly alive with interest. It found its consensus in the questions, 'How can that be? What does it mean, anyway?'

Usche could add little. 'I'm not sure, but that's what Andawyr said, anyway. He did a simple teaching transference when I was demonstrating something and . . . nothing. Andawyr thinks it's perhaps something to do with Antyr's ability to enter dreams but, whatever it is, I've no doubt that it'll be the subject of considerable debate shortly.' She gave Antyr a guilty look. 'I'm sorry, we're talking about you as if you weren't here, aren't we?'

'It's all right,' Antyr said, content just to be sitting and with someone he knew. 'I can understand your curiosity and I'm gradually growing used to the idea that everyone here knows who I am and asks questions incessantly. I've never encountered anything like it before and it's a very peculiar feeling. But it's reassuring in a way.'

'I wouldn't say everyone knows who you are,' Usche said. 'They know your name and a little about your unusual ability, but mainly they know to leave you alone if you're found . . . unconscious.' Her face looked pained, as if she were seeking confirmation of this. Antyr gave it.

'Yes, that, above all, you *must* do,' he said insistently, briefly taking control of the group and looking at each of them in turn. 'You'll put yourselves and quite possibly me in great danger if you don't.'

'It seems an odd thing to do,' said a young man sitting next to him.

His earnest manner provoked a soft laugh from Antyr. 'From what I've heard about this Power of yours – and seen,' he acknowledged Usche, 'I'd say you should be used to odd things by now.'

Flustered, the man said, 'I meant, oddly callous – just to leave someone lying there.'

Antyr regretted his laughter and gripped the man's arm, at

114

once fatherly and man to man. 'It would be, normally,' he said. 'But not in this case. You'll just have to take my word for it. It really is important that everyone understands this.'

'The wolves are dangerous, then?' someone asked.

Antyr gave his usual homily about Tarrian and Grayle. 'It's in their nature to protect me, but they're their own animals. They go their own way, beholden to no one for anything. They're neither trained nor tame. Don't make any attempt to touch them unless they seek you out, which, generally speaking, is unlikely.'

'You come with a lot of warnings hung about you,' said his neighbour, making Antyr laugh again.

'I suppose it seems like that,' he conceded. 'But there's only the two, really. Leave me to lie and leave the wolves.'

'Where are they now?'

The question prompted some anxious head turning.

'I've no idea,' Antyr replied. 'Except that *they* won't be lost. And by now they'll probably know every source of food in the entire place. Don't worry. As I said, they avoid getting involved with people as a rule. To be honest, they think we're rather an inadequate species.'

'Splendid,' came an acid comment from someone. 'First we have the felcis treating us as inferiors, now we have wolves. I think Andawyr should bar any more animals coming into the place before we end up at the very bottom of the mammalian ladder.'

'What are these felcis like?' Antyr queried.

'Don't worry, you'll find out soon enough,' said the man sitting next to Antyr, echoing Andawyr's earlier comment. 'In fact, with all the talk there's been about you, I'm rather surprised they've not been round to look at you. They're nothing if not nosy.'

'Inquisitive is a kinder word,' Usche said.

'Nosy feels better.'

Before the argument could continue, there was a flurry of activity at the far end of the room and the sound of raised voices.

Chapter 10

There was a quality about the noise that Antyr immediately associated with Tarrian: the clatter of people suddenly obliged to jump aside and loud voices raised in an explosive mixture of alarm and anger. Even without looking he could see the wolf, and presumably his brother, barging through anything that was in the way in their haste to get somewhere. An excited bark and the crash of something falling over, followed by a string of oaths, confirmed his assessment.

'I think they're here,' he said, levering himself up off the low couch wearily. Then another sound reached him that was quite new. A swooping and remarkably loud whistling. Curious now, he joined the others in craning to see what was happening. As he did so, he caught a fleeting glimpse of a brown, sinuous animal, flitting rapidly through the confusion. Involuntarily his feet came together protectively and preparatory to jumping on to the couch.

They must have flushed out a rat, he thought. And a big one, by the look of it.

A combination of relief and embarrassment swept over him. At least it wasn't anything more serious they were up to, but then it was hardly the mark of a good guest to expose the more unsavoury inhabitants of his host's dwelling: still less to engage in a frantic pursuit through it.

Abruptly the animal was in front of him. Before Antyr could stop it, one of his feet came up and rested on the couch. Only an apparent lack of concern by Usche and her friends kept the other one on the floor. And, indeed, the animal was not moving. It was sitting back on its haunches with its forelegs dangling. Slowly it tilted its head on one side as it looked at Antyr intently with bright, penetrating eyes.

It looked remarkably composed.

And whatever it was, it wasn't a rat.

It must be a pet, Antyr realized in horror as Tarrian and Grayle arrived, cascading to a claw-skittering halt on the polished floor. A vision of a violent, bloody and very public skirmish resulting in the brutal destruction of someone's dearest filled him. It was followed immediately by a clutch of the dire and humiliating consequences that must surely ensue for both him and the wolves if this happened. He was just about to call out to Tarrian and Grayle when the animal, still on its haunches, calmly looked over its shoulder at the panting pair.

'This is him, isn't it?' it said, in a languid but quite clear voice.

Tarrian and Grayle were quite still now except for their lolling tongues and wagging tails. Antyr caught a hint of a reply from one of them and the animal returned to its scrutiny of him.

'Hm. Gapes rather, doesn't he?'

Through the bewilderment rapidly taking possession of him, Antyr became aware of Usche standing close beside him. Her hand on his arm, she had the protective aura of a guide particularly anxious to ensure that an inadvertent but important meeting should be carried off successfully. As casually as he could, he removed his errant foot from the couch.

'This is Kristabell,' Usche said quickly and with heavily forced geniality. 'She's a felci. I gather from what you were just saying that they're not an animal you're familiar with.'

'Close your mouth.' Tarrian's voice hissed unexpectedly in Antyr's mind. 'You look ridiculous.'

Caught between Tarrian's indignation, Usche's anxiety, this strange creature's inspection of him, and the incipient suspicion that he was perhaps being made the butt of some elaborate prank, Antyr smiled weakly and uttered a brief string of incomprehensible sounds before managing to say, 'Hello, Kristabell.'

The Felci nodded with each word like an adult coaxing a carefully rehearsed greeting out of a child. 'Very good. I didn't quite catch the first part of that but the rest was fairly intelligible. He seems personable enough. Do you have much trouble with him?'

Tarrian carefully kept his reply from Antyr, but Kristabell gave a knowing nod. 'I understand,' she said.

'Kristabell, behave yourself,' Usche said through clenched teeth. 'Antyr's our guest.'

The felci gave her a long look, then dropped on to all fours. Following the wolves' spectacular entrance, the group had become the focus of everyone in the room and a substantial crowd was now standing around them, awaiting developments. Usche sat down and motioned Antyr to do the same. As he did so – and to his considerable alarm – the felci clambered on to his knee. After an elaborate and disconcerting adjustment of her position, she squatted on her haunches again and continued her study of him.

'Antyr, eh? Strange names you creatures give yourselves. I thought maybe the pups had got it wrong, but there you are. I should have trusted them a little more, shouldn't I?' Kristabell's voice was deeper and more resonant than might have been expected from such a comparatively small animal. It was also unusually powerful and, the creature being immediately in front of his face, indicated to Antyr that if he was indeed being made the butt of a joke it was an extremely well-made one. Was it, perhaps, someone giving him a benign demonstration of this Power that so dominated everything here? It seemed improbable: the creature, its mannerisms, its voice, were all very realistic. It did not help him, though, that he could clearly sense a faint suggestion of amusement behind the voice.

'Kristabell!' Usche hissed. 'Stop that!'

As before, the felci ignored her and continued its study of Antyr. He found her bright-eyed, intelligent gaze disconcerting.

'You are a strange one, aren't you?' she concluded eventually. Her tone was serious and intrigued and the faint touch of humour had gone. She curled her lip back and absently tapped one of her teeth with a forepaw. Antyr noticed that the teeth and the claw protruding from the paw both looked very powerful. Coupled with the musculature he could sense beneath the creature's sleek fur he decided that this could be a frighteningly ferocious animal if need arose.

'There are depths here. There's something very old about you, young man. *Very* old. Well, well, how interesting.' Humming tunelessly to herself she bent even closer, her eyes searching deep into his. Then they closed, the humming stopped, and she was sniffing at him, her nose twitching energetically.

Abruptly, she was conversational. 'The pups tell me that you and they roam the dreamways. Tell me, how do you think you do that?'

'Kristabell!' Usche brought her determined face next to the felci's. 'I'm sure if Andawyr wants you to interrogate our guest, he'll ask you.'

'He'd be wise to, child,' Kristabell replied. Antyr felt Usche stiffen at the word 'child'. 'He won't make much of him if I'm not there, believe me.' She gave a laugh that ended in a joyous whistle. 'Poor Andy, he's going to have real trouble finding this one in his calculations, I can tell you. I'll make a point of speaking to him about it, otherwise he's likely to be lost without trace.'

'I'm sure he'll be indebted.'

Kristabell looked at her, then clambered down from Antyr and on to Usche's lap. She gave a low reproachful whistle and clicked her tongue. 'Sarcasm really doesn't become you, child.'

'Don't call me child,' Usche muttered darkly. It was obviously not a new injunction, but even as she spoke it, she was stroking the felci affectionately.

'Sarcasm *and* such over-sensitivity. Not endearing traits in a *young woman*, Usche my dear. Don't you agree, Dream Finder?'

Antyr found himself stammering again at being suddenly dragged into this private and very female exchange.

'I think perhaps Usche is trying to be – is being – a good hostess. Helping me to adjust to the . . .' He was about to say 'strange' but caught himself in time. '. . . Unusual . . . things that are to be found in this place.'

Kristabell's gaze returned to him. 'Ah, a gallant. How refreshing.' She looked round at the watching Cadwanwr significantly, before speaking to Antyr again. 'You find me unusual?' she asked.

In some desperation and aided by a prompt from Tarrian, Antyr opted for the truth.

'Yes, to be honest, I do,' he said. 'I've never even heard of – felcis – before, still less seen or met one. In fact, I've never met an animal that could actually talk.'

'Really?' Kristabell said. 'Well, your frankness does you credit, but I presume you mean you've never met anything other than *human* animals that talk your rather awkward and inadequate language.' A paw indicated the still-watching group.

Antyr gave up. 'I suppose so,' he conceded.

Kristabell was reassuring. 'Don't fret, young man. I wouldn't dream of reproaching you. You're not alone, by any means. I'm afraid there's many a dim creature out there that thinks its own kind are the totality of everything. And you, at least, can speak to the pups.'

Before Antyr could say anything, Kristabell had jumped down from Usche's lap and was scratching vigorously. 'Well, well. Must be off. Things to do. A delight to meet you, Antyr. Truly. We must talk. At length. You're more interesting than you know. You could even be one of us. There's a thought.' Her voice became suddenly softer. 'Dar-volci would have been so excited to see you. I wish he . . .' She stopped and was silent for a moment. Then she was brisk again. 'Still, he'll be back when he'll be back and fretting won't make that any earlier, will it?'

To Antyr's alarm, she stood on her hind legs immediately in front of Tarrian. His alarm, however, became surprise as the wolf lay down and rolled over submissively. Grayle did the same, flattening himself low and pushing his muzzle gently between the two of them.

'And lovely to see you two again, pups,' Kristabell said, tickling Tarrian's stomach and making his back leg twitch. 'You've grown into fine animals. And you've done well for yourselves finding this . . . Dream Finder – very well. I'll

121

tell everyone you're back. And the Alphraan. They'll be delighted. Splendid, splendid. We'll sing soon.' And she was gone, slipping between the legs of the crowd, whistling and laughing.

'Pups?' Antyr said to Tarrian and Grayle witheringly as the sound of Kristabell's departing faded. 'What was all that about?'

'Later. It's too complicated,' Tarrian replied as he stood up and shook himself noisily. Antyr did not pursue the matter. He could feel something rising from the wolf that he had never known before. It carried too much of the animal's deeper nature for him to be able to identify it, though it was unmistakably joyous in character. He knew that the two animals were sharing this with him deliberately and that they could say nothing more about what they were experiencing. He bent low and stroked both of them by way of acknowledgement.

'Are you all right?' It was Usche. As was invariably the case when he had touched near the wolves' true self, the human voice sounded harsh and crude. For an instant he understood Kristabell's remark about their language being both awkward and inadequate.

'I'm sorry,' he said. 'I was just talking to Tarrian and Grayle.'

Usche was brushing hairs from her robe. She stopped and looked first at him and then at the two wolves. 'Well, I suppose if our felci surprised you by talking out loud, we'll have to get used to your talking silently to your Companions,' she said. 'Although, I have to say, I think it's the stranger of the two.' Then she asked the question that Oslang had asked. 'Could they speak to me like that?'

'They could, but they won't,' Antyr said, anticipating Tarrian's refusal. Usche's brown eyes looked at him, disappointed.

'I don't know why they won't,' he felt obliged to add. 'And it wouldn't do any good for me to press them.' Then, unable to prevent himself from explaining further, 'I think they find our thoughts unsettling. There's something about us – something they can't reach, just as I can't reach fully into them – something that frightens them.' He shrugged. 'It's only a thought. It's a subject I've learned to avoid over the years.'

122

'I understand,' Usche said, though Antyr could see that the topic would arise again sooner or later. Then she frowned and gave the wolves a sidelong look. 'You said "thoughts", didn't you? They can't pry into my thoughts, can they? Tell what I'm thinking?'

'No,' Antyr lied confidently, as he always did when this question was asked. All the Serenstad Dream Finders lied about it both routinely and with great conviction. It was the Guild of Dream Finders' only true secret. No one knew why but there was a strong presumption that the practice had its origins in a violent past.

Usche looked relieved, if a little suspicious. However, she was prevented from pursuing the matter by the mounting curiosity of her watching colleagues. Everyone in the room was now gathered about them and each newcomer naturally gravitated towards them. They were beginning to ask questions of Antyr.

Usche stood up and raised her arms for silence uncertainly. Antyr saw why: it was obvious that several of those present were senior to her.

'Can I ask you for a little patience, Brothers? We've all got so many questions to ask, but, as you know, Antyr has only just arrived after a long journey and, as you also know, he had very little sleep last night. In courtesy we should let him relax and get used to our ways and this place before we start badgering him.' Her speech ended rather lamely, but, together with a plaintive expression and some hand-wringing, it was enough to disperse most of the spectators. Slowly the hall became as it had been when Antyr first entered, though, from the glances that were continually thrown his way, he knew there was only one topic of conversation.

He tried to start a new one of his own, indicating the extensive view of the mountains and the plains.

'Are these proper windows or are they mirror stones?' he asked. 'I haven't seen anything so far that's this big.'

'They're mirror stones,' Usche replied casually. 'All the windows are. The Cadwanen is completely isolated from the outside except for a few entrances, and they're all well protected.'

123

Antyr found the contrast between the seeming openness of the bright hall and the dark claustrophobia of Usche's statement disturbing.

'Always the fortress, eh?' he heard himself saying.

'Always the fortress,' Usche confirmed. She sensed his mood. 'But at least we're a fortress of light,' she said. 'Like Anderras Darion. We seek knowledge, we disseminate it. We illuminate.' Suddenly she was excited. 'Just look around you, Antyr. Every aspect of this place is such an achievement. I shouldn't imagine you've seen a fraction of it yet, but have you met anything that made you feel you were buried deep inside the mountains, or that you were in anything other than an ordinary building, and a fine one at that?' She answered for him, tapping her temple with her forefinger. 'No, because the knowledge, the learning that animates everything here has brought even the sunlight and the air into the depths so that we can live like civilized people.'

'You could say that was using your knowledge to deceive, to misrepresent where we really are,' Antyr retorted, somewhat to his own surprise, rising to the hint of challenge in her voice.

Usche cocked her head back and a broad smile broke through her earnest expression. 'What is the function of a window, Antyr?' she said.

Antyr opened his mouth to reply, then closed it again. 'To let the light in – and perhaps the air – and to see what's happening outside,' he admitted after a moment's thought.

'Dear, dear, dear.' It was Tarrian. 'Walked into that one, didn't you? Ask her if there are any children round here for you to argue with – someone more your own weight.'

'Shut up,' Antyr growled back, adding venomously, 'Pup.'

It had no effect other than to make both Tarrian and Grayle chuckle.

Then Usche was standing up in some confusion, as were her friends. 'We're late,' she was saying. 'That's Kristabell's fault, keeping us all talking. She's no idea what has to be done around here.' She put her hand on Antyr's arm. 'I'm sorry about this, but we've got to go. I'll see you later.'

Thus abandoned, Antyr found himself once more the focus

of much of the attention in the hall. He was about to retreat with a view to continuing his trek when Yatsu and Jaldaric entered. They acknowledged warm greetings from many sources as they came towards him.

'Is there anyone you don't know here?' he asked as Yatsu dropped down beside him.

'Oh yes. There are always lots of new faces and lots of gossip in this place,' Yatsu replied. He looked at Antyr and laughed. 'You've the look of a week-old novice. Come on, own up. How badly did you get lost?'

'I get enough abuse off these two without you adding to it,' Antyr said, nudging Tarrian with his foot. 'This is a very confusing place. And it doesn't help that I can't understand any of these symbols written up everywhere.'

He recounted the details of his day's walking, concluding with his encounter with Kristabell.

'You're privileged,' Jaldaric told him. 'They're delightful creatures, felcis, but they do have a habit of treating people as if we're were rather slow-witted pets.' He looked around the hall. 'And they regard this place as just an extension to their own system of tunnels and burrows – an extension they graciously allow us to use.'

'And Kristabell's very fussy about who she takes a shine to,' Yatsu added.

'I thought at first that someone was playing a joke on me.'

'I can see that a felci would be a surprise to you, for all you're used to talking to your wolves.'

'How do they get in here? Usche told me there are only a few well-guarded entrances to the place.'

This amused the two men. 'You've hit on one of the many mysteries that surround the felcis,' Yatsu said. 'And one of Andawyr's greatest banes.' He laughed. 'He gets so frustrated. They just come and go as they please and no one's ever found out how they do it. They seem to be immune to the Power in some way.'

'I imagine someone's asked them?' Antyr said, striking for the obvious.

'Oh yes, many times,' Yatsu said, still laughing. 'But to no avail. All they ever say is we're too young to understand.'

'That's odd, she said I was old – or part of me was.'

He had half expected more laughter from Yatsu at this but, instead, the Goraidin pursed his lips appreciatively. 'Interesting. Felcis know a great many things that we don't, for sure. I can't hazard what she meant but it could well be significant. I'd mention it to Andawyr if I were you.'

'She said she was going to do that anyway. She seemed very amused about it.'

'They laugh a lot, felcis.'

Antyr was hesitant about his next remark. 'I noticed that she had very powerful-looking claws and teeth. It occurred to me that she could be quite fierce. Are they dangerous?'

'Very,' Yatsu said simply. 'But not gratuitously so. They're not like people, they're like most other animals. If you want to see how dangerous they are, you have to provoke them – and at some considerable length, I might add. But then you take the consequences.' He drew a finger across his throat. 'On the whole they prefer to cut you down with a caustic comment rather than anything else, but those claws can open you from top to bottom and those teeth can snap your thickest bones like twigs.' As was often the case when he spoke on such matters, Yatsu's matter-of-fact delivery added a vividness to what he was saying that many a storyteller would have envied. Antyr winced. 'They're mountain creatures,' Yatsu went on. 'Their claws are designed for burrowing through the rock, and designed very well. And they can eat rocks with those teeth, though I've a feeling they only do it to watch us cringe at the noise it makes.'

'You seem very impressed by them.'

'I am. As will you be when you get to know them a little better. And if Kristabell's taken an interest in you, you probably will.'

'It's all very strange. Insofar as I ever thought about it, I don't know what I imagined this place was going to be like. Probably something similar to one of our Serenstad Learning Houses. Dignified if rather decrepit buildings peopled by dignified if rather decrepit sages, droning on about the same things they've been droning on about for years. Certainly I didn't expect this bizarre mixture of siege thinking and open inquiry. Nor this convoluted maze of passages and rooms peopled by the likes of Andawyr and Oslang and strange talking creatures who call me old and eat rocks.'

'Well, I suppose if you put it like that, it *is* rather unusual. You'll soon get used to it.'

Antyr suddenly felt light-hearted. 'Yes, I think I will,' he said. 'In fact, I'm quite looking forward to it.'

Andawyr's study presented a scene very different from the one Antyr had seen the previous night. There was tumbled confusion on some of the shelves, several drawers hung open with documents spilling from them, and the various tables were all littered with books and papers – as was the floor.

In the midst of the disorder was its architect.

Sitting sideways in a deep, well-upholstered chair, his legs thrown over one arm, Andawyr was massaging the remains of his nose between his thumb and forefinger. In his other hand was a piece of paper covered with symbols. From time to time he glanced at it.

Oslang was sitting at one of the tables, stiff and upright and staring blankly ahead. One finger was tapping out an indeterminate rhythm on the table.

The paper slithered from Andawyr's hand to follow an oscillating pathway down to the floor where it gracefully settled on top of many others.

'We're going nowhere,' he said, swinging his legs off the arm of the chair and standing up. He began pacing. The papers rattled about his feet like dead leaves. 'Nowhere, nowhere, nowhere.'

'You're being impatient again,' Oslang said. He gestured across the tables. 'We've plenty of information, it's only a matter of . . .'

'There's too much information,' Andawyr interrupted irritably.

'If you'll allow me to finish,' Oslang said sternly. 'We've plenty of information, it's only a matter of working through it methodically, painstakingly. Ordering it . . .'

'We've been doing that all day, and we're going *nowhere*!' Andawyr insisted.

127

'This is our first look. We can get the others to help shortly. I think there's a pattern emerging.'

'No, there isn't. Not unless you count randomly increasing confusion as a pattern.'

As Oslang prepared to reply, the door opened and Kristabell entered. She gazed around the room for a moment and then looked at Andawyr.

'It's a great pity that your nobility of both intellect and soul doesn't manifest itself more conspicuously in the more mundane matters of this world, Cadwanwr,' she said with some distaste.

'I can do without any of your mother-hen lectures today, thank you, Kristabell,' Andawyr retorted. 'What do you want? Can't you see we're busy?'

'Ah. Charming as ever. And such a contrast to the gentleman I've just met. The new one the pups brought in – you know – the old one – the Dream Finder. Leapt to Usche's defence as though she might actually need it. Such a happy instinct. Being with the pups has helped, I suppose, but I wonder how long it'll be before he falls under your disorderly influence.'

'Kristabell, what are you talking about?'

The felci jumped up on to the table and, humming to herself, began nosing through the papers.

'Still going the long way round, eh? Ploughing your interminable furrow and marking the way with your arcane symbols.'

Catching a signal from Oslang, Andawyr made a noticeable effort not to respond to this taunt. He forced a conciliatory note into his voice.

'Kristabell, we do have a problem that needs our immediate attention.'

The felci stopped her inspection and sat back on her haunches. 'Yes, you do, don't you? I heard all about it.' She scratched her stomach. 'I think you're going to have more. I wish Dar was back. He has a surer touch than I do.'

'What do you mean?' Andawyr asked, concerned by the felci's sudden and unusual seriousness.

'I don't know. The Song's disturbed. All the ways feel cloudy and dangerous. It's like a storm brewing. A bad one.

Things are coming together that shouldn't. Old things. Deep things.' She flicked some of the papers to one side. 'This won't be enough, I fear. Another way will have to be found.'

She gave a low doleful whistle, then jumped down from the table. When she reached the doorway she stopped and turned.

'You should take the Dream Finder to Anderras Darion, Andawyr. It's a stronger place than this. Take him now. Don't delay.'

Chapter 11

The sun was setting. Farnor Yarrance leaned on the gate and gazed at the reddening sky streaked with thin lines of cloud that were slowly turning from grey to black. Marna and the others had been gone less than a week but it was as though they had been gone for years. It had been his firm intention when he said goodbye to them to put the dreadful events of the past weeks behind him once and for all, and begin the rest of his life: a life that would have been a continuation of what it had been before the arrival of Nilsson and his men and the murder of Farnor's parents; a life that he knew they would have wanted for him and indeed that he wanted for himself.

Prior to Marna leaving he had thought that this must be the way ahead of him. It was still the way he wanted and many of the old normalities of his life had already begun to close about him protectively: the demands of the farm, the bustling help of his friends and neighbours, all familiar, comforting. But before she and the others had been gone a day he began to see that it was not to be. It was not that *something* had changed. It was that *everything* had changed. Everything about him, everything about the village. Nothing was truly as familiar and comforting as it had been, nor ever could be again.

So many things had come together in so short a time and so fatefully. Nilsson's men seizing the village after being mistaken for the king's tithe gatherers. Marna's flight to seek help from the capital and meeting instead Yengar, Olvric, Jenna and Yrain, four soldiers from a distant land who had been relentlessly pursuing Nilsson and his men so that they could be brought to justice for past crimes. The encounter between Rannick and the creature from the caves, which had turned the

131

surly and ill-tempered farm labourer's strange natural gift into a murderous power and given him control over others while feeding his own bitter and uncontrollable nature: a nature that had led him to murder Farnor's parents. Then had come Farnor's desperate flight into the Great Forest, the home of the tree-dwelling Valderen, and the discovery of his own mysterious gift, the gift that, amongst other things, enabled him to touch the will of the ancient trees of the Great Forest and that he sensed he had not yet begun to measure. Even now, so far from the Forest, he could hear the whispering of the nearby trees and know that they were watching him and would do so wherever the will of the Forest could reach. For though he had won their trust, as far as any human – any Mover – could, he knew that they too had no true measure of him and that it troubled them.

And finally there had been the terrifying conclusion. So much fear and pain of every kind. The villagers driven to attack the castle, the brief but bloody battle between Nilsson's men and the Valderen, and Farnor returning to face the crazed Rannick and his grim familiar.

Farnor closed his eyes. This last was burned into his mind. The bruising and stiffness from his fight with the creature were easing, but he must surely remember for ever the hauntingly beautiful worlds that lay beyond this one, worlds which Rannick, or the creature, or both, had somehow torn a way into and which drew Rannick to his death as, in his lust for yet more power, he had reached ever deeper into them.

Farnor was trembling. His mouth was dry and his brow was damp when he opened his eyes again. It was always so when he thought about what had happened. And he could not avoid thinking about it – over and over. Sometimes, for no reason that he could understand, it seemed he was actually back in the heart of those desperate moments again. He held out his hand as he had then, vainly reaching out to save Rannick while at the same time sealing the rent that had been torn between the worlds.

His hand returned to the top rail of the gate and he gripped it tightly.

What was he? How had he done such a thing?

132

He shied away from the questions.

Looking down he saw the old timber, weathered and polished smooth with years of usage. The sight and the touch of it were deeply ingrained in him, yet even this was different now. The last few days, the days he had intended would be a beginning, had had a quality so unreal about them as to be almost that of nightmare. Every least task, tasks he had performed for years, had felt false and empty. All the things that should have enabled him to gather together the threads of his old life had instead seemed to conspire to tear him apart.

The questions returned but this time he did not shy away from them.

He squeezed the rail affectionately, as if absolving it from blame for his dark mood. He had no choice, he knew now. It was not possible that he could become Farmer Yarrance in the stead of his murdered father. It was not possible to bring back what had gone, nor any part of it.

What was it his father used to say? 'Celebrate what you have while you have it. It helps when it's gone.' A remark that, notwithstanding his father's deeply optimistic disposition, he had thought rather gloomy at the time but that, like most parental remarks, had largely passed over him anyway. Now he suspected he was perhaps beginning to understand. He had always felt a contentedness – a stillness – in his father, underneath his everyday moods in the face of the daily exigencies of farm life. And there had been something similar in the four who had come in pursuit of Nilsson, though people more different from his father it would have been difficult for him to imagine. Yengar, straightforward and, when all was over, quite genial. Olvric, quiet but unsettling. And the two women who had made such an impression on Marna. Even now Farnor found it difficult to accept all the stories he had been told about the way Jenna and Yrain rode and fought.

They had suggested that he go with them to their own land.

'There are people there who will understand your strange gift and what should be done with it,' Yengar had said to him. 'And people who can help to ease your deeper pain.'

'Knew me better than I knew myself,' Farnor said out loud to the dimming sky. He patted the gate and turned back to the farmhouse. The sight of the old building, still partly gutted from the fire that Rannick had set, and cluttered with the planks and ladders and general paraphernalia of repair work, jarred with his memories of how it should be and confirmed the rightness of the decision he had just made.

He would go after them.

A few days later he was well on his way.

The parting had been harder than he had anticipated, especially parting from the stock, and particularly his dogs, but he had been able to shed such tears as he needed to shed as he rode alone, north towards the Great Forest. It had helped him that Gryss, the Senior Elder of the village, had agreed with his decision. It had helped him even further to note the almost sprightly air that was pervading the old man. He remarked on it.

'The whole business has given me a shaking that I probably needed, young Farnor,' Gryss said with a smile that was not without sadness. 'Perhaps we all needed it, though, pity knows, I'd have wished it in a happier form: so many people have been so cruelly hurt. But what's happened has happened and it's up to each of us to make what we can of it.' He gave a rueful laugh. 'The very least we'll have is a change of drinking stories. And it'll be interesting to see how much they do change over the next few months – how many trembling legs and churning stomachs are conveniently forgotten.' Then he looked at Farnor keenly, his mood sombre again. 'You'll be missed, Farnor, not least by me. But you're right to go. Don't have any doubts about that. To be honest, I was rather surprised you didn't go with them right away.' He lowered his voice. 'There's something very special about you, Farnor, and you must learn about it. There's no one here who can help you, and if you stay, choose to ignore it . . .' He hesitated. '. . . Perhaps it might fester unseen . . . like Rannick's. Who can say?'

It was a dark thought, touching as it did on the knowledge hanging silent between them that, in so small and isolated a community, Farnor and Rannick must surely have some common ancestry, common blood. Hadn't Rannick called him 'cousin' at the end?

'All this time you've been the same as me and we never knew.'

Scorching, frightening words. Perhaps more than anything else, it was these that disturbed Farnor and urged him forward.

The rest of his conversation with Gryss had been full of the practical details of his intended journey – horses, food, clothes, and, not least, the tenanting of his farm during his absence. They parted with an unexpectedly long embrace and, after a day's preparation, Farnor left the valley quietly, in the half-light before sunrise. He forced himself not to look back along the dark-stained trail he had made through the dew-sodden grass.

His journey into the Great Forest was markedly different from the first time he had made it. Then he had been frantic with terror, clinging for his life to his equally terrified mount and heading towards a world about which he knew nothing save old fireside tales. Now, he was riding at ease and feeling the welcome that the trees were offering him. Yet even now, there was a hint of urgency about his journey that was due to something other than his need to catch Marna and the others.

Before entering the Forest he had sought its permission, after the way of the Valderen.

'You are ever welcome, Hearer,' had come back the many-voiced reply. 'Much has changed. The spawn of the Great Evil is gone from this place and the darkness in you is not as it was.'

'I'm following my friends to a place where I might learn about that darkness.'

The Forest had trouble with the idea of friends, of such strange togetherness and separateness, but he felt their approval. Yet he sensed also an unease beneath it.

'What troubles you?' he asked.

Then had come the faint but recognizable voice of the heart of the Great Forest, reaching out to him from that vast and silent enclave of trees to the north where few were allowed to travel and which the Valderen knew as the place of the Most Ancient.

'The worlds are troubled still, Far-nor. And the Great Evil still strives to return.'

135

The worlds!

As he heard the words he was almost overwhelmed by a flood of images. He had experienced them during this early contact with the Forest, yet still they meant nothing to him. And still they were deeply disturbing.

For a moment he was tempted to seek an explanation but he knew that it would serve no purpose. Though the Forest trusted him, and though he could communicate with it as apparently no one had been able to do in generations, what they held in common was the merest flickering candle in the deep darkness of their differences.

'I Hear your fears,' he said. 'I shall protect you if I can.'

'And we, you, Far-nor. It is good that you seek the light.'

'Good day to you, young sir.' The voice startled Farnor. Though it sounded loud and intrusive, even as he spun round Farnor knew that the speaker would have been whispering and this betokened both knowledge and respect.

'Marken?' he said, smiling and opening his arms in greeting. 'What are you doing here?'

The old man, narrow-faced and slightly built, swung down from his horse and gave Farnor a long look.

'I *live* here, Farnor, if you recall. The question is, what are *you* doing here? Not that you're other than welcome, of course.' He took Farnor's arms in the powerful grip that was a characteristic Valderen greeting.

'I meant, how did you know I was here?' Farnor said in some confusion, trying not to rub his arms.

Marken's eyebrows rose. 'You're not the only Hearer in the Forest you know. They told me you were coming, and that I – that all of us – should help you on your way. Incidentally, I'm Hearing much better than I used to – I don't know whether it's me or them, but it's . . . a good feeling.' Farnor smiled at his friend's conspicuous pleasure. 'I must confess to being surprised to see you again so soon, though. I thought you were going back to live on your farm.'

Farnor explained what he was doing. Marken nodded sympathetically. 'I understand,' he said. 'Many things other than my Hearing are different here, too. Quite possibly for the better, for all the pain we suffered. I don't know. Time will doubtless tell.' He became brisk. 'Will you come to Derwyn's lodge? Stay with us awhile?'

'I can't, Marken. I have to catch my friends. They won't be hurrying but they're several days ahead and I really don't know where I'm going, except east. Besides, I'm still sore after fighting that creature of Rannick's. I think I'd frighten you to death trying to climb one of your ladders.'

'You always did,' Marken said bluntly. 'You're a natural born Faller, without a doubt. Are you sure you don't want to come to Derwyn's? He'd be . . .'

'He'd be annoyed if he thought I was idling in his lodge when I'd urgent matters to attend to.'

Marken looked at him shrewdly.

'Help me find my friends, Marken,' Farnor pressed. 'They came this way with your permission, and I'd be more than surprised if you didn't know not only where they are, but every step they've taken.'

Marken cleared his throat self-consciously. 'We watch . . . newcomers . . . in the Forest, naturally. They made need help, guidance – it's easy to get lost.'

'Hm.'

'And, of course, we're curious too,' Marken conceded. 'They did great service. We honour them.'

'I know,' Farnor said reassuringly.

Marken leaned forward and became confidential. 'The young girl – Marna – is awkward – like you – a Faller – though she's tried hard and she's learning quickly. But the others are remarkable. So light in their touch. They've great respect for everything around them. Their passing leaves no sign. They could almost be Valderen.'

It was a considerable compliment.

'How far did you go with them?' Farnor asked knowingly.

'Just a day's ride,' Marken admitted, his manner indicating that he regretted it had not been for longer. 'Then we had to get back to the lodge.'

'We?'

'There were . . . a few . . . of us.'

'*That* many, eh? Things *are* different.'

'I suppose I'd better see you on your way, then, if you're so anxious to be off. You'd like me to give your affection to Derwyn and his lodge, I imagine?'

'Of course. You know that.'

Marken rode with him for half a day and with his guidance the steady trot they were able to maintain carried them a long way.

'Let the Forest guide your horse,' Marken told him as they finally parted.

'I don't think that's going to be necessary,' Farnor said, pointing to two riders approaching them.

'Probably not,' Marken said with a broad smile. 'I've sent messages ahead. I think it's unlikely you'll be alone for long, if at all. You might have to tell your story a few times, but you'll make good progress and you'll save a lot of your supplies.' He took Farnor's arms again. 'I don't know if I've said this before, I don't really have the words to say what I feel, but thank you for all that you've done – for me, and for the Forest.' He released him. 'Travel well, Hearer. And come back to us one day.'

'I will.'

The journey proved to be just as Marken had said. Farnor was accompanied all the way and he not only saved his supplies but had them supplemented, as lodge after lodge pressed gifts on him.

Then, early one morning, he was at the edge of the Forest. The ground had been rising for some time and the trees ended abruptly, sweeping up the lower slopes of a range of mountains like a still and silent wave.

'We must leave you now, Farnor,' said the eldest of his latest companions. 'This is not a place where we can guide you.' He pointed to a col between two small peaks. 'Up there. That's the way your friends have gone.' There followed the grip on his arms, then, 'Go safely, it's been an honour to ride with you . . . Faller.' The familiar jibe was made both affectionately and tentatively and Farnor knew that he was giving more true thanks in his laughing at it than in his actual words. He spoke them nevertheless, then set off up the rocky slope.

He turned when he reached the dip. The Valderen were still at the edge of the Forest. He waved to them, then led his horses over the top of the rise. The Valderen returned his salute and in their turn disappeared into the Forest.

For a while, as he walked down the far side of the col, he could hear the horns of the Valderen speeding him on his way. It was a good sound, full of meaning for him. Gradually it faded.

He looked along the valley. It was much narrower than his home valley but it was green and lush and although the mountains bounding it were high and stern they were not oppressive. He mounted and clicked his horse forward.

For the first time since he had left home he felt alone. In the Forest he had been accompanied throughout not only by the Valderen but by the will of the Forest itself, unintrusive but powerful. It reaffirmed for him that the Most Ancient were indeed watching him and that wherever their consciousness touched the lesser woods and forests beyond the Forest – the remnants of what they had once been – they would be watching him there also.

But here there was nothing.

He felt a little afraid.

Had he made the right decision, leaving a home and the friends of a lifetime to go in search of . . .

Of what?

Doubts came to him more than once as he rode on, but each time, whenever they reached the point of making him draw in his horse, he realized again that he could do no other. He must go forward, find Marna and the others and go with them to the people who might understand what his gift was and what it meant. The fear that his gift, if ignored, might turn him into another Rannick persisted. In the end, the doubts, like the notes of the horns of the Valderen, faded into nothingness.

Towards evening, he fancied he caught a glimpse of a thin column of smoke rising through the still air. Briefly it caught the light of the setting sun shining along the valley, then it twisted and parted and was gone. He looked at the lengthening shadows around him and did his best to estimate the distance to where it had been.

He could do it, he decided, urging his horse forward.

It was a mistake, as he discovered shortly afterwards when

the sun finally dipped behind the head of the valley and the gloaming deepened abruptly. He glanced upwards. The tops of the mountains, some still dull red against the darkening sky, were becoming shadows, wrapping themselves about with wisps of dull grey cloud. A solitary silver star shone clear and bright in the east, like a guiding beacon, but, beautiful as it was, he realized that its light was treacherous and deceptive, serving only to deepen the darkness in the valley ahead.

Reluctantly he reined his horse to a halt and, after a final glance towards where the smoke had been, he began hurriedly preparing a camp in what was left of the light.

As had been the case since he left home, he slept well.

He woke to rain, fine and vertical. It hid much of the valley while the peaks above were completely hidden by cloud. Oddly enough, the cold greeting roused Farnor to action more than sunlight streaming through the entrance to his tent would have done. Years of living on a farm had made him an early waker and comparatively brisk and orderly in the execution of morning duties, but sunlight always seemed to fan his idleness while a colder kiss made him resolute, if a touch grim. And today, of course, there was the added incentive that he was now very near to catching Marna and the others.

Thus he had tended the horses and broken both the camp and his fast – albeit with cold fare – within a very short time of waking. Bearing in mind the implicit strictures of Marken he examined his camp site carefully to ensure that he too would 'leave no sign'.

As he mounted his horse and pulled his hood forward he began to plan the pending meeting. It was very early and it was unlikely his prey would be choosing to break their camp with the same alacrity as he had. With luck he might be able to surprise them before they even woke. He did not hurry, however. The valley floor rose a little and he could see sheets of rock jutting through. He would have to walk over these. Whatever the rights and wrongs of his journey, it would become a disaster if he or one of his horses were injured trying to negotiate such terrain too quickly.

Nevertheless, for a while he was buoyed up at the prospect of at least reaching his goal. He tried to envisage their reactions. Marna almost certainly would be abusive, but he found that he could not begin to guess how the others would respond. Yengar would probably greet him with a smile, Olvric would be as silent and enigmatic as ever. As for the two women, he had no idea.

He was still thinking about this when he came to the top of a rise and found himself looking down on their camp. It was nestling discreetly in between two rocky shoulders and he did not notice it at first. Suddenly, and chillingly, it occurred to him that perhaps this camp might not be the one he was seeking. There was no reason why there should be only him and them in the valley. Had not Nilsson and his men roamed all over before stumbling on the village? What if this was the camp of others of his ilk? It was a bad thought.

Then, between two tents of an unusual design, he saw a smaller one that he recognized as Marna's. He let out a sigh of relief and his previous excitement returned. It was mixed with smugness as he surveyed the still and silent scene. Whatever their reactions were going to be, they would be surprised at least. Perhaps he could start a fire for them. That would be a welcoming gesture for them. On the other hand, he might be left looking extremely foolish as they woke to find him wet and dismal as he struggled to light one in this rain.

He decided against any firm plans and, carefully leading his horses, began to make his way down the slope.

He reached the bottom without incident and was again debating how he should announce himself when a hooded figure emerged silently from behind a rock, sword in hand.

Chapter 12

The thoughts he had had when he first sighted the camp tumbled into Farnor's mind. What if Marna and her companions had been waylaid by a group such as Nilsson's? Was he walking into the aftermath of a new horror, into a new danger?

'An ill way to approach a camp, my friend.' The figure's voice cut across them. It was a man's, soft and calm, but with a quality in it that, while not directly menacing, nevertheless made Farnor feel cold and defenceless.

Even so, he had to make a deliberate effort to stop his hand flicking towards the knife in his belt. It was not a gesture he would even have contemplated making a few weeks ago, but then he had not been the person he was now. He made the movement into an adjustment of his robe and took a slow, unobtrusive pace backwards. If necessary he should be able to mount and flee.

The man seemed to be aware of this brief inner conflict for his sword moved slightly as if it too were debating. Then his head tilted to one side and he leaned forward a little.

'Farnor?'

Awkwardly, and taking another discreet step backwards, Farnor yanked back his hood. Slowly, the figure did the same, to reveal Olvric. He gave a hint of a smile, sheathed his sword, and offered his hand. 'Whatever's brought you here, it's good to see you, young man. But for the future you'd be advised to give a hail when you approach a camp if your intentions are friendly.' An eyebrow was raised to accompany the faint smile. 'And if they're not friendly, you'll need to go more quietly.'

'I *was* going quietly,' Farnor protested.

'Oh.'

'Farnor, what are you doing here?' This voice and its cross-examining tone were unmistakable and an old relationship re-established itself immediately.

'Nice to see you again, Marna,' Farnor said to the bleary-eyed face squinting out of the smallest tent.

Marna's face became concerned. 'Nothing's wrong at home, is it?'

'No, everyone's well. Or as well as can be expected, given all that's happened. I just decided I should come with you.'

Marna contemplated the news for a moment, then looked up at the rain-shrouded valley, grunted and disappeared.

Yengar appeared from one of the other tents. As Farnor had envisaged, he smiled warmly and held out his hand to greet him.

'Or should I greet you in the way of the Valderen?' he said, laughing. He mimicked the movement with clawed hands then massaged his own arms in mock pain.

'It takes a little getting used to,' Farnor said, taking Yengar's hand quickly in case he intended to fulfil his threat.

'It certainly does. I'm black and blue.' It was Marna again, emerging from her tent and combing her hair with a ferocity that made Farnor wince. 'And all those damned ladders and walkways. I've never been so frightened in all my life.' She faltered. 'Well, not like that, anyway.'

'You stayed in one of their lodges?' Farnor said in surprise.

'Indeed we did,' Yengar said. 'And a rare experience it was, too. They're a fascinating people. I'd like to have spent much longer with them. Perhaps one day. They invited us to return.'

'They must think very highly of you.'

Yengar gave a self-deprecating shrug. 'We fought in a common cause. It breaks through barriers that seem insuperable in quieter times. But I think it's you who's their hero, they were full of your exploits.'

'Perhaps we should talk about it out of the rain,' Marna said tartly, tugging hairs out of her comb. She eyed Olvric. 'When you've lit the fire. I did it last night.'

'Yes, and filled the valley with enough smoke to frighten

every tree in the Great Forest,' Olvric rejoined.

'That's not true. It was just . . .'

'Come on. Put Farnor's horses with the others and I'll show you again. Just pay attention this time.'

Farnor felt a faint frisson of resentment at seeing the new friendship that had obviously developed between Marna and these people. It caught him by surprise, but vanished as Marna took the horses from him with a conspiratorial 'In trouble again,' grin.

Yengar was crouching down, fiddling with something around the entrance to his tent. As he stood up, it came with him and with a couple of practised flicks the tent was opened and a canopy set up in front of it. Yengar bowed and motioned an astonished Farnor into it with exaggerated courtesy. Inside, he found the tent much bigger than he had imagined and he remarked on it. Yengar produced two small folding stools which he placed under the canopy.

'A little thought, a little experience, a little ingenuity,' Yengar said, looking around the spacious interior as if he had not seen it for a long time. 'Actually, more a lot than a little, now I think about it,' he added. 'But!' He clapped his hands. 'What are you doing here?' Before Farnor could reply, Yengar leaned forward confidentially. 'Everything *is* all right at home, is it?'

'Everything's fine,' Farnor confirmed. 'Different, but fine. If it's still open I've come to accept your offer to take me to wherever it is . . . whoever it is . . . who can help me find out what's happened to me.'

Yengar smiled understandingly. 'A wise decision, I suspect, and I'm more than glad to see you. As much for our sakes as yours. I was fairly certain that, once we'd given our accounting of what happened here, we'd probably have been asked to escort someone back to talk with you. Perhaps even Andawyr himself. And, with no disrespect to your friends and kin, I'd like to spend a little time in my own home for a while.'

'Andawyr?' Farnor asked.

'He's the Leader of the Cadwanol – the people most likely to know about the kind of thing that happened to you. You'd like him.' Yengar chuckled. 'He's as far away from being like the head of a great Teaching Order as you could imagine. But very clever – and very wise.'

Their conversation was underlaid by the steady drumming of the rain on the roof of the canopy and the splashing of its irregular dripping from the edges. Marna's raised voice drifted across to them. She and Olvric were bent over a pile of rocks from which a faint wisp of smoke was rising. Marna was protesting about something.

Farnor felt the need to apologize. 'She's quite headstrong, Marna,' he said. 'Not the easiest of people to get along with sometimes.'

Yengar indicated the other large tent. 'We're used to head-strong women,' he said, adding loudly, 'and idle ones.'

A thought occurred to Farnor. 'I'd no idea how long we were going to be travelling so I brought lots of supplies. Then the Valderen gave me lots more. It's their way once they know you, they're very generous.'

'So we gathered,' Yengar said, wide-eyed. 'We weren't certain whether refusing them would be an insult so we just smiled, said "Thank you" and loaded the poor pack horses some more. I think we'll have enough food to see us into the winter, let alone home.'

'Well, you have mine now, as well.'

They were interrupted by Yrain and Jenna emerging from the other tent. As they did so they threw up the canopy as Yengar had done but even more quickly.

'Marna, air your tent,' Jenna shouted as they moved across to join the two men. There was no reply, but Farnor noticed Marna's shoulder's hunch. He was standing up to offer his seat to one of the women when they seized and embraced him vigorously.

'Good to see you, young man,' Yrain said, releasing him, then dropping down and sitting cross-legged beside him. 'I'm glad you've decided to come with us.'

Farnor looked at Yengar in surprise.

'They were listening,' the Goraidin explained dismissively. 'You probably woke them when you arrived. They'll have been cowering there, fearful of an attack by some mountain demon.'

146

'It's your turn to cook the breakfast, isn't it?' Jenna said to him before Yrain could voice the acid reply that was making its way from her eyes to her mouth.

Yengar patted Farnor on the shoulder, then left them and went over to the horses.

'Don't make anything for me,' Farnor shouted after him. 'I've eaten.'

Yrain looked up at the sky. 'Early riser,' she said with some admiration.

'The animals don't lie in,' he said. She smiled and squeezed his arm affectionately.

As the others ate, Farnor told them about the few things that had happened in the village since they had left and then explained why he had decided to follow them. His reasons surprised no one and they all reiterated Yengar's welcome and his opinion that they would probably have had to come back to see him anyway.

'Even so,' Yengar said as the conversation flagged momentarily. 'A hard decision for you. Accepting that something's gone for ever is never easy.'

'I'm not sure that it has,' Farnor said quietly. 'At least, not all of it. I think what my mother and father gave me, and Gryss, and all my friends, my whole life in the valley – even Rannick, in the end – *will* stay with me for ever.'

The others exchanged glances and Jenna turned away.

'I'd say I was at least ten years older than you before I learned that,' Yengar said. 'Well done.'

Then the camp became brisk. The two large tents were dismantled and stowed on the pack horses with the same alacrity with which Yengar had erected the canopy. Marna's took a little longer and involved more robust language. The fire was dowsed, latrines sealed, and the whole site carefully examined until they were satisfied that it was as they had found it.

Farnor helped where he could. 'Marken said your passing leaves no sign,' he told them. 'It impressed him.'

He watched Olvric turning over a stone before he finally mounted.

'Why such care?' he asked as they set off.

'Habit now,' Olvric replied. 'Training once. And the nature of the work we do.'

'Work? I thought you were soldiers.'

This provoked a mixture of laughter and stern reproach.

'There's a little more to soldiering than just charging in and killing people – or getting killed,' Yengar said. 'We go deep into enemy territory to find out what they're doing – where their army is, how big, how many infantry and what kind, how many cavalry and what kind, how well equipped, disciplined, supplied they are, and so on. Then we take the information back to our own people so that they can decide what should be done for the best. Occasionally we have to go in and do damage.' Farnor looked at him in anticipation of a tale but Yengar became unexpectedly serious. 'Our profession is the study of ordered violence, Farnor. If we do our work well, then fewer people die than might have been the case. If we do it *really* well then perhaps none die, perhaps the battle never happens.' His manner lightened again. 'And part of our work – a part we relish, I might add – is staying alive. That's why we do our best to leave no sign.'

'There's no enemy round here,' Farnor protested.

'You know these mountains, this land, do you?'

'Well, no, but . . .'

'Well, no, but, indeed. Still, you're probably right, I doubt there's any enemy around here. But our work can be dangerous and frightening. Believe me, when someone's hunting you, he'll spot a broken twig, an upturned rock, scuffed grass, and be on you like a summer storm. As Olvric just said, we rely first on good training and then on good habits – habits we can't risk letting slip just because there's no immediate threat. Hard experience has taught us that – both ours and other people's.'

Farnor acknowledged the explanation.

'Besides,' Yengar went on. 'Leaving the place a mess is disrespectful to the other creatures that live here, isn't it? So if the idea of fighting offends you, you can think of our tidiness as simply good manners.'

'It doesn't offend me. It frightens me – frightens me a lot.' He paused. 'And it puzzles me. I understand it and I don't

148

understand it. When I reached the Most Ancient I was full of hatred for Rannick. I had a vision of him dead – killed by me – like I'd slaughter a pig – and I wanted their knowledge so that I could come back and overwhelm him and make it so. But when I came away, I was different. The hatred was still there, driving me on, but changed somehow. I knew then I had to try to stop him doing what he was doing. I didn't seem to have a choice. I couldn't see any life beyond it.' He laughed weakly. 'I remember having some vague idea about bringing him before the law, to be tried. But I knew in reality I'd have to fight him – and that creature – and that I might die. I convinced myself it wasn't just for me any more, that it was for everyone else as well. It was to stop him hurting people like he'd hurt me. But it was still the same hatred. And still as much a desire for vengeance as it was for justice.'

He fell silent, rapt in thought. No one disturbed him.

'And in the end I forgave him. Forgave him the murder of my parents. How could I do that?' He gave a gulping laugh that was almost a sob. 'And that destroyed him as surely as if I'd cut him open like that damned creature of his.' He threw back his hood and turned his face upwards to let the rain fall on it. 'I held out my hand to help my parents' murderer and it destroyed him. Do you think I knew that was going to happen? That that was the sure way to destroy him?' He shook his head and wiped his hand down his face. 'It's too complicated. I don't understand.'

There was a long silence.

'Wiser men than you or I have struggled to understand the darkness we have inside us, Farnor,' Yengar said eventually. 'And failed. I suppose we all have to make our own peace with it as best we can – strive to do as little harm as possible. What you did you did for a purpose that any of us would consider just. And you did well. In fact, you did magnificently. Circumstances put you where you were and, dark and frightening though they might have been, you found the resources to survive – in every way. Any blame – any guilt – was Rannick's. He had the same choices as you, but where you used your crueller nature to a good end, he allowed himself to be consumed by his.' Farnor made to speak but

149

Yengar pressed on. 'There *is* no understanding the likes of him when they pass a certain point. They cut their own demented path through the lives of others, and bring about their own destruction.'

There was a soft murmur of agreement from the others.

'Gryss thinks that I might have the same power as Rannick.'

The words hung in the rain-filled air.

'Maybe you have,' Yengar said casually. 'I don't pretend to understand these things, but coming from a small community like yours you're bound to be related in some way if that's of any relevance. Not that it matters.'

Farnor was taken aback by his offhand manner. 'Not matter? But . . .'

'But nothing.' Yengar looked at him powerfully. 'You've been tried and tested. More than many so-called fighting men I know. If you were going to turn into another Rannick it would've happened by now. Trust me.' He swung an arm across his companions. 'There are always choices – and always the heart and the head to guide. You made yours and you chose well – as you said yourself, what your parents gave you will be with you for ever. Even now, by coming with us, you're choosing. You've chosen to learn more about yourself. And if it transpires you've some skill with the Power – or something else – then learn whatever you can about it. You'll make mistakes with it, as sure as fate, but you'll put it to no ill use.' He put a reassuring hand on Farnor's shoulder. 'For now, all you need concern yourself with is staying in your saddle and enjoying our journey home.'

Farnor frowned. 'You've thought a lot about this, haven't you?'

Yengar threw his head back and a loud, generous laugh rolled out of him. Jenna and Yrain too laughed. Olvric smiled quietly. Farnor and Marna looked at one another, uncertain about the cause of this mirth.

'Yes, I certainly have,' Yengar replied, still laughing. '*Many*'s the time all of us have had cause to think "What am I doing here?" And if I can teach you in ten days what it's taken me ten years to learn then I'm only too happy to.'

'Could you teach me to be like you?'

Yengar reined in his laughter and gave Farnor a strange look as if the young man might be teasing him. 'What do you mean?' he asked.

'I mean, be like you. Someone who can protect people against the likes of Nilsson and his men. A warrior.'

Yengar's mouth opened and closed twice before he managed to say, 'You challenged Nilsson and survived. You challenged Rannick and survived. You challenged the Great Forest and survived. You plunged into the depths of your own fears and doubts and survived. And, not least, you fought and killed what was almost certainly a Sierwolf and came away with nothing more than a few bruises. You need no lessons from me, Farnor, you're everything you need to be.'

'I was lucky.'

Yengar laughed again, though this time with an air of exasperated disbelief. 'You quite probably were,' he said. 'But being "a warrior" . . .'; he laid a mocking emphasis on the words '. . . doesn't mean that you don't need your share of luck.'

'You know what I mean.'

'No, I don't. Why in pity's name would you want to be like me – or any of us?'

'Because I would! Because I can still remember the helplessness I felt when Nilsson beat me. It was like nothing I'd ever known before. I could do nothing. I was something less than a child's doll to him. You're right, I did survive, but only because Gryss intervened and talked our way out of it. I don't want to experience anything like that ever again!'

Yengar did not speak, surprised and a little disconcerted by this unexpected passion.

'Even Gulda threw me around as if I was nothing,' Farnor added, almost petulantly.

'Gulda?' exclaimed Yrain, suddenly taking a keen interest in the conversation. 'Why would she throw you around?'

Farnor turned to her sheepishly. 'She took me by surprise,' he said defensively, clearing his throat. 'She sneaked up on me when I was by my camp fire. I . . . I lashed out at her with a stick.'

'You did *what*!' Both Jenna and Yrain were wide-eyed.

'I . . . lashed out at her with a stick. Then . . . I tried to stab her.'

'I don't believe I'm hearing this,' Yrain said. 'You never told us about it before.'

'You never asked,' Farnor said weakly.

The two women moved their horses to ride either side of him, Yrain casually displacing Yengar despite the fact that he was equally enthralled by this revelation.

'What happened?' they both urged him, abruptly gossiping jades.

'I don't know,' Farnor replied, taken aback by this sudden interest and beginning to regret he had mentioned this encounter. 'I was poking the fire and, all of a sudden, there was this figure behind me. I just swung round with the stick I was holding.'

'And . . .'

Farnor hesitated for a moment. 'I remember the clearing turning upside down. And then I hit the ground . . . some way away. Twice, I think. And without my stick. *She* was poking the fire with it when I gathered my wits.'

This caused a great deal of laughter and brought down a combination of back-slapping and precarious embracing that nearly tumbled Farnor out of his saddle.

'Swinging a stick at Gulda,' Yrain said, at the same time wiping her eyes and righting him again. 'I'd have given a lot to see that.'

'No, you wouldn't,' Yengar intruded. 'You'd have been hiding behind the nearest tree. As would all of us.'

'You're probably right.'

There was more laughter.

'It's not funny,' Farnor said indignantly.

'Yes, it is,' Yengar replied. 'You don't know Gulda like we do.'

'She's just an old woman,' Farnor said, knowing that this was not true even as he spoke. Then, anxious to end his tenure as the butt of their mirth, he asked, 'Can she use this . . . Power . . . that you were talking about? Is that how she did it?'

The laughter faded.

'No one knows what Gulda can do. Or even who she is. Most of us had thought never to hear of her again after the war.' It was Olvric. 'She's like Hawklan – deep and puzzling. Very deep.'

'And formidable,' Yengar added. 'In every way. I wouldn't be surprised if she could use the Power, but she wouldn't have needed it to deal with you. If it's any comfort to you, none of us here would choose to threaten her. Nor any that I know.'

Farnor gave a defiant shrug. 'But still . . .'

Yengar met the young man's pained gaze, then looked skywards. 'All right. I can see it's something that's troubling you. We'll do as you ask. We all know what it's like to receive a beating. Things like that do harm that lasts a long time. We'll show you what we can. A few tricks and a little thought will soon have you feeling more confident in yourself.' He became serious. 'But I meant what I said about you before. Warrior's not a word I'd choose, but you have the heart of what you need already: a profound determination to survive. Without that, weapons, fighting skills, they're all worthless.'

He cast a glance at Marna. 'It must be something in the water in that valley of yours. Now we have two pupils. However . . .' He looked at Farnor significantly. 'While I might possibly be able to give you the benefit of ten years of thought about conflict and violence in ten days, when it comes to learning how to fight and all that that involves – including such matters as talking your way out of problems, like Gryss, and surviving out here – then I'm afraid you have to go the long way.'

'I understand,' Farnor replied, a little nervous now that his request had been granted. 'When can we . . . start?'

Yengar raised an eyebrow and his previous laughter returned. 'We'll start right now,' he said. 'Here's your first and most important lesson in self-defence. Remember it well.' He leaned across to Farnor and placed a confidential arm around his shoulders. Farnor bent towards him keenly.

'Don't swing a stick at Gulda again.'

Laughter floated into the rain-soaked air as the small procession wended its way along the valley.

A little later, the rain stopped and the clouds thinned to

reveal streaks of blue sky and occasional shafts of sunlight. Coming to the end of the valley they stopped to rest the horses and to eat. And to decide where to go next, for the valley opened into an even broader one running north and south.

'Pick a gap,' Yengar said to Farnor as they surveyed the peaks along the far side.

Farnor looked at him blankly. 'Where are we going?'

Yengar smiled. 'Second rule of self-defence – ask questions like that before you set out.'

Farnor scowled at him.

'They're like this all the time,' Marna said, her mouth full of a large Valderen pie. 'And they laugh a lot – except him.' She waved the pie at Olvric who inclined his head slightly towards her by way of reply. 'Their main rule of self-defence is keep inventing new rules to make sure everything your students do is wrong.'

'To make sure your students understand that everything they do can always be done better,' Yengar intervened.

'See what I mean?' Marna declared with heavy fatalism.

'Even so, it's a good question,' Jenna said. 'Where *are* we going now? We were going to go to Vakloss, to give our accounting to the Geadrol, but . . .' She indicated Farnor who shifted uncomfortably as all four turned to look at him.

'Anderras Darion,' Olvric said flatly, turning back to the strap on one of the panniers that he was repairing. 'Gulda will be there.'

Farnor felt an uneasiness pervade the group momentarily. Yengar ended it by looking at the others for any sign of dissent.

'It's there or the Cadwanen,' Jenna said. 'There's no one at Vakloss who can answer *his* questions. And the quickest way to the Cadwanen will be past Anderras Darion anyway.'

'We'll take you to Hawklan's castle, then, Farnor,' Yengar said. 'He's the best man to advise you from there.'

'And Gulda?' Farnor asked. 'Will she be there?'

Again he sensed the uneasiness.

'What's the matter?' he asked, unable to prevent the question.

Without any apparent signal, everyone was standing and preparing to set off again.

'Gulda has a way of . . . gravitating . . . towards trouble,' Yengar told him, as they began leading their horses down into the valley. 'To be honest, from what you've told me I don't think she'd have left you in the Forest unless she'd some other more urgent errand in mind.' He made an effort at a reassuring smile. 'Still, that's all conjecture, isn't it? We'll find out if she's there soon enough. All we need bother ourselves with at the moment is which gap you've picked for us to go through.' He pointed across the valley.

'*I* don't know,' Farnor protested in some alarm. 'Don't you have some way of telling which is the best way?'

'Yes,' Yengar said pensively. 'It's called guessing.'

It took them the rest of the day to cross the valley. Apart from a search for a shallow stretch by which to cross over an otherwise fast and turbulent river, the journey was without incident and they camped near the top of a col which they had agreed looked 'as good a way as any'.

Alone in his tent Farnor pondered the events of the day from his first nervous encounter with Olvric. It had been good, he decided, though the sense of some hidden darkness when Gulda was mentioned disturbed him a little. Still, these people were soldiers and by all accounts they had fought in a bitter war long before they came in search of Nilsson and his men. There were probably many things that they would not wish to share with either him or Marna. Then he realized that this was the first time since his parents had been killed that he had lain in a bed and felt both security around him and a future ahead of him. He was looking forward to it as he drifted into sleep, his thoughts fragmenting and scattering into disjointed nonsense.

Then he was wide awake, with fear crawling through every part of him.

Chapter 13

Farnor started upright, his heart pounding. It took him a little time to remember where he was and a little more to realize that the strange noise rasping through the tent was his own breathing. It took him even longer to bring it under any semblance of control, for the fear he had woken to was still with him. At one point he was tempted to call out, but something stopped him. Slowly it came to him that the fear was not fear. It was more like the response he might have had to fingernails drawn down glass. And it was familiar.

Then there was fear.

This was how he had felt when, as he had confronted Rannick and his terrible familiar, a gash through this reality had been torn to reveal the myriad worlds beyond. As the memory returned, so now, as had happened then, he found part of himself reaching out to make right this affront – a part that he did not understand and that seemed more to be controlling him than he it. His helplessness brought fear of another kind. Not least because a struggle developed. Some power was opposing this other part of him!

Then, abruptly, the struggle was over. The gash was gone, as was this inner self. Everything was whole again.

He was leaning forward supporting himself on one arm as though, with opposition removed, he had stumbled forward. And he was shaking violently.

What had happened?

A nightmare?

No.

The feeling had been real, without a doubt, but what it had meant he had no idea. This time there had been no vision of the rent through into the worlds beyond. There had been just the darkness of the tent all around him. Nor had it been so intense. But it had been the same, without question. Except that this time, something had opposed whatever it was in him that sought to right the injury.

Again he was tempted to call out but again he forced himself not to. Whatever had happened, it had definitely passed and, welcoming though his new hosts had proved to be, it was unlikely they would take kindly to being wakened in the middle of the night by what *they* would almost certainly have considered to be a nightmare. For he doubted that he would be able to describe the incident adequately.

Nevertheless, the following day, as they broke camp, he told them about it.

His story met with an uncomfortable silence.

'I don't know what to say,' Yengar said. 'It's . . .'

'Did you sense danger?' Olvric intruded quietly.

Farnor thought before he replied. 'I was afraid,' he said. 'But I think that was because of what had happened before, and I couldn't do anything – not deliberately, anyway – I was helpless. The sensation wasn't frightening in itself.' He floundered. 'I'm sorry, I don't really have any words for it. It was just wrong, unnatural, something that shouldn't be. It made my flesh creep.' He shuddered noisily, then looked round at the others. They were watching him intently. Silently Marna pulled her horse alongside him in a small show of support against these potentially hostile strangers.

'Did you sense danger?' Olvric repeated his question.

Farnor found himself being thankful for his cold, searching manner. It carried no judgement, only a need to know.

'No,' he said firmly. 'No danger. But it was still a bad thing, something that shouldn't have been. And this time something resisted whatever it was I was doing to close the rift. That didn't happen before.'

'You've said before twice, this hasn't happened at any other time since you faced Rannick?'

'No.'

'Wake us if it happens again.'

'But . . .'

'Wake us.' Olvric's tone was both matter-of-fact and unequivocal and seemed to dispel the uncertainty pervading the others.

'I'm sorry if we gaped at you,' Yengar said. 'You caught us all by surprise. Olvric's right. Wake us next time – if there's a next time. Other things may be happening which you're unaware of and which we'll be able to see.'

'But . . .'

'Information, Farnor,' Yengar went on, explanatory now. 'I told you. Our job. Gathering information. The more we can tell Hawklan or Andawyr about what's happening to you, the better.'

'And if there's nothing for you see – or feel – or anything?'

'That's information in itself, isn't it? It may be just as significant. Who are we to say? What we have to do is note events accurately so that we can describe them to others accurately.'

'I suppose so,' Farnor conceded reluctantly. The mood of the group was lightening. 'It just seems – fussy.'

Yengar mulled over the word. 'Well, we've been called worse. I prefer to think of myself as being obsessive. Fussy sounds rather petty, don't you think?'

Farnor eyed him suspiciously, testing the self-deprecating humour that seemed to be a common feature of the group. His response caused some amusement.

'Never underestimate the effects of the small action,' the two women said to him in unison, obviously recalling an insistent teaching.

'Sumeral's in the details,' Yrain said in a strident, authoritative voice that Farnor thought he should know.

'Ethriss is in the details,' Jenna echoed in the same vein.

Then they both laughed.

'I'm sure Gulda will be greatly heartened to find how carefully you listened to her,' Yengar said with affected sternness. Farnor remembered the voice.

'*Memsa* Gulda, Goraidin. *Memsa*,' the two women chimed, to even greater amusement. Yengar resisted for a moment, then capitulated. 'It doesn't concern me, I can always have Farnor chase her with a stick, I suppose.'

'I told you, they're like this all the time,' Marna said to the bemused Farnor through the ensuing clamour. 'When they're not getting someone else to do all the dirty work,' she added loudly.

'A necessary part of your training, cadet,' Jenna said, maintaining Gulda's persona.

Marna gave Farnor a knowing look and dropped back to join them. Olvric replaced her.

'Don't confuse our humour with frivolity, Farnor,' he said after they had ridden a little way in silence. 'We've done many things together. Many things. We know and trust one another deeply.'

'I understand,' Farnor replied, Olvric's remarks bringing to him the memory of the friends and the laughter he had left back at the village. It all seemed to be such a long time ago. Then, abruptly, he did understand, and though the laughter behind him did not change it was suddenly different, echoing into the depths of who these people were.

'It's what Marken called your lightness of touch,' he said, turning and looking directly at the enigmatic Goraidin.

Olvric raised his eyebrows and bent his head forward slightly in appreciation.

Farnor straightened as if a weight had been lifted from him.

'But *you* don't laugh much,' he heard himself saying.

Unexpectedly, Olvric chuckled. 'I do in my own way,' he replied as the sound rumbled through him to break out in an equally unexpected, if brief, smile. 'Have no fear about that.' He became pensive for a moment then said, 'It's good to have you both along,' before easing his horse forward a little to ride alone.

The sky was overcast, but the clouds were high and light and seemed set to remain so for the rest of the day. Towards midday, however, a wind sprang up and began to disperse them. The valley that they had chosen twisted and turned, but it carried them generally eastward and the going was easy. Farnor was gradually inducted into the ways of their travelling, now walking, now riding, now resting, now eating. And throughout, he was aware that both he and Marna were being gently instructed.

When they stopped in the late afternoon to make camp for the night he was given the task of choosing a suitable site. After some wandering about and a disproportionate amount of fretful thought, he chose the lee of a rock face.

Jenna looked at it critically. 'Dry ground, out of the wind, no sign of loose rocks above to give us a rude awakening, near a stream but no so near that it'll disturb us or cover unwelcome sounds. Not bad.'

Later, they sat around the fire, eating.

'I'm afraid we're not going to be able to give you much hunting experience, Farnor,' Yengar said, dropping a well-gnawed bone on to the fire. 'Not with the quantity of supplies that we've still got left.' He pulled a rueful face. 'In fact, I think some of the food will be going bad before we can eat it. We'll have to leave it for the local scavengers.'

'I've trapped rabbits and foxes,' Farnor told him.

'Can you use a bow?' Olvric asked. Farnor shook his head. 'Not really. There were quite a few in the village, but I don't think anyone could use one properly. Gryss wouldn't allow anyone to take one when we first went looking for the creature.'

'It's not a good idea to have a weapon you can't use,' Olvric went on.

Farnor shrugged. 'If they were ever for anything it was probably hunting, and there was precious little need for that. I don't think anyone ever thought about them being used as weapons. We'd no need at all for weapons.' His voice faded. 'Well, we thought we'd no need.'

'An apt epitaph,' Olvric said, staring bleakly into the fire. 'And an old one.'

'Speaking of which, what's that?' Yrain was pointing to a sword lying by Farnor's saddle.

'It's a sword,' Farnor replied, with a hint of indignation.

'May I look at it?'

Farnor held out his hand towards it by way of invitation. Yrain took the sword from its scabbard and brought it back to the fire. She was grimacing as she lifted it.

'It's just an old thing I found,' Farnor said.

'It certainly is,' Yrain agreed.

161

'I wanted a Threshold Sword. Like the Valderen. I think everyone in the village has one now. I know the blacksmith's been kept busy making new ones and repairing old ones. Better late than never, I suppose.'

Yrain tested the edge and her expression changed. 'Almost everything about this thing leaves a lot to be desired, but this edge is good,' she said, openly surprised. 'Did your blacksmith do it for you?'

'No, *I* did that. I could always put a good edge on things.'

Yrain's surprise became frank admiration. The sword did the rounds of the four soldiers who all reacted similarly.

'I don't suppose you know how to use this either?' Olvric said, returning it to Farnor.

'What's to know?' Farnor replied, making a mock fighting gesture with the sword to the considerable consternation of the others.

'A lot,' Olvric said tersely as his grip closed powerfully around Farnor's wrist and he gently prised the sword from his hand. He signalled to Yrain.

'Come on, you two, over there,' she said to Farnor and Marna.

After some ritual opposition from both of them, they spent the next hour receiving instruction in basic swordsmanship.

'Keep it *very* basic,' Olvric emphasized to her after watching them for a little while. 'Just enough to make sure we don't get cut down by our own fireside and they don't cut their own heads off.'

When finally Yrain finished with them, it was almost dark. Farnor and Marna, red-faced and breathless, collapsed gracelessly by the fire. Farnor was wriggling his shoulders and massaging his right arm. Yengar made to speak but Farnor gave him a baleful look. 'Don't tell me to relax, that's all I've heard for the last hour.'

'You won't want to do any close-quarter, unarmed fighting, then?' Yengar grinned at him. Farnor's look became grimmer.

'I'll take that as a refusal,' Yengar said, this time laughing.

Olvric gave Yrain an inquiring look.

'Not bad,' she said. 'I've dealt with worse. Just impatient with themselves like most young people.' She became serious.

162

'But they're both clearer in their minds than most.'

'That's only to be expected,' Yengar said sadly.

Farnor levered himself into a sitting position. 'How long does it take to learn all this?' he asked.

'All what?' Yengar asked in turn.

'All this . . . stuff you know about fighting, riding, camping, hunting, surviving on your own in places like this . . . everything.'

'Stuff!' Jenna said with mock despair.

'See what I mean about impatience?' Yrain interjected.

'You asked the wrong question, Farnor,' Olvric said.

'What?'

'The wrong question,' Olvric repeated. 'You should have asked, how do I learn about "all this"?'

'Very well, how do *I* learn about "all this"?'

'By taking one step at a time.'

'Thank you, that's a great help,' Farnor said caustically. 'And how long's that going to take?'

Olvric nudged the fire gently with his foot, sending up a small flurry of sparks. 'A lifetime,' he said. 'It's as well you started tonight. Keep at it, you'll go far.'

Jenna took pity on Farnor. 'What Olvric's telling you is that if you really want to be like us, then you never stop learning. There's never a time when you've learned "all this . . . *stuff*". Learn *that* and you've learned a lot. Learn that and most of your impatience will drop away from you.'

'Sounds like hard work.'

'It's as hard as you make it. Certainly no harder than getting up at dawn every day to tend the farm. It just becomes a habit after a while, once you start thinking properly.'

Farnor grimaced as any semblance of a reply to this refused to come to him. 'Well, my next learning will be to find out how cold that stream is, because I'm going to have a wash after all that.'

'I'll come with you,' Marna said.

As the two strolled off into the gloaming, the four Goraidin looked at one another.

'Teach them everything we can,' Olvric said in answer to an unspoken question. 'They're intelligent, braver than they

163

know, and full of good heart, for all they've been through.'

'I don't know,' Jenna said doubtfully. 'We became what we are because we'd wars to fight. An enemy to face. They don't have that.'

'There are always enemies to face,' Olvric said.

'You know what I mean,' Jenna said heatedly.

'And *you* know what *I* mean,' Olvric replied. 'Would you be other than you are? Marna's still burdened by the man she killed and, if nothing else, Farnor's burdened by the beating that thug Nilsson gave him. We can help him with that. It's the least we can do. And then there's this . . . gift . . . of his. From what I can gather, it seems as if it might have something to do with the Power. I think he's going to need great trust in himself sooner or later.'

Jenna looked uncomfortable. 'Don't forget we've seen no manifestation of this so-called gift for ourselves,' she said.

'I haven't forgotten,' Olvric said flatly. 'But there's more than enough First Face evidence to confirm there's something special about him. Not least is the fact that, one way or another, single-handedly, he dealt with Rannick and that creature. You might recall that we, with our vaunted fighting abilities, only survived when we faced Rannick *on his own* because something made him abandon us! And none of us here doubt that Rannick used the Power, do we?'

'Or that he stank of Sumeral,' Yrain added viciously. No one demurred.

Olvric pressed on. 'Then there's the Valderen. They need no convincing. Farnor's *very* special to them. They might be strange, but I'd judge them to be practical, clear-sighted. Whether or not he's seeing through into "worlds beyond this one", whatever they might be, is probably irrelevant. He believes that's what's happening and everything we've learned about him, from Gryss, Marna, the villagers and our own observations confirms that he's a decent lad – troubled, as well he might be, given what happened to him – but level-headed and down-to-earth. He's neither a madman nor a liar. We can do no more than accept his own judgement of his condition and watch him so that we can give a proper Accounting when asked.'

He looked round at his friends and received their silent assent.

'And in the meantime, help him to become more self-reliant. My instincts tell me the lad has dangers to face yet. I can't begin to guess what's really driven him to leave his home and come to us, but he's come in trust, and for guidance of some kind. While we have him – which shouldn't be for more than a few days anyway – we should teach him what we can. It's little enough. I think Hawklan would expect that of us.'

'Gulda would, for sure,' Yengar agreed. 'I'm still concerned that she left him in the Forest when he patently needed help.'

'Gulda's Gulda,' Yrain said. 'She sees further than any of us. If she didn't help him, she couldn't. Or perhaps she'd done all she could by the time they parted. There's always that dreadful time when you *have* to stand by and watch someone learn the hard way.'

'Well, if she's at Anderras Darion when we get there, you can ask her,' Yengar said.

'I think I will.'

This determined pronouncement brought united derision down on Yrain, during which Marna and Farnor returned.

'That was quick.'

'Yes, we're quick learners. We learned very quickly that it was very cold,' Marna replied for them both. 'Have you been talking about us behind our backs?'

'Of course,' Yengar confessed. 'It's much more fun than when you're here.' He changed the subject before Marna could reply. 'Did you enjoy the sword training?'

'Yes.' Marna's reply was immediate and enthusiastic. Farnor was a little more reticent. 'It wasn't quite what I was expecting.'

'What were you expecting?'

Farnor thought for a moment. 'I don't know, now you mention it.'

'Ah. So you've learned at least two things, then?'

Farnor looked at him blankly.

'That few things in life are as you expect them to be, whether you do or whether you don't.'

He paused significantly.

'And?' Farnor prompted suspiciously.

'You don't always learn what you think you're learning.'

Marna leaned over to Farnor and said, 'They're going to laugh now.'

And they did.

Abruptly Farnor lurched forward. Yengar's arm shot out and caught him before he tumbled into the fire. Jenna and Yrain took hold of him and were easing him upright when Olvric's voice hissed through the sudden commotion.

'Quiet!'

Instantly Marna found Yrain's free hand across her mouth and the Goraidin's urgent eyes confirming the command. She nodded quickly to indicate she understood. Yrain withdrew her hand. Olvric was peering intently into the darkness. Silently Yengar eased a thin slab of stone over the fire to douse its light. Equally silently, Jenna and Yrain laid Farnor down, Jenna whispering to him, then testing his pulse and finally bending low to listen for his breathing.

Yrain drew her knife.

Marna wanted to speak, but she had known the Goraidin long enough to know that in such circumstances she must just do as she was told and stay alert. She became aware of Olvric pointing. Following his direction she saw a movement some way away from the camp. She screwed her eyes tight in an attempt to bring it more clearly into focus, but to little avail. The movement was not that of a figure, human or animal. Rather it was an odd shimmering, as though the night air were dancing above hot coals. And, too, she realized she could not judge where it was, near or far. For an instant it was almost as if it were not beyond the camp, but dancing in her mind. She drew in a sharp breath and, as she did so, the shimmering was beyond her again.

Jenna was still trying to win a response from Farnor but without success. Frighteningly she could see that his eyes were wide open, dull white in the darkness.

The others were silent and watching.

Marna could contain herself no longer. 'What is it?' she whispered.

'Watch. Listen,' came the reply.

Then she felt a faint, unpleasant tingling. It shifted and changed, echoing the mysterious movement in the darkness. The hairs on her arms rose in revulsion and she clenched them tight to herself as though a cold wind had sprung up. She became aware of a scuffling behind her. Glancing quickly over her shoulder, she could just make out Farnor struggling to pull himself upright, Jenna helping him, her hand hovering about his mouth to stifle any inadvertent cry.

The tingling in Marna's arms grew worse, and started to spread down her back. She wanted to turn away from the dancing shape, but, serpentine now, it held her fascinated. A thin wavering light started to cut an unsteady thread through it. As it too moved, parts of it flared brightly, like ghastly jewels, then it faded and slowly widened, becoming a foaming grey, turbulent and troubled.

Still Marna could not decide how far away it was, or even whether it was on the ground or floating in the air. Her stomach lurched.

She felt Farnor moving again.

'No,' she heard him saying hoarsely. 'No!' Then she could sense Jenna's hand gently but very firmly silencing him.

A convulsion shook the grey, storm-cloud turbulence.

And into it came the black silhouette of a horseman.

Chapter 14

M arna felt a scream forming but no sound came from her constricted throat.

'No.' The hoarse cry became a rumbling growl. Though she knew it was Farnor she could barely recognize his voice, so full of angry defiance was it. And though it was not loud, there was a deep resonance about it that seemed to echo all around her. The boiling greyness shivered at the touch of it and both rider and horse became momentarily still. Then, slowly, as though the movement were tearing through the air itself, the rider's head turned.

Marna could sense a burning gaze searching through the darkness. Already crouching low she had to fight an almost overwhelming urge to throw herself flat to the ground to avoid this unseen scrutiny. Then an arm was raised and a hand was pointing towards them and the horse was prancing and rearing violently as though struggling to move forward. The unpleasant tingling that was now suffusing her became a wave of horror, biting and acidic. Though she could hear nothing, she knew it was the rider, calling out. She turned away and raised her hands protectively as if against a blistering wind. As she did so, she had a fleeting impression of other riders appearing behind the first.

Then Farnor, free of Jenna, was pushing past her, his arms extended.

It seemed then to Marna that suddenly there were two great forces opposing one another – balanced – and she could do no other than hold her breath for fear of disturbing this frightening equilibrium. Slowly it shifted. There was a sensation of something tearing within and around her – a noise that was not a noise. Looking up hesitantly, she saw the storm-cloud greyness beginning to shrink. She willed it on its way desperately as, with a painful slowness, it closed about the riders. Then, quite suddenly, it dwindled into nothingness, leaving only a thin, baleful red line that quivered and twitched unpleasantly before fading in its turn. As it vanished, so the awful tingling slipped away from her, though she kept rubbing her arms.

For what seemed to be a very long time there was a deep silence. Then Yengar was barking out orders, his voice low but coldly urgent, and Jenna was rushing forward to catch Farnor who was slowly sinking to his knees. Even as Yengar was speaking, he and Olvric were moving into the night towards where the mysterious image had appeared. Yrain, eyes and knife scanning the darkness, remained protectively by Marna who was still rubbing her arms.

The silence returned.

Marna watched the strange, flickering movement of the two men as they searched. Bright swathes of light came and went suddenly, now here, now there, as they used the tightly focused lanterns fastened to their wrists to slice open the darkness. Anything caught in their beam would be both dazzled and exposed – either to the sword in the light-bearer's other hand, or to that of his companion, now silent and dark. Yengar and Olvric moved to a deadly, long-practised rhythm.

For a while the lights bobbed and jerked like sinister fireflies, then they were gone and the two men were returning.

'Nothing,' Yengar said, disbelief dominating the exasperation in his voice as he unfastened the lantern from his wrist, checked it and laid it down by the fire. 'No sign of anything. Not a stone moved, not a blade of grass bent. No sound of riders moving away. There's nothing and no one here or anywhere near.' He addressed no one in particular. 'What in the name of Ethriss was that?'

'Help me with Farnor,' Jenna said, ignoring the question.

The group rallied round, seeking temporary solace from the eeriness of what they had just witnessed in a common concern. Farnor, shaking and patently distressed, was gently brought back to the fire and sat down. Olvric gingerly eased the slab from the fire and soon had it blazing again. Its light banished the darkness of the empty valley around them but not the memory of what they had just seen.

For a long time Farnor sat motionless and silent, staring into the fire, his eyes wide and unblinking. No one spoke. Each seemed to be waiting for the other.

'Something awful is happening,' he said eventually.

Despite this ominous remark, there was an almost palpable sense of relief in the group.

'Can you tell us what happened?' Jenna asked softly.

'I must learn about this thing inside me,' Farnor went on as if he had not heard her. He turned towards where the apparition had appeared. 'And that. All that out there.' He looked around the watching group, his face desperate. 'I'm so frightened. They'll be able to help me, these people we're going to see, Hawklan, Andawyr?'

'More than we can,' Yengar replied. 'And it frightened all of us, don't fret about that. At least there doesn't seem to be any danger now – if there ever was.'

'There was.' Farnor's tone was unequivocal.

'Well, it's gone. In fact there's no sign that anything was ever here. Are you all right now, in yourself?' As he spoke, Yengar put his hand on Farnor's forehead, then tested pulses in his neck.

Farnor paid no heed to the inspection, but looked down at his hands. They were trembling and he was obviously struggling to gain control over himself. Yengar's expression telling them that he could find nothing immediately untoward in the young man, the four Goraidin exchanged a look and turned to their own needs.

'What did we each see?' Olvric asked. 'Marna?'

Marna started slightly at being drawn into this conversation. She was still rubbing her arms slowly, though the tingling had passed. 'What did you see?' Olvric pressed.

Hesitantly, she described the greyness and the rider – perhaps riders – and their vanishing as the greyness had closed about them.

'That's what I saw too,' Olvric said when she had finished. The others concurred. 'Well done,' he said to her. 'At least we know that it was something outside ourselves. One of us having an hallucination is one thing, but five of us sharing it is unlikely, to say the least.'

'But what was it?' Marna burst out, her voice shaking.

Olvric became wilfully instructive. 'First, we need to be clear what we saw and heard. Then what we felt. Then perhaps we can speculate.' He took her hands and held them. He was unexpectedly gentle. 'Seeing things as they are is rarely easy, but it's invariably our greatest protection. It'll be yours too in due course. You've a clear vision. Clearer than you know. It's a great asset.' He released her. 'Why were you rubbing your arms like that?'

Marna told him. This time when Olvric turned to the others he was greeted by head-shaking. Yengar summarized their responses. 'I didn't hear anything – or feel anything unusual – apart from being frightened out of my wits.'

Olvric looked thoughtful. 'It's possible you've some distant kinship with Farnor back along the line,' he said. 'Maybe that's something to do with it. Anyway, just remember what it felt like. It'll help you if it happens again.'

'Happens again!'

'Why not?'

Marna went cold, though whether it was the prospect of the riders returning or Olvric's casual acceptance of the possibility, she could not have said. Olvric was talking to Farnor. 'How are you now? Can you tell us what happened?'

The fire was casting deep shadows on Farnor's face, ageing him. He held out his hands again. They were still now. 'I saw what you saw,' he said. 'But what I felt I can't begin to describe. It's as though every part of me was filled with rage and horror – except that it's not just me, it's parts of me I know nothing of. I'm sorry.' He smiled weakly.

Yengar snatched at an idea.

'Was that what happened when you destroyed Rannick?' he asked.

'It was similar, yes,' Farnor replied. 'Though that was far more . . . intense. This felt . . . crude, forced, even more unnatural, if such a thing were possible. And whatever it is inside me that reached out to put it right was opposed

172

again . . .' He paused. '. . . Just like last night. Something was fighting to keep it open. That didn't happen when Rannick was lost. And what I saw then was very different.' He pressed his fingertips against his forehead. 'It was as though I were seeing with my entire body. I "saw" sights that can't be seen just with the eyes. I know that sounds ridiculous, but that's how it was.' He became almost scornful and his hand waved out into the darkness. 'But this was just out there. A hole deliberately torn into this place from . . . somewhere else . . . and riders struggling to come through.'

'Marna thought she heard – or she sensed – a cry. Did you hear anything?'

Farnor touched his head again. 'Yes, but nothing I could identify.' He shuddered. 'Just a dreadful sound in my head. Full of triumph, then anger and hate.'

'And you still don't know how you . . . reach out . . . and end these things?'

Farnor shook his head slowly. 'Nothing. Nothing at all.' Suddenly his hand seized Yengar's wrist and his face was contorted with anger as he voiced again his own desperate need. 'We *have* to find out about *all* of this as soon as possible. I can't begin to imagine who or what just tried to come into this place, or why they'd want to be here, but they *don't belong*.'

'How can you know that?' It was Yrain. 'It was alarming but that's because it was strange – unexpected. We don't know those riders meant any harm. Perhaps, wherever they are, they're just wanderers like ourselves. People who suddenly found themselves confronted by a mysterious phenomenon and . . .'

Both Marna and Farnor were shaking their heads.

'There was malice there,' Farnor said with a quietness more telling than any ranting declamation. 'Just by being here they'll bring harm.' It was he now who became instructive. 'Their not belonging here is harmful in itself. It was reaching out into other worlds – places where *he* didn't belong – in search of the power he wanted that destroyed Rannick. It's *so* wrong – so dangerous. And while some part of me has sealed these . . . rips, tears, doorways, whatever they are . . . so far, I

173

don't know what I'm doing. I know less about it than my horse knows about flying.' His anger returned. 'And I refuse to tolerate the helplessness of standing by vaguely while something else makes use of me, whether it's for good or bad!'

'Maybe these people at Anderras Darion can get rid of whatever's inside you,' Marna offered.

Farnor turned on her, but both guilt and despair flitted across his face when he saw her flinch away from him. 'It's not something that can be taken away, Marna. I know that much about it. There's nothing I'd like more than for all this to go away and for everything to be as it was. But that's not going to happen.' He flicked an almost dismissive hand towards Olvric. 'It's like he says, we're safer seeing things the way they are. Not that I didn't know that already.' He gave a cold laugh. 'Another learning, eh? All lessons have to be learned and relearned over and over.' Then he squeezed Marna's hand affectionately, in a manner quite at odds with his demeanour. 'And the way things are, someone or something deliberately tried to tear its way into this world: someone or something that doesn't belong here and that can only bring harm, like Rannick.' He paused and took a deep breath. His tone was bleak. 'And for some reason, I can't walk away, any more than I could from Rannick. Perhaps it's because it's the right thing to do. Perhaps it's because I think they'll follow me anyway. I think – I know – they're frightened of me. I threaten them in some way. Given that, I don't seem to have any choice but to understand what I really am.'

He fell silent, and no one spoke for a long time.

'I'm going to bed,' he said eventually. 'I need to be alone for a while – to think.' He smiled ruefully at Olvric. 'I'll wake you if anything happens this time.'

The group was subdued after he had gone.

'Too many questions and not a vestige of an answer to any of them,' Yengar said.

'Still, the lad has my sword,' Olvric said. The others looked at him.

'And mine,' they each said in turn.

'And mine, for what it's worth,' Marna said, struggling with tears.

Jenna put an arm around her. 'It's worth a lot, Marna,' she said. 'You're his friend more than we can ever be, and that's important. He relies on you more than either of you know.'

The night passed without further incident, though, unbeknown to either Marna or Farnor, the Goraidin took turns at standing guard. The following morning, their mood was lighter but, before leaving, they agreed to search the area where they thought the apparition had appeared. Determining this proved to be harder than they imagined and, by way of compromise, they searched an area that covered each of their estimates of the location. Their findings were no different from those of Olvric and Yengar the previous night. There was no indication anywhere that any riders had been near the camp. No one seemed surprised.

'You're Orthlundyn: is there anything unusual about this place?' Yengar asked Yrain and Jenna, looking round at the mountains.

The two women looked around indifferently. 'We're not carvers,' Jenna replied. 'You know that. That's why we're soldiers. We're both of us the despair of our parents.' Both she and Yrain mimicked a head-shaking parental tone. 'Quite rockblind.'

'Even so, you're more sensitive to these things than we are,' Yengar pressed seriously.

'Maybe, maybe not, but I can't feel anything unusual,' Jenna dismissed the subject as she mounted her horse.

'Nor I,' Yrain added.

'Carvers?' Marna queried.

'Great stone carvers, the Orthlundyn,' Yengar said. 'They live by farming, but they live *for* carving. They've an amazing instinct for working stone. And how to use light-shadow lore, they call it. You'll see for yourself when we get there.'

'Just don't ask anyone about it if you don't want to be kept there for a day and a half while they explain it to you,' Olvric warned theatrically. He seemed set to expand on this but changed his mind after a purposeful nudge between the shoulder blades from Jenna's boot.

Later that day, they reached the edge of the mountains.

'Eirthlund,' Yengar announced as they paused on a rocky

175

prominence. 'Not too far now and much easier going when we get down there.'

Gently rolling countryside lay spread out below them, gradually disappearing into the distance as the cloudy sky seeped down to obscure the horizon in a light haze. Farnor and Marna looked at in silence. Eventually Marna gave a nervous laugh.

'Funny. It feels strange. I suppose it's because I'm used to having mountains all around. It makes me feel . . . unprotected, somehow.'

'How much longer before we reach Anderras Darion?' Farnor asked impatiently.

'It depends exactly where we are,' Yengar replied. 'And how near to any of the river bridges. But only a few days at most.' He grinned. 'A lot less than our supplies will last, for sure. We'll probably be sharing Valderen food with the good souls of Pedhavin when we arrive. It seems you're not destined to learn anything about hunting on this trip.'

Unexpectedly, Farnor's lip curled. 'Then teach me how to fight – and how to ride quickly.'

Yengar inclined his head in acknowledgement, though there was some sadness in the look he gave his friends as they set off again.

Nevertheless, the four Goraidin did as Farnor requested and their first day's journey through the Eirthlundyn countryside proved to be unexpectedly fast. It was thus a very stiff young man who levered himself out of his saddle when they finally stopped. No one remarked on it or offered to help him. He felt the need to spend some time leaning against his horse before Yengar's instruction to 'Get the horses sorted out, they've worked hard today' prodded him into action. As they went through the routines of establishing their camp, he moved slowly and with great concentration and when he finally sat down he advised his companions that he had pains in places he didn't even know he had. This relevation was greeted with some cursory nodding, but no one seemed inclined to be overly sympathetic, though Yengar did tell him he was 'doing well,' and that he should just 'try to relax a little more'. He complemented this advice with a brisk slap on the back which rendered Farnor wide-eyed and motionless for some time.

Marna, being naturally more relaxed than Farnor, had fared a little better on the journey but in any case was sustained by a personal vow she had made before she had left her home and father, to learn whatever lessons these four people had to teach, without comment. Thus it was that she joined in the Goraidin's unspoken plot and stood up with an affectation of enthusiasm when sword practice was mooted. Farnor hesitated for a moment but, caught between Yengar's encouraging smile and Marna's betrayal, contented himself with giving her a brief unforgiving look as he creaked to his feet.

To Farnor's considerable alarm, Olvric decided to join them. 'Good idea,' he said, cracking his entwined fingers. 'It'll help us wind down a little.'

In common with the rest of the day, it proved to be an energetic interlude and following it both Marna and Farnor retired to their tents exhausted.

The low rumble of conversation around the camp-fire filled the darkness around Farnor as he drifted through the twilight between waking and sleeping. Whirling images of Olvric's instruction filled his mind. There was such an intensity in everything the man did, yet, paradoxically, a variation of Marken's judgement came to Farnor: Olvric's touch was the lightest of them all. Farnor's last waking thoughts were full of puzzlement. Why was this man, with his frighteningly effective fighting skills, so much more gentle, so much less warlike in his teaching of them than the woman, Yrain? His final image was of Yrain casually watching as he and Marna were being shown something. He had caught a fleeting glimpse of her eyes. They were as intense as Olvric's and full of realization. This capable and resolute woman was still learning . . .

Still learning . . .

And glad to be . . .

Farnor slept well and the momentum of his long-established habits woke him easily the next morning. The same momentum also lifted him from his bed, though markedly less easily thanks to the stiffness that the previous day's rigours had

177

blessed him with and that had diffused through his entire frame during the night.

He emerged painfully from his tent to be greeted by a cool and damp dawn that was full of the promise of bright sunshine to come. Despite his discomfort, it felt good. He drew in a deep breath and released it slowly, then began flexing his reluctant limbs carefully. As usual he was awake before the others. For reasons he could not identify he suddenly felt a great goodwill towards them and by the time they stirred he had quietly tended the horses and was preparing breakfast.

It brought him fulsome praise, though Marna could not forbear reverting to their old relationship and passing an acid comment about 'teacher's pet'. A jibe he endured by adopting a wilfully saintly demeanour.

They travelled as they had the previous day, making good progress.

'Does no one live in this land?' Farnor asked, looking for topics of conversation to take his mind off his discomfort as they rode relentlessly on.

'Not many,' Yengar told him. 'A few villages here and there. It makes Orthlund look positively crowded and there's precious few live there.' He thought for a moment. 'Then again, I suppose even Pedhavin's bigger than you're used to. And I can't imagine what you'll make of Vakloss if you ever get there.'

Scarcely had he made this observation than they came upon a road. It was unmetalled but ruts and hoofprints testified to its recent usage. After a brief debate they decided to follow it. 'All roads lead to Anderras Darion,' Yrain declared.

It took them through an Eirthlundyn village where they became the object of much attention and where their steady progress ground to a halt as the curious but very amiable populace plied them with questions.

'You're very patient,' one elderly man told them, just before signs of impatience were about to show. 'We don't see many travellers and we can be a bit overwhelming when we do. Not much happens around here.'

That delayed them even longer.

'Crafty old beggar,' Yengar diagnosed as they finally made

their escape. 'He's made me feel guilty for not taking the rest of the day to tell him about everything we've been doing. Still, at least we know where we are now.'

'Their clothes are beautiful,' Marna said. 'Such colours. And the embroidery. So elaborate. I've never seen anything like it.'

'They're famous for their weaving and the like,' Jenna said. 'They sell it all over Orthlund, Fyorlund and Riddin. They're considerable traders. That's why the old man kept wringing tales out of Yengar. He'll be drinking free on what he's heard for days now.'

As they rode on, the road widened and with every cross-roads they passed they began to meet more travellers, moving in both directions. Some were on foot, carrying large packs, a few were on horseback, but most were riding in steep-sided carts, ornately carved and painted in the same style as the highly embroidered Eirthlundyn clothes. Everyone they met offered a friendly greeting and more than a few tried to lure them into making a purchase of some kind. Farnor found their persistence a little daunting, for even the admission that they had no money provoked nothing more than a broad understanding shrug followed immediately by some form of bartering proposition. In the end the two Goraidin parted with some of the still extant Valderen supplies in exchange for three bags of radiant stones, two leather belts and two brightly coloured kerchiefs. Yengar tied his about his neck and preened himself before the others. Both the women shook their heads and Jenna addressed Farnor conspicuously. 'Not bad when it comes to using a sword or bow, these two, but as for bartering, I'm afraid they're a sorry pair. Little to be learned there except what not to do.'

Shortly after that, however, following another encounter with an Eirthlundyn traveller she became the proud possessor of a beautiful scarf. Yengar said nothing, but whistled to himself irritatingly.

'Maybe we should trot for a while,' Farnor suggested.

They would have trotted over the bridge when they came to it, but both Farnor and Marna dismounted and walked to the edge of the river to look at it in wonder. Stout stone arches reached out into the river from both banks, rising gently to a wide central span over which rose a single arch of elaborately woven and jointed iron and timber.

'It rises up in the middle so that boats can pass underneath it,' Yengar said, before Farnor asked. 'That's what I've been told, anyway. Though there's precious little river traffic these days, and nothing that couldn't easily slip under the shore arches, let alone the middle.'

'It's big,' was all Farnor could manage to say. And big it was, being so much wider than the road that served it that, Farnor judged, it could accommodate at least six of the carts he had seen, side by side.

'Who built it?' he asked. 'And why, with so few people living here?'

Yengar shook his head. 'I've no idea. There are a lot of buildings and structures in this part of the world whose origins are long forgotten. It was probably built during the wars of the First Coming. There are features in its design we still use in temporary crossings and presumably it's the size it is to take a great deal of heavy traffic very quickly – that usually means an army.' He seemed anxious to leave the topic. 'Come on, you can look at it as we cross. It's even more impressive when you're on it.'

Since no one else was using the bridge, the six of them rode on to it side by side and widely spaced. They moved steadily up the gentle incline but as they neared the central span Farnor and Marna exchanged a quick glance and, without comment, dismounted again and ran to the nearest edge to peer down into the water. The four Goraidin stopped and watched them for a moment, then, exchanging a glance of their own, dismounted in their turn and joined them.

'I think I should do this more often,' Yengar said, picking up a stone and dropping it into the slowly swirling waters below.

Olvric nodded and leaned forward over the stone parapet, his feet leaving the ground, in imitation of Farnor and Marna. He threw a stone after Yengar's.

'Perhaps you two should bring your little wooden boats to play with,' Yrain said, leaning with her back against the parapet and gazing with heavy indifference at the arch rising up ahead of them.

'Good idea,' Yengar replied. 'We could put your little dollies in them. Or would they be seasick?'

Before Yrain could offer any rejoinder to this challenge, both Farnor and Marna cried out.

A large black bird had skimmed closely over their heads, startling them both. It dipped down, almost touching the waters below, then soared up in a high, sweeping arc. At the peak of its climb it seemed to hover. Then it was dropping towards them again. There was a faintly undignified hustle as Farnor and Marna debated whether they should stand or flee as the bird drew nearer. In the end they did a little of each, but Yengar and Olvric reached out to prevent their flight becoming a rout.

As they did so, the bird halted its rapid descent and landed on the parapet.

It was a large raven.

It had a wooden leg.

Chapter 15

Vredech had been a Preaching Brother in the Church of Ishrythan. Now he was travelling northwards, away from his homeland of Canol Madreth, with his wife Nertha and two companions, Dacu and Tirke. On their journey, they had passed through Arvenstaat where they had been joined by a young Caddoran, Thyrn, and his friend, Endryk.

Like Antyr and Farnor, both Vredech and Thyrn were troubled men. Vredech had found himself transported into strange other worlds as he struggled to exorcize a force that had possessed his friend and fellow Preaching Brother, Cassraw, and that through him and his wife Dowinne had threatened to possess the whole of Canol Madreth and thence lands beyond. Thyrn, by contrast, had accidentally thwarted the vaulting ambitions of his powerful master Vashnar, the Chief Warden of Arvenstaat, and, with a few reluctant allies, had been driven into the Karpas Mountains to be hunted as an outlaw. City dwellers all, they had survived there only because of a chance meeting with Endryk.

Like Antyr and Farnor also, both men had faced malign powers beyond their understanding with skills that they were unaware they possessed and of whose use they knew nothing. Each at some point had feared for his sanity and both had nearly perished violently. Now, though they had prevailed, their old lives were gone for ever. They had placed their faith in the companions that chance had thrown their way and were looking to find answers to their many questions at Anderras Darion.

Dacu and his younger companion, Tirke, were Goraidin. Together with Yrain, Jenna, Jaldaric and Yatsu they had been

183

part of the force which had accompanied Hawklan and Andawyr into the heart of Narsindal to face the returned Sumeral. They had stood at the edge of Lake Kedrieth as Derras Ustramel had tumbled to its destruction following Hawklan's fateful confrontation with its creator. At the same time, Yengar and Olvric had stood in the front ranks of the battle against Sumeral's Uhriel and His grim army.

Dacu and Tirke and many others had travelled abroad at the suggestion of the Cadwanol. Not, in their case, to bring fugitives to justice, but to learn more of the world that lay beyond Fyorlund, Orthlund and Riddin and to see how far Sumeral's corrosive and silent influence had spread this time. Alarmed by what they had witnessed in Canol Madreth they had advised Vredech to return with them to Anderras Darion. Their subsequent meeting with Thyrn and the recounting of his story had served only to heighten their alarm.

Endryk was a Fyordyn High Guard. He too had stood in the ranks that faced Sumeral's army, but the horror of the day and all that had led to it had proved too much and, like many others, he had left the victorious battlefield not to return home but to wander aimless and lost. Eventually he had come to Arvenstaat and found some solace in a long, lonely vigil as a shoreman. There it was that he had encountered the fleeing Thyrn and his companions and in helping them had found the strength to return to his own country and perhaps some part of his old life.

Nertha was a physician. Her trust and clear-eyed vision had anchored Vredech as his conflict with Cassraw had pushed him to the edge of insanity: her courage had saved his life in his final and tragic confrontation with the dark force that was seeking a way to this world.

Despite their past ordeals and the shadows that these threw on the present, all the travellers were in good heart and looking forward in their different ways to reaching Anderras Darion. Thyrn in particular was much easier in his manner than the haunted youth he had been when Endryk had first met him. The Caddoran were an ancient Guild of Messengers. Their origins were obscure, lying probably in the battles of the First Coming, long since forgotten in Arvenstaat. Now they were merely servants to rich merchants and high officials, though they plied a subtle and unusual trade. Not only did they memorize messages, they memorized also the nuances of the senders' intonations and expressions – they were invaluable in the conspiratorial underworld of Arvenstaat's trade and government. Thyrn had been exceptionally gifted and was the youngest person ever to become Caddoran to the Chief Warden. Now his Caddoran skills gave him a swiftness in learning things that was a constant source of amazement to his new friends.

A companionable group, they talked a great deal, often long into the night, each telling of their own lands and lives. The Goraidin spoke about Fyorlund with its Queen and its many Lords and their High Guards, about Orthlund with the great castle of Anderras Darion at its heart, about Riddin with its society seemingly built entirely around the Riddin-volk's love of horses and, not least, about the First and Second Comings of Sumeral, though they made little mention of their fears that perhaps His hand was to be seen in what had happened to both Vredech and Thyrn. Thyrn was much taken by the aspects of these stories that were part of Arvenstaat folklore, but Vredech found this same coincidence with many of the features of his erstwhile religion unsettling.

'I can understand you being upset,' Dacu said to him. 'The basis of your beliefs – indeed, your chosen calling – being so shaken, but, to be honest, I've the greatest difficulty in grasping the fundamental idea of religion anyway. It seems to me that something based on unreasoning faith is intrinsically doomed to such a fate.'

Dacu's quiet and easy manner allowed him to confront without causing offence.

'Your people have no god? No religion at all?' Vredech retorted, not without some surprise.

'None,' Dacu replied with hesitation. Then he smiled and conceded, 'There are one or two strange little sects and cults, and plenty of people with peculiar ideas, but nothing like a state religion such as your Ishrythan was.'

Vredech objected. 'It wasn't an instrument of government.

No one was obliged to believe or to go to the Meeting Houses.'

'It was the "done thing", though,' Dacu pressed.

Vredech looked at him narrowly and moved on to the attack. 'I suppose so,' he said. 'Rather like one of your young men "volunteering" to spend a period of his life in one of your Lords' High Guards.'

'That's character-forming,' Dacu chuckled.

'Hm. I think we can rest evens on the imperfections of our respective social conventions, but I find it difficult to imagine that your people don't ask questions such as "Where do we come from?" and "What are we here for?" '

'And Ishrythan has the answers to these questions?'

'It seeks to find them – in faith.'

This time it was Dacu who indulged in the narrow look. 'On the whole, I'd say that when we ask such questions, we seek answers not in faith – not in the blind acceptance of a doctrine laid down by someone else, however profound – but in constantly questioning – using reason – reason and tested observation.'

'And reason and tested observation have the answers?' Vredech returned sharply. 'And bring comfort to the afflicted?'

Dacu laughed ruefully. But as his laughter faded, he became more serious. 'No, I'm afraid they don't give all the answers. In fact they merely provided more questions. It's all they can ever do. But I think they protect us from some of the excesses that the darker side of our nature can lead us to.' He moved on quickly. 'As for offering comfort. I think we each of us find that where we can. For myself, and my friends and companions who've found themselves following a soldier's way like me, I'd say we take comfort in trying to see things clearly – as they are.'

Vredech looked at him. 'A harsh creed,' he said gently.

Dacu nodded. 'Possibly. But on the whole, better a harsh truth than a soft lie. And perhaps a little more clarity of vision – a little more questioning – might have spared your people some of their pain.'

'That, I can hardly deny. Though, in fairness, the mindless

bigotry that poor Cassraw fostered in his madness was no part of the teaching of Ishryth – your Ethriss. How it took the hold it did . . .' He threw up his arms. 'I don't know. It was very frightening. As was the impotence of both the church and our leaders in the face of it. Which is why I'm here, I suppose, travelling through strange lands to a strange destination. Putting my faith in you.'

Dacu put his hand to his head theatrically in an attempt to lighten Vredech's mood. 'Now I understand how a god must feel – burdened by such unquestioning trust. Still,' he went on sympathetically. 'Looking back on what happened, being frightened was the only response you could have had. And for all my countrymen's vaunted reason and our tried and trusted way of government – far superior to yours, I can tell you, as an observed fact – we too faltered and were led astray – plunged first into civil war and then into a war of aggression. Desperate times, desperate events. I think we can both accept that notwithstanding the answers to the "great" questions, we know there are people – powers – in the world that are bent on doing harm even if we can't begin to fathom why.'

'Possessed by evil, perhaps.'

'I'm not even sure what that means. I'm more inclined to think that, like Thyrn here, they're people born with attributes that have come down through time to us. Reason unknown. Except that in their case, it's not a gift, like Thyrn's, but rather an omission. Something missing. They're faulty, incomplete. They lack the fetters that *we* have on our inner darkness. Fetters that have been forged as we've moved from crueller times, when life must have been a constant struggle against hunger, cold, uncaring nature generally. In a sense, they're our past, come to haunt us.' He looked squarely at Vredech. 'But however they come to be, they *are*, as we both know all too well, and to ignore them is to court disaster. And the likes of you and I who know these things betray ourselves and those who trust us if we don't watch for them.'

He fell silent.

'Watch for them and deal with them,' Vredech added. There was a questioning note in his voice.

Dacu nodded. 'With all that that means. Head, heart and

sword. Wilfully removing our own fetters if we have to.' He gave a grim smile. 'It seems we've a gift of our own, haven't we? We can't see such things and do nothing.'

'Evil prevails while good lies abed.'

'You two aren't going to be allowed to ride together if your conversation's going to be so relentlessly cosmic all the time.' Nertha's smile came between the two riders. 'Why can't you talk about the weather for a while?'

'It's sunny,' Dacu said hastily, taking her hand.

'Yes,' Vredech agreed, taking the other. 'But it might rain later.'

'Very droll,' Nertha retorted caustically, studiously withdrawing her hands to fumble with the ribbon that was holding back her long black hair. 'Perhaps you'd care to talk about where we are, then? Where we might be tomorrow? When we'll be in Anderras Darion?' Pulling the ribbon ferociously tight, she slapped the sleeve of her jacket. A pale reddish dust rose up from it. She looked down at her grimed hands, gave a sigh, then fixed Dacu with a stern gaze. 'They *do* have running water there, I trust.'

'Well, when it rains, they . . .'

'They've everything you'll need, Nertha.' Tirke intervened rapidly as Nertha's brown eyes narrowed dangerously. 'As for where we are, I think the short answer is, we don't know.'

Nertha let out a pained breath. 'Tirke, I don't wish to seem unkind, but I have to tell you, you're not reassuring me.'

Tirke floundered. 'I mean, we don't know *exactly* where we are. We're heading north all right – towards home – but we didn't come this way. We were further east on our way out – more towards the coast. But there are towns there – the Wilde Ports – that we thought it would be better to avoid on the way back.'

'I know where we are.' It was Endryk. 'We're at the south end of the Thlosgaral.'

This provoked only inquiring looks.

'I wandered around this region, long ago,' he explained. 'The Thlosgaral's a . . . rocky desert . . . for want of a better description. Dusty, barren, dangerous. The only people who go into it are miners and the bandits who prey on them.' He grimaced, then shuddered. 'It's a bad place. And it moves.'

'Moves?' Tirke and Nertha exclaimed simultaneously.

Endryk did not flinch before their combined doubt.

'Moves,' he confirmed. 'Slowly, but quite definitely. It's like an ocean caught in a different time. I spent a night here once – and only one night. I couldn't get out fast enough. And there seems to be something unhealthy about the rocks themselves. You'll understand if we see any miners. They all look the same – as if the life's been wrung out of them.' He turned to Dacu. 'We should go around it. It's longer, but it'll be quicker and much safer.' Dacu inclined his head and motioned Endryk to take the lead.

Towards evening, Dacu began looking towards the eastern sky, puzzled.

'That redness in the sky is the Thlosgaral,' Endryk told him. 'It's like a permanent sunset.'

'More like an inflamed wound,' Nertha said, frowning.

Thyrn was riding alongside Endryk. 'It feels like the place in the Karpas mountains where Vashnar attacked us.' The young Caddoran looked decidedly unhappy as he too glanced towards the eastern sky.

'It does indeed,' Endryk said tersely. 'Perhaps they're outcrops of the same thing.'

Dacu frowned. 'If it's like the place you described to us, then we really should have a look at it. Andawyr and the others will want to know about it for sure.'

'Andawyr and the others can come and look at it for themselves, then,' Endryk said bluntly. 'I've been in it once, I won't go in it again.'

'Nor I,' Thyrn said, hunching his shoulders.

It was the nearest they had come to a dispute on their journey so far. Dacu held up a peacemaking hand. 'Just habit, that's all. It's in my nature to find out about things. But I can see the idea upsets both of you. Sorry.'

Endryk became conciliatory as they rode on. 'There's every chance we'd get lost. Once you're in there it's as though you've been transported to another world, it's so different from anywhere you've ever been before. And it *does* move. Sometimes you can actually feel it – everything around you shaking, shifting. Suddenly nothing's fixed – not even the ground – you feel dizzy, sick – it's very frightening. Then you're disorientated when you find all the landmarks have subtly changed. And there's nothing to see – just reddish-grey rocks everywhere. No natural erosion patterns, no trails, no vegetation, no animals, nothing. The whole place looks blighted. And it makes noises as it moves. Like something being tortured.'

'You've made your point,' Dacu said. 'Quite vividly. But we should still find something out about the place if it bears any relationship to the place where you fought Vashnar. You mentioned miners. Perhaps we can speak to some of them if we see any. By the way, what do they mine that's so precious if the place is as awful as you say?'

'Crystals, though I don't know what they are or why they're valuable. I imagine they trade them in Arash-Felloren or the Wilde Ports.'

'Arash-Felloren? That's north-west of here, isn't it? I seem to remember hearing about it when we passed through the Wilde Ports.'

'It is,' Endryk said. 'I've been there once too.'

Dacu looked surprised. 'You never mentioned it.'

'It was long ago. And I was in a sorry state then. It was only the dust on Nertha's jacket reminded me where we might be.'

'What's it like?'

Endryk pulled a wry face. 'Big,' he said. 'Very big. Far bigger than Vakloss.' Dacu raised doubting eyebrows. 'And very confusing. Full of hills and winding streets. I've vague memories of all kinds of buildings – big, small, old, new, rich, rotten – wide avenues, cramped alleys. And people every-where.'

'Sounds peculiar, but interesting. Are the people friendly to strangers?'

Endryk's expression became pained. 'At my best I was no Goraidin, Dacu, and in those days I could hardly remember my name, let alone pay attention to what was going on around me. I remember the people as being neither friendly nor unfriendly – just indifferent. Almost as if, were you to fall over in the street, they'd let you lie there until you died or found the strength to stand up again. People would step over you.' Dacu frowned at the image, but Endryk continued. 'The whole place was full of clamour and noise, everyone buying and selling all the time, everyone in a hurry, rushing everywhere. It probably suited me then. On my own in a vast crowd. Surrounded but alone.'

Dacu searched anxiously into the High Guard's face. 'I'm sorry,' he said. 'I've stirred memories you'd rather have left to lie. It sounds like an awful place.'

'I wouldn't judge,' Endryk said. 'It *was* a long time ago and, as I said, I was in a sorry state then. People did help me, I know, though, to my shame, I can't remember either names or faces. When I think of the place now I remember only confusion, but that could've been as much me as the city. There must be countless good souls there or so huge a place would've destroyed itself by now.'

'Can we go into it?' Thyrn thrust the enthusiastic question between the two men. Reaching safety in some vaguely rumoured 'great city in the north' had been constantly in his mind during his flight across Arvenstaat. Dacu gave Endryk an inquiring look.

Endryk looked at the pack horses. 'There's no special reason why we should, we've plenty of supplies. And we've no local money so we'd have to barter if we wanted anything.' He shook his head. 'And I *do* remember they're hard bargainers. I doubt any of us here are match for one of them in a haggle.'

'We don't have to buy anything, we could just look – wander around for a while,' Thyrn insisted.

His enthusiasm made the others smile.

'Well, if Endryk's happy there's no threat to us and if it's not too far off our way we can spare a day to have a look at this place, can't we?' Tirke inquired generally. 'I'd certainly be interested to see a city that's bigger than Vakloss.'

'I don't see why not,' Dacu said. He looked at the others challengingly. 'The sight of some different faces might do all of us some good.'

The next day they came to a road heading north. When they first joined it there were few other travellers using it but as the day passed it became much busier, traffic entering at almost every junction. They made several brief travelling acquaintances as they rode along: people in groups; people alone; families in orderly, courteous procession; families in excited, disorderly confusion; heavy-booted farmers on heavy-wheeled carts loaded with hay and produce; slouching stockmen, herding cattle and sheep; craftsmen and tradesmen of all kinds, walking, riding, leading pack horses, pushing and pulling precariously loaded hardcarts of every conceivable shape and size.

'It seems you were right,' said a stunned and unusually agitated Dacu to Endryk as he managed to extricate himself from one individual. 'They all want to buy or sell something.' He indicated his recent companion, who misjudged the gesture and gave him a knowing salute in return. 'I *told* him we were just passing through, that we were on a long journey, but he insisted on trying to sell me glass for my windows – *windows*! – for my tent, presumably!' He growled. 'Or in my saddle, for all I know! I doubt he cared. My "lucky day", it was, to have met him before any of his rascally competitors. His glass was "not cheap", he admitted.' Dacu laid his hand on his heart in imitation of the man's expression of sincerity. 'But "very special. Double thickness". It would "last a lifetime", though he didn't say whose, now I think about it.' His eyes widened in shock. 'I wouldn't mind, but I nearly bought some. This place must be worse than the Gretmearc.'

Endryk stopped trying not to laugh. 'A soldier of your experience should know when he's outmatched. There's no disgrace in retreat under such circumstances.'

'It's not even seeing the ambush that's bothering me. These people are the commercial equivalent of a combined Goraidin and heavy infantry unit.'

'We need a new leader if you can't take the strain,' Endryk advised him solemnly. He nodded towards Nertha who was in the middle of an agitated debate with a red-faced man pushing a bright yellow cart full of garments. Vredech was trailing in her wake with the air of a child who has just been given the sternest parental instruction to stay quiet. Amid a great deal of emotional arm-waving, Dacu and Endryk learned, amongst other things, that the carter had a family of sickly children on the very edge of penury somewhere, while Nertha's horse had developed a debilitating complaint that needed her every worldly resource to cure. Being a physician, Nertha had a wealth of ominous words and alarming symptoms at her command. In the end, Vredech was presented with a stout jacket of undeniable quality and the carter went on his way, still concerned for the well-being of his family, whose condition was apparently worsening by the minute, but carrying now an elegant gown with which, presumably, to comfort his much afflicted wife.

'It was no use to me,' Nertha replied to her husband's protestation. 'I don't know why I brought it in the first place. And you need a good jacket.'

There were less entertaining meetings though. At a cross-roads a band of uniformed but unsavoury-looking individuals passed over the road in front of them, heading east towards the Thlosgaral. With them were two conspicuously well-dressed men.

'Private guards escorting someone across the Thlosgaral,' Endryk told Dacu. 'There are lots of such people in the city, protecting individuals, businesses, properties.'

'They have no civic authority to do this?'

Endryk's lip curled. 'After a fashion. There's the Prefect and his Guards – the Weartans – but they're corrupt. Much worse than Arvenstaat's Wardens.'

'The more I hear, the more I feel this city's a desperate place,' Dacu said.

'Well, now you make me think about it again, I suspect it's just the size of the place. Too many people too close together. They can't be governed by force any more than we could be, and there are too many conflicting factions and interests to reach any semblance of a consensus for an effective form of government.'

'Destined to destruction?'

Endryk was unexpectedly optimistic. 'I don't think so. Destined to permanent change, yes, but they're probably used to that. Some of their qualities might have protected us better. Made us more alert, suspicious. I don't know.'

Dacu was silent for a while before saying simply, 'You may well be right.'

Later, while they were walking the horses, they were overtaken by a hooded figure striding out, high-shouldered and tense. Both Dacu and Tirke started as he passed them while Thyrn reached out and gripped Endryk's arm tightly.

'Good day to you, sir,' Dacu said to the man with a geniality that his friends saw was taking some effort.

The figure hesitated, then turned to him as if surprised.

'Good day to you,' came a harsh and unpleasant voice after a moment. Then the figure was on its way again.

A passer-by, a middle-aged man, spat noisily and sneered after the departing figure.

'You know him?' Dacu asked.

'I know *them*,' the man replied, his voice as full of contempt as his face. 'Kyrosdyn. The lot of them should be burnt.'

'That seems rather extreme.'

'You're strangers around here, aren't you?'

'Yes, we're heading north.'

'Well, welcome to Arash-Felloren, my friends.'

'I don't wish to buy anything,' Dacu said hastily.

The man's expression changed. He chuckled. 'I see you're not complete strangers, then. Don't worry, I'm not selling anything, I'm just going to watch one of the animal fights tonight. But I'll give you this advice for free. While you're in the city, keep your eyes on your goods, your hand on your wallet, and your business well away from the Kyrosdyn.'

Dacu's eyes narrowed at the mention of animal fights, but he asked, 'Bad people, are they, these Kyrosdyn?'

'Yes, very,' the man replied starkly. 'Crystal workers they're supposed to be, but they've got fingers in everything.'

'What are crystals?' Dacu asked.

The man looked at him in open surprise. 'You *must* be from a long way away. They're used in everything. Expensive jewellery, toughening iron for ploughshares, knives and the like, fancy decorations for those who can afford them, medicines . . .'

'Medicines?' Nertha queried.

194

The man looked her up and down as though she might be an item for sale. 'Ointments, potions, lozenges. Draw the badness out of anything, they do.' He leered. 'Or put life into it if it's . . . sagging a little.' The leer faded as Nertha did not respond. He tried for another effect. 'There's some grind them and cut them straight into the blood.' He made a scratching motion with his finger on his arm but the action seemed to disturb him more than it disturbed Nertha, to whom it obviously meant nothing. He rejoined the men. 'Kyrosdyn do it all the time, if you ask me. That's why they all look the same.' He gestured towards the rapidly retreating figure. 'All tight and jerky.' He sneered again, then took Dacu's arm confidentially. 'Mind you, their star's falling a bit, what with Imorren getting killed and all.'

'Imorren?'

'Their Ailad – their chief. Right bitch she was. Good looker by all accounts, but a bad lot. Good riddance, that's my feeling.'

Before Dacu could question him further, the man had acknowledged a salute from the driver of a passing cart and, without any leave-taking, was clambering on to it.

'Certainly short on social graces, these people,' Nertha said.

'Did you make anything of that?' Dacu asked her.

She shook her head. 'These crystals sound strange, though.' She mimicked the scratching that the man had demonstrated. 'And that sounds very peculiar.'

Dacu's eyes narrowed as he looked after the now distant figure of the Kyrosdyn. 'I'd swear I felt a touch of the Power as he went past,' he said to Tirke who nodded grimly but did not speak. 'Thyrn, something startled you, didn't it?'

'I don't know. I felt for a moment as if Vashnar . . . I don't know . . . I . . .'

He was obviously distressed. Dacu stopped him. 'Don't worry. There's no danger. Just remember it for later.'

Then he said softly to Tirke. 'And you too. If that *was* the Power then Andawyr and the others will be more than interested.'

'Should we follow the man?'

Dacu thought for a moment. 'No. We can't leave the others

and there's no saying what we might run into in the city. I'm certainly not disposed to seek out anyone who can use the Power without a Cadwanwr by my side. We'll have to leave it. Just include it in our Accounting.'

As the day passed, Nertha succeeded in transforming a few more unwanted items into the local money.

'It'll come in handy if we go into the city,' she claimed, dropping the coins into her belt purse.

'Speaking of which, I think we'll have to decide soon,' Dacu announced. Ahead of them, at the bottom of a gentle slope, were crossroads. Some of the traffic travelling their way was moving east and a little was moving north, but most of it was turning west.

Set some way back was a large building surrounded by rambling outhouses and stables. A sign hanging from an arched timber frame over the gate to the courtyard declared it to be 'The Wyndering'.

As they drew nearer, an appetizing smell drifted over the group, drawing them to a spontaneous halt. They looked at one another.

'Let's see how far your new-found wealth goes, Nertha,' Dacu said, voicing their common thought. 'It'll be nice to sit on a chair and have a meal cooked by someone else. We can decide what we want to do while we eat. What do you . . .'

The others were already heading for the gate.

Chapter 16

The owner of The Wyndering was Ghreel. He was very fat and very unpleasant. Had The Wyndering depended on his charm for its survival, it would have long since fallen into decay. As it was, it prospered, though, admittedly, little sign of this prosperity could be noted in its outward appearance which was that of a genteel house which had fallen on hard times. Its success was due almost completely to its location. Past it moved most of the traffic travelling from Arash-Felloren to the Wilde Ports, and all of such traffic as moved north and south in that region. In fairness, it had to be said that Ghreel was a good cook, being a keen judge of his own cooking – he had not always been fat – and, for most regular travellers, this was adequate compensation for his sour disposition. There was also a thriving subculture where these same travellers would exchange ever wilder stories about his rudeness, giving him, if not mythic status, at least high standing in the local canon of alehouse tales.

He was at his usual station, leaning against a robust but crude wooden counter and glowering at his regular customers, when the door creaked noisily to announce the entrance of Dacu and the others. His beady eyes examined them as they stood blinking in the comparative gloom, but he made no other movement. The door creaked again as Thyrn tried awkwardly to close it quietly. Nertha wrinkled her nose in distaste at the smell of the place, as did Vredech, though more discreetly.

'Food, landlord?' Dacu inquired.

Ghreel's eyes widened slightly. Then, without replying, he flicked his head towards a double door standing open at the end of the room. They threaded their way through the drink-soiled furniture to be confronted by four long tables as they passed through the door. There were several people eating but plenty of space for the newcomers.

'At least it doesn't stink of stale ale like that other room,' Vredech said, sitting down with some relish.

A slightly conspiratorial interlude followed during which Nertha was delegated to negotiate their meal with one of the young boys serving the tables. On the road, she had bargained fiercely, with much finger-jabbing and lying. Here it was a combination of studied womanly foolishness and slowness with the local coin that saw her quietly winning the day.

'I can see why you married her,' Dacu said.

'I'm learning more every day,' Vredech replied, enigmatically.

A little later, the meal had appeared and been devoured, largely in silence, and they were all both relaxed and replete.

'Excellent,' was the consensus, this being announced with some surprise, given the demeanour of the landlord.

'I'm not sure it was such a good idea, though,' Tirke remarked, closing his eyes ecstatically. 'It's really going to make camp food heavy going.'

'It usually is when you cook it,' Endryk remarked.

'Talking of heavy going, the landlord's been taking quite an interest in us,' Thyrn said, without looking up. 'He keeps casually wandering in, by the way, and looking over here.'

'I noticed,' Dacu said. 'He seemed surprised when I first spoke to him.'

'He's probably deciding how much to charge us for watering the horses,' Nertha said.

Vredech gave his wife a wilfully reproachful look. 'You're getting quite cynical, my dear.'

'I'm getting quite used to the people around here,' she replied emphatically. 'I think they'd charge for the air we breathe if they could work out how to do it.'

'Well, we'll soon find out,' Dacu said. 'Here he comes.'

They all turned to witness Ghreel's lumbering approach.

'A good meal, landlord,' Dacu said genially, as Ghreel

198

lurched to a halt and began collecting their plates. 'You seem very interested in us. What can we do for you?'

'Subtle,' Nertha muttered.

Ghreel nearly dropped the plates. 'Careful,' Dacu said, reaching out to steady the teetering pile. A broad smile pressed his question.

Ghreel emitted a series of peculiar sounds that eventually concluded in something that sounded vaguely grateful. Then he said, 'I hope you lot haven't got any rats with you.'

An odd silence descended on the group as they looked first at him, then at each other and then back to their host.

'Rats?' Dacu queried hesitantly, as if he might have misheard. 'Why would we have rats with us?'

'You're from up there aren't you?' Ghreel replied.

'Up there?'

'The north.'

'Some of us are,' Dacu said, obtusely not identifying the guilty parties.

'Knew as soon as you walked in,' Ghreel declared knowingly. 'The way you talked. Funny.'

'I always try to please,' Dacu said, but the sarcasm bounced off its target.

'We don't get many northerners passing through here.'

'Strange, I'd have thought they'd have flocked here,' Dacu said, still to no effect. Ghreel's concern, however, now released, had a momentum comparable with that of his frame as he thrust the dishes through a hatch and bowled back towards the table.

'We had one of your kind in the other day – with his rat. And I don't want any more, I can tell you. Do you keep them as pets or something up there?'

'Well, we've been away quite a time,' Dacu said thoughtfully. 'But keeping rats wasn't common when we left.'

Ghreel looked unconvinced. His story had to make its full way out.

'Vicious little swine it was. And teeth like I've never seen on any animal before.' He made a futile effort to straighten up and draw his stomach in. 'Mind you, my dogs would've had it if I hadn't taken them in hand.' He frowned. 'And I had to, I

199

can tell you.' He indicated two large dogs asleep in the corner.

Dacu nodded understandingly. 'Rest assured, landlord, we've no rats or any other pets with us that you might need your dogs for. And if I hear of anyone coming this way I'll advise them to leave their rats outside.'

This began to impinge. Ghreel's face crumpled into a scowl. Dacu intercepted the pending reproach by standing up and taking his arm in a companionable manner. 'I understand. You've a business to run here. Obviously you can't have strange animals wandering in and out as they feel like it. It'd soon get the place a bad name. What was the man like? There aren't many of us up there, as you might have gathered from the number who come here, so we might know him. We can speak to him about it if we see him.'

Partly mollified, Ghreel described the offending customer, concluding with, 'And he'd a big hat, even though the sun was belting down.'

Dacu's expression of recognition was not feigned. Nor was Tirke's. 'And the rat?' Dacu pressed. 'Are you sure it was a rat?'

Ghreel scowled again, though this time in thought. 'He said it was a welci, or flooky, or something.'

'A felci?' Dacu suggested.

Ghreel nodded grimly. 'Still looked like a rat to me.' A fat finger prodded the table. 'And I don't want any more. You tell him, if you see him.'

'I certainly will.'

'And tell him I wasn't impressed by that trick he did.'

'Trick?'

'Making it look as if it could talk.' Dacu raised an eyebrow. The finger prodded the table again, then indicated the doorway. 'Just when they were leaving. Stood on its hind legs over by the counter next door, thanked me for the meal, then laughed.' He snorted scornfully. 'Told me he was a teacher. Lying sod. If you ask me he was just another street clown who hadn't the nous to make a living here and went scuttling home. Tell him I've seen better acts washing dishes. Him and his talking rat.'

'We'll be sure to mention you didn't appreciate it if we run into him,' Dacu said, signalling to the others to leave. 'Was he heading back north?'

Jowls shook in indignant dismissal. 'How would I know what he was doing? He had some halfwit with him. I think he went north.'

In the courtyard, as they mounted, Dacu and Tirke looked at one another.

'Atelon,' they said, at the same time.

'And Dar-volci, I'll wager,' Dacu added. 'He wouldn't be able to resist a parting jibe at the likes of our friend in there. What in the name of mercy were they doing out here? And who's this "halfwit" he's got with him?'

'You know this "northerner", with his talking rat?' Nertha asked.

'It sounds like an old friend of ours,' Tirke replied. Suddenly he was quite serious. 'Atelon's a Cadwanwr. He's probably only about my age, but he's lifetimes older. He stood with Oslang and the other Cadwanwr and kept Sumeral's Uhriel from destroying the army with the Power. It took a toll I don't think we can begin to understand.'

'I didn't mean to sound flippant.'

'It's all right. It's just a little disturbing to hear about him like that.'

'Do you think he might be in danger?'

'I doubt it, he's a Riddinwr.'

'Meaning?'

'Meaning that like all the Riddinvolk, he and his horse together make a lethal combination. And, for a Learned Brother, Atelon's more than a fair hand with a sword.'

But Dacu had reservations. He turned to Thyrn. 'I've no reason for this, but I feel uneasy about what we've just heard. I'd like to press on towards home. See if we can catch up with him.' He held out a hand westward towards the unseen Arash-Felloren, his face questioning.

Thyrn looked in the direction he was pointing, then thought for a moment. 'Some other time. I decided not to come here once before, it's not hard to do it again. I'm sure it'll be here for some years yet.'

'Thank you,' Dacu said.

201

'Besides,' Thyrn added, 'I'm intrigued by this talking rat.'

They moved out of the courtyard and, after watching the busy crossroads for a while, turned on to the emptier road that ran northwards.

'This talking rat is almost certainly Dar-Volci,' Dacu told Thyrn. 'He's a felci. One of the few that take a serious interest in people and probably the only one who'll travel anywhere. They're rock dwellers and they look nothing like rats.' He smiled to himself. 'If I'm any judge of our erstwhile host, he's tried to set his dogs on Dar and they've been seen off.'

'They were big dogs. I wouldn't like to argue with either of them,' Vredech interposed.

'Size doesn't really come into it,' Dacu said. 'They're strange creatures, felci. Full of life, energy, mischief – lots of mischief – but very dangerous if they have to fight.'

'And they actually talk?' It was Nertha.

'Oh yes. As I said, they're strange creatures. They say their ancestry goes back to the time before the very beginning of things.'

'*Before* the beginning?' Vredech exclaimed.

Dacu gave a disclaiming shrug. 'You're the theologian: you tell me. That's what they claim. I'm sure Dar-volci will be only too happy to discuss it with you – at great length.'

Vredech gave him a suspicious look. 'I'll confess to having passed the time with the occasional dog from time to time in the past, but I find it difficult to see me discussing theology – or anything, for that matter – with a talking rat.'

Both Tirke and Dacu laughed. 'Well, if you'll accept a word of advice, I wouldn't call Dar-volci a rat to his snout,' Dacu said. 'He can be quite cutting. And I'd reserve your judgement on his intellect if I were you.'

Vredech's suspicious look deepened. He looked to Endryk for aid. 'Are you joining with your countrymen in this?' he asked.

Endryk tried not to laugh at Vredech's discomfiture, but failed. 'I'm afraid so,' he replied. 'I've never had the privilege of a conversation with a felci, but I've seen one or two and I'm afraid Dacu's telling you the truth. And from what I've heard, they regard us as a rather inferior and troublesome species they have to keep an eye on.'

Vredech looked to his wife. 'I'm beginning to suspect there's something in the humour of these people that doesn't travel.' He returned to Dacu. 'I suppose you'll tell me next that this Dar-volci is a sort of king felci.'

Dacu chuckled. 'No. They'd regard that as being very peculiarly human – extremely eccentric, not to say downright dangerous.' Then his manner was abruptly almost sombre. 'But he is exceptional.' He glanced at Endryk to draw him into the conversation. 'It was Dar-volci who killed Sumeral's most powerful Uhriel, Oklar. The man – the creature – who cut a swathe through Vakloss with a gesture. Killed him just like that.' He snapped his fingers. 'Whatever the felci are. Wherever . . . or whenever . . . they come from, they're not to be underestimated, and the Power seems to hold no terror for them.'

The expression on Endryk's face told Vredech more vividly than any reassurances that he was not being made the butt of even a gentle joke.

'I see there's a great deal I have to learn about your country and its people,' he said.

'There's a great deal we all have to learn about each other,' Dacu retorted. 'And many other things as well. I find it hard to come to accept these "other worlds" that you say you've been mysteriously transported to, and that Thyrn says he's seen.' His sombre mood fell away. 'But I'm looking forward to finding out about everything.'

The road ran directly north and they followed it for the rest of the day, at Dacu's urging and under his guidance, travelling faster than they had done hitherto. They camped eventually in a small stand of trees on a low hillock. As the sun sank and the sky darkened, there was a persistent glow above the western horizon. It puzzled them for a while until they realized that it must be from the lights of Arash-Felloren.

'What a strange sight,' Dacu mused. 'It's as though the place were ablaze. You can see Vakloss from far away at night, but only if it's in direct sight. Not beyond the mountains. Why would these people choose to light the sky as well as their streets and byways? Do they envy the stars? Or would they seek to emulate them?'

Vredech laughed. 'I can't say that the direction of the street lighting was ever a concern in Canol Madreth,' he said. '*I've* certainly never thought about it and I presume it's the same with these people. Thoughtlessness at the worst. Not the greatest of sins in this case, surely?'

'It just makes me uncomfortable, that's all,' Dacu said. 'Thoughtlessness it may well be but I'm not sure I can forgive it as readily as you. Of an individual, yes, but not of an entire city. It's a symptom of the place. Almost every aspect of it we've touched on has been tainted with it. Not least towards other people. And if they disregard their own kind so casually, what regard will they have for anything else around them?'

Vredech gave him an arch look. 'You *are* stern, aren't you? I'd never have taken you for a zealot. "Thou shalt not shine a light at night." Are you sure you haven't studied religion at some time?'

The taunt made Dacu smile but he issued a challenge. 'Just fault my reasoning, priest. The more we learn about the place the more it feels as though Sumeral's touch is all over it. I wonder if it was once one of His citadels?' The question was half to Tirke, half to himself, but neither pursued it. 'Anyway, I'm glad we found out about it, but we were probably wise not to go into it.'

'Some other time, though,' Thyrn reminded him.

'Some other time, certainly. When Nertha has taught us all how to haggle properly.'

The next day, maintaining the same faster pace, they continued along the road, which still led steadily northward. They had met little traffic the previous day and such as there had been had lessened with each junction they came to. Now they met no one travelling in either direction and gradually the road itself began to disappear as the surrounding countryside encroached on it. Eventually it was gone, and all suggestion of the influence of Arash-Felloren passed from the landscape. Their mood lightened.

'Do you think your friend has come this way?' Vredech asked.

'Oh yes,' Dacu replied.

'You sound very confident.'

'If he was going home, this is the most direct way. There's no reason why he should wander off the road. And he's left signs for us to follow.'

'Signs? I've seen nothing. And he didn't know we'd be following, did he?'

'No, I'm sorry. I meant because he wasn't deliberately hiding from us, he's left a trail for us to follow if you know what to look for. So far it's been easy – scuffs in the dirt, an occasional hoofprint in damp ground.'

'And not forgetting Dar-volci's paw prints,' Tirke added.

Vredech looked at them both, wide-eyed. 'You make me feel blind and useless. I'd be interested to look for these "signs" myself if you'd care to help me.'

'And me,' Thyrn said. 'Endryk taught me how to leave no sign when we were being chased through the mountains. He said we'd left a trail across Arvenstaat like a runaway haycart.'

Soon, moving still northwards and with all of them now searching enthusiastically for the faint reminders of Atelon's passing, they were leaving the grasslands and ascending into mountains again. Unlike others they had passed through though, these were of no great severity and the way proved to be quite easy. At one point as they moved along a valley floor, Dacu, who had been looking back and forth for some time, reined to a halt.

'This has been a proper road at one time. And no farm track, either. I'll wager you could see the line of it from up on the ridge,' he said. 'Fascinating.' He spoke to Tirke and Endryk. 'We really must study this region in detail. We can start as soon as we get back to Anderras Darion: there are all manner of maps and plans in the library there.'

Thyrn's eyes narrowed at the word 'study'. 'How far ahead do you think your friend is?' he asked quickly.

'Not far, I would imagine,' Dacu replied. 'We've been making good progress and I doubt he was hurrying particularly. We might reach him today.'

And they did. Towards evening, riding towards the head of the valley, they saw the light of a distant camp-fire.

'Let's see how alert our warrior-Canwanwr is.' Dacu and Tirke enjoyed a private joke. As they drew nearer a tent similar to those used by the two Goraidin came into view, but there was no sign of any occupants.

'Ho, the camp,' Dacu shouted.

'Ho yourself, Goraidin,' came a voice from close nearby. Both Dacu and Tirke laughed and then applauded as a figure emerged from the shade of some rocks. It held a lantern that shone in their faces.

There followed a brief confusion of greetings and abuse typical of long-separated friends meeting unexpectedly and in happy circumstances, then Atelon was more soberly introduced to the others.

'So you're a Cadwanwr?' Thyrn said as he found himself looking into a weather-beaten face and deep-set eyes. 'They said you wore a big hat.'

Atelon's face cracked into a bright smile. 'Only when I don't want to fight,' he said. Then, still smiling, he looked at his inquisitor intently. Briefly a look of pain came into his eyes and his hand flicked as if it were about to reach up and offer consolation. He turned the movement into a gesture towards his camp-fire.

'Welcome to my hearth. I was just about to . . .'

'Aren't we forgetting something?' Except for Atelon and the two Goraidin, everyone looked round for the owner of this peculiarly deep voice. Nertha gave a faint 'Oh!' and Thyrn jumped as the sinuous form of Dar-volci emerged from the shadows. 'After all, it was me who told you they were coming.'

'I'd heard them,' Atelon replied defensively.

'Hm.'

Without any warning, the felci jumped up into Atelon's arms and thence on to his shoulder. 'Let's have a look at our visitors,' he said paternally. 'I have your names, but some of you smell very interesting.' Following this injunction, Atelon took him to each of the new arrivals in turn. Dar-volci stared intently at each one separately, his triangular head jutting forward a little and his muzzle twitching. Throughout he maintained a soft, absent-minded whistling.

'Very interesting indeed,' he concluded finally. 'I think we're going to have a lot to talk about. Introduce them to Pinnatte, then let's eat.'

206

Pinnatte, slight in build and with disorderly fair hair and disconcertingly black eyes, was the 'halfwit' that Ghreel had referred to. Except that he was not a halfwit.

'The Kyrosdyn used him in an experiment,' Atelon told them as they sat around the fire eating.

Nertha frowned but did not speak. In travelling with the Goraidin she had soon learned that when they explained something, it was clearly and thoroughly done, and when others explained, they listened. She deemed the last in particular to be a great virtue. In her experience it was rare.

Atelon continued. 'They "infected" him, for want of a better word, with a compound they'd formulated. Something involving crystal products, I imagine.' He paused and looked directly at Dacu. 'This is wickedness, the like of which I find hard to speak of calmly. I take some bitter pride in the fact that I was able to play a part in the destruction of its architect.'

'Imorren?' Dacu queried, untypically interrupting. 'Their leader?'

Atelon showed no great surprise that Dacu knew of this. He nodded.

'The whole story's a long one,' he said. 'And far from clear in my mind yet. Suffice it to say I'm expecting a long Accounting when I get back to the Cadwanen.'

'I understand. But tell us what you can.'

Atelon thought for a moment. Perhaps telling a new audience about what had happened might give him an insight that had been denied him in his own inner speculations. But where to start?

Andawyr's words came to him. 'When you don't know where to start, start.'

So he started. 'Briefly, as I said, they used him as part of an experiment. Exactly what they had in mind I couldn't say, but what they finished up doing was trying to make him into something that couldn't be.'

'What do you mean, something that couldn't be?' Thyrn interrupted, provoking a reproachful glance from Endryk.

Atelon looked at him and his voice became that of someone obliged to deliver a difficult lecture. 'Tell me, young man, what do you know about the Power?'

Chapter 17

'I've heard of it,' Thyrn replied, indicating his companions as the source of his information. 'It's something that's supposed to pervade everything. These mountains, this food, us. And some people – such as yourself – Cadwanwr – can use it deliberately, to move things, change them.' He looked uncomfortable. 'I know Dacu and Tirke wouldn't lie to me, and I know from my own experience there are some strange things in the world, but, to be honest, the whole idea seems very far-fetched.'

'Your scepticism does you credit,' Atelon said, smiling now. 'Keep it sharp and strong, it's your sword and shield. *Always* question. You're not alone in struggling with the idea of the Power. There's a great deal we Cadwanwr don't understand about it and we've been studying it since Ethriss founded our Order. We know much more than we used to – in fact, over the years since Sumeral's Second Coming, our knowledge has increased enormously. But it seems the nearer we get to its true nature, the more elusive it becomes.' He became suddenly thoughtful. 'Perhaps we can never fully discover what it is because we're a part of it.' He smiled to himself. 'Anyway, accept it for the moment, Thyrn, just as you'd accept any fireside tale. There'll be plenty of time for doubt later.' He looked round to draw in the rest of his audience. 'This isn't an easy idea to grasp, but, in the course of our studies, one of many conjectures was that there could be other worlds existing at the same time and in the same place as this one we see around us.' A gesture took in the darkening mountains and he paused as if expecting a reaction from his listeners. None came, however. They were watching him expectantly. Dacu correctly interpreted his momentary confusion.

'Strange as it may seem, we're all of us familiar with the idea, Atelon,' he said. 'Thyrn and Vredech particularly so. They've tales of their own to tell. But finish yours first.'

Atelon's surprise was quite open. 'Well, I must admit that's not the response I expected. You intrigue me.' He looked at Thyrn and Vredech keenly for a moment before recollecting himself. 'Still, as I said, this was conjecture. There was some logic to it, but much of it was speculative. Recently, however, we've come increasingly to the conclusion that the existence of these other worlds is not only a real *possibility* but a strong *probability*. Further, given particular conditions – admittedly, as yet far from fully known – we think that certain individuals should have the ability to pass between them.' He turned his empty plate over. 'What is *not* possible any more than that this plate could have only one side – and this we *do* know – is that anyone who has the ability to use the Power could also have the ability to make such a journey. It's intrinsic in the nature of things. Which brings us to the Kyrosdyn. They're supposed to be crystal workers – simple craftsmen. Their true interest, however, lies in the Power.'

'Like you,' Thyrn said as Atelon paused. Endryk nudged him.

'Yes,' Atelon admitted. 'But *we* study the Power out of both intellectual curiosity as one of the great mysteries of our existence and also to understand something that has the potential to do terrible harm if abused. *They* study it so that they can use it to acquire control over others. And the way they study it can only be described as diseased, obscene. It's contrary to everything *we*'ve ever believed in or done.' His lean face became taut as he struggled to control an obvious anger. Then he spoke directly to Dacu. 'Arash-Felloren was once His place beyond any doubt, and the Kyrosdyn are His servants, whether they know it or not.' He hesitated and his voice fell. 'From what I could discover about Imorren herself, and from my own feelings, having met her, I think she may well have gained her knowledge from His hand directly – at Derras Ustramel.'

Both Dacu and Tirke frowned at this but did not speak.

210

Thyrn fidgeted but followed their example and remained silent. Atelon took Pinnatte's hand protectively.

'The reason they infected him,' his mouth curled in disgust, 'they called it Anointing – was to change him so that he'd serve as a vehicle for Sumeral's return.'

The final words almost tumbled out. Tirke stood up abruptly and turned away from the fire. Thyrn felt Endryk start violently. Dacu did not move, but his eyes became grim.

'I was there at the end,' Atelon said, answering their unspoken questions. 'I felt Him gathering and preparing to come forth again.' He shivered and fell silent.

'But, obviously, it didn't happen,' Tirke said, still facing into the darkness, his voice shaking and full of doubt. 'You prevailed.'

Atelon nodded uncertainly. 'We survived,' he replied. 'Pinnatte, Dar-volci and myself. Imorren died. Though I don't know whether it's right to say we prevailed. Maybe the whole thing was doomed from the outset, maybe not. I think if I were superstitious, I'd be inclined to say some higher force intervened, but setting that aside, it was chance – very fortunate chance – that brought us through it. A chance accident to Pinnatte that marred their experiment and left him with enough humanity to be reached when the time came.'

'What happened?'

Pinnatte lifted his right hand to encase Atelon's, still holding his left. It was extensively bandaged.

'Shortly after he'd been infected – here, on the back of his hand – he grazed it badly – bravely too, but I'll tell you about that later. A simple cleaning ointment was applied to it and that was it. The Kyrosdyn's experiment was suddenly changed into something beyond any controlling. Like a small stone tumbling down a mountainside and causing a rock fall instead of just coming to rest. I don't know what was meant to happen but in the end Pinnatte became someone who just shouldn't be – someone who could both use the Power and move between the worlds.' Atelon closed his eyes. 'It was a nightmare. The terrible instability of it all. I've never been so frightened in all my life. Not even when I stood with the army facing the Uhriel.' He began breathing deeply as a trembling in his voice threatened to take control of him. Dacu leaned forward and took his arm supportively.

'May I look at his hand?' Nertha asked into the ensuing silence.

Atelon glanced at Dacu, who nodded, then he looked at Pinnatte for his permission. The young man gave no sign but held out his hand to Nertha. She smiled at him and began removing the bandage. Her face lit with approval as she did so. 'This is as neat as anything I can do,' she said. 'And I take some small pride in my bandaging. I gather you've had some training as a physician.'

'I know a little about healing,' Atelon replied non-committally.

Nertha's face was studiously blank as she finally exposed the hand, though there was a tightness about the edges of her mouth. Pinnatte's fingers were clawed and rigid and the back of his hand was badly misshapen.

'What happened here?' she asked Atelon quietly but very firmly. 'This is more than a graze and an infection, this looks as if it's been under a wagon wheel.'

'A Sierwolf bit it,' Atelon replied flatly.

'What?' Tirke exclaimed.

'A Sierwolf.' Dar-volci's deep voice cut through the pending confusion. 'You shouldn't be too surprised, we've told you often enough that there are many of His creatures still lurking in the depths.'

'Yes, but . . .'

'Dar-volci fought it. Killed it.' It was Pinnatte. From his general manner, a more faltering voice might have been expected, but he spoke quite clearly, albeit with obvious difficulty. He had the hard-edged accent typical of the street citizens of Arash-Felloren.

Dar-volci chuckled darkly. 'I did, too. Foul piece of work that it was.' He spat into the fire which replied with a hissing cloud of steam and a few half-hearted sparks. 'Mind you, it was both a privilege and a pleasure to cut chunks out of such an abomination.'

'Where in the name of pity did a Sierwolf come from?' Dacu demanded of Atelon, again visibly disturbed.

'There are tunnels and caves under the city. As far as we can tell, the Kyrosdyn somehow captured it down there to fight in the animal pits. But it escaped and became linked with Pinnatte.'

'Linked?' Dacu queried.

'I was it, it was me,' Pinnatte said painfully. He offered no further explanation. Atelon made a sign to Dacu not to question the young man.

'Something to do with what they'd done to him – or what he'd become.'

'Yet it attacked him?' Nertha said.

'It bit him when he intervened to save my life,' Atelon said. 'I'll tell you about that later, too.'

The atmosphere around the fire was uneasy.

'And can Pinnatte still use the Power and move between the worlds?' Thyrn asked hesitantly.

Atelon shook his head. 'No. His condition was as unstable as it was dangerous.' He picked up his plate. 'What happened to him was more improbable than me throwing this on to the rocks over there and having it land on its edge and stay perfectly balanced. Even if it happened it wouldn't be for long, would it? If things had happened differently he'd probably be dead now – or possessed. Fortunately, they didn't. As it is, he's normal – whatever normal might mean – though I'm afraid he's lost most of the use of his hand. And he's tormented in ways I don't seem to be able to help him with. Which is why I'm taking him to see Hawklan. There's nothing for someone in his condition in Arash-Felloren.'

Tongue protruding slightly, Nertha was rebandaging Pinnatte's hand. 'It's certainly a nasty injury,' she said. 'But I've seen worse. I think, with a little exercise, we might be able to get some movement back into it. If you want to try.' She smiled inquiringly at Pinnatte who nodded almost imperceptibly.

As she released his hand and sat back, Dar-volci sidled around the fire and flopped down against her. Without thinking, she began to stroke him. After a moment, he dropped his head into her lap and closed his eyes.

'I see what you mean about your Accounting being a long

one,' Dacu said to Atelon. He looked round at the others. 'So much seems to be happening. Wait until you hear what Vredech and Thyrn have to say.' He rolled his shoulder as if it were troubling him. 'So many questions. And all so . . .' He let out a noisy breath, then slapped his knees briskly. 'But everything in its time. That's for then, this is now. What were the two of you doing down here, anyway? I presume you didn't come looking for trouble.'

'We certainly didn't,' Atelon replied ruefully. 'And more than once I was nearly heading back for home, I can assure you. And at speed. But . . .' He shrugged.

'Another one with the gift,' Vredech said to Dacu wryly, hoping to lighten the Goraidin's mood. Atelon looked at him quizzically. 'It was something we were talking about the other day,' Vredech explained. 'We all seem to have the gift of not standing idly by in the face of wickedness.'

Dacu accepted the gesture. 'Vredech's a priest, he exercises the gift by virtue of a higher moral authority. You and I just don't know any better,' he said provocatively.

Atelon smiled broadly. The exchange told him a great deal about this disparate party that had descended on him so unexpectedly. 'Always looking for a fight, eh, warrior?' he said. 'Take no notice of him, Vredech. A few more people with that particular gift wouldn't go amiss in Arash-Felloren. If ever there was an example of what we can descend to, that place is a good signpost.'

'So we gathered,' Dacu said. 'So what were you doing there?'

Atelon looked rueful. 'Now you mention it, I'd almost forgotten, it seems so trivial now – and a long time ago.' He drew out the word 'long', then he stretched luxuriously, easier for having told at least part of his tale, despite its grim implications. 'We came across crystals being sold at the Gretmearc – which was a surprise, to say the least. Andawyr was concerned. He asked us to see if we could find where they were coming from.' He gave a guilty moue. 'He's due for a shock. They all are.'

Dacu's brow furrowed. 'What are these things – these crystals?' he said, with a hint of irritation. 'I'd never even heard of them before I came here. And what's the Cadwanol's interest in them?'

Atelon turned round to root in the pack he was leaning on. From it he produced a small flat box which he opened and held out for inspection. In it lay two rows of large many-faceted jewels. They were all different colours and they glittered seductively even in the firelight.

Nertha leaned forward with an enthusiastic 'Ooo,' but before she could touch any of them, Pinnatte reached out and closed the box. The movement was silent but determined. His face was pained.

'Sorry,' Atelon said to him. 'That was thoughtless of me.' He dropped the box back in his pack, leaving Nertha frowning at him, her 'Ooo' now a disconsolate 'Oh.'

'He can't even stand to look at them now. Not long ago, like many another in Arash-Felloren, I suspect there's little he wouldn't have done to acquire those.'

'No,' Pinnatte said, his eyes fixed on Nertha. 'Couldn't sell. Too many others.' He ran a finger across his throat.

Atelon nodded understandingly. 'There's apparently a hierarchy amongst the thieves in the city. The greater steal from the lesser.' He tapped his pack. 'And there's enough in that box for someone to kill for – enough to give them financial security for a lifetime.'

'Why are they so valuable?' Dacu asked.

'They've many uses,' Atelon replied. 'More than we ever thought, to be sure. As for their value, I don't really understand how or why, but much of that seems to be arbitrarily maintained by some kind of arrangement between the Kyrosdyn, the crystal traders and the people who control the miners. One of Arash-Felloren's few redeeming features is that it's so big, so crowded, that no one faction or individual has ever controlled it and the people there set great store by that. So even the Kyrosdyn with their wealth and their skill in using the Power have to use cunning and stealth to achieve anything they want.'

'What do they use them for?' Dacu pressed. 'Come to that, what do *you* use them for?'

'Mainly we study them. It was trying to understand them

215

which led us to realize there could be other worlds around us. They can change the characteristics of space itself, and even time . . .' Dacu's raised eyebrows halted the explanation. Atelon gave a worldly sigh and raised his own eyebrows in retaliation. 'Do you want me to get technical?' he demanded.

'Just being sceptical,' Dacu returned, reminding him of his advice to Thyrn.

'You've used the Slips to move about the Cadwanen, haven't you?' Atelon continued.

'Before you closed them, yes. Never liked them, though. Now you're here, now you're there – creepy.' He gave a laboured shudder. 'And all to save a little time.'

'Well, that's as may be. Andawyr used one to escape from the Gretmearc when he and Hawklan were attacked once, though I doubt anyone but him could have done it. But they use crystals. It was when we began to learn more about them that we stopped using them.'

Dacu pursed his lips doubtingly. 'Andawyr told me he stopped you using them because you were all getting too fat and idle.'

'Just our great leader's little joke, that's all,' Atelon rebutted, defensively. 'He wouldn't want to worry you.' Then he was serious. 'It's the same with using the Power generally. The more we've learned, the more circumspect we've become about using it.'

Dacu nodded. 'Why were you surprised when you found crystals being sold? How did you come by yours?'

'Ethriss gave them to us, but no one knows how he came by them. Insofar as anyone ever thought about it, it was always assumed he'd created them just for us. It all seems rather naïve now.'

'Well, if these things are being mined, then, in a manner of speaking, perhaps he *did* create them. He was the first of the Guardians,' Dacu offered.

Atelon gave a self-deprecating laugh. 'It's a nice thought but I'm afraid we're beyond the help of pedantry on this. The fact is we *didn't* think about them, we took them for granted, and we've no idea where they came from. Finding them for sale on a market stall was more than a surprise, actually: it was a considerable shock. As if you might have come across Hawklan's sword casually dumped in the clutter at the back of a blacksmith's shop.' He half turned towards his pack. 'Oddly enough, though, while they might be dug out of the ground like any other precious stone, my feeling – and it's only a feeling, I'll admit – is that they're *made* things – that the many uses to which they're put are simply an inadvertent consequence of some deeper purpose. Something even Ethriss didn't understand. The way they can be used to manipulate the Power, I can't shake from my mind the idea that they're intended for use as some kind of a weapon.'

Dacu watched the Cadwanwr thoughtfully. 'Trust your judgement, Atelon,' he said. 'I wouldn't hesitate to. The light will break through eventually, you know that.'

Nertha's face had darkened as she listened to this conversation. The image of Pinnatte silently closing the box returned to highlight what Atelon was saying about the crystals.

'Are those things dangerous now?' she asked, pointing to his pack.

'They can be,' Atelon replied. 'If you're sensitive to them – particularly the green ones. That was Andawyr's main concern when he found we weren't the sole possessors of them. There are lots of people in Riddin, Fyorlund and Orthlund who've got some aptitude for using the Power and given that, even if it's a scarcely noticeable trait, then an accidental misuse of a crystal can do them a great deal of harm.'

'How?'

Nertha delivered her question like a punch and Atelon floundered momentarily before managing to gather together a reply.

'Forgive me, it's difficult without knowing how you approach your healing but, put simply, the Power underlies the energy that suffuses us and just as the crystals can focus and transform the Power so they can do the same to this energy. Consequences range from simple contact burns to ulcers to a permanent imbalance of the body's ability to mend itself.'

'Fascinating. We'd heard they were used in medicines,' Nertha said. 'But I can see why you were concerned.'

They fell silent.

Dar-volci opened a bleary eye, gave a small, explosive sneeze, then closed it again as Nertha continued stroking him.

Night filled the valley and stars could be seen between thin, slowly drifting shreds of cloud. Now and then, a distant animal cry echoed through the darkness. The fire burned a quiet red and the occasional soughing hint of urgent nightbird wings came down to the silent group.

Suddenly Pinnatte pointed to Vredech. 'Your tale,' he said. He flicked his ear. 'Listening.'

The gesture and his manner caused a crackle of amusement around the fire. Endryk prodded it into life and threw on some more wood, sending up a flurry of sparks which briefly rivalled the stars.

It was much later by the time Vredech and Thyrn had recounted their own strange stories and fatigue was beginning to take its toll. Pinnatte was the first to succumb, but the others did not remain by the fire for long after Nertha and Atelon had helped him to bed.

The next day, neither Pinnatte nor Vredech could be woken.

Chapter 18

The raven cocked its head on one side as it examined first Marna, then Farnor. It craned forward as if to examine Farnor particularly thoroughly. Shimmering rainbow colours scattered and rippled across its shining plumage as it moved. Then it tapped its wooden leg on the stone coping and turned its attention to the Goraidin.

'Dear boys, dear girls, how nice to see you all again,' it said in a deep and cultured voice. 'And such a surprise. I was just in the area . . . visiting a friend . . . when I noticed this small army riding determinedly over the bridge. Invaders, I thought, as one would. Doubtless intending to bombard us with Eirthlundyn ribbons and laces. So I thought I'd better pop down and shoo you all away. And here you all are. Delightful. And quite timely, too.'

Overcoming her initial shock, Marna grasped Farnor's arm excitedly. 'A talking crow,' she exclaimed. The Goraidin winced in anticipation. The raven turned slowly and stared at her.

'And you've brought guests with you. How nice. Just what we need – young people,' it said acidly. Then it turned back to Yengar and spoke in a loud whisper. 'Do tell them not to gape, dear boy, it gives me this overwhelming urge to fill their little mouths with worms. It's a fatherhood thing, I think. Quite disconcerting in its way.'

'Marna, Farnor, allow me to introduce you to Gavor,' Yengar said. 'Hawklan's companion. We've told you about him.'

Farnor's eyes widened as he realized to whom he was being introduced. Gavor had featured highly in the Goraidins' fireside accounts of the war of the Second Coming.

His hand extended automatically to hover vaguely in front of the raven before dropping awkwardly to his side.

'It's an honour to meet you . . . sir,' he said, uncertain how to address the bird.

Gavor bowed his head by way of acknowledgement. 'Farnor, eh? Now this *is* a surprise. Given the odd names you people choose for yourselves, I'll warrant you must be Farnor Yarrance. The young man that Memsa Gulda met in the Forest. Delighted to meet you. I've heard such a lot about you. The Memsa mentions you often. She was most concerned at having to leave you the way she did. Said you were lost and full of darkness. There's something odd about you, for sure, though I can't put a claw on it, but you seem bright enough – for a fledgling. Anyone who stops to watch the river going by can't be all bad, can they? And, to be honest, the Memsa's apt to be a touch doom-laden at times.' Before Farnor could reply, Gavor was speaking to Marna.

'You'll be his mate, I imagine, I must say, you're . . .'

'I am not!' Marna interrupted indignantly. She flicked a thumb towards the smirking Goraidin. 'I came with them.' The thumb moved to Farnor. 'He . . . just followed, later.'

Gavor flapped his wings and hopped back nervously in the face of this powerful denial. 'Sincerest apologies, dear girl,' he said. 'But an understandable error on my part. I was about to remark how attractive you are and how fortunate he was to have won the charms of someone so lovely.' Marna's jaw dropped, prompting Gavor to add with weary confidentiality, 'When your mouth's not hanging open, that is, dear girl. Do take care, it really doesn't do you justice.'

Yengar intervened protectively. 'You're a long way from home, Gavor.'

'Just giving the old wings a stretch as it were. Didn't realize how far I'd come. Out for a little solitude. Anderras Darion's rather crowded these days. It seems the whole world's being drawn to it. It's getting to be positively raucous.'

'I'm sure Memsa Gulda will bring some semblance of order to things,' Yrain said. 'How long has she been there?'

'Well, you know how it is with the Memsa. Disappears for years on end – gone forever, as far as we knew – gone to take her place in legend. Then she's back and picking up the last conversation she was having with you as if she'd never been away. And she is, as you quite rightly surmise, bringing order to things. Which is one of the other reasons I thought I'd pop out for a while.'

His desolate tone prompted some laughter.

'And how are you, sky prince?' Yrain asked. 'Have you missed us?'

With an alarming flurry, Gavor took off and propelled himself from the parapet to land on her shoulder. 'Unceasingly, dear girl. How could I not, with such radiance gone from the castle? You've been constantly in my mind. Both of you,' he added with a hasty glance at Jenna.

'Gavor, how you've avoided the pot for so long defeats me,' Yrain said, trying unsuccessfully to remove him.

'Charm, patience, wit, stalwart fidelity, to name but a few of my many sterling qualities. And I'm an excellent listener, as you know. Do be still, dear girl, you're making me quite giddy.' He jumped up on to her head and addressed the whole group. 'Now, tell me everything you've been doing. Don't miss a thing. I desperately need to be able to tell the Memsa something she doesn't already know.'

'No,' Yengar said unequivocally. 'We'll be at Anderras Darion soon enough and we don't want to be telling everything twice.'

'Dear boy,' Gavor purred coaxingly. 'Just a little. Just enough to enable me to look skyward and say "I know" when she tells me something.'

Yengar pursed his lips and shook his head. 'Our Oath as Goraidin specifically forbids us from becoming involved in disputes between formidable old ladies and birds – of any ilk. It's in the part about self-preservation.'

Gavor's wooden leg began tapping an impatient tattoo on Yrain's head.

'Very droll. But I have to tell you it's probably in your best interests to have a quick run through your Accounting, Goraidin. Just to get it clear in your mind. You'll certainly have to go through it more than a few times when you get to Anderras Darion.'

Yengar eyed him suspiciously. 'Why?'

'I told you. The place is alive with people asking questions.'

'It was when we left, if you recall. We haven't been gone that long. What can you expect with so many people travelling abroad these days? Besides, the Memsa needs only one telling, you know that. She's a joy to account to.' He signalled to Farnor and Marna. 'Come on, you two. Mount up. Let's be on our way. If we keep up a good pace, we can be there before midday tomorrow.'

'Andawyr's there as well,' Gavor announced, extending his wings to steady himself as they set off, much to Yrain's annoyance.

Yengar looked surprised but did not yield. 'Excellent, that means we won't have to trail up to the Cadwanen as well and we'll all be able to get home much sooner – something I'm looking forward to after all that's happened.'

'Which was?'

'Ah.'

'Gavor, will you get off my damned head?' Yrain ended the exchange. 'You're heavy.'

Gavor let out a conspicuous sigh as he jumped to avoid her flailing hand.

'And don't sit on mine,' Jenna said fiercely. 'Not after what you did last time.'

'I did apologize, dear girl. It was the merest slip. These things happen when one's engrossed. No personal criticism was intended. And it really doesn't become you to be so unforgiving.' Jenna's expression, however, remained unremittingly baleful. Olvric held out his hand. Gavor bounced on to it, then up on to his head. As his broad wings spread out, it seemed to Farnor that Olvric was wearing an ancient battle helm. The sight made him catch his breath.

'Can you still Hear the trees – and talk to them?'

Gavor was talking to him. Taken by surprise, Farnor had managed only a few inarticulate sounds before the raven was complaining to Yengar that he was, 'Gaping again. It's really most disconcerting.'

'Yes, I can,' Farnor finally said. 'Though only faintly. We're a long way from the Great Forest.'

'The Great Forest is everywhere, really,' Gavor said, leaning forward and staring at him. 'Still, it's remarkable. A rare gift indeed. Even amongst the Valderen. And yours is exceptional even by their standards, the Memsa tells me.'

'So I believe. You know about the Valderen, the Great Forest?'

Gavor did not answer. 'The will of the Great Forest goes back beyond any knowing,' he said.

'I wouldn't know,' Farnor retorted. 'They were difficult to understand sometimes – most of the time actually. Very difficult. And it disorientated me badly when they touched on ancient things. It's as if they remembered everything they ever knew, all the time. Almost as if time didn't exist and everything was happening at once.'

'Remarkable indeed,' Gavor said softly, as if to himself. 'You must keep them with you – touch them often. Don't let their voice be drowned by the clamour that your own kind makes.' They were off the bridge now and Gavor nodded significantly towards the clusters of trees that dotted the Orthlundyn landscape.

'I will,' Farnor promised, unexpectedly moved by the raven's manner.

'What's Andawyr down for?' Yengar asked with a casualness that did not prevent Gavor from gloating.

'Oh, this and that,' he replied, equally casually. 'I'm sure he'll tell you if he can find a moment.' Suddenly the banter was gone from his voice. 'Actually, he only arrived yesterday, so I don't really know. Yatsu and Jaldaric are with him, too. And now you're coming back, with this remarkable young man. It seems the whole world's converging on Anderras Darion. As if the old mother were drawing her children together.'

'They're well, Yatsu and Jaldaric?' Yengar interrupted his musing.

'Yes, well enough. A little travel-weary, like yourselves, but in good heart.'

'Did they find the men they were looking for?'

'They did, I believe. Quite the uplifting tale, actually, though I haven't got all of it yet. It seems whatever folly they committed in serving Oklar, they apparently atoned for it and more with loyal service to a good lord. And did you find yours?'

'Oh yes, eventually. But there's nothing uplifting about their fate. Those who aren't dead are in captivity until we can arrange for them to be brought back to give a full Accounting.'

'One would have expected little else, given who they were. But, as I recall, you were just supposed to find out where they'd gone, not start a war with them.'

'It's a long story.'

'Do tell.'

Thus, as they rode on, and despite Yengar's previous avowal, much of the remainder of the day was spent in telling Gavor of their journeying: of the seizure of Farnor's valley by Nilsson and his men, of the emergence of the Sierwolf, of Rannick's terrifying transformation, and of the destruction of all three.

'A weighty tale,' Gavor declared when it was finished, though his manner was a little subdued. 'And so many questions to be asked.'

'Well, those I am definitely not answering,' Yengar told him firmly.

'Wouldn't dream of asking you, dear boy,' Gavor replied. 'You've been generosity itself. Besides, I'm not sure what I should ask. And my pinions tell me that Yatsu and Jaldaric will have as much to say. I suspect they also became involved in some rather heated exchanges while they were away.' He gave Farnor a sidelong look and lowered his voice. 'And this Antyr they've brought with them is . . . strange, to put it mildly.'

'You're sounding ominous, Gavor. Who's Antyr?'

Gavor was abruptly himself again. 'Nonsense, dear boy. How could I be ominous? It's not in my nature. I'm a bringer of light and joy. This you know. Speaking of which . . .' He bent forward as though to avoid the ears of eavesdroppers. His listeners found themselves doing the same as he kept lowering his voice. 'Andawyr's brought this delightful little acolyte with him. I'd never have credited him with that much discernment, to be honest. Usche, she's called – typical clunking

Riddin name – but she's a treat – a real treat. So fetching in those Cadwanwr robes, you have no idea – you know the way they . . .'

'Who's Antyr, Gavor?' Yrain's voice came through clenched teeth and cut across Gavor's increasingly enthusiastic description.

Untypically, Gavor stammered. 'Ah, Antyr . . . he's . . . a Dream Finder, I believe.'

'A what?'

'A Dream Finder. It seems you're all bringing back interesting people. I really do have to be off now. Things to do. Can't spend all day chatting. They'll be worrying about me being gone so long.'

And before anyone could speak Gavor's great wings were spread wide and he was swooping down towards the road prior to soaring up into the evening sky.

'I'll tell them to expect you tomorrow,' he called down.

'I think that bird must practise being aggravating,' Yrain growled as the black speck dwindled into the distance.

'More of a gift, I'd have thought,' Jenna said. 'He does it so well and with such ease.'

'What's a Dream Finder?' Farnor asked of no one in particular.

'A Dream Finder's an exercise in patience that Gavor's set for us,' Olvric replied. 'We have to wait and see.'

'Sounds intriguing.'

'So does Andawyr's . . . aeolyte.' Yengar and Olvric exchanged a look and a laugh. Yrain and Jenna just exchanged a look.

'Just concentrate on staying on your horses, you two,' Yrain said scornfully. 'And where we're going to camp. Unless you're so *intrigued* you fancy a night gallop.'

As it was, they spent the night at a nearby farm, eating with the farmer and his wife but sleeping in their tents in one of the fields. The only difficulty they experienced was in persuading the farmer, a large and jovial man, to accept a contribution of Valderen food towards the meal.

In many ways, the warm friendliness of the greeting that Farnor and Marna received made them feel as though they were back at home but that very familiarity conspired to wash occasional waves of homesickness over them as they ate and talked. All too well understood by the Goraidin, these were noted but allowed to subside in their own time. The darkness of such moments, though deep, did not linger, however, for though the hospitality was familiar, the farmhouse was very different from anything either Farnor or Marna had ever known. This was not only their first meeting with the people of Orthlund, other than Yrain and Jenna who, by their own admission, were unusual, it was their first contact with the Orthlundyn love of stone carving.

There were examples of it everywhere. It was not the Orthlundyn way idly to grace tables, mantelshelves, window-sills and any other convenient horizontal surfaces with a few fond ornaments. Examples of their art formed a deep integral part of walls, ceilings, staircases, door surrounds, fireplaces, mullions and transoms, anywhere that a chisel and ingenuity could reach. But none of it was reckless or indiscriminate. Always there was order and intention, even though this might not be clearly apparent at first glance. Indeed, it was rarely so, because the Orthlundyn were not only skilled carvers, they were also subtle thinkers, and masters of shadow lore.

Thus it was that Orthlundyn carvings could stand constant examination, each one linking to its neighbour, either directly, physically, or by some discreet, understated implication, and each seeming to move and shift as the changing lights of the day fell on it.

As the evening passed Farnor became more and more engrossed with them. 'I've never seen anything like these before,' he said eventually. 'They're incredible – so complicated – so fine.'

The farmer chuckled and bowed to him. 'Well, I'm no Isloman, but I try. And the judgement of your outlander's eye is appreciated.'

By contrast, Farnor noted, the wooden table at which they were sitting was almost completely devoid of any decoration.

'Don't you carve wooden things?' he asked.

'No,' the farmer boomed disparagingly. 'Doesn't get to the heart of things, wood. Stone has the history of everything written in it for the finding if you're prepared to look.' He cast a mischievous glance at Olvric and Yengar. 'It's more a Fyordyn kind of a thing, messing about with wood. And, to give them their due, they're quite good at it, in their way.'

'The Valderen do it in the Great Forest,' Farnor said. 'You'll come across carved animals and figures peering out of the branches in the most unexpected places. In and around the lodges mainly, but sometimes in the middle of nowhere – far from any of the lodges – just because someone's taken a liking to a particular tree or bush, or clearing.' He leaned forward and began drawing in his audience enthusiastically. 'They've a huge meeting hall with a great arched ceiling that looks like a tangle of roots from a tree so big it would reach up into the clouds. When people speak, it carries their voices to everyone there. I spoke there once, but I wish I'd looked at it more carefully while I had the chance. In fact, I wish I'd paid more attention to everything. I will when I go back, for sure. The Valderen do everything with wood – everything – build, decorate, work the soil, make fine threads and great ropes, even medicines and perfumes. And never a thing without first asking the permission of the Forest itself.'

The farmer was impressed. He had heard of the Great Forest as an ancient myth but never thought that any part of it still existed. Thus Farnor found himself explaining the ways of the Valderen and, as well as he could, of the Forest itself. He needed no signals from Yengar to avoid the darker aspects of his time with them. When he had finished, the farmer was staring at him thoughtfully.

'I'm in your debt, young man,' he announced, slapping the table and making his wife flutter. 'What a tale. You've given me enough ideas to last a lifetime.' He looked down at his empty plate. 'And if the Valderen's carving is as good as their food then it'll be worthy of respect at least.' He looked upwards. 'A ceiling of roots that carries words to everyone, you say – sheltering the people and binding earth and sky – and small animals carved to be unseen for most of the time – and wood used for everything.' His gaze moved to the rest of the room and he became increasingly preoccupied until his wife discreetly rapped him with a spoon to bring his attention back to his guests.

'This is a beautiful land,' Farnor said to Olvric as they left the farmhouse and went to their tents. 'There's something special about it. I've felt it more and more since we crossed the bridge.'

'You're right,' Olvric replied. 'Orthlund's a very special place.'

'And are all the people like him – the farmer – and his family?'

'People are people,' Olvric replied unhelpfully. 'No two are alike, you should know that by now. But, yes, generally speaking, the Orthlundyn will offer you trust and hospitality.'

'Yet they've a Threshold Sword hanging by the door.'

'That's a Fyordyn tradition we seem to be exporting. They've only been doing it here since the war.' Unexpectedly Olvric gave a sad smile. 'Part of me thinks I should be unhappy about that but it's difficult to be unhappy about anything the Orthlundyn do, they bring such qualities to their actions. I could be sad about your people – they took to the Threshold Sword because the darker realities of the world beyond their valley had impinged on them. It's something they did with regret and they'd happily be without it. In a way, they lost their innocence. I could even perhaps be sad about my own people – we maintained the tradition religiously – had the symbol constantly before us – yet didn't see what it meant – not even us, the Goraidin, the elite of the High Guards, Morlider War veterans, who, above all, should have seen clearly.'

'I'm sorry,' Farnor said. 'I didn't mean to upset you.'

Olvric was offhand. 'Don't worry, you didn't. A day doesn't pass when some memory of the war doesn't intrude. It can't be avoided, but it's no burden. It's just one of the differences between you and me, that's all.'

Farnor made to enter his tent but he paused. 'What did you mean, the Orthlundyn bring such qualities to their actions?'

'Just that.' Olvric stood a few paces away from him now, shadowy in the light that shone from the farmhouse windows. 'Even in a simple thing like adopting the Threshold Sword, they did it not as an unfortunate necessity, like your people, but almost as if they were renewing some ancient pledge. Yet, at the same time, they did it . . . lightly.'

'I don't understand.'

'Don't worry, neither do I. As individuals they're like you and me. As a people, they're deep.'

'Why?'

There was an untypical hint of exasperation in Olvric's reply. 'Farnor, it's been a long day and I'm tired. You pick a rare time to ask questions like that.'

'Sorry.' Olvric half turned to continue to his tent, then he stopped. He spoke into the darkness.

'The Orthlundyn are the remains of the people who stood first and longest against Sumeral at the time of the First Coming. They were Ethriss's firmest allies. They paid a terrible price. Their innocence has long been lost.' He turned to Farnor. 'Unlike my people and the Riddinvolk, they've no military tradition. All they're interested in is their farming and their carving. If we ever thought about them at all, it was with amused affection, I suppose. Not that we ever thought about them much. But when He returned, they mustered an army out of nothing, moved it across the mountains and fought battles as if they'd been trained to it not only from birth but through countless generations.' Farnor could not see Olvric's face, but he saw his clenched fist raised in emphasis. 'And you should've seen them fight, Farnor. Such courage, discipline. Incredible. A match for the finest we had. Even their elite, the Helyadin, their Goraidin. That's what Yrain and Jenna were, Helyadin – that's Gulda's influence for you.' The fist was lowered. 'And when everything was over, they . . .' He shrugged. 'Disbanded. Went back to their homes, their farming, their carving.'

'As if nothing had happened?'

'Oh no. No one could do that. Too many were too cruelly hurt, in every way. They're changed, as are we all. But where we and the Riddinvolk have been moved to a different awareness of our lives and our history, it's as though the Orthlundyn were simply awakening – becoming something that they used to be – but still at ease with it.'

He fell silent.

A door closed in the farmhouse, and somewhere a dog barked.

'Good night, Farnor.'

'Good night, Olvric.'

The following morning it was raining and a strong breeze was blowing, but Farnor, first awake as always, found he could do no other than join the farmer with his daily tasks. Apart from an initial, surprised greeting, the farmer accepted his help in companionable and appreciative silence.

When they had finished, Farnor stood looking at the farmhouse, inevitably contrasting it with the memory of his own home, both as it had been and as it had become. The memory distressed him and for a while there were more than raindrops running down his face.

After they had breakfasted with the farmer and his wife, the party set off again, though, to both Farnor's and Marna's relief, not at the pace they had maintained for the previous days. Soon they were moving through hedged and cultivated land along metalled roads and encountering a modest amount of traffic. Each person they met offered them a greeting, which they returned, and there were one or two more prolonged intervals as old friends were occasionally recognized.

Farnor began to feel nervous. The memories stirred by his brief stay at the farm had disturbed him. What was he doing in this place, so far from his home and friends? Why was he learning these dark Goraidin ways? What was it inside him that could reach out and touch the Great Forest and the ways to these worlds beyond? And what was Marna doing here, dark-haired and contrary Marna who had leapt into the blazing castle to rescue the four Goraidin? But there was his answer, he knew. Both he and the Marna he had known were changed, and that change had set them both on this journey and to whatever followed. His thoughts slipped back momentarily to the help he had given the farmer that morning. That had been good. That would always be good. That would always be there.

Almost without realizing it, he was listening to the voice of the Great Forest within him. He had not consciously done that for some time.

'You must keep in touch with them,' Gavor had said. 'Don't let their voice be drowned by the clamour that your own kind makes.'

'I am here,' Farnor said inwardly. 'All is well. This is a place of light.'

And even as the words formed, his unease slipped away. Orthlund was indeed a place of light. He could feel it all around him. His nervousness became anticipation.

'Are you all right?'

He jumped as Marna seemed to bellow her concern at him.

'Yes,' he said, shaking his head. 'Just thinking about something.'

They were walking up a small rise.

Marna turned to Yengar. 'How much further . . .'

Yengar lifted his hand for silence and they stopped at the top of the rise. As they stood there, the only sounds to be heard were the soft creak of the horses' tackle and the flapping of Farnor's cloak, flying loose in the blustering wind.

Yengar pointed to the horizon. The rain had stopped and the clouds had been scattered. In the distance ran a long range of sunlit mountains and between two of the peaks the sun was reflecting off something with diamond brightness.

'That's the Gate to Anderras Darion,' he said.

Chapter 19

Farnor found his nervousness returning. It alternated with an increasing excitement. What was this place going to be like? And what were its people going to be like? Gulda he knew, or at least had met, albeit only briefly, though while she had made a powerful impression on him he could not fathom why she was held almost in awe by his otherwise commanding and apparently fearless companions. What would Andawyr be like? The descriptions he had been given did not seem to fit the leader of what was apparently an ancient and wise Order. And, not least, what would this great leader, the owner of Anderras Darion, Hawklan, be like? Old? Young? Ferocious and grim? Massively strong? Battle-scarred? Clad in heroic armour, sitting on a great throne with an armed retinue about him?

He fought down a powerful urge to pester the Goraidin with questions, and he could see that Marna was doing the same. More than once as they drew nearer to the castle they exchanged uncertain anticipatory glances. It did not help him that they were now travelling at a very leisurely walking pace. In the end he voiced his concern, 'Can't we go a little faster?'

'Yes,' Yengar replied. But they didn't.

Then they were entering Pedhavin, the village that lay on the tumbling slopes at the foot of the steep ascent to Anderras Darion. Farnor and Marna had been silent for some time, their gaze fixed on the increasingly dominant presence of the castle. For though it was dwarfed by the mountain peaks on either side, dominate it did, like a matriarch between two hulking offspring. Above the blank and windowless wall in which was set the Great Gate could be seen a jostling forest of

233

towers and spires. They ramped back far out of sight in a seemingly random array as though, like a mountain flood, they had crashed down the valley to surge up against an immovable dam. As Farnor stared up he thought from time to time that he could see a pattern in them, but whenever he tried to study it, it slipped away, like a strange shadow at the edge of a dream.

The Goraidin smiled at one another, seeing the wonder written on the faces of the two young people. But their smiles had little in the way of adult indulgence because, though they themselves had seen it many times, Anderras Darion always drew the eye and never failed to stir the spirit.

Only as they entered the village and the castle slipped from view did Farnor and Marna feel able to speak.

'So big.'

Marna whispered through the clatter of the hooves on the stone streets, as though too loud a voice might bring an echoing rebuke down on her. 'I thought the castle in the valley was big, but this . . .'

'Yes,' Farnor agreed inadequately. He could feel countless questions bubbling inside him but he could not find the words to ask them though, in tones as hushed as Marna's, he did manage, 'Who built it?'

'The Orthlundyn,' Yengar whispered in reply before he realized what he was doing. He cleared his throat and spoke normally. 'At the time of the First Coming. They were a powerful people then, ruled by lords and kings, but free and strong. Ethriss made it his own after . . .' He stopped himself. '. . . After they were almost destroyed in a terrible battle against Sumeral's army.'

'It looks incredible.'

'It's a wondrous place, Farnor, but, like everything, it's not without darkness, by any means.' Yengar frowned as though he had said something he did not intend to. Farnor scarcely noticed the reservation, however, his attention having turned to the village. Like the castle, this too was unlike anything he had seen before. Most of the stone-built houses were two storeys high, with heavy, low-pitched roofs that jutted out provocatively at the eaves. They were dotted about seemingly at random, forming a bewildering maze of narrow, hilly streets punctuated occasionally by bright squares and court-yards. And everywhere was overlooked by balconies.

Had he known Pedhavin before the war he would have seen one conspicuous difference. There were gardens and trees, and bright flowers and foliage hung from eaves and balconies and specially made stone brackets. Previously, Pedhavin, in common with most Orthlundyn villages, had been decorated only by its carvings. Now the Orthlundyn seemed to feel a need to have about them reminders of blooming and fading, beginnings and endings that were not beginnings and endings. Not that there were any fewer carvings to be seen. In fact there were many more, as the Orthlundyn could do no other than draw inspiration from the new lines and shadows that these incessant changes offered them.

Though his few hours at the farmhouse had to some extent acquainted Farnor with Orthlundyn carving, he found himself quite bewildered by the intricate scenes that now surrounded him. Men and women worked in the fields under gathering clouds and burning suns, they worked in their homes, engaged in debate, fought in battles, quarrelled, loved. Some scenes even showed carvers watching carvers. Others patently told stories that needed a close study not possible when riding past. Yet others were just patterns, simple, elaborate, obses-sively symmetrical, achingly random, angular, sinuous. And it seemed that virtually nowhere had escaped attention. So much so that where some surface stood blank it attracted attention.

'Two reasons, usually,' Yengar told Farnor when he inquired. 'Someone didn't like what he'd done and has removed it . . .'

'They'd take part of a house wall down just for that?' Farnor interjected, incredulous.

'They do it all the time,' Yengar replied, adding, not without some amusement shared with Olvric, 'If you're not a good carver there's always a job for you in Orthlund as a mason.'

Farnor puffed out his cheeks in disbelief. 'What was the other reason?'

'Ah, a little more profound, that. It's a gesture towards the better carver who's yet to come.'

Pedhavin was quite large for an Orthlundyn village though it did not take them long to pass through it. But despite trying to observe the Goraidin teaching of always noting where they were going, neither Farnor nor Marna would have claimed to be able to say what route they had travelled by the time they were on the winding road that led up to the castle.

Despite its steepness the road was quite busy and the greetings to the Goraidin that had been an increasing feature of their journey became constant, much to Farnor's scarcely hidden irritation. Though it was virtually impossible to see the castle from much of the road, Farnor could sense its massive presence above him. It seemed to pull him forward. As they rounded a bend that brought them on to the final stretch of the road Farnor heard a breathy, 'Uh uh' behind him. It was Yrain.

Looking up the hill he saw a small black figure standing in the middle of the road. It was leaning on a stick. He smiled and, without thinking, urged his horse forward. The others made no attempt to keep up with him.

As he reached the top of the slope, the road opened into a flat grassy area and his attention was drawn from the familiar figure he was approaching to the wall towering above him and its Great Gate. He stopped and stared at it, transfixed.

'Gavor did tell me you'd taken to gaping, young Farnor. I see you have. Still, it's understandable in the circumstances.'

'It's enormous,' Farnor said hoarsely.

'I've heard more poetic responses, but I suppose that's not bad for a farm boy from the middle of nowhere.'

Farnor recollected himself and hastily clambered down from his horse. 'I'm sorry,' he said, smiling and flustered. 'I've been looking at it for most of the day, but it still took me completely by surprise. I . . .' He gave an apologetic shrug. 'I'm sorry. I'm making a fool of myself, aren't I It's good to see you again.'

'It's good to see you again, too, young man,' came the reply. 'And you're not making a fool of yourself. Anderras Darion has tied better tongues than yours.' Farnor found himself transfixed by piercing blue eyes that seemed to be searching to the heart of him. They were overshadowed by a determined forehead that was buttressed by a long nose which, in its turn, loomed over a stern mouth. Memsa Gulda, dressed in black as ever, remained leaning on her stick and, stern though her mouth was, it was smiling.

'You still have the stick I gave you,' he said.

Gulda grunted and with alarming and quite unexpected speed spun the stick round to land with a determined slap in her other hand. The movement took Farnor immediately back to the time when they had stood alone in a clearing in the Great Forest and he had offered the stick to her just before they parted. 'Of course,' she said. 'A fine gift. It's done well for itself since you tried to hit me with it.'

Farnor looked at her shrewdly, then risked, 'I don't think I'm going to apologize twice for that. You shouldn't have sneaked up on me.'

'I'm not sure you apologized even once, actually,' Gulda replied. 'You just gasped as you hit the ground.' She chuckled darkly.

'It's still good to see you ... Memsa ... Ashstock. What should I call you? Yengar and the others seem to be very nervous of you.'

'That's because they're more worldly-wise and less discerning than you, young Farnor. *You* may call me Ashstock. We're kin to the Great Forest, you and I, aren't we? A rare thing – even amongst the Valderen. We should carry it with us always.' The blue eyes were searching him again, even more disconcertingly than before. 'You've changed. And for the better. Much better. You can see more of the depths in yourself. But there's still darkness there. You're still troubled, aren't you?'

Her hand came up to indicate she did not want a reply. Farnor became aware of the others arriving. As they dismounted, Gulda thrust her stick into Farnor's hand, then gently eased him to one side to welcome each of them in turn. She gripped the men by the arms, Valderen style, and to their surprise, not to say their consternation, enfolded the women in a black-shrouded embrace.

'How splendid to see you all again. You're looking well.' She gave Olvric a quick head-to-toe appraisal, smacked Yengar's stomach with the back of her hand, and gave a reluctantly approving nod. 'And doing our best to age with dignity, I see.'

Though they were obviously delighted to see the old woman, Farnor had never before seen the four Goraidin quite so unsettled.

Gulda turned her attention next to Marna. She held out a hand in conventional greeting. 'Gavor told me about you, Marna, who definitely isn't Farnor's mate. Light be with you. Welcome to Anderras Darion.'

She took Marna's arm before she could speak, at the same time snapping her fingers at Farnor to signal for the return of her stick. Farnor jumped at the whipcrack sound and thrust the stick towards her quickly, then found he had to stride out to keep up with her unnervingly fast walk as she led Marna towards the Gate.

'Farnor, I suspect, like me, has little choice but to be here,' she was saying to Marna. 'The castle always seems to call to its own. But what are *you* doing in the company of these ne'er-do-wells?'

Gulda's grip on her arm, though gentle, prevented Marna from turning to her companions to seek help in how to deal with this strange woman.

'I . . . don't really know,' she stammered eventually. 'I think perhaps after all that happened at home, the valley, the village, felt too small – too vulnerable. I'm sorry . . . I . . .'

'She saved our lives. And she's Goraidin. Or will be with a little . . .'

Gulda's stick was raised for silence. 'As patient as ever, eh, Yrain?' she said, without looking round.

Yrain winced.

'I killed someone,' Marna said suddenly, her voice soft.

'What?' Farnor exclaimed, but Gulda's stick flicked up to silence him also.

'Son of a bitch tried to rape her. It was a clean kill. She did well. We've talked a few times, but it still bothers her.' Yrain braced herself for another rebuke even as she spoke.

It did not come. Instead, Gulda just nodded and her grip on Marna's arm became a reassuring squeeze. When she spoke, her voice was almost casual. 'These things do tend to upset a little, even when you've had no real choice. You can tell me the details later but Yrain's judgement in these matters is sound, Marna, absolutely sound. Make what peace you can with what happened, but carry no blame. You're just a little wiser, that's all. Some things can't be avoided.' She cast a glance at Marna's now pale and uncertain face and then at the still stunned Farnor and her eyes narrowed. 'And I suspect what's really burdening you is not so much what you did as that you've kept it from someone.'

Marna started violently and she came to a sudden halt. Gulda took one pace ahead and turned to face her. Marna's eyes flickered between Gulda and Farnor several times before finally settling on her old friend. She seemed to wilt inwardly.

'I'm sorry,' she said unhappily. 'I didn't know how to tell you. I don't know why. And it got harder the longer I left it.'

Farnor's throat was dry and he felt woefully inadequate in the face of what he had just learned and the pain he could see in Marna's whole posture.

Something in him reached out to her. 'It doesn't matter,' he heard himself saying. 'It was none of my business anyway. And I wouldn't have known how to help you. I suppose you did what you did because of where you were, like me with Rannick,.' He looked at Yrain and Gulda. 'And, without any disrespect, I don't need anyone else's judgement to tell me you've done nothing wrong.'

He gave her an awkward embrace with one arm and, for a moment, it seemed that Marna was going to cry, though she fought down the urge and muttered something unintelligible. Gulda gave an approving grunt and began propelling them both towards the Gate again.

As they approached, Farnor saw that a wicket door stood open. Two figures were coming through it, one tall and powerfully built, the other shorter but barrel-chested and, despite the difference in their heights, looking more than a match for his companion.

'Late as ever,' Gulda announced as they came forward to greet the newcomers. Farnor noticed immediately that, as with the Goraidin, the two men had an aura in the presence of Gulda not dissimilar to that of anxious children constrained to

239

best behaviour. It made him want to smile, but he didn't . . . not with Gulda there.

Her stick serving as a pointer she indicated each in turn, the shorter one first.

'This is Loman. Hawklan appointed him as Castellan, but he's a smith really.' The stick gave him a prod that was almost affectionate, 'And no mean commander of men when the need arises.' The stick moved on. 'This is his older brother, Isloman. Pedhavin's First Carver. A fair hand with a chisel, without a doubt. These are our guests, gentlemen, Farnor and Marna.'

Farnor saw his hand disappear first in Loman's furnace-browned fist and then in Isloman's paler but even larger one. Both grips, however, though purposeful, were unexpectedly gentle, and the warmth of their greetings began to dispel Farnor's more nervous thoughts about the inhabitants of this place of which he had heard so much and towards which he had been travelling for so long.

There then followed a noisy exchange as the two men greeted the Goraidin. This involved, amongst other things, Isloman seizing Yengar and Olvric, one in each arm, and lifting both of them off the ground at the same time. Warning looks from the two women saw them merely lightly embraced.

Gulda was looking round. 'Where's Hawklan?' she demanded. 'And Andawyr?'

'Gavor's looking for them,' Loman said.

'Show these young people their quarters, Loman, get them settled in, then bring them to the small dining hall. You are hungry, aren't you?' she asked over her shoulder, answering, 'Good, good,' before anyone could reply.

There was a small group of people standing very close to the Gate, apparently examining it in great detail. Some were talking excitedly, others were running their hands over the Gate, absorbed in thought, still others were making copious notes and sketches.

'What are they doing?' Farnor whispered to Gulda.

'They're studying the Gate.'

Farnor frowned, puzzled. He was about to emit an incredulous 'What?' but changed it instead to 'Why?'

240

Gulda halted the procession. 'Go and look at it,' she said. 'You too, Marna.'

Rather self-consciously Farnor did as he was told, Marna following him. As he came to the Gate, however, he saw that the shimmering he had seen from a distance was caused by elaborate and intricate patterns cut into its metal surface. He saw too that they were sharp-edged and clear and quite unaffected by the summers and winters of what must have been many generations.

'This is incredible,' he said, talking to himself as much as to Marna. 'Gryss would have loved this place so.' Then, like the people he had been looking at but minutes previously, he was gently running his hands over the Gate. Scenes and text seemed to come and go, forming and reforming through the whirling complexity of the carving. Here was a chariot, with white-eyed, foam-flecked horses, manes streaming wildly as they strained to the will of their furious driver. So vivid was it that Farnor thought he could hear the gasping breath, the pounding hooves, the rattle and creak of axles and tackle. But was it near or far? Then he realized that chariot, horses and driver were formed from countless other smaller scenes, each as detailed. He blinked to clear his vision, then saw that these were formed in turn from the overlapping features of yet other, larger carvings. A thin cloud drifted over the sun, sending a faint shadow dancing across the Gate. He gasped and stepped back as the whole Gate seemed to come alive with movement. His gaze was drawn inexorably upwards to the wall towering high above him.

'Careful.' A powerful hand between his shoulder blades prevented what would have been an inglorious tumble as he leaned ever further backwards.

He turned to thank his saviour but it took him a moment to focus properly. Then he found himself looking at a tall figure in a simple black robe. He was about the same height as Isloman but, though not as powerfully built, he gave the impression of being far stronger and, even though he was standing still, Farnor could sense an economy of movement in him that he knew would be the envy of the likes of Olvric and the others. In an instant he knew too who served as their example.

241

'You're Hawklan, aren't you?' he said, looking into a lean, weathered, yet strangely ageless face. Angular, with high cheek-bones and a prominent nose, it was dominated by bright green eyes.

'I am,' Hawklan admitted with a slight bow. 'And you are Farnor, I presume, if Gavor's description is to be trusted.' He extended a hand toward Marna. 'And you'll be Marna, the young woman who rides with the Goraidin and who quite definitely isn't Farnor's mate. You made an impression on our bird.'

Marna nodded, untypically overawed by this new arrival.

'You like the Gate?'

'I don't think I can say anything without stammering,' Farnor said.

Hawklan looked up at it. 'Not an inappropriate response by any means,' he said. 'People have made a lifetime's work of studying it, but no one has even managed to draw it in its entirety. Not even Orthlund's finest carvers seem to have the eye for it. You ran your hands over it, I noticed.' Farnor guiltily wiped his hands on his trousers and surreptitiously put them behind his back. 'Had you been blind, you'd have seen pictures and read tales quite different from those that we can see. At least, so I'm told. And if you have the ears for it, it sings at the touch of the least breeze.'

Farnor looked at him uncertainly. Hawklan laughed gently. 'You, above all, shouldn't doubt that, Farnor. You who can Hear the Great Forest.'

Before Farnor could reply he and Marna were being shepherded back to the others. There was a brief interlude as Hawklan greeted the four Goraidin. His greeting was not as raucous as Loman's and Isloman's but just as heartfelt, if not more so.

Some time later they were all together in a bright, airy room that overlooked an expansive garden area, one of many such within the confines of the castle. Both Farnor and Marna were oscillating between excitement and a numb bewilderment as a result of discovery after discovery. Loman had taken them to the quarters he had prepared. Large, elegantly furnished and bedecked with the elaborate carvings that seemed to be everywhere, the rooms, like so much else they were encountering, quite unlike anything either of them had ever known. It had taken Loman some time to assure the two young people that the rooms were indeed theirs while they remained in the castle. Now, bathed, changed into clean clothes, and replete with a substantial if simple meal, they were sitting in well-upholstered chairs and awaiting events.

They were not long in unfolding. Farnor was trying to tell Loman that he could not accept such lavish hospitality without offering some form of payment – 'I'd be happy to work on one of the farms. Or repair things. Or just sweep the floor – anything' – and Loman was trying to assure him that it was unnecessary when a commotion in the doorway interrupted them.

Andawyr staggered into the room with an oath, having been unbalanced by Tarrian and Grayle as they pushed roughly past him. The four Goraidin were on their feet immediately, all of them reaching for knives at the sight of the two wolves.

'It's all right,' Hawklan shouted hastily. 'There's no danger. Please. Sit down.'

It was with the utmost reluctance that they did as he asked and all of them were sitting on the edge of their chairs as the two animals moved around the room unceremoniously sniffing at everything and everyone. Andawyr was followed by Antyr, Oslang, Usche and an uncomfortable looking Ar-Billan.

After a plethora of introductions and chair-moving, Andawyr took charge of the gathering.

'This is difficult. I've no beginning to what I want to say, because I'm far from clear about what seems to be happening. However, suffice it that I came here with my colleagues because Yatsu and Jaldaric came to the Cadwanen with Antyr and a very disturbing tale.'

'Where are those two?' Gulda demanded curtly.

'They'll be here shortly,' Loman said.

'As I was saying,' Andawyr went on pointedly. 'Antyr has a very disturbing tale. One that coincides in its details with other matters that I . . .' He extended a hand towards Oslang. 'That we, at the Cadwanol, have been growing increasingly concerned about for some time. Now, from what I've heard from Gavor, it seems that our new guest, Farnor, also has a disconcerting tale for us. As we've none of us had much of a chance to talk so far, may I suggest we start now?'

The door opened and Yatsu and Jaldaric entered. Under Gulda's beady gaze they sat down sheepishly.

'We should start with the Goraidins' Accounting,' Gulda said. 'Then, if they feel up to it, Antyr and Farnor can make their own contribution.'

The various tellings took a long time, not least because both Gulda and Andawyr asked a great many questions. However, so thorough were the Goraidin in their reporting of events that both Antyr and Farnor had little to do other than explain their own parts in the events that had been described: Antyr telling of Ivaroth and the blind man who had controlled him, and Farnor telling of Rannick and the Sierwolf.

When all was finished the room was silent. It was dark outside, the sun having dropped behind the castle wall. As the light had faded, so lamps around the room had slowly blossomed into life.

'Strange, strange, tales,' Gulda said, tapping her stick absently on the floor. 'And disturbing, as you say.'

'You haven't told us why you came back, Memsa,' Hawklan said, asking the question that Andawyr had been wanting to ask throughout.

Gulda shrugged. 'I was drawn here,' she said simply and in a tone that indicated no further explanation would be forthcoming.

Hawklan looked at Andawyr. 'Any conclusions?'

Andawyr shook his head. 'Not yet,' he replied. 'Only a lot more questions. Though I'm even more concerned than I was. Something bad's afoot, but . . .'

'No buts, Andawyr,' Gulda said firmly, banging her stick on the floor, startling everyone. 'Something bad is indeed afoot. You and I need to address these questions now, and at length. There's nothing to be gained by delay.' She stood up. 'I've no doubt the vulgar soldiery here want to get down to some serious reminiscing, and our guests have done all they can for the moment. Loman, could you . . .'

The door opened and a red-faced boy barged into the room. He wove a nimble if breathless way through the seated figures, heading straight to Loman and oblivious of Gulda's basilisk glare.

'The Watch say there are riders coming from the south, Castellan, coming fast.'

Chapter 20

Long-shadowed in the light of the setting sun, a small, shifting crowd stood in front of the castle, waiting for the approaching riders. When they arrived, it was immediately apparent that they had been riding hard for some distance. The horses were exhausted and the riders were in little better shape. Hawklan was at the forefront of the group that ran forward to meet them. Surprise heightened the concern on his face as he recognized the riders.

'Dacu, Tirke! What's the matter?'

The two Goraidin declined help as they dismounted wearily but they gratefully accepted the removal of their steaming horses. Dacu wasted no time in greetings, delivering his message to Hawklan immediately. It was as clear and straight-forward as it was urgent.

'You're needed. We have two men down.'

Only after a brief explanation did he notice the presence of Andawyr and Gulda. Though obviously surprised to see them he made no pause for inquiry, merely bowing respectfully to them both and saying to Andawyr, 'Come yourself, if you can.'

Thus it was that, shortly after their arrival, the two Goraidin, mounted on fresh horses, were moving back down the steep road towards the village. They were accompanied by Hawklan and followed at a distance by Andawyr and Isloman driving a soft-wheeled cart. Despite their fatigue, Dacu and Tirke had restricted their rest and refreshment to the brief interlude while the new horses were saddled and a plunging of their travel-grimed faces into the icy stream that surged up by the Great Gate after an uncharted passage deep beneath the castle.

Passing through Pedhavin, the group turned south and began to ride faster. As they travelled, Dacu and Tirke told Hawklan of all that had happened on their journey through Canol Madreth and Arvenstaat and of their meeting with Atelon. Hawklan listened impassively as the strange tales of Vredech, Thyrn and Pinnatte unfolded.

Though they had powerful Riddin horse lanterns to light their way, they were not able to ride as quickly as the Goraidin had dashed to the castle and it was the middle of the night before a swinging light signalled them into the camp that was their destination.

They were greeted warmly by a fretful Atelon.

'Nertha's with her husband and Pinnatte,' Atelon told Hawklan, speaking softly as if to avoid disturbing anyone. 'Thyrn and Endryk are asleep – they're exhausted. Come to that, so is Nertha, but . . .' He gave a disclaiming shrug.

'She's a healer as well as a wife, Dacu tells me,' Hawklan said. 'Doubly blessed with insomnia, under the circumstances.' He turned to Dacu and Tirke. 'Speaking of which, you two must rest now. You've done well and there's nothing else you can do, at least not until Andawyr and Isloman arrive. Get what sleep you can. Atelon will tend the horses, then he'll sleep too.' Tirke seemed inclined to protest, but Hawklan's raised eyebrow coupled with a nudge from Dacu kept him silent. Atelon bowed slightly, then took the horses.

Nertha emerged from one of the tents. Her face was drawn and anxious in the dancing shadows that an unsettling mixture of flickering firelight and staring lantern light was casting about the camp. Seeing Hawklan, she straightened her jacket, pulled herself erect and came towards him briskly, her hand extended. Hawklan took it and felt immediately the strength of her healer's will vying with the weakness and doubt that were an inevitable consequence of tending someone close.

'Dacu's told me what he knows about your husband and Pinnatte,' he said, leading her back to the tent. 'Which is both a great deal and very little. Has anything changed while they've been away?'

'No,' Nertha replied, her consciously adopted physician's

manner barely managing to keep the tremor out of her voice. 'They're still . . . asleep.'

There had been considerable alarm in the camp when they had been unable to rouse Vredech and Pinnatte. It had been eased more by Nertha's sternly controlled manner than by her diagnosis after she had examined them.

'I don't know what's happened, but the last time my husband was like this – seemingly asleep, but unwakeable – he, or some part of him, was alive and conscious in another place, perhaps another time.' She ruthlessly crushed any debate. 'He told you about it. Now I am. A similar thing's happened to you, Thyrn, hasn't it?' Thyrn nodded but did not speak. He was clutching Endryk's arm like a child. 'I've no explanation,' Nertha went on as if fearful of stopping. 'Seeking reasons is why we're here. When it happened before, he just woke up. I think all we can do now is keep them comfortable and . . . wait.'

Dacu looked at the two apparently sleeping figures and frowned. 'Hearing about such a thing around the camp-fire is one thing, seeing it is . . . unsettling . . . to say the least.' He took refuge in practicalities. Looking around at the camp he said, 'We can't wait here. These mountains are hardly formidable but they're more than enough to kill us. Our supplies won't last indefinitely and if the weather changes we'll be in serious trouble.'

Thus it was that they had spent the day and much of the night continuing their journey, carrying the two prostrated men. The terrain for the most part was too uneven and difficult for the use of horse-drawn litters and it proved necessary to carry Vredech and Pinnatte on hastily rigged stretchers. Though neither man was particularly heavy, it was nevertheless desperate and wearying work. Throughout, their condition did not change and when the group finally stopped and made camp, Dacu decided that after a few hours' sleep he and Tirke should head for Anderras Darion as quickly as they could, to bring help. Atelon and the others were to stay where they were but, as it transpired, they ignored this injunction and, at no small cost to themselves, had made useful further progress northwards by the time the Goraidin returned with Hawklan.

Nertha turned up the light of the lantern as Hawklan examined the two men. Routinely he checked their pulses and various other vital signs, though he judged from what he had both heard about Nertha and concluded from his brief acquaintance with her that nothing untoward would be found.

'They seem simply to be asleep,' he confirmed. 'I can't find anything other than the normal stresses and strains I'd expect to find in people who've been travelling for a long time. In fact, they're so relaxed I'd say they were dreaming, except their eyes aren't moving.'

'My husband says he doesn't dream,' Nertha said absently.

Hawklan took Pinnatte's injured hand. 'This is peculiar, though. It's almost as if it's part of something else, something . . . beyond him.' He shook his head thoughtfully. 'Still, they don't seem to be in any danger.'

'Not here, anyway,' Nertha said, watching Hawklan's face intently. 'They *are* somewhere else, though, I'm sure.'

'Yes. So Dacu's told me,' Hawklan replied. He saw her eyes testing his doubt. 'I'm a healer, like you,' he said. 'There are a great many things I don't understand, but I've learned to accept what is, however odd or frightening. It's a strange tale, I'll admit, but I've heard stranger.' He gave a soft, self-deprecating laugh that seemed to warm the tent. 'In fact, I've been in stranger.'

His brow furrowed, then, on an impulse, he knelt down between the two bodies and placed his hands on their foreheads. 'You are safe and watched-over here,' he said. 'Do not be afraid. All is well. All will be well.'

Then he stood up. 'There's nothing we can do now that you haven't already done. There's a cart following behind us. We'll get them to Anderras Darion as quickly as we can. There're more facilities, more knowledge, more everything there. In the meantime, you should sleep.'

Nertha shook her head. 'I belong here.'

'You've done all you can, you know that,' Hawklan said. 'I'll be here and I'll wake you if anything happens.' Nertha's face became uncertain.

'If you're needed you'll be needed rested and strong,' Hawklan insisted.

250

Nertha looked at him earnestly, then came a little nearer to the point of capitulation. 'You're probably right,' she admitted. 'But I may as well stay with you. Needing sleep and being able to are two different matters.'

'I understand,' he said. 'Allow me.'

Without waiting for permission and with a movement that was as swift as it was easy, he passed his hand slowly over Nertha's face, then caught her as she fell.

'You always did have a way with women, didn't you?'

It was Dar-volci, greeting Hawklan as he carried Nertha out of the tent, her head cradled on his shoulder.

'Good to see you, rock eater,' Hawklan acknowledged. 'Though it seems I can't let you wander off on your own for more than a few days without you turning the world upside down. Which is her tent?'

Settling Nertha and checking that everyone else in the camp was asleep, Hawklan placed a signal lantern to guide Isloman and Andawyr, then sat down by the fire. He threw a handful of small branches onto it and watched the sparks scurrying up into the night sky. Dar-volci curled up opposite him.

'What do you make of this?' Hawklan asked the felci.

'Nothing good. Sumeral's taking shape again, somewhere, and He's struggling to return.'

Hawklan felt as though he had been suddenly plunged into icy water. For an instant he could hear nothing but his own heartbeat, and his vision was filled with Dar-volci's triangular head. The felci's mouth was moving. 'Arash-Felloren stinks of His presence.' A matter-of-fact tone helped draw Hawklan out of his shock and back from the memories of the war that were suddenly threatening to overwhelm him. 'It must have been one of His citadels once – ancient, corrupted roots. And those damned Kyrosdyn nearly brought Him back, using Pinnatte.' He chattered his teeth angrily, then scratched himself. He was silent for a moment. 'You know, I'm not so sure that mightn't have been a bad thing, now I look back on it.' The expression in Hawklan's eyes turned from shock to incredulity, but he said nothing. 'Whatever the Kyrosdyn had turned Pinnatte into, it was unstable. Very unstable. It couldn't have lasted. How it ever came to be defeats me.' Dar-volci's tone became

251

briefly ironic. 'Andawyr would probably be able to show you a calculation proving it these days, but all you needed to feel it was to be there. Ask Atelon. I think if He'd taken Pinnatte's body it might have doomed Him utterly. Still, ever impetuous, we went and leapt to the rescue, didn't we? And Pinnatte's a nice enough lad in his way.'

Hawklan was hoping he would be able to accuse the felci of playing some dark, mocking fantasy for him, but it was patently not so. Even Dar-volci's sense of humour was not so dark. Hawklan dropped his head into his hands and shook it slowly. It was some time before he could speak.

'You talk about it very casually. I can hardly bear even to think it.' He looked up into the night sky, after the fleeing sparks. His face was pained. 'It can't be true, surely, Dar? You've made a mistake. How can He return?' He knew the questions were futile. Dar-volci would not have spoken as he had without being certain. Nevertheless Hawklan had to ask them. They were part of his way towards acceptance. 'At least, so soon after He was . . . destroyed. There were countless generations between the First and the Second Comings.'

Dar-volci allowed no relief. 'We don't know how long He'd been in Narsindal before we learned about Him, do we? It was Oklar's folly that exposed Him, not our vigilance. Nor do we know what brought Him back or in what form He came. But Derras Ustramel wasn't built and the Uhriel weren't resurrected and sent out to infest the world in any short span.' The felci's summary was coldly accurate. It was not new. The manner and moment of Sumeral's return had been the subject of much debate amongst the Fyordyn and their allies after the war. It could not be otherwise for, however and whenever it had happened, it was a devastating measure of their failure in their ancient responsibilities.

Hawklan stared silently into the fire.

'It can't be, it can't be,' he said, more a plea than a statement. 'All those people killed. Every kind of suffering. Suffering that's still with us – endless consequences. I doubt there's anyone who was involved who doesn't have some memory of the war return to them every day. We couldn't fight Him again, not like that. It was supposed to be over. He was destroyed before He gained His full strength. He destroyed Himself. Scattered Himself who knows where?'

'Precisely,' Dar-volci said. 'Who knows where? From the very beginning no one ever knew what He was, where He came from, or why He was the way He was. All that even Ethriss knew was that, like himself, He had come from the beginning – the Great Searing. That, and the fact that He would return, though he never said how he knew that. I suspect he just guessed. But return He did. And He's coming yet again if we don't find a way to stop Him.'

Hawklan's thoughts flailed. 'Perhaps you and Atelon defeating Him in Arash-Felloren may have destroyed Him.'

Dar-volci shook his head. 'We thwarted Him, that's all. I sensed no destruction. And the destruction of such a thing I'd have felt, I know. Now, in addition to what happened to us, we have Vredech's experience. Dacu's told you, I presume?'

Hawklan nodded. 'His friend – Cassraw, was it? – was possessed by something and tried to possess others through some kind of demented religion . . .'

Dar-volci interrupted him, his manner emphatic. 'Always His favourite way, religion, you know that. The easy way. Ignorance masquerading as certainty. Endless opportunities for all manner of horrors when that kind of claptrap's poured into the minds of the weak and the gullible.' He uttered a low whistle. 'You're easily led, you creatures. Then there's what happened to Thyrn. These things aren't coincidences.'

'You think Thyrn has been touched by Him also?' Hawklan said warily. 'That it was Sumeral who took possession of this man who employed him?' He searched for the name.

Dar-volci found it for him. 'Vashnar. Some kind of high-ranking government official.' He stretched, then curled up again. The tension in his voice was replaced by thoughtfulness. 'I don't know about Thyrn. What happened to him feels similar but very different at the same time. Whatever it was that possessed this Vashnar character used the Power, if Thyrn's description is to be trusted – and it is, as you'll learn when you get to know him. But there's something in the way he talks

about it. It's because he's a Caddoran, I suppose. He repro-
duces what he's heard with great subtlety. It's remarkable. You
must have him tell his own tale to you personally, you'll
understand what I mean then. When I listen to him talk about
Vashnar and the power . . . the entity . . . whatever it was that
was driving him, I get the feeling of something . . . truly
ancient . . . something that perhaps comes from a time before
the Great Searing. It's very odd. Very disturbing. I can't put my
claw on what it is but I can't shake it off.'

Dar-volci was not normally given to uncertainty and his
hesitation added to Hawklan's unease. He risked an element
of levity in his reply. 'You can attend to that, then. You felcis
are supposed to come from a time before the Great Searing,
aren't you?' he said, unclear himself whether he was being
serious or not.

'We do,' Dar-volci replied flatly. 'Or our line does, to be
more accurate.' His half-closed eyes opened suddenly, bright,
wide and challenging. 'How do we know such a thing, you
ask? It's buried deep in the spiralling knowledge that lies at
the heart of every least part of us.' Then he responded to
Hawklan's need, becoming ironic again. 'But I'm afraid we
don't have it written on a piece of paper somewhere to show
everyone,' he said, his manner heavily confidential.

Hawklan laughed, grateful for the humour, though it served
only to dispel briefly the darkness into which Dar-volci's
original analysis has plunged him. As he pondered it now he
saw that, in many ways, it was a darkness that had perhaps
been growing since the war itself. It was quite separate from
the pain and the suffering he had seen and tended. That was
something he had been able both to accept and yet detach
himself from. That was a necessary part of his lot as a healer.
This was different. It was unclear, ill-formed. It came from
another place within him and it hung around the words that
Sumeral had spoken to him as, Ethriss's Black Sword in his
hand, he had run along the causeway across Lake Kedrieth
and towards the mist-shrouded fortress of Derras Ustramel to
destroy this returned abomination.

'*Greatest of my Uhriel,*' He had called him.

Whenever this memory returned to him, he was running

again on that dank and empty causeway with no sounds about him other than his own soft footfalls and the icy lapping of the lake. A coldness had possessed him as Sumeral's voice had rung through him, as beautiful as it was fearful.

'*Greatest of my Uhriel.*'

Every part of him had screamed out in denial. This could not be so! Had not Ethriss's own hand snatched him from the point of death on an ancient battlefield of the First Coming to bring him to face Sumeral in this time?

'*That hand was mine, Hawklan. Ethriss spared none of his creations. I saw your true worth and took you to be mine when I should rise again.*'

Soul-shaking words.

'*See your inheritance and deny it if you can.*'

Then had come His vision of Ethriss's world and those beyond, and how they were to be remade in His image. Flawless, perfect, without the least impairment. Even now, it lingered hauntingly in Hawklan's thoughts, though he rarely spoke of it. He seemed to have no ability to go beyond it, to question it. It was there. Finished. A totality.

And with the memory came another. One that racked him. Numbed by Sumeral's revelation, and tempted by His words, he had let slip the Black Sword. '*Ethriss's cruel goad.*' That had been a deed of the profoundest folly, he had come to believe, though any reason for this certainty was denied him. He needed no sword in this now-peaceful world, and even if he should there were countless in the Armoury at Anderras Darion that would serve him perfectly well. Yet something that was a part of him had been lost.

He felt his hand opening and the Sword tumbling from it. It could only have fallen into that grey, cold lake, surely? But he remembered it falling for ever, through the darkness, falling, falling, until a ringing chime had signalled . . . what? He tried to rationalize what he had heard. There had been so many other sounds dinning through that dank Narsindal greyness as Sumeral and his great fortress had been destroyed. It could not have been as he remembered it. Yet . . .

'At the lakeside again?' Dar-volci's voice shattered his reverie.

'Despite your denials, I still think you read minds,' Hawklan replied, looking up.

Dar-volci shook his head. 'I prefer both depth and quality in my reading.'

He spat into the fire.

'Bad taste in your mouth?'

'At the lakeside again,' Dar-volci said sourly.

'Do you think we'll ever leave it?'

Dar-volci's firelit eyes glinted at him. 'I left it that same day,' he said. 'I only go back because you're still there.' He shook his head with an irritated growl and spat into the fire again.

Hawklan bowed apologetically. 'I'm sorry,' he said. 'But I value your company.' Then he heard himself saying, 'I shouldn't have dropped the Sword.'

For a timeless moment, there was nothing anywhere save the man and the felci by the fire, hovering in a universe of absolute silence. Dar-volci slowly inclined his head.

'Well, well, well. It's taken you some time to say that, hasn't it?'

Hawklan let out a long breath. There was a feeling inside him such as a vast and still ocean might know as the unseen forces holding it imperceptibly eased past a point of balance and turned its smooth rippled equilibrium from ebb to flow.

'I think you may be right,' he said.

'You're not contemplating sending another batch of poor volunteers out to plumb that foul lake, are you?'

Hawklan hurriedly disclaimed that notorious enterprise. 'Fortunately that was never my idea. Besides wherever it is, it's not there, I'm sure of that now. It's gone as mysteriously as it came.'

Dar-volci turned towards the tent where Vredech and Pinnatte were lying. 'Somewhere else, eh? Like our two friends, perhaps? Maybe they'll come across it for you.'

A companionable silence settled between the two.

Dar-volci eventually broke it. 'Do you ever have the feeling that at some deep level everything is coming apart, unravelling?'

Hawklan gave him a perplexed look.

256

Dar-volci stood up and shook himself. 'It doesn't matter. Just a fancy. I'm sure if anything's amiss, it'll show itself soon enough.'

'Andawyr says he feels things are not so much coming apart as coming together,' Hawklan said. 'You, Atelon, Thyrn, all the others, suddenly appearing with your frightening stories is going to give him even more to think about.'

'Andawyr's at Anderras Darion?'

Hawklan catalogued. 'And Yatsu and Jaldaric. And Yengar, Olvric, Jenna, Yrain. All of them, like you, with unusual guests. *And* Gulda!'

Dar-volci was sitting on his haunches. He emitted a series of excited whistles. 'Do tell, dear boy,' he said, imitating Gavor. Then he cocked his head sharply on one side and muttered something under his breath.

'Don't bother, they're here.'

'Don't be afraid,' Vredech said.

'Hush' came the urgent reply.

No sun was to be seen and the sky rang with a dark and peculiar blue. Beneath it was a harsh and rugged landscape. Blue-in-black shadows shaped out a curving line of jagged peaks and crags that lowered over a wide plain. Stretching to a blue-echoing horizon, it was cracked and split by deep ravines, which gave it the look of something dead and long decayed.

Vredech did not know why he had said, 'Don't be afraid,' because he was very afraid himself. A habit brought with him from his pastoral duties, doubtless, he decided. Trying to bring comfort even though he saw cause for none.

He and Pinnatte were standing near the top of a broad col which rose up on either side of them to buttress sharp and cruel peaks. Where they were, how they had come there, how long they had been there were mysteries to him. He had gone to bed quite normally, then, abruptly, without any sense of change that he could recall, he had been here, Pinnatte crouching by him.

Pinnatte's instincts, as a street thief, had been to remain still and silent in the face of an unexpected development until he

257

could properly assess it. For danger there was here, he was sure. He too had found himself in this place without any recollection of how he came there.

He peered through the heavy blue twilight, seeking some clue in the mysterious and unpleasant terrain. But there was nothing. Yet, he realized, he was more himself here, more the Pinnatte who had flitted through the crowded streets and byways of Arash-Felloren, confident, sure-footed, ever watchful for both opportunity and danger. Gone was the haziness that seemed to have come between his mind and his speech since the Kyrosdyn had started their damned experiments with him. It was good.

'If I didn't dream, I'd say this was one,' he said softly.

'I don't dream either,' Vredech said. 'And wherever this place is, it's real. This kind of thing has happened to me before.'

'What has?'

'This moving to . . . other places . . . without warning. I don't understand it. One of the reasons I was going to Anderras Darion was to find out about it. At one stage I thought I was going mad.'

'Perhaps we've both gone mad,' Pinnatte said.

Vredech shook his head and laid a reassuring hand on Pinnatte's arm. 'There's no madness here. Not in us, anyway.'

Releasing Pinnatte, he put his hand to his face. Although no wind was blowing, there was a sensation on his face as though one were.

'Your hands are shaking,' Pinnatte said. 'I thought you said this had happened to you before.'

'I didn't say I enjoyed it or that I wasn't afraid,' Vredech replied. He looked around. 'And I was never anywhere like this. No clouds, no sun, no stars, this place is like nothing I could have even imagined.'

'And the air smells funny.'

'Acrid,' Vredech agreed. 'Like a smithy, burning metal, but cold instead of hot.'

'How do we get back?' Pinnatte asked hesitantly.

'When it's happened before I've found myself back where I was, just as unexpectedly as I . . . left,' Vredech said, though he knew there was no comfort in the words. He closed his eyes. Faintly he could feel another part of him, lying in the tent. Nertha was watching over him. But how indeed to get back there? Pinnatte's question started a panic mounting that took him some effort to control. There was nothing he could do. Nothing except wait. He passed his conclusion on to his companion.

Pinnatte was rubbing his hand. 'Do you think it's something to do with what the Kyrosdyn did to me?'

'I've no idea, I . . .'

'Look.' Pinnatte was pointing.

Vredech followed his hand, reaching out over the fractured plain.

'I can't see anything.'

'There, look.' Pinnatte jabbed the air in emphasis.

Vredech blinked, then narrowed his eyes in an attempt to penetrate the all-pervading blue light.

As he saw the figures, so the sound of them reached him.

Chapter 21

It was no welcoming hail. High-pitched, tearing and cruel, it cut through Vredech and Pinnatte as it cut through the acrid blue air. Both men brought their hands to their ears to keep out the awful sound, but to no avail. It seemed to Vredech that the mountains themselves quivered and rang at its touch. Pinnatte dropped low. Feeling doubly exposed, Vredech followed him. Crouching side by side, they watched the approaching figures.

Apart from the difficulties posed by the light, they were too far away for any detail to be seen, save that they were riding and that there were three of them with one leading and two following on either side. They maintained their stations so meticulously and kept to so straight a line that they had the appearance of an arrowhead as they moved across the plain. Both Vredech and Pinnatte gasped as the three riders jumped over a wide ravine without changing either speed or formation.

'Who are they?' Pinnatte whispered.

Alarm made Vredech's reply irritable. 'I told you, I've never been here. I've no idea who they are – or what.'

Pinnatte ignored his tone. His instincts spoke. 'I think we should keep away from them.'

Another cry reached them. It was joined by others, screeching and frightening. Though he could detect nothing intelligible in the sound, the hairs on Vredech's arms rose in response. A ghastly conversation was being held. 'Yes,' he said. 'That's probably a good idea. They don't sound particularly hospitable.'

'They sound terrifying,' Pinnatte corrected him, his eyes

wide. 'I'm glad we're halfway up a mountain.' He pointed to some rocks nearby and, following his unspoken command, he and Vredech slipped silently into their lee. 'This feels a bit better,' Pinnatte whispered as Vredech joined him. 'We can watch them from here.'

The noises stopped.

'Keep quiet, keep still!' Pinnatte said urgently. It was another command, but although the figures were a considerable distance away, Vredech did not feel inclined to dispute it. Though there was silence now, the cries still seemed to be ringing through him. They stirred such darkness within him that it was all he could do to stop himself from praying.

Where was this place? And how had he and Pinnatte come here? Or, for that matter, why? That was a bad question. He shied away from it and closed his eyes again to reach out for the part of him that he could feel lying safely under the watchful eye of his wife. It was still there, though there was something strange and confused about it now . . .

Pinnatte was shaking him, returning him to this eerie blue world.

The figures had come to a halt. They were standing side by side, completely motionless. Vredech found he was holding his breath. This place was unnaturally quiet, he realized. There was not even a hint of the susurration of distant tumbling streams and the blowing of the wind through low cols and around high peaks that was always present in the mountains. It was as though the peaks themselves were standing in fearful obeisance to these new arrivals.

Or were they too perhaps trying to avoid their attention?

Vredech forced out a gulping breath. *Relax*, he ordered himself. This predicament was strange enough without letting his imagination overwhelm him.

Then, with a slowness that was as unnatural as the silence draping down from the waiting mountains, the figures were moving again, this time behind one another. Very gradually, the gap between them increased and the line began to turn until they were equally spaced and moving in a wide circle. Soft mewlings reached Pinnatte and Vredech, but for all their softness they were as disturbingly unpleasant as the screams

262

that had first announced the arrival of the figures.

Like hunting creatures trying to lure out a shy prey, Vredech thought.

A further pattern was emerging. While the riders maintained their respective positions, the circle was slowly shrinking. At the same time they were increasing their speed. Unsettling in its precision, it became a giddying and hypnotic sight that seemed to stretch time itself for the two watchers.

The cries that accompanied this taut and inward spiralling changed in harmony with it, rising and falling in a broken, uneven rhythm, like a rasping incantation. Vredech leaned forward and narrowed his eyes. There was something at the centre of the circle, he was sure – something forming.

'Be careful,' Pinnatte whispered, drawing him back.

'Can you see what they're riding around?' Vredech asked.

Pinnatte squinted in his turn. 'No,' he replied then, 'There might be a light or something. Moving about. I can't see properly through this blue air.'

A wave of sound broke over them in an unexpected and jangling climax, making them both start. Then, as sharply as though a sword had cut through it, it stopped.

The sudden cessation was as jolting as the first hearing. Vredech shook his head. Were the sounds still reverberating in his ears, nothing more than a physical response, like the images that linger in the eyes after looking at too bright a light, or were they real? Echoes of the riders' cries leaking down to him as they resonated from peak to peak, carrying their message to the farthest extremities of this bleak place. Pinnatte too was shaking his head as though to clear it, but neither of them spoke. They renewed their observation of the distant figures.

Still now, the three riders were standing side by side again. In front of them, Vredech could see a vague haziness. It was moving fitfully from side to side. As though held there against its will, Vredech thought. And it was twisting and turning, he was sure. It had the quality of the elusive shapes that flit across the resting eye, at once real and unreal, and though Vredech could see it, he could not focus on it nor even, he realized, judge exactly where it was. Was it just an illusion?

He blinked deliberately to see if it would move in response. For an instant he was close to the riders and peering into the growing light. It was like a rift in the blue reality of this place. And there was something within it, beyond it . . .

Then the cries were ringing about the mountains again, triumphant and malevolent, and he was crouching back down behind his distant shelter.

'Are you all right?' Pinnatte was asking. The street thief was holding his arm and looking at him anxiously.

Vredech nodded. 'Yes. Just felt a little dizzy, that's all.'

'It's the smell of this place,' Pinnatte diagnosed, wrinkling his face to mark his own distress. 'It's setting my teeth on edge. And this damned light. It makes it difficult to see anything clearly. And it feels as though it's shining right through me. As though I'm drowning in it . . . or not really here.'

The riders' voices silenced him. Though still unintelligible they were obviously in a state of great excitement. Their ordered line had broken up and their mounts were rearing and kicking. Gone was all sign of the obsessive symmetry that had marked their approach and their circling of the light. As he watched them, something else disturbed Vredech. The movements of the horses were alien and strange.

Almost serpentine, he concluded. He let the thought pass and turned his attention back to the light that seemed to be the source of the riders' celebration. It was no clearer to him than before, shifting and wavering erratically, though, at times, it moved to the pattern of the riders' cries. Then their tone was different. Excitement was mounting, tilting now towards frenzy. One of the riders moved directly towards the light. It shifted and changed as he reached it as if trying to avoid him, and the cries reaching Vredech and Pinnatte became a mixture of shrieking defiance and frantic urging.

The two other riders joined their fellow in this mysterious assault, but each time the first rider reached it, some unseen force turned him away.

'What are they doing?' Pinnatte asked, but Vredech waved him silent. Something about the unfolding scene was reaching deep inside him, shaking him, pounding him. It was both

264

obscene and terrifying. Abruptly, he turned and vomited.

Pinnatte let out a hissing exclamation filled as much with alarm and disgust as concern.

'I'm sorry,' Vredech said, leaning back against the rock and wiping his hand across his now clammy forehead. 'I don't know what . . .'

Something had changed. Another sound was echoing through the mountains. It was full of despair and fury. Turning, Vredech saw its cause immediately.

The light was changing, slowly both shrinking and fading into the all-pervading blue of this strange place. For a while it faltered, growing fitfully as the pitch of the cries rose, looking set to return, then falling back again, smaller each time.

Its fate was inevitable, Vredech saw, though he could not have said why. No urging from the three riders could forestall it.

As it finally disappeared he turned away and covered his ears against the raging cacophony that he knew would follow. Pinnatte did the same.

They remained thus for a long time, then both were suddenly aware of silence around them again. Looking up, they saw that the three riders were standing silent and motionless again, equally spaced about a circle centred on the vanished light and facing where it had been. Vredech could feel a tension mounting that was far more menacing than anything he had felt before. Both he and Pinnatte stayed very still. It was not difficult: the mountains themselves seemed to be awaiting some decision.

'They know we're here,' Pinnatte whispered, very softly. His eyes were wide and he was shaking.

'No,' Vredech said, rubbing his leaden stomach. 'They can't. They're too far away.' But even as he spoke he heard the lie in his own words. Nothing could be hidden for long on this desolate, ringing blue world. Some insight told him that each part of this place touched all others.

A solitary, almost coaxing cry rose up from the plain. Its unsteady tones rang round the trembling peaks like the keening of a hunting falcon. Vredech and Pinnatte both held their breaths as the eerie sound folded around them, echoing and fragmenting on the rocks that sheltered them before coming together again and swooping treacherously back down to the riders.

Pinnatte's shaking infected Vredech. *They can't see us, they can't see us*, he repeated inwardly, over and over, as if repetition might make it so.

Another cry came. Harsher and taunting. Again the mountains carried the message and returned an answer.

Vredech saw Pinnatte's hand close about a large stone. He tried to find a reassurance which a glance of the eyes might communicate to the young man, but could not. Though he had found himself in other worlds before, none of them had been as strange and disconcerting as this, and his leaving them had always been as involuntary as his arriving. Whatever it was about him that allowed such things was beyond his control. Should he be angry and frightened in order to carry himself and Pinnatte out of here? Or relaxed and calm? He did not know. He was helpless.

A third cry reached them, goading and confident.

The three riders began to move.

'They're coming for us,' Pinnatte said.

'You don't know that,' Vredech tried.

Pinnatte looked at him, almost scornfully. 'I know when people are looking for me. I've known it all my life. That's why I haven't been caught very often.' He became urgent and practical. 'We need to get back where we came from, find a better hiding place, or get ready to deal those three.'

'I don't know how to leave this place,' Vredech said, doing his best to hold Pinnatte's gaze.

'Well, whoever they are, I don't want to meet them face to face,' Pinnatte retorted, without any hint of reproach at this admission.

Vredech glanced down at the approaching riders. 'They're not hurrying,' he said. 'And they'll never get horses up here.'

Pinnatte was less sanguine. 'I don't know about the horses, but if they're not hurrying it's because they don't have to. It's not a good sign.'

With a grimace, Vredech bowed before the young man's greater experience in such matters.

'That leaves us with finding a hiding place,' he said. 'Or perhaps running.'

Pinnatte looked around desperately. 'It's not my kind of country. I'm used to streets and alleys and lots of noise and people.'

Vredech too was searching the terrain. He still clung faintly to the hope that the riders would not be able to make what looked to be a long and difficult climb to reach them.

A mocking cry circled around them. Pinnatte clamped his hands over his ears.

'They don't care what we do,' he said, breathing heavily and obviously struggling to retain control of himself. 'I've had to deal with people like that before. This is their place, their territory. All of it. Wherever we go, they'll find us, and there's nothing we can do about it.' He seized Vredech's arm. 'Are you sure you can't get us back?'

'I told you, I don't know how,' Vredech snapped, snatching his arm free.

Pinnatte put his hand to his face momentarily, then swore and began scrabbling about, gathering more stones.

'Perhaps we can talk to them,' Vredech said weakly. 'Perhaps we're worrying unnecessarily. Maybe they can help us find a way back.'

Pinnatte was openly scornful. 'Use your ears, man,' he said. 'That's not some clerk and his family out for a quiet evening's ride. I don't know what they are. I'm not even sure they're people, making a noise like that. But they're bad, that I do know.' He waved an encompassing arm. 'And look at this place. Anything that lives here is going to be like nothing either of us have ever met.' He thrust some rocks into Vredech's hand. 'I don't suppose you can fight either, can you?'

Vredech toyed with the stones nervously. Irregular and jagged, with sharp edges and many facets, they were unlike any stones he had ever seen before.

'You suppose right,' he said. 'I'm a Preaching Brother, not a warrior.' He glanced down again at the riders. They were still making the same unhurried progress. Almost as if they had seen him watching, a rasping cry greeted him. It was a

267

chilling sound and it gave Pinnatte's remarks a grim validity. 'But if we get caught, we still try talking before using these,' he said sternly, rattling the stones in front of Pinnatte's face. 'If we start throwing first we'll only have one option then.'

Pinnatte paused and thought for a moment, then nodded and returned to gathering his ammunition. Vredech looked again at where they were. Born amongst mountains, this ought to be more his kind of country that it was Pinnatte's but it did not help. There was a newness about this place, a harsh violence, that was quite different from the age-sculpted landscape of Canol Madreth. Sheer rock faces swept up to improbable peaks and ridges that looked as sharp as crystal and which seemed to be striving to tear down the sky itself. Like the stones that Pinnatte had given him there was nothing about them that indicated the touch of wind or rain or any of the rigours of an endless parade of summers and winters. And, too, there was a barren monotony, a deadness, about the place that weighed on him and that he could not properly identify.

In front of them – the way the riders would have to come – was a rough slope that, reassuringly, fell quickly out of sight. On either side of them the ground swept up with increasing steepness to high peaks and offered nothing but more exposure and no escape. To their rear, the ground rose a little to the top of the col.

'You wait here. I'm going to have a look over the top,' he whispered to Pinnate. 'There might be somewhere to hide on the other side. Or we might be able to lay a false trail.'

'No!' Pinnatte exclaimed anxiously, seizing his arm again. 'We came here together, we must stay together. I don't want you going over there, then suddenly, *poof*, you're gone and I'm left here on my own.'

'Or the other way round, for that matter,' Vredech said soberly. 'We'll go together, then.'

Another glance told him that the riders would soon be out of sight beneath the curve of the slope. As they finally disappeared, he and Pinnatte set off up the short scramble to the top of the col. It did not take them long. Pinnatte was nimble, Vredech was mountain-bred, and both were frightened.

In so far as he had expected anything, Vredech had

assumed that the col would leave him at the top of a slope down into another valley, and, he hoped, with choices to make. It was thus with a cry of outright terror that he came to a sudden halt, swaying precariously on the very edge of a vertical drop. Indeed, he might have fallen had not Pinnatte, a few paces behind him, hastily seized his jacket and dragged him roughly backwards.

It was some time before either of them recovered sufficiently to talk coherently.

'I'm all right,' Vredech gasped several times, patting Pinnatte's supporting arm with an urgency which showed quite clearly that he was not. Pinnatte returned the reassurance, then eased himself forward on his stomach to peer over the edge into the dark blue void that had nearly taken his companion. Not unused to the rooftops of Arash-Felloren, he prided himself that he was unafraid of heights. This, however, was different. The edge was as abrupt and clean as that of any man-made wall, and the rock face that fell away from it plunged giddyingly into an unseeable blue darkness that seemed to reach up into Pinnatte as he involuntarily drew in a sharp breath. With an effort, he forced himself to look from side to side. The edge curved away, fading into the same impenetrable shadow. The view disorientated him, not least, he realized, because though there was the darkness of shadow to be seen everywhere, there was no sun to cast it, nor any other light than the pervading blueness.

Even more carefully than he had approached it, Pinnatte pushed himself away from the edge and rejoined Vredech.

Though still breathing heavily, Vredech was more himself. He was looking upwards at the surrounding peaks and gesturing for silence. Pinnatte became still. As he did so he became aware of a faint whining all around them. It tinged the bitter air mockingly.

'My cry,' Vredech said, his face pained and fretful. 'Echoing and echoing. If they didn't know we were here before, they do now.' His lip curled into an uncharacteristic snarl. 'These mountains must carry every sound as far as they reach. They're like nothing I've ever known.'

'I gathered that, the way you nearly ran over that edge,' Pinnatte retorted acidly.

An unexpected touch of humour in his manner cut through Vredech's frustration and anger and drew a soft, snorting chuckle out of him. As if in confirmation of his estimation of the treachery of the mountains, the sound bubbled up to join the fading echoes of his cry, shaking and disturbing them. But, too, something was lifted from him. Nothing had changed about their predicament, and his heart was still pounding from his near accident but he felt a little lighter.

'It seems we've nowhere to go but down – towards our hosts,' he said, standing up shakily. Pinnatte's eyes widened. 'Well, have we?' Vredech pressed, before he could voice any protest.

'I . . . I suppose not,' Pinnatte stammered. 'But . . .'

Vredech laid an earnest hand on his shoulder. 'They come up one way, we go down another,' he said.

'And if there's only one way up and one way down?'

Vredech shrugged. 'Then we meet them a little sooner, that's all.'

'But . . .'

'Come on!' Vredech tugged Pinnatte's arm encouragingly and set off down the slope. They had only gone a few paces when Pinnatte looked down at his hand and swore.

Vredech turned to see the young man sucking his hand and then spitting.

'What's the matter?' he asked.

'I've cut myself, that's all. Everything's so sharp.'

Vredech quickly examined the cut. It was at the base of the thumb and though it was not deep it was very fine and bleeding quite profusely. Pinnatte sucked on it and spat again, splattering an uneven purple stain on the ground. Vredech unearthed a kerchief and bound the hand. 'It looks clean,' he said. 'Just keep this tight if you can.' Then he looked at his own hands. There were one or two thin scratches there that he had no recollection of receiving but none of them was bleeding. It was a timely warning, he thought. Every edge in this place did seem to be relentlessly sharp. Another cruel difference between here and the mountains he knew.

As they reached the place where they had first found themselves, Vredech paused, trying to estimate which way the riders might be coming. With nothing to guide him, however, he opted for what looked to be the easiest way. Pinnatte followed him without question.

With his recent experience still vividly in his mind, Vredech moved very slowly, peering intently ahead and placing every step with exaggerated care. Occasionally, an exchange of high-pitched cries would well up to let them know that the riders were still nearby and, presumably, still searching for them. Each time this happened, they stopped, momentarily paralysed by the sounds, but now they had decided on a course of action, however futile it might prove to be, Vredech found that he was greeting the cries of their pursuers with a growing defiance. Gradually, however, and as he had feared, the slope became steeper and the choice of ways down more problematical, forcing them to move with increasing caution. Though the sides of the mountain were covered with sheets of tumbled rocks and boulders, these were sharp-edged and viciously spiked like miniatures of the peaks towering above them, a clamouring family scrabbling at the knees of their parents. And, too, it was not easy to see in the blue light, nor breathe easily in the clinging unpleasantness of the sour air.

They halted in the lee of a large rock to catch their breath.

'We don't seem to be any nearer the bottom,' Pinnatte said unhappily as he looked first up, then down the slope.

'We've come quite a way,' Vredech reassured him. 'It's just that mountains are bigger than you think. You tend to lose your sense of size and distance. What seems to be no more than an hour or so's walk away takes half a day.'

'Well, at least we'll all be on foot,' Pinnatte said, gazing round. 'I mightn't know much about mountains, but no horse I've ever seen could walk across this. It's hard enough with two good feet and two good hands.' As he looked down at his hands he turned over the one that the Sierwolf had crushed and began examining it closely. 'Your wife thought she could bring some use back to this, didn't she?' he said, softly, as though to himself. 'I'd like that. She's got a way with her, your wife.'

Pinnatte's harsh city accent gave the compliment an edge that prompted Vredech to give him a sidelong look despite their circumstances. Pinnatte caught it. He stammered. 'I meant . . . she's kind . . . clever. Atelon saved my life when this thing was festering – burning me up – but I don't think he even thought about how it could be made to work again.'

He leaned forward and took Vredech's arm in a powerful grip. 'If we get out of here – get back to the camp – and my head's choked up with . . . cobwebs . . . again, tell her "Thank you". Tell her, yes, I want my hand back, if she can do it. I'll do whatever she says. Tell her – tell all of them . . .' He tapped his head. 'I'm in here. I'm listening, I'm learning. And I'm grateful.'

Vredech was taken aback by this passionate outburst. 'I will,' he managed to say, but Pinnatte had not finished. He bared his teeth. 'And tell them I'm angry, too. Angry at what those foul crystal meddlers did to me. I might have been precious little use to anyone as a street thief, but I didn't deserve that. And I don't deserve this either. I . . .'

Vredech reached out and put his hand over Pinnatte's mouth gently.

'I understand,' he said urgently. 'I understand. And I'll make sure everyone else does when we get back. And it *is* "when" we get back, not "if". Do *you* understand?'

Pinnatte's nodded reply was interrupted by a paean of triumphant shrieking high above them. Both men started violently, so abrupt and awful was the noise. Instinctively they flattened themselves against the sheltering rock. Vredech's defiance faltered as his protestation about their ultimate destination felt empty and futile in his suddenly dry throat.

'How did they get above us?' Pinnatte whispered.

'As you said, this is their place,' Vredech replied as he began to recover from the shock. Though, even as he spoke, he realized he could not properly answer Pinnatte's question. It did not seem possible that anything could have clambered up this slope so quickly.

'More to the point is why do they sound like that? As if they've found something they've been searching for.'

'Probably because they have,' Pinnatte replied tersely. 'Perhaps they weren't after us at all.'

Vredech looked at him unhappily. There was logic in what he was saying, but every part of him denied it. The riders were searching for them, and the triumph in their calls did not bode well.

'Do we stay or do we run?' he asked.

'Run,' Pinnatte said without a pause.

Not that anything approaching running seemed possible, but they immediately moved away from the sheltering rock and continued their painstaking descent.

The shrieking above them continued, first one voice, then another, rising and falling. A debate was being held. A leisurely debate, Vredech thought. Just as they had moved across the plain, so the pursuers were moving towards their prey quite unhurriedly. Though nothing in their cries was intelligible, their general tenor was unequivocal: there was nowhere for Vredech and Pinnatte to go, nowhere to hide, nowhere in this entire terrible place.

As if giving a blessing to this conclusion, a low, moaning cry of satisfaction folded around them.

They stopped and turned at the same time.

Above them, on the rock they had been sheltering under, black against the dark blue sky, and still mounted, stood the three figures.

Chapter 22

Both Pinnatte and Vredech looked around, but flight still did not seem possible across this vicious terrain. Vredech became aware of Pinnatte slowly reaching into his pocket.

'Talk first,' he reminded him, quietly but urgently.

Pinnatte stopped moving but his hand remained in his pocket.

Not that Vredech had much confidence that talking would make any impression on the new arrivals. Though they were motionless, the three figures had a powerful and menacing presence and there was an aura about them which more than confirmed Pinnatte's remark that this was *their* place.

Then they were moving and a further fearful quality was added to the scene. For though their mounts appeared to be horses, there were differences that transformed them into obscene caricatures: a subtle harshness to their lines; malevolent, almost glowing eyes; hooves that looked like claws; too-long heads on too-long necks that swayed unpleasantly as if to some sound only they could hear. It brought back to Vredech, with chilling vividness, the impression he had formed as he had watched their futile assault on the strange light that they had conjured up. Serpentine. And the way they stepped over the jagged rocks further marked their strangeness, for they moved with the silent, untroubled sureness of great cats.

The riders halted, side by side. The heads of the mounts continued to sway hypnotically while their cruel, hunting eyes remained fixed on Vredech and Pinnatte. Their rasping breath filled the silence. Vredech forced himself to stand straight. With an effort he tore his gaze from the watching mounts and looked at their riders.

Not that his inspection told him a great deal for, like so much in this place, they were difficult to see – an unsettling patchwork of blueness and shadows that should not be shadows shifted in and out of focus. Yet they were all too real. There was no doubting that. And a frightening sight. Was that armour they were wearing? Black and glistening? Spiked and protected like the whole of this landscape? And what lay behind those visored helms? Vredech tried to still his imagination as he struggled to retain some semblance of calm under the silent scrutiny of the three figures and their mounts. He was about to speak when the central rider leaned forward suddenly. Vredech felt the intensity of its inspection increase almost to the point of tangibility. It was all he could do not to step backwards under its force.

It did not lessen as the rider sat upright again. Rather it increased, though Vredech thought he could sense surprise and doubt in the rider's posture. These were unexpectedly human traits. As, too, was an excitement that was beginning to emerge through them, though this was so febrile that it snatched away the solace that the previous doubt had momentarily offered.

Then there was an exchange between the riders. A complex mélange of eerie sounds reminiscent of, but quite different from, the shrieks they had announced themselves with. Awaiting its outcome, Pinnatte glanced over his shoulder, again searching for some means of escape. One of the mounts craned forward and hissed at him. It bared its teeth, predatory and feral. Pinnatte froze.

The exchange faded away, whistling echoes of it drifting into the distance.

'Welcome,' the rider said.

The voice was jarring and repellent and the word seemed to be not so much spoken as wrung out of one of their awful shrieks. It was surrounded by quivering overtones and dissonant harmonies that set Vredech's teeth on edge.

As grotesque and unnatural as everything else in this benighted place, he thought. He opened his mouth to speak, but no sound came.

'You are not as we thought.'

'You are not of this place.'

Vredech could not make out which one of them was speaking.

'We are strangers,' he managed to say, his own voice sounding alien to him.

There was dark amusement in the reply.

'Yes. There are few indeed left here who have not received our blessing since this world became His.'

'Blessed be His name. Great are His works.'

The words were intoned by all three riders. The sound struck Vredech like icy water dashed in his face. Vivid memories washed over him of the mechanical responses he had heard so many times from his own congregations.

'Take us to the Opening of the Ways.'

Vredech and Pinnatte stood silent in the face of this abrupt command for a moment, then they exchanged an awkward glance.

'Take us to the Opening of the Ways,' the voice came again, this time impatient.

'I . . . we . . . don't know what you mean,' Vredech replied hesitantly. 'We know of no such things. We don't even know how we came here. We . . .'

A gesture silenced him. 'Take us to the Opening of the Ways!' The speaker's mount took a soft, menacing step forward, its neck extended and its head no longer swaying. Vredech quailed. One of the others reached out and touched the advancing rider who, with some reluctance, retreated.

'You must forgive us,' said the interceding rider. 'The purification of this place since we were drawn here is both our duty and our delight and we honour Him in the joy we bring to it. As we do to the Search. Now you have been sent to guide us. Mysterious are His ways, Allyn Vredech.'

Vredech's eyes widened in shock. 'How do you know my name?' he asked.

There was a sound that might have been laughter except that no laughter could have been so depraved.

'Am I so changed that you don't recognize me? You whose loving touch set me on this glorious way?'

The rider reached up and removed his helm . . .

277

Her helm.

For Vredech found himself looking not into the face of some grim and cruel warrior but into that of a monster worse by far. Leaner and harsher than it had been, with glistening black eyes, it was nevertheless unmistakably the face of Dowinne, the wife of his erstwhile friend, Cassraw.

Vredech drew in a sharp breath and took an unsteady step backwards. His foot caught on a rock and he would have stumbled had not Pinnatte caught him.

'But you're dead,' he burst out, his face alive with horror. 'I . . . I killed you myself . . . plunged you into that awful abyss.'

'How could you kill such as me, Allyn? All things are to His design. You were but an instrument of His will, as are we all. Your role then was to free me from the cringing flesh of that world so that a greater destiny could be fulfilled.'

'You're dead,' Vredech repeated feebly, though the words jangled meaninglessly in him.

Dowinne inclined her head slightly in the manner of a teacher dealing with a capable but headstrong pupil. Her arm swept over the plain and the mountains but her dead gaze remained on Vredech. 'You are not so blind, surely? Through the perfection, the purity that we have made here and are making yet, His will has reached out and brought you and I together again, touched on your great gift so that you can lead us back to that place which is the heartworld of His need.'

Vredech was leaning heavily on Pinnatte. His mind was whirling. Though Dowinne had brought her own death on herself, his part in it had been a source of distress to him ever since. His only solace was the knowledge that he had had no alternative, that he had done what he had done not out of hate but to prevent a greater evil, that he had been justified. But still it troubled him.

'It always will,' Dacu had told him. 'Be truly afraid when it doesn't.'

But now Dowinne was standing before him like a judgement.

He felt Pinnatte's arm tightening about him strongly, fingers pinching into his arm.

'Stand up, damn you!' came a whispered but snarling reproach. 'We'll never get out of this if you collapse. You're the one who said we should talk first, remember?'

The three riders seemed to be disputing with one another. This time, Vredech could make out Dowinne's voice vying with the impatience in the others, though the excitement that he had noted before pervaded all of them. It was a grasping, clawing thing. And it was growing.

Talk.

Vredech clung to the word. And more of Dacu's words came to help him. However frightening, however improbable, whatever was happening here *was* happening. He must see it as it was and accept its reality. All else would lead to futility or worse. This was Dowinne, beyond any dispute. The Dowinne whom he thought he had killed. The Dowinne who had killed his friend. The Dowinne who even then had possessed strange and dangerous powers. How she had come here, resurrected, was irrelevant. What was important was that, whatever she had become, he had known her. A link existed, however tenuous.

He drew in a breath of the tainted air and gently prised away Pinnatte's supporting arm.

'I understand none of this, Dowinne,' he said, trying to prevent his voice from trembling. 'I don't know how we came to be here and we want only to leave. We . . .'

'Your understanding is not needed. Only your obedience.'

The tone was dismissive and the attention of the riders was turned suddenly to Pinnatte. They were silent for a long time. Vredech, gradually overcoming his initial shock, moved now to protect his former protector. He edged a little way in front of him.

Who are you?' Dowinne asked Pinnatte.

'Jedred, your honour,' Pinnatte replied immediately, bowing slightly and lying freely, as was his habit under such circumstances. 'Apprentice saddler to the Faldine Guild. This man and I are strangers. One moment we were sharing an evening's camp in the mountains, then suddenly we were here. It's all very alarming. Personally, and no disrespect to yourself and your good friends, but I can't help thinking I'm dreaming, and . . .'

279

An angry wave from Dowinne silenced him. He gave another curt bow and began rubbing his hands submissively.

'You are strange indeed,' Dowinne said slowly, thoughtfully. 'There are signs about you that . . . should not be. One such was promised. One that would be His vessel. But you are flawed and imperfect. He would not use so poor a thing. Yet . . .'

'Perhaps if you asked Him . . .' Pinnatte began.

Abruptly, the three mounts were rearing, their eyes glaring and their clawlike hooves flailing wildly.

'Blasphemer!'

Dowinne's voice, barbed and awful, hissed towards Pinnatte like a burning arrow, drawing in its wake a tangled skein of sound torn from the rasping cries of the other riders.

Vredech stepped in front of him, a hand raised protectively even as he winced away from this ferocious rebuke.

'Leave him alone,' he shouted into the din. 'He's only a boy. If you want something of me, Dowinne, ask, but let him go, he's here by chance.'

'There is no chance. There is only His will.'

'Blessed be His name. Great are His works.'

'He wishes only to leave,' Vredech said.

'His wishes are of no concern. He is here to serve, as are we. As all will serve when He returns. You have been sent to guide us, he . . .' She pointed at Pinnatte, then paused. 'We shall determine. Somewhere in him His purpose will be written. We shall find it. Come.'

She held out a hand and beckoned Pinnatte.

Vredech stretched out both arms sideways to prevent Pinnatte from passing. Not that such a gesture was needed, for Pinnatte had decided that there had been more than enough talk to fulfil the bargain he had made.

'They're Kyrosdyn,' he breathed into Vredech's ear. 'All of them. They stink of it. This whole place does. I'm not going with them.' The desperation in his voice made Vredech turn sharply. Pinnatte was reaching into his pocket again.

Vredech seized his arm. 'No! We must . . .'

'Must what?' Pinnatte's eyes were wide with a mixture of terror and an almost manic rage. 'Go with them? Never. I

280

know what the Kyrosdyn can do.' He snatched his arm free. 'We've a simple rule on the streets for dealing with situations like this. They're not going to take us anywhere for our good, so whatever else we do, we *don't go with them.*'

Vredech faltered in the face of Pinnatte's certainty. There was a dreadful truth in it that chimed with the fear knotting his stomach. He looked round at the jagged terrain and then at the three riders. Dowinne had replaced her helm, hiding her face. Her hand was still slowly calling them forward.

Don't go with them!

'Last chance,' Pinnatte said.

Vredech took a deep breath.

'Let's try to keep together,' he said.

Then they were running down the slope, jumping from rock to blue-sheened rock, reflexes alone keeping them upright. And, without either sound or signal, the three riders were moving after them, their mounts striding out easily and unhurriedly but with deceptive speed.

For the briefest of moments, Vredech was a child again, wilfully disobedient, running recklessly down a rocky hillside. He had only done it once and it had ended in bruised ribs, a twisted ankle and a response from his father that was at once thunderously furious and frantic with relief.

As the memory flitted by he felt a hint of 'What will this end in?' threatening, but it was swept aside by the desperate needs of the moment. He was vaguely aware of Pinnatte just ahead of him, but he could neither help him nor seek help from him. Everything now was filled with the sound of his gasping breath and the pounding of his heart, and only instinct was guiding his feet.

Then that same instinct was intruding into his mind.

He must slow down.

The slope was becoming steeper and steeper. Soon they would not be running but falling and that must surely mean terrible injury or death in this place.

Yet his legs would not respond. Could not respond. He was already going too quickly. He could do nothing. Nothing except plunge towards the outcome of this catastrophic flight. Panic began to coil inside him.

The screeching cries of the three riders reached him but he dared not look over his shoulder to see how close his pursuers were. Yet there was a peculiar urgency in them – a concern, almost.

Then something was touching him, twining itself about his body, holding him, slowing him, promising to stop his tumbling descent. But all that he could feel for this restraint was revulsion. It clung to him like the viscous discharge of an infected wound.

He could see that Pinnatte too was being affected by something. The young man was moving as through strongly flowing water, though Vredech could see no apparent cause. Both of them had been brought to a halt.

Pinnatte was turning to face the oncoming riders, his whole posture alive with rage and fear. As Vredech too turned to face them, he became aware of Pinnatte's arm moving and a stone arcing its way through the stinging air. An angry shout rode with it and the rider it was aimed at flinched and hastily raised a defensive arm. The stone struck him ineffectively on the shoulder but his gesture had been peculiarly human and it stirred something inside Vredech – a distant, flickering hope that he could not properly identify. He could identify a faltering in the mysterious force that was holding him, however. As apparently could Pinnatte, for another stone and another oath passed by Vredech on its way to the same target. This one, though, struck nothing. With a sound almost like that of an animal in pain, it shattered into dust and fragments in mid-air as the intended target casually raised towards it the hand that previously had betrayed him.

But, at the same time, Pinnatte and Vredech found themselves free. The faint hope in Vredech flared suddenly, like a fire caught by a gusting breeze and, scarcely realizing what he was doing, he seized his companion in a powerful embrace. As he did so, the hope became a blinding light and the two of them were falling through it. All around them, clamouring and tearing at the fabric of the brightness itself, came the frenzied cries of their pursuers.

The terrible noise was still tangled about them as, wide-eyed and gaping, they both jerked violently upright.

The room they found themselves in was shaking with the shrieking frustration of the three riders.

As it faded, Nertha was the first to recover. Emotion broke free from the control she had been exerting ever since Pinnatte and her husband had been found comatose, and with a wordless cry of her own she dropped down by Vredech's bed and wrapped her arms around him.

Andawyr, though visibly shaken, dashed to Pinnatte. Echoing Nertha he repeated, 'You're safe, you're safe,' over and over, until eventually he began to gain the young man's attention. Not that Pinnatte seemed too sure about the message he was being given so fervently as his eyes gradually focused and he found himself staring into Andawyr's battered face. He jerked away from him and gazed wildly about the dimly lit room. Catching sight of a tall figure standing in the shade near the foot of the bed he pushed himself backwards, his hand grasping for more stones with which to defend himself.

The figure did not move, however.

'Don't be afraid,' it said, its voice calm and reassuring. 'Wherever you've been, you're safely returned, and nothing can harm you here. I'm going to let a little more light in: will that be all right?'

'Yes,' Vredech said hesitantly on behalf of his companion.

Hawklan touched something by the window and an intricate weave of shutters began slowly to disentangle itself, folding back silently layer upon layer to become part of the window surrounds. Bright sunlight unfurled into the room to reveal elaborate traceries carved across the walls and ceiling. Vredech and Pinnatte, still shocked as they were by their sudden return, stared in wonder, for at the touch of the sunlight the carvings seemed to ripple and turn towards it in welcome. Vredech drew in a deep breath and felt the light washing away the last remnants of the sour blue air that scarcely heartbeats ago had been pervading him.

Pinnatte did the same. He gesticulated vaguely and said, 'Where?'

'Anderras Darion, young man,' came a stern voice. 'More to the point, where have you been to come back bearing such a gift?' He turned to see an old woman sitting nearby. At least, he thought it was an old woman, though there was an ageless quality about her face that made it difficult for him to tell. Bright blue eyes held him fixed, however, preventing him from either replying to her question or asking his own.

Hawklan turned to her sharply. 'Gently, Memsa,' he said with both reproach and surprise. Gulda tapped her stick on the floor impatiently and seemed set to dispute with him for a moment. Then, with a curt nod, she released her captive.

Pinnatte and Vredech, together with the other sleepers, had been brought back to Anderras Darion as quickly as the night and the road would allow. Both Hawklan and Andawyr had examined them again as soon as they reached the castle, but neither had been able to reach any conclusion as to what had happened. In the end, there being no danger to the two men immediately apparent, and bearing in mind Nertha's strange but unequivocal pronouncement that they could well be in some other place, they had reluctantly had to settle for making them comfortable and watching them, pending fresher thoughts the following day.

They had been joined shortly after dawn by a grim-faced Nertha, well rested but less than grateful for the sleep that Hawklan had given her. Gulda had been with them throughout. She had confined her own examination of the two men to laying her hand on their foreheads but otherwise she had said nothing. For what was left of the night she had sat motionless in her characteristic pose: hands clamped over the top of her stick and her chin resting on them.

When the two men suddenly woke and the room filled with the piercing screams of the riders, Andawyr, Hawklan and Nertha all cried out and covered their ears. Gulda, however, straightened up sharply and gazed about her, as if following every echoing nuance of the sounds as they clamoured about the room like trapped and demented animals.

Hawklan knelt down between the two beds. 'Are you all right?' he asked both of them.

'I think so,' Vredech said, though he was pale and visibly confused. 'This is really Anderras Darion?'

'Yes,' Hawklan replied. 'Welcome to my home.'

Vredech levered himself upright. The movement made him feel light-headed and he took his wife's arm for support. He realized that his legs were shaking, a reminder of his reckless dash down the mountainside. He looked at his host and managed to smile.

'So you're the man we've journeyed all this way to meet.' He held out his hand. 'I don't know how we came here, but I think we owe you a debt of thanks . . .' He stopped abruptly and turned to Pinnatte guiltily. Swinging off the bed he leaned forward and looked at his companion anxiously. 'Are *you* all right?' he asked earnestly.

Pinnatte nodded, then shook his head.

'Cobwebs back?' Vredech asked, his face pained.

Pinnatte grimaced and nodded again.

Vredech squeezed his arm encouragingly. 'Don't worry. I'll remember. I'll make sure everyone knows. You'll not be left out. And thanks for whatever you just did.'

Pinnatte shrugged. 'You,' he said.

Vredech shrugged in his turn. 'It's not important,' he said. 'What's important is that we're safe here.'

'No,' Pinnatte said flatly. 'No one's safe.' He looked around the room. 'Tell.'

'Yes,' Gulda said, tapping her stick forcefully on the floor as she stood up. 'Tell.'

'No,' Nertha intervened, placing herself resolutely between the two men and the advancing Memsa. 'Talking can wait. These two need to wash, change their clothes and have something to eat before they do anything else.'

The two women stared at one another for a long moment, then Gulda gave a brief grunt. 'You're right,' she said. 'I apologize.'

Hawklan and Andawyr exchanged a look of open surprise, though they ensured that Gulda did not see it.

The door opened and Atelon entered, his face flushed and concerned. 'What was that noise? Oh.'

The exclamation came as he saw Vredech and Pinnatte awake. His concern became relief and then concern again. 'You're bleeding,' he said to Pinnatte.

Nertha swore under her breath and with an angry look at

285

Hawklan and Andawyr pushed them both aside as she moved to Pinnatte.

'He wasn't bleeding before,' Andawyr protested plaintively as he was drawn into her wake.

'Well, he's bleeding now,' Nertha retorted, untying Vredech's already slack kerchief and looking closely at the cut. 'It looks worse than it is, I think.' She smiled at Pinnatte. 'At least it's clean. Get my bag, and some water.'

While Pinnatte was being attended to, Vredech looked at his own hands. Just as they had been in that strange blue world, they too were scratched. What else had he brought from there? he thought. And what had he left?

Andawyr took Atelon aside. 'Take care of Pinnatte and Vredech.' He lowered his voice. 'And Nertha. Keep a close eye on them. And stay alert.'

As Atelon took his charges in hand, Gulda flicked her stick at Hawklan and Andawyr. 'Come with me, you two, we need to talk.'

She led them along a bright corridor at the end of which was a door that opened on to a broad, circular balcony. It overlooked a small park and children's voices rose up to greet them. Gulda leaned on the stone parapet and watched the children for some time before speaking. She seemed to be unusually uneasy.

'What's the matter, Memsa?' Hawklan ventured.

'What indeed?' she replied, maintaining her vigil over the playing children. 'What indeed?'

Hawklan and Andawyr looked at one another but found no enlightenment.

'No slight thing, I'd deduce, from your manner,' Hawklan said. 'Indeed, I'd deduce that from the fact that you've come back to Anderras Darion. I'd thought never to see you again.'

Gulda looked round at the towers and spires of the great castle, then at her questioner. 'I thought I'd never be back,' she replied. 'I thought that with the Uhriel slain at last and Sumeral destroyed so totally there'd be no more need for me.' She turned back to the children. 'Except as a wandering teacher.'

'But?'

'But . . . little signs everywhere. Little signs – and doubts deep within myself that, though chance and courage had conspired to give us victory, perhaps all was not truly over. That what was scattered might come together again, as it had before.' She drummed a brief tattoo on the parapet with her long fingers. 'Only vagueness, Hawklan. A strangeness in the wind that says that rain is coming, winter, spring, something. A call beneath the senses.'

'It's a deep call if it's beneath *your* senses,' Hawklan said, without irony.

'Who can truly assess the effects of the least thing?' she replied. 'Who knows what things we truly know? Who knows how we guide ourselves?'

She abandoned the children and began walking around the balcony. 'Suffice it that I sensed a coming together of some kind. It was a dark and ominous feeling. And my feet turned me towards here.'

Unusually, Andawyr showed a hint of impatience. 'We'll talk about that over the next few days, together with everything else.' He put his hands to his temples. 'So *many* things are happening so quickly we mustn't confuse coincidence and cause. We'll have the tales of our visitors – and, from what I've heard so far, these are mightily strange – and we'll have the Accounting of the Goraidin. If there's a pattern there, we'll find it, you know that. We're all of us wiser than we were.' Following Gulda's deceptively fast stride, they moved into the shade of the tower. The sound of the children was replaced by the clatter of horses' hooves in the stone courtyard below. 'But that's not why you dragged us out here, is it?'

Chapter 23

'No, it's not,' Gulda replied, tapping her stick on the mosaic floor as she strode around the balcony. Both men declined to press her. Experience had taught them that Gulda did what she wanted, when she wanted, and that even to try to force events was to risk a memorable rebuke. They were torn, however, for, very unusually, she seemed to be openly disturbed.

She stopped abruptly, then moved off again. As they came back into the sunlight she sat down on a long bench and motioned them to sit by her. She was about to speak when something caught her eye. It was Gavor, high above them, black and purposeful against the blue sky. Wings wide and still, save for pinions lightly testing the unseen pathways of the air, he began gliding down in a slow, graceful spiral. As was often the way, though, he landed less elegantly, with a great deal of flapping and a muttered oath as he bounced to a halt.

'You sedentary souls really should make the effort and learn to fly,' he said as he recovered. 'It's not at all difficult and it's such a joy up there.' He looked beadily at each in turn. 'Ah, I see that a sparkling demeanour is inappropriate. Do tell.'

'Just listen, bird,' Gulda said. 'And all of you, say nothing of this to anyone else.' A curt movement of her hand silenced the pending protests. 'Nothing,' she insisted. 'For the simple reason that I don't know the significance of what I've just heard yet, and nothing's to be gained by adding needless alarm to what's already happening.'

'Dar-volci's already told me that Sumeral is whole again

and struggling to return,' Hawklan said bluntly. 'And he was quite unequivocal about it. What could be more alarming than that?'

Gulda did not reply. 'Just listen,' she said.

A ringing burst of childish laughter rose up from the park below.

'The sound that we heard when Vredech and Pinnatte awoke. What did you make of it?' she asked.

'It was peculiar, to put it mildly,' Hawklan replied after a moment's pause to assimilate the unexpected question. 'In fact, it was extremely unpleasant. I wouldn't have thought a human throat could make such a noise, but then, their whole condition was peculiar. To all intents and purposes, just sleeping, yet apparently unwakeable.'

'It's not unknown for people to wake up screaming from nightmares, you know,' Andawyr contributed dismissively. 'And from what I can gather, they've both been through a great deal in the not too distant past.'

'They didn't dream,' Hawklan said, casually but categorically. Then he frowned as if taken unawares by his own remark.

Andawyr too looked puzzled. 'Didn't dream?' he echoed. 'What do you mean?'

'I mean they didn't dream,' Hawklan replied as though he were testing the answer.

Andawyr pursed his lips and shook his head. 'You must be mistaken. Everyone dreams. It's deep in the roots of the way our minds work. Stop someone dreaming for long enough and they'll go mad.'

'I know that,' Hawklan said irritably, his frown deepening. 'And I'm not mistaken. I've sat through enough night vigils to recognize different kinds of sleep. In fact, now I think back on it, the behaviour of both of them was unusual. I don't know why it didn't strike me sooner. They didn't toss and turn like ordinary sleepers and they definitely didn't dream.' Andawyr looked set to protest again but Hawklan did not allow him. 'No spells of deep relaxation or flickering eye movement. Not one.'

Andawyr was unpersuaded. 'It isn't possible,' he said

testily. 'You probably missed them, that's all. You were tired yourself. You probably dozed off from time to time without realizing it. It happens.'

'I know. I heard you snoring.'

An impatient tap from Gulda's stick ended the burgeoning argument and drew them both back to her question. 'The noise,' she demanded stonily.

'I don't understand what you want, Memsa,' Hawklan said, still a little querulous at Andawyr's off-hand rejection of his idea. 'They woke up screaming, presumably after some frightening experience – dream or otherwise. But we won't know anything about it until we can talk to them properly – that's to say when Nertha lets them go.'

Gulda gave a menacing snort. 'Think back to when they awoke. Both of you!'

Her tone forbade any dispute or return to their disagreement but Hawklan still protested. 'I really don't know what . . .'

'Think!'

Gavor chuckled and, stepping to the edge of the parapet, peered precariously down at the playing children. Hawklan yielded and did as he was told, taking his mind back to the sudden awakening of Vredech and Pinnatte.

There had not been a vestige of a warning. At one moment the two men were lying motionless and asleep, the only sound in the softly lit room being the breathing of its occupants and the faint background buzz of the activity that pervaded the castle. Then, as though an ambush had been sprung, the room was full of the overpowering sound of the sleepers' screaming as, suddenly, they were awake.

Even now, sitting in the sunlight with the friendly guardian towers of Anderras Darion about him, Hawklan shuddered as he recalled the scene. Despite Gulda's stern injunction to reflect on what had happened, he found he was strangely reluctant to return to the event. And why was Gulda so interested in the noise the two waking men had made?

Because it wasn't they who had made it!

The realization struck him almost like a blow.

The sound had had no focus, no single point of origin. Nor had it grown to a climax. It had suffused the entire room the instant that Vredech and Pinnatte woke. And it had died strangely: not collapsing back on to its creators in all too human sobs or choking gasps, but fading into the distance like dying echoes across a rocky valley. He had a fleeting image of Gulda's eyes searching the room.

He voiced his discovery.

Andawyr shuffled uncomfortably. Part of him wanted to decry the idea but he had been coming to the same conclusion himself.

A breeze wafted over the balcony. Gavor's shining wings fluttered as he steadied himself. Gulda turned her head into it and drew in a deep breath, her nose cutting the air like the sail of a tiny, tacking yacht.

'Which prompts the question, who – or what – *did* make the noise?' Hawklan said.

'And where did it come from?' Andawyr added.

'Which brings us back to the need to talk to them,' Hawklan concluded.

Gulda laid an unexpectedly gentle hand on his arm. 'In time,' she said softly. 'But there's something else you need to know about what you heard.' She paused. The sound of the children drifted up to them again, silvery in the sunlit air. Gulda waited until it passed before she continued, as if she were afraid of marring it.

'It was more than just a noise,' she said. 'It was a language.'

The words emerged as though against her will. Even more disturbed by her manner than intrigued by what she had said, both men looked at her keenly, but neither spoke. She answered their unasked questions.

'It is His language. And the sounds that filled that room were voices – three distinct voices. The voices of His Uhriel.'

Involuntarily, Andawyr circled his hand over his heart in the ancient Sign of the Iron Ring. It was a gesture that represented the Fyordyn High Guards who had surrounded Ethriss at the Last Battle of the First Coming and making it, in these more enlightened times, was generally regarded as being rather foolish. Embarrassed at this betrayal by his hand, Andawyr coughed uncomfortably and transformed the movement into an unconvincing straightening of his robe.

'The Uhriel are dead,' Hawklan said in a voice that was little more than a whisper. 'You . . .' He stopped sharply. 'You know that. The bodies of Creost and Dar-Hastuin were burned and their ashes scattered to the winds. And both Andawyr and I saw Oklar die. They're gone, utterly. However Sumeral restored them, it can't be done again.'

'Yes,' Gulda said, still seemingly having to force out her words. 'As you say, they were killed. But the sounds that came with Vredech and Pinnatte *were* the voices of the Uhriel, nevertheless.' She tapped her stick sharply on the floor and, as if at a signal, was abruptly her normal self again. She did not give Hawklan and Andawyr an opportunity to speak. 'Gentlemen,' she announced. 'I'm afraid we must accept that the Uhriel have been . . .' she curled her lip '. . . born again. Somewhere His will is whole and He has found new vessels for His old evil, vessels doubtless willing to be as well versed in His ways as their predecessors.' She sniffed. 'Worse, from what we just heard, I'd surmise that while their corruption is as ancient as Sumeral Himself, their hearts are strong and green, and full of the surging zeal and righteousness that's the invariable hallmark of the newly enlightened.'

Both men turned away from the unusual passion and anger in her voice. Despite what she had said, however, they both knew that nothing was to be gained by asking her how she came by such knowledge. Gulda was a deeper enigma even than Hawklan. Certain questions were never asked of her and even those who speculated about them tended to do so in hushed tones. Those who knew her knew too that they must take what she offered and confine themselves to matters earthbound and practical. Andawyr spoke first.

'I've no serious qualms about accepting what you say at first face, Memsa,' he said, with a crisp frankness in his voice that was quite belied by his posture and his expression. 'But, grim prospect though it is, there's nothing in what you've said that needs to be kept away from the testing of open debate, is there? Why are we discussing it out here like conspirators?'

'Because of the language, Andawyr, the language,' Gulda replied. 'Not His . . . renewed . . . existence, nor even the rebirth of the Uhriel. Your people will come to that soon enough. The one has always been a probability, though, I'd thought, a far lower one than seems to be the case, and I suppose the other's an inevitable consequence of it. But they know nothing of the language. That was His, and His alone. It's the true language of the Power – His closest-held secret. He gave only the merest hint of it to His first Uhriel. Sufficient for their needs. Or, rather, sufficient for *His* needs. And such as He allowed them to know He constrained them to using only rarely.' She paused, uneasy again. 'The voices that we just heard were steeped in it.'

'Which means?' Andawyr asked.

'Which means that whoever they are, wherever they are, He's chosen to give them knowledge of the Power far greater than he allowed the original Uhriel. *Far* greater.'

Andawyr closed his eyes and leaned back, turning his face to the sun.

'It can't be,' he said, more a plea than a statement. 'Oklar alone cut a swathe of destruction through Vakloss with a mere gesture. And when Oslang and the others faced the Uhriel on the battlefield it taxed them to limits they could scarcely have imagined. Even though we've learned more since then that in who can say how many generations previously, I'd be loath to face them again as they were, let alone stronger.'

Gulda was pitiless. 'You're less than dust in the face of the power they have now.'

There was a stark silence. Even the children below seemed to be waiting for something, their play now hushed and whispered. Gavor's wooden leg clunked softly as he paced up and down the parapet. He stopped.

'You're certain about what you heard?' Andawyr asked cautiously.

'Oh yes, very certain,' Gulda confirmed, without a vestige of the irritation that could normally be expected of her at such a question. Hawklan leaned forward, dropping his head into his hands, and the silence folded around them again.

'It's a frightening picture you're drawing for us, Memsa,' he said eventually. 'I don't know where to begin making sense of it all.' He grimaced and drew his hands down his face. 'I've never been truly at ease since the war. Now this. It can't happen again. It can't be allowed to. But all I can think of is why would He give such knowledge to these new Uhriel if He denied it to those who'd served Him so long and so faithfully before?'

Gulda looked at him and then at Andawyr.

'It was always said that He *took on* human form. Took it on because it was the best suited to His needs. But no one truly knows what He is.' She paused. 'We can be sure however, that whatever He is, following His destruction – or perhaps I should say, His *dispatch* from this world – He'll be even further removed from whatever humanity He had. And like you, Andawyr, and the rest of the Cadwanwr, like all of us, He'll be wiser by far, now.'

'Wiser?'

Gulda's mouth tightened into a grim smile. 'You're begging the question, sage, assuming that all wisdom is for *our* greater good! Let's say He'll be more *knowledgeable*.'

'And how will He use this knowledge?' Hawklan asked.

Gulda gripped his arm. It was a grip he was familiar with, not remotely that of an old woman, but powerful and determined, the grip of a swordsman. It was also both reassuring and appealing. It told him she needed both his help and his trust.

'The Uhriel were always mere weapons,' she said. 'Devices honed and sharpened for the execution of His will. We've no reason to presume they're not still so. But where once they were weapons of stealth and silent insinuation, at least initially, perhaps now they're weapons of sheer, brutal force: lions to be set amongst the sheep.'

Despite his protestation about the frailty of the Cadwanwr before the Uhriel, Andawyr shifted uneasily at the comparison and risked giving her a resentful look.

'Sheep you are,' Gulda said firmly, though not without a hint of dark humour. 'The Guardians are long gone and now He knows that for certain. He knows too that He foundered the last time only because He *didn't* know that. He knows that He could have swept out of Narsindal and carried all before Him when Oklar's folly betrayed His return.'

There was no denying that conclusion. In the agonizing that

had followed the war, it had been reluctantly accepted by most of those involved that good fortune had contributed at least as much as courage and determination to the victory.

'What shall we do?' Hawklan asked.

Gulda's grip tightened and her piercing eyes blazed through him. 'Fight. What else can you do?'

'But . . .'

'But what? Do you expect to reason with Him? He was ever a breaker of promises and treaties, but given that He didn't even offer to negotiate last time, I doubt He will when He returns. As He surely will. Your choice then will be as before: fight or die – or, at best, perhaps be allowed some dismal span in cruel bondage.' She slapped his arm. 'These are dark and awful thoughts indeed, Hawklan, but many strange tides are moving and we're caught in them whether we wish it or not. If we don't seize them, ride them, they'll sweep us where they will and only destruction and misery will ensue. You're stronger and wiser than you've ever been, as are all of us. All that's gone before has merely been to bring us to this point, to prepare us.' She stood up. 'Now we must talk to our guests – see what threats and promises these tides have washed to our feet.' She waved an admonishing finger at both of them, and at Gavor.

'Mention nothing of the Uhriel's language and what it means,' she said. 'My judgement is that it's too fearful a revelation at the moment. I told you about it so that you can guide the debate that we're about to have.' She turned to Andawyr. 'Conduct the debate well. We need to listen, both to what's said and what's not said. Somewhere amid the tangle of it all, there'll be the knowledge to come to the heart of this – perhaps even a chance of putting an end to it once and for all.'

The following days did indeed require a great deal of listening by the Cadwanwr and travelling scholars whom Andawyr discreetly chose from those currently visiting the castle. There were many questions and much discussion as the returned Goraidin gave formal Accountings of their travels and the newcomers were asked to explain in their own fashion what had driven them to leave their homelands and make the long journey to Anderras Darion.

Though Antyr and the other outlanders, by virtue of travelling with the Goraidin, had had some experience of the painstaking ways of the Orthlundyn and their allies in such matters, it was nevertheless strange for them at first. It was particularly bewildering for Vredech and Thyrn, who were more familiar with the institutions that governed Canol Madreth and Arvenstaat. Both these worthy bodies affected to be centres of ordered and reasoned debate where the wishes of the people could be given true voice. In reality, however, they were predominantly theatres for the ambitious, the vainglorious, the vacuously loquacious who were incapable of earning a similar stipend in an honest trade and, not least, those who lusted for power while shunning the responsibility that it carried. The quality of the debate they offered generally differed from that which could be heard daily in any children's playground only in its superior vocabulary, its greater pettiness, and the deeper depths of its hypocrisy. By contrast, Antyr, coming as he did from the city-state of Serenstad, was used to government largely by Ducal Edict and thus accepted the idea of the Orthlundyn's rational congress quite easily. Farnor and Marna simply took it for granted, being both young and from a small, isolated village and thus completely unused to the collective follies that larger societies can manufacture for their governance.

Andawyr, with a silent Gulda sitting in the background, handled the proceedings as he would any meeting with his colleagues at the Cadwanen, that is to say along the lines that the Lords of Fyorlund conducted the business of serving their Queen and the people in their own formal assembly of government, the Geadrol. Individuals spoke for the most part without interruption, although occasionally Andawyr would prompt gently to elucidate a particular point or direct them from some rambling byway back to the main thrust of their account. Only when each speaker had finished were questions allowed. Finally, if it was possible, such facts as had been gleaned were ranged in an order of their probable reliability. At Andawyr's urging, discussion about what was being revealed was to be left until the end. The whole was taxing and stern, but its relentless, truth-seeking thoroughness invariably enthralled even the most indifferent of observers.

Andawyr chose, as a venue for this exposition, not one of Anderras Darion's many great halls but a comparatively small room high in one of the towers. Circular in shape, one half of its circumference was occupied by windows that rose up from the floor and swept across the ceiling. They overlooked the castle's great wall and, beyond it, the rolling farmlands and forests of Orthlund. The other half was carved with a representation of that same view, giving the impression that the room was without walls.

Despite the discipline of the majority of the participants, the unfolding of the various tales proved to be no quiet or simple affair. Questions and ideas abounded.

Tarrian and Grayle were reluctantly impressed.

'These are civilized people,' Tarrian conceded. 'For humans. People who take joy in learning and from whom much can be learned. They're the least tainted by His past deeds and the most knowledgeable about them. They're the ones who both see the need and have the will to face and oppose Him.'

'Praise indeed,' Antyr said, not without some irony. 'But you sound rather pessimistic about it.'

'No. I'm just frightened. I'd be pessimistic if they didn't see the need or didn't have the will,' Tarrian concluded tersely.

Gulda took charge of the newcomers, guiding them around the castle whenever Andawyr deemed a break necessary in the proceedings. In common with most new arrivals to Anderras Darion, they were rendered almost speechless by the wealth of strange and beautiful things they met.

'Why was it built?' Farnor asked, as Gulda led them into a small cobbled courtyard.

'One of the problems with young people is that they always ask such lethal questions,' she said conspicuously to Vredech and Nertha. 'It was built as a castle, oddly enough, young man. A place of strength, a place of refuge for the people against Sumeral's marauding armies. And it served that purpose well for a long time. But what Ethriss turned it into later . . .?' She shrugged. 'He alone knows. Though I have some doubts even about that, to be honest, when I look around.'

'It's a wonder in its own right, just like a fine painting or a piece of music,' Nertha said.

'Once, perhaps, yes,' Gulda mused. 'When the world was young and Sumeral hadn't yet tainted it. But not when much of this work was done. Beautiful it is, and wondrous, beyond argument. But I suspect – I've always suspected – there's a deep purpose to it somewhere.'

'Don't let Him build anything,' Vredech said.

'I'm sorry?' Gulda looked at him quizzically.

'Don't let Him build anything,' Vredech repeated, as though to himself. 'The Whistler said that to me. He was adamant about it.'

'The Whistler? Ah, the man, the creature, the strange flute-player you encountered in your dreams,' Gulda said.

'I don't dream,' Vredech said firmly. 'Never have. And whatever, whoever, the Whistler was, he was no more a figment of my imagination than you are.' Gulda grunted but said nothing. 'He sounded a solitary note,' Vredech went on, his face thoughtful as he recalled the encounter. 'It echoed. "There's a quality in the rock that responds to the touch of the note," he said. "So it is with Him. Who responds to His Song builds a way for Him. And there are many ways He can come. Ways of the mind, the spirit, the heart, the flesh. Don't let this friend of yours build anything." He meant Cassraw. "No monuments, palaces, nothing. Such a place could draw Him down on you like lightning down a tree." '

Gulda was watching him narrowly. 'Tell this to the others when you speak again,' She said. 'I'll give it some thought myself.'

She ran her forefinger idly over an intricate and finely detailed scroll that was part of a carving on a nearby wall. There were many similar features in Anderras Darion and they were the envy of Orthlund's finest carvers. For when inspected with a glass they revealed finer and finer detail. So much so that it was conjectured by some that, contrary to reason though it was, they dwindled beyond any possibility of sight.

'All infinity in less than the width of an eyelash,' she muttered, then her gaze followed the scrolling into the greater whole of the carving and thence to the shapes made by the windows and balconies and all the shadowed nooks and crannies of the three-and four-storey buildings that surrounded the courtyard. Upwards it went, beyond the line of the jostling rooftops, to towers and spires, each one different from its neighbour, and beyond again, to the mountains, still and patient.

'Patterns within patterns forever,' Gulda said to herself, softly. 'And resonances, resonances. Echoing who knows where?'

Then her stick was tapping the visitors on their way again.

The Goraidin's Accounting had been given, and the tales of Antyr, Farnor, Vredech, Pinnatte and Thyrn all told. It had taken a long time.

Andawyr addressed the gathering.

Chapter 24

'Now we begin,' Andawyr said, looking round at the faces of the small assembly.

A sense of wilful control over tumbling questions filled the hall. It was underlaid by a deep unease. Andawyr addressed it directly.

'Now we begin to make a coherent picture of what we've learned over these past days – if we can. I can't see that it will be easy. I can't see that it will be comforting. Indeed, I fear it will be the very opposite. The listening alone has been taxing, and some grim shadows have been cast. I'll not ask you not to be afraid: I think we've learned enough already to know that that would be asking too much, but I *will* ask you not to allow your fear to cloud your vision, and to bring your every faculty to bear until we can say we have at least a semblance of the truth about what all of this means. I know I'm stating the obvious.' A quick glance took in the faces of Farnor, Marna and Thyrn. 'Something most of us have learned already. But "obvious" is a treacherous word and I'd rather repeat a thing a dozen times than have it go by default. However bad it is, the truth is always preferable to ignorance. When the fears and the doubts become too much, hold firm to that. You're all people of proven ability and resolve. Remember who you're with and where you are.' An airy wave encompassed the view beyond the hall, though much of the Orthlundyn countryside was hidden in a fine drizzling rain.

He sat down and swung one leg on to a table. His manner became matter-of-fact. 'We'll need our heads and our hearts to deal with this, my friends – our intellects and our intuitions.' He hesitated. 'And, on that very point, I have to say that

301

what concerns me most is the . . . feeling . . . that we don't have a great deal of time before some resolution not of our making breaks over our heads.' He lifted both hands to silence any questions even though none were being voiced. 'Just a feeling,' he repeated. 'My stomach, not my head. But bear with me in this, please. Be thorough in your inquiries and your work, but *be urgent*!'

He opened his arms towards Antyr and the others. 'I'll admit I'm at a loss to know what to say to you. You've each faced your own terrible trials, trials that have been cruel enough to drive you far from your homes and friends in search of help. And what have we done for you? Badgered you with our interminable questions. We're not normally so inhospitable. We owe you at least an apology. All I can do is ask . . .'

'No apology is necessary,' Antyr interrupted, drawing all eyes to himself. 'I can't speak for the others, of course, but this Accounting, as you call it, has been like a keen wind blowing through my mind, clearing away dust and clutter. It hasn't solved any of my problems. I'm still no wiser about my . . . gift. And some of the things I've heard have been very disturbing. But I feel great hope in this place and amongst you all. It's where I think I need to be and, right now, it's certainly where I *want* to be. You owe me nothing, and I owe you my thanks.'

Unused to compliments, Andawyr swung his leg down from the table and cleared his throat awkwardly. He coloured.

'He does speak for all of us,' Vredech added after a glance that took in Thyrn, Farnor and Pinnatte.

Andawyr cleared his throat again, then glowered at Usche, who was smirking, and at Ar-Billan who was trying not to. He stood up, made a futile attempt to straighten his robe and gave Antyr a brisk bow. Then he was issuing needless instructions.

'We must search the castle's library for references to Dream Finding and anything that tells of or even implies travelling between different worlds – mythology, superstition, children's tales, ancient science, abstruse mathematics – anything. We must find it, study it, and relate it to the information, *the facts*, we've learned. I suspect this strange ability of Antyr's is fundamental.' He fidgeted with some papers lying on the table

302

in front of him. 'This too needs to be pursued, but I don't see how we can do it in a hurry – I seem to have run into a wall or, rather, a maelstrom with it. Still . . .' He drummed a brief, pensive tattoo on the papers, then picked them up and thrust them at Usche. 'Let me know what you think,' he said. 'Work with Ar-Billan.'

Others were given the task of helping Pinnatte to find a way to clear his mind of the 'cobwebs' that he had told Vredech about and which seemed to bind him largely to silence. Nertha attached herself determinedly to these. Yet others were to study two translucent blue stones that Pinnatte had found in his pocket after his precipitate return from the world of the Uhriel. He had caused a small stir when, discovering them, he had cried out and frantically thrown them away.

'Crystals,' he said, putting an unsteady but determined hand on Andawyr to restrain him as he stooped to pick them up. 'Dangerous.'

Andawyr looked at him, then held his open hand over the stones for a while before nudging one of them gingerly with his finger. What he felt he did not say, but he frowned and said, 'I think you're right,' picking them up quickly with a cloth. He also gave a strong injunction to 'Be careful' when he gave them to his fellow Cadwanwr for study.

Later, having been chased away by his various charges, who insisted they needed no immediate help with their allotted tasks, Andawyr sat alone in his own room. His feet on the table, his chair pushed back precariously on two legs and his hands behind his head, he was staring up at the ceiling. A soft scratching at the door disturbed his reverie. Opening it, he found himself looking down at Tarrian. He knelt inquiringly in front of the wolf who stepped a little to one side and, head lowered, peered into the room.

A reproach filled Andawyr's mind. 'Such a mess,' Tarrian said despairingly. 'Still. None of my business, I suppose. Time to talk. Grayle's gone for Gulda and Hawklan.'

'But . . .'

'Come along, don't dawdle. It's not as if you were doing anything useful – like tidying your room, for example.'

Tarrian was retreating along the corridor but the insistence in his voice moved Andawyr's feet before he was aware of it.

'Where are we going?' he asked as they clattered down a winding flight of stairs.

'Forward.'

Andawyr's eyes narrowed. 'I see,' he caustically. 'Out of the past and into the future. From here to there, and so on. An accurate and totally useless reply. I've got enough to think about without bandying bad philosophy with you, wolf. Where, specifically, are we going, and why?'

They were walking along a wide, brightly lit corridor. Statues stared out at them from semi-circular apses which reached up to a high, steeply arched ceiling. Tarrian's nails clicked purposefully on the mosaic floor, tapping a sharp and rhythmic counterpoint to Andawyr's shuffling footfall.

'To see Antyr,' Tarrian replied, just as Andawyr was about to repeat his question.

At the end of the corridor was a large double door. They had to pause by a wicket-door to allow a noisy and cheerful group – Riddinvolk, by their accents – to enter, before leaving the building and heading across a broad lawn. The grass had recently been cut and, touched by rain that had fallen earlier in the day, its scent was strong and heady. Tarrian stopped for a moment and sniffed vigorously, his head swinging from side to side. Almost mimicking him, Andawyr too closed his eyes and drew in a deep breath.

Then they were moving again, Tarrian leading the way up the sweeping steps that led to the top of the castle wall. Puffing a little as he reached the top, Andawyr saw Hawklan and Gulda standing with Antyr. They were looking out over the countryside. The sun was low and very bright, hiding much of the landscape under an elaborate patchwork of long, gold-flecked shadows.

'Fine evening,' Andawyr said as he joined the others. The bland courtesy emerged unbidden and sounded empty in the face of the sun's splendour. Tarrian jumped up on to one of the embrasures. Grayle and Dar-volci were already there, sprawled out luxuriously. Tarrian dropped down beside them. The eyes of the two wolves glinted yellow in the sunlight.

Andawyr looked at Gulda and then at Hawklan. Both of

them returned his inquiring gaze.

'We thought you needed to talk,' Dar-volci said.

'We?' Gulda asked, turning to him darkly.

'Me, Tarrian, Grayle, Gavor.'

'We've been talking for days, or hadn't you noticed?' Andawyr said with some impatience.

'Oh yes, we noticed. You made quite a reasonable job of it, too,' Tarrian intruded, addressing all of them.

Andawyr gave Antyr a world-weary look. 'It's hard enough having patronizing felcis all over the place without the wolves joining in.'

Antyr gave a disclaiming shrug.

'Just sit quietly for a little while,' Tarrian said, conspicuously ignoring the sarcasm. 'Watch the sun go down and Anderras Darion's stars rise.'

Radiant-stone lanterns were already releasing their sun-stored light into parts of the castle that were deep in shade. They changed in intensity as need arose, casting a gentle light that eased the darkness aside rather than slashing through it as though it were an enemy.

A black shape, flickering shadows in the gloaming, landed on top of the wall and then hopped on to Hawklan's shoulder.

'Sorry I'm late, dear boys, Memsa,' Gavor said. 'Just talking to a friend.'

Gulda reached up and tapped his beak, then chuckled and sat down by the wolves, motioning the others to do the same.

They sat in silence for a long time, watching the sun sink slowly beyond the horizon, returning the landscape to them for a little while before the darkness finally enfolded it. Evening was a time when the Orthlundyn tended to wander their streets, watching what the changing shadows did to their carvings. Orthlundyn carving frequently produced results that its creators had not intended. In so doing, it asked questions and opened ways, and the Orthlundyn relished it.

As the western sky dimmed and stars began to appear, so more lights began to bloom into life about the castle. Occasionally, sounds drifted to the watchers, deepening the silence: voices, distant and indistinct; laughter; a closing door; the cry of a nightbird or an animal.

'Excuse us,' Tarrian said, as he and Grayle scrambled to their feet and jumped down from the embrasure.

'Patronizing they might be when it suits them,' Gulda said as the two wolves trotted off along the wall. 'But they have a sureness of touch that we have to work hard to attain and even harder to keep.'

'I thought it was a good Accounting,' Andawyr said in a slightly injured tone.

'It was,' Gulda replied. 'An excellent one, insofar as excellent is a word to be used for what we've learned. But a little silence, a little stillness, a little freedom doesn't go amiss, does it? Let the castle soak into us, as it were.'

She looked upwards. Where lights decked the towers they had an intensity and were arranged in such a way that it was often difficult to distinguish them from the stars.

'It seems that Ethriss's patterns stretch out into the very heavens,' Gulda said softly. 'Vying with the constellations.'

'Like those in the hilt of the Black Sword,' Hawklan said, equally softly.

Andawyr looked at him. 'What did you make of the appearance of yourself and the Sword in my dream?' The question was more abrupt than he had intended. 'The one I had back at the Cadwanen when I hustled Antyr into demonstrating his art on me.'

Hawklan did not answer immediately. His thoughts had drifted back to the mountain camp when he and Dar-volci had discussed the loss of the Sword and when Dar-volci had so casually announced his belief that Sumeral was whole again and bent on returning. He voiced the thoughts he had had then.

'I don't know. I've no conceivable need for a sword, yet it haunts me still that I let it slip so easily from my hand.'

'Don't underestimate the power of Sumeral's voice,' Gulda said. 'Had I been a little wiser, perhaps I might have prepared you better.'

Hawklan shook his head and affected a casualness he did not feel. 'I doubt it. But it's of no account. The deed's done and the Sword lost.'

'But it still troubles you?'

' "Troubles" is too strong a word. But the recollection comes to me from time to time and there's always a wrongness about the memory. I can't do other than reproach myself for what happened.'

'Time to time?' Andawyr's voice was shrewd. 'Wouldn't it be more accurate to say that scarcely a day passes without you thinking about it?'

Hawklan grimaced and avoided his gaze. 'I suppose so, yes,' he admitted reluctantly. 'Particularly lately – since I discussed it with Dar – but . . .'

'No buts,' Andawyr said. 'It mightn't be giving you sleepless nights, but it's troubling you all right. And, to be honest, it troubles me too, though, like you, I don't know why. You and it are joined in some way. It almost literally fell into your hand when it was needed. How did it come to be in the Armoury? It couldn't have been there before. A smith like Loman would have sensed its presence years earlier. And on the few occasions you used it, it was like a trumpet call. It rang out, clarity and truth swirling in its wake.' He became very still, then pressed the heel of his palm to his forehead. 'How couldn't I have seen it before?' he said, his eyes suddenly wide and intense. 'It's so obvious. He was afraid of it. Afraid of it.'

'As you said yourself, a treacherous word, "obvious",' Gulda said. 'Who was afraid of it?'

'Him! Sumeral!' Andawyr replied, swinging his still wide-eyed gaze round to her. 'The Sword's some kind of extraordinary artefact of the Power, but if He'd been able to use it, He'd simply have taken it. Hawklan can't use the Power himself. He was no threat that we could perceive. He was running towards Derras Ustramel in faith and the vainest of hopes. Sumeral's least effort could have bound him there and taken the Sword.' He turned to Hawklan and prodded a satisfied finger into his chest. 'But instead, He stopped you, long before you reached the castle, before you could even see it through the mist. And He made you drop the Sword into the lake.'

'No, not into the lake,' Hawklan said. 'Somewhere else.'

Andawyr bared his teeth in a moue of annoyance and his

elation faltered. He sagged a little. 'Well, that's as maybe. It's still lost, isn't it? As you said, the deed's done, there's no point fretting about it.'

'There's rarely any point about fretting over anything,' Gulda said sharply. 'But given that our healer still feels the absence of it after so long – increasingly so, it would seem – and the venerable leader of the Cadwanol sees it in his dreams, and even now is still standing on that misty causeway where it was lost, I think it would be worth bringing a little purposeful thought to it.'

As she looked significantly at the two men, a low moaning cry came out of the darkness. Another followed it. All of them turned towards the sound.

'It's Tarrian and Grayle,' Antyr said, as the noise of the wolves' howling gradually gathered force. Dar-volci stretched, then sat up, his head cocked to one side.

No one spoke, no one moved, as the voices of the wolves swelled to fill the starlit darkness. Long notes rose and fell, tumbling one over the other, echoing round the tall and silent towers of Anderras Darion and the steep crags of the mountains that sheltered Hawklan's castle. They sang the Great Song, telling the ancient tale of the wonder and mystery that was in all things. And of the joy of being.

No one spoke, no one moved for some time after the final notes had dwindled into the ringing distance.

The two wolves padded back out of the darkness.

'I needed that,' Tarrian said, sitting down and scratching vigorously.

Gulda bent down and stroked their heads. 'The Alphraan will value it,' she said softly before returning to the others. 'The Sword, gentlemen. Time to come down from the stars and turn to our more mundane problems.'

She levelled her stick at Andawyr. 'As memory serves me, you surmised that when you saw the Sword in your dream it wasn't actually part of the dream but, somehow, Antyr's strange gift had actually brought it to you – or you to it – or opened a way between the worlds for you to reach it?'

Andawyr looked at her suspiciously, uncertain of her tone. 'Yes,' he said somewhat defensively. 'I did think that was a possibility.' He straightened up and met her gaze. 'In fact, after what we've heard I'm quite certain now that it was a *possibility*. But such a remote one.' He shook his head. 'I'm still finding all these clear affirmations of the existence of other worlds unsettling – ideas, theories, calculations and experiments are one thing, but to have them all suddenly given such form . . . still . . .' He massaged his ruined nose with a fist. 'The Sword actually being present certainly makes sense of the alarms being set off the way they were.'

Gulda turned to Antyr. 'Do you think this too?'

'I don't know. It could be. I don't have Andawyr's knowledge of why these places should be but I also don't have his reservations. I know they're there and that moving to them involves not just the mind. The body – a body – *your* body – is there, no different to how it is here, and you can live and die there just as here. And objects can be moved as well – like the blue stones Pinnatte brought back. The incident in Andawyr's dream wasn't as clearly obvious as the other times when I've moved into some other world, but it was certainly no ordinary dream.'

'You're the expert,' Gulda said. 'But it sounds reasonable to me in the light of what we've heard. Though in all conscience, for all we know Pinnatte might have had those stones in his pocket since he left Arash-Felloren. He is a thief by profession, after all. It's quite . . .'

'No.' Andawyr interrupted. 'Whatever those stones are I've never felt anything like them before, and they *are* dangerous. Far more even than green crystals, I'd judge, and *they*'re frightening enough for anyone who can use the Power. They're certainly far too dangerous for anyone to carry idly in his pocket, and, street thief or no, he didn't throw them away with the attitude of someone creating a diversion to gull a gawping crowd. I've someone looking at them as a matter of urgency.'

'Both he and Vredech *are* Dream Finders,' Antyr blurted out. The revelation caused some surprise.

'You didn't mention this before,' Andawyr said.

'I wasn't sure. But listening to Vredech and speaking to him, and discussing Pinnatte with Atelon, and thinking about everything else that's happened, I'm fairly certain now. They're untrained, of course, and without Earth Holders, but they're Dream Finders nevertheless. Not only that, I think they're like me – able to move between the worlds.'

'Adepts?' Andawyr, looked at him closely. 'I thought – you told me – they were very rare.'

'I thought they were non-existent,' Antyr replied. 'Until the blind man called me one, "Adept" was nothing more than a word – a Dream Finding myth. Even now I don't feel easy with the name. "Adept" implies a considerable and *conscious* skill. I'll own to being a competent, perhaps good Dream Finder, but if I'm an Adept I'm frankly a floundering one. I'm at the behest of something inside me that seems to be quite beyond my control.'

'Yet you think both Pinnatte and Vredech are Adepts also?' Gulda queried, ignoring this repudiation.

Antyr wilted a little under her stern gaze but held his ground. 'In Serenstad there are many Dream Finders, but the whole idea of Adepts – people who can find Gateways to the Threshold – other worlds – and perhaps even the Inner Portals to the Great Dream – is thought of as so much nonsense. No one thinks they actually exist.' He curled his lip in distaste. 'Least of all anyone in the Guild of Dream Finders – all *they*'re interested in are the fees their inner circle can charge. But, having been forced to think about it, perhaps there may be more Adepts than we know – if I'm one, then Ivaroth was for sure. And, occasionally, Dream Finders die mysteriously.' He sat down and stroked Tarrian's head. 'My own father did. And all their Earth Holders can say is that they just . . . slip away. Perhaps there've always been Adepts but, for some reason, we've stopped being able to recognize them. Or perhaps it's always been an uncontrollable gift.' He grimaced as he reached this last conclusion.

Gulda's gaze relented but she turned to Tarrian. 'Wolf, can you explain this any better?'

'No,' came the immediate reply. 'It's in a part of me – of us – that's beyond your understanding, just as much of you is beyond me. The other worlds are there – we "see" them as we "see" the darkness around us right now through the many

310

scents that pervade it. But you're blind to this knowledge, just as you're blind to the rich perfumes of the night and I can't truly stand in your place. How can the living explain life to the unborn? Earth Holders move between the worlds. I've no other words for you, still less the kind of explanation you need – only the knowledge. But the Gateways aren't for us and if our charge chooses to pass through one – or is drawn there – or stumbles upon one in his blindness – they disappear, as Antyr said – just slip from our view. I had a flickering awareness of the Great Dream when Antyr's father died but . . .' Strange, wild images filled the minds of his four listeners, leaving them bewildered and shaking their heads. 'We hunt for them – we've no choice – but . . .' Tarrian's thoughts faded away.

Gulda anchored the group again. 'You told us that Dream Finders were once known as Dream Warriors,' she said to Antyr.

'That's the tradition,' Antyr replied, grateful to be away from Tarrian's disturbing thoughts. 'People who guarded the spirits of others.'

'From what?' Gulda's question was like the slamming of a door caught by the wind. Antyr looked at her.

'I . . . don't know,' he stammered.

Gulda tapped her stick on the floor idly, then swung it up and looked at it thoughtfully. 'Farnor gave me this before he went into the heart of the Great Forest,' she said. 'I was very loath to leave him then, but he'd problems only he could deal with.' She frowned and was briefly silent. 'It had been a long time since I'd spoken with the trees myself – touched their strange and ancient memories. It was salutary, to put it mildly. We're so obsessed with ourselves. We forget how many ways Sumeral assailed this world at the time of the First Coming. In fact, we never even fully knew. No single record exists of the totality of that war, but each account we have implies – some even state directly – that many other battles were fought elsewhere – by people who had mysterious skills – by creatures other than humans – high in the clouds – deep in the oceans.' She paused and looked at Antyr.

'Whatever I am, I'm afraid I'm no warrior,' he said,

311

disconcerted by her renewed scrutiny. 'It's not all that long ago since I was just a drunk.'

'Yes, you told us,' Gulda said. 'But you stayed sober and kept your sanity when you discovered your ability to move between the worlds, you killed Ivaroth in personal combat, and you faced and defeated the blind man, as you called him, the Mynedarion, the user – or abuser, should I say, of the Power. No small achievement, any one of those.'

Faced with this heroic catalogue, Antyr could do no more than shrug weakly. 'I was lucky,' he protested incongruously. His manner made Hawklan and Andawyr laugh and even Gulda raised her eyebrows.

'An invaluable trait in a warrior,' she said, slapping his arm, then gripping it affectionately. 'Would that we had a training programme for it.' She began guiding him along the wall. 'It's a fine evening. Let's go down into the parks and walk and talk, speculate awhile, as your good Companions have suggested.'

A swift double tap with her stick transformed the suggestion into an order and Hawklan and Andawyr set off after the now retreating couple.

Gavor spread his wings and floated silently into the darkness.

Tarrian, Grayle and Dar-volci looked at one another. Then they all stretched and dropped down from the embrasure to bring up the rear of the small procession.

Chapter 25

There were many parks within the confines of Anderras Darion and many people enjoying the quiet calm of the evening. Maintaining an unusually modest and relaxed pace Gulda led her entourage to one of the parks that was quite populous. As they moved through the delicate shifting shadows thrown by Anderras Darion's myriad lights, they passed also through a winding avenue of soft and friendly greetings before she sat them down finally at a circular array of short benches set on top of a small hillock. Double seated, the benches looked both inwards and outwards. As they sat down, facing each other at Gulda's directing, a solitary lantern high above them bloomed gently into life. Its light had the quality of moonlight, but without its coldness. In nearby trees, night songbirds began contesting with one another as at a signal. Gavor floated down out of the darkening sky to rest on the back of the bench by Hawklan. The two wolves curled at Antyr's feet while Dar-volci clambered unbidden on to Gulda's knee.

For a long time, no one spoke.

'Whatever else happens, I am so glad I made this journey,' Antyr said eventually, his voice low as though he were talking to himself. 'There's such wonder about this place. Such touches of perfection.'

No one replied and silence enfolded the group again until Gulda clicked her tongue, wrapped her hands over the top of her stick and leaned forward to rest her chin on them, displacing Dar-volci from his roost in the process.

'What do we have, my friends?' she said. 'Or rather, let's start with *who* do we have?' Her tone was rhetorical. Still resting on her stick she looked at Antyr. 'There's you, with

313

Tarrian and Grayle and the strange ability you have between you to delve into the minds of others and seemingly into worlds beyond this one. Worlds whose very existence has previously been little more than speculation to us. Then there's Farnor, scarcely more than a boy, brutally orphaned, with the ability to touch the mind of the Great Forest and some kind of a gift for healing rifts between the worlds, if I read his telling correctly. And his friend Marna, a woman who wants to be a soldier when we've no war to fight. Declared by no fewer than four of our Goraidin to be a young woman of considerable resource and courage, which is praise indeed.'

'I'm not sure she wants to be a soldier,' Hawklan remarked.

'I wouldn't dispute about that,' Gulda replied. 'But warrior skills aren't confined to fighting, are they? And if she wants to learn them she probably needs to.' She reverted to her summary. 'Then there's Vredech. An erstwhile Preaching Brother.' Her eyes narrowed and her mouth became disapproving.

'They're not all bad,' Andawyr announced, anticipating a need to defend Vredech in his absence.

'You've not seen as many as I have,' Gulda retorted acidly. 'Believe me, religion was Sumeral's greatest gift after war itself.' Andawyr bridled but Gulda became conciliatory. 'Don't fret, old man, I'll take him as he is, you know that. As his own Santyth says, "Judge not lest ye be judged". And I'm long past judging anyone.' A knowing glance passed between Hawklan and Andawyr, though they contrived to keep it hidden from Gulda as she continued. 'If Antyr's correct then it seems he too is a Dream Finder, maybe even an Adept, as also is Pinnatte. Another young man, barely Farnor's age, I'd say, but probably much older in his ways, though you'd never guess it from his speech.'

'We'll do our best to help him through that,' Andawyr said. 'I'm sure it's only some kind of shock. But there's something about him which eludes me.' Anger began to roughen his voice. 'Those damned Kyrosdyn, experimenting on people. They . . .'

'Ever His way.' Gulda cut him short. 'You know that.'

Andawyr bit back the denunciation with difficulty. 'I don't know what they did to him, but I think part of it's still with him,' he said, more calmly.

Gulda nodded but did not pursue his concern. 'And lastly we have Thyrn. Yet another young man. The youngest of them all, in many ways. Over-protected, by Endryk's Account – cultivated, almost – by his parents, then plunged head first into the highest levels of Arvenstaat's politics. He seems to be making plenty of friends here. Which is nice. I doubt he'd had a childhood worth speaking of.' Her face became pained, as though the thought particularly disturbed her, but she pressed on. 'What a strange talent he has. When he speaks of others they're there, you can feel their presence. Remarkable. He makes the Goraidin look clumsy and inaccurate.'

'He's also got the same healing touch as Farnor,' Hawklan added.

'I've got people searching into the history of the Caddoran,' Andawyr said. 'There could be something of interest there. It's probably no more than a relic of battlefield message-carrying, like the Goraidin's Accounting, but it's odd we've none of us heard of it before.' He became thoughtful. 'And I find his story more disturbing than any of the others.' He stretched out his legs and, putting his hands behind his head, gazed upwards past the solitary lantern and into the star-filled sky. 'The blind man that Antyr faced, Farnor's Rannick and what was almost certainly a Sierwolf, Vredech's Dowinne, the Kyrosdyn and their crystals and what was *definitely* a Sierwolf, by Atelon's account. All these had a quality of familiarity about them – they all involved the use of the Power in some way. And there's a pattern in them – a frightening pattern, granted – but a pattern nonetheless – a clear indication of Sumeral struggling to take form in this world again. But what happened to Thyrn feels entirely different.'

'In what way?' Hawklan asked. 'He found himself an inadvertent witness to an exchange between Vashnar and . . . someone . . . some *thing* . . . full of hatred and malice, someone intent on coming into this world and destroying it. Surely it must have been another manifestation of Sumeral, or one of His creatures?'

Andawyr's face wrinkled in reluctant disagreement. 'One would think so, but, as I watched and listened to Thyrn, of all the many things I felt I did *not* feel myself in the presence of

Sumeral. Not a hint of Him. And I fully expected to.' He glanced at Gulda as if for support in this finding, but she had pulled her hood forward, plunging her face into shadow, and she gave no sign.

'That's probably just the lad's way of telling his story. Maybe we're reading too much into this skill of his,' Hawklan pressed.

Andawyr's reply was firm. 'No. If you recall, I journeyed through the Pass of Elewart with Sumeral's presence all around me. Journeyed in some terror, I might add. And with you into Narsindal. I'm well attuned to Him.' He indicated Antyr. 'I could feel His presence when you told us about the blind man, and it was there in some degree when all the others told their tales. I know it as well as I know the Cadwanen. And it wasn't there when Thyrn spoke.' He wrapped his arms about himself and closed his eyes briefly.

Despite this disavowal, Hawklan nevertheless looked set to pursue his objection. Andawyr, however, gave him no opportunity. 'Everything that Thyrn told us was deeply strange. The very place he described where Vashnar and this figure – this entity – met was unlike anything I've even heard of. None of the intricate, elaborate, obsessive patterns, the stark points and edges that typify His work – the frantic scratching after His notion of perfection. And what the figure actually said.' He leaned forward, drawing the circle of listeners tighter. Only Gulda remained motionless. His manner became intense. 'Remember, think back. Thyrn's telling was so vivid, he had us all standing next to him in that strange grey half-world – there and not there – eavesdropping on this exchange. We could feel the figure's appalling cruelty and bloodlust. And also that it was all too human. When it first appeared it seemed to be a manifestation of many wills, but then it became one distinct individual. Yet when Vashnar asked it who it was, it was puzzled at first, then amused.'

' "I am remade in my old image by forces that I do not fully comprehend." '

It was Gulda, reciting the words that Thyrn had put into the mouth of Vashnar's mysterious companion. Her voice was flat and without emotion but Hawklan noticed that her hands, folded over the top of her stick, were tense, as though she were gripping it to prevent herself from trembling.

'Yes,' Andawyr said, slightly unsettled by this unexpected assistance. ' "For aeons I have been scattered, without form," it said. "Such an event as we have here – such a coming-together – does not happen once in ten thousand generations." These aren't the words of Sumeral or any of His acolytes. Apart from the fact that Sumeral was amongst us less than a single generation ago, He'd never admit to any ignorance, least of all about how He came to be. He perceives Himself to be the true beginning – the very fount – of all things. And His followers always bear His stamp – the mark of the chains by which He binds them – *always*. It's unmistakable.'

Hawklan made to speak, but a slight gesture from Gulda kept him silent. Andawyr snapped his fingers, speaking now as much to himself as to the others. ' "How I came to be thus I do not know." ' Andawyr was shaking his head as his conclusion became more certain. 'More ignorance admitted, you see. It's not Sumeral, definitely. Nor anything of His. Everything that Thyrn recounted cries out with that.'

'Who was it, then?' Hawklan asked bluntly.

Andawyr frowned. 'I've no idea,' he said flatly and with no small sense of anticlimax. 'That's to say, I've no idea who the individual was – the hooded figure. But . . .' He stopped and squeezed his nose, then ran his hands through his disordered hair a few times.

'Say what you've got to say, old man,' Gulda said.

'It's vague, unclear,' Andawyr protested.

'Nor likely to become otherwise if you don't spit it out.' Gulda flicked her hood back and leaned towards him, her stick beginning to tap the turf impatiently.

Andawyr made a series of opening gestures before actually continuing. 'There was something else the figure said to Vash-nar. Though he seemed to be like we are – only just discovering something – somehow he knew that both he and those he called his enemies had been defeated. He spoke of a – conjunction – of some kind. A coming-together that shouldn't have happened. He referred to it as his enemy's treachery but I've the feeling it was some kind of simultaneous attack in which everything was destroyed. A mutual killing.' Andawyr's voice fell. 'He said that a brightness moved across the land – and across the oceans. It moved through everything that lived – what an odd phrase. Even odder, it moved "at scarcely the pace of a walking man", growing relentlessly, sustaining itself. The Power can be used with infinite delicacy if needs be, but it can't do that. Everyone fled before it – "Believer and heretic alike", but none escaped.' Andawyr raised his arm to his eyes, mimicking Thyrn's gesture as he had related the tale. ' "And then there was only a brightness beyond bearing – a reshaping – a remaking." A brightness beyond bearing.'

Andawyr's final words were given a power by the very quietness of his manner that made them seem to hang in the night air, ominous and grim. No one said anything. Even the nearby nightbirds fell silent.

Then Hawklan spoke. 'Assuming that Thyrn's tale is true – and I've no reason to doubt it – what is it about it that so concerns you? Wars enough have been fought in the past. Armies have been destroyed themselves before now. Perhaps the brightness is a metaphor for some military disaster.'

Andawyr was disparaging. 'I doubt it. You felt the character of the man when Thyrn spoke. Ruthless, powerful, *fanatical*. He spoke of armies and war machines beyond imagining – that could well be exaggeration. But war machines that would "unravel the very essence" of his enemies? It's a phrase that's lodged itself in my mind and won't go away. Nor will that strange, slow-moving brightness.'

Hawklan intruded, 'But . . .'

'Listen!' Gulda said sharply, silencing him.

Andawyr nodded gratefully. 'This is very difficult,' he said. 'Ideas are coming together – rushing together – that are shaking the very foundations of almost everything I know – or thought I knew.' He gave a rueful smile. 'When Ethriss formed the Cadwanol, it was a desperate time. He gathered all manner of learned men and women together from everywhere to search into ways of opposing Sumeral. But even then he told them they must "go beyond". Insofar as any of them thought about it they presumed it was his way of telling them to pursue every avenue in search of the skills and the knowledge that would bring Sumeral down – something they were determined to do anyway. Later, in safer times, the phrase was handed down, and mouthed a great deal – not least by myself – but I wouldn't say that any great thought was given to what he really meant. Now, I suspect, its real meaning is becoming apparent.' He looked around at his audience before continuing, rather self-consciously. 'As we've studied, thought, tested, experimented, through the generations, learning more and more about . . . everything . . . we've unearthed and explained many great mysteries – particularly so since the war. Some of our discoveries – the true turbulent, flickering nature of the roots of existence – the strange, vast arches of time and distance out there . . .' he glanced upwards '. . . present great challenges to the way we think about and perceive things, but strange though they are – and they really are very strange – there's a rightness about them that builds on what has gone before, that truly measures the world and its many parts and that draws us forward. But there've been other problems, in many ways less profound, that have brought us to a halt like a ship suddenly striking hidden rocks.' He brought his fist into his palm in emphasis. 'In the past we've always tended to resolve – I should, perhaps, say dismiss – these by saying that, despite our best endeavours, our theories must be flawed, our measurements insufficiently accurate etc – quite often with some validity. Lately, though, this hasn't been enough. Now we know that our latest theories aren't *that* flawed, our most recent measurements aren't *that* inaccurate.' He held out an arm towards the mountains, their hulking presence now only implied by the absence of stars. Then he took a deep breath and concluded in a rush, 'It appears that the mountains are older than they should be.' He looked down at his hands. '*We* are older than we should be. The stars themselves are. *Everything* is older than it should be. It isn't possible that the world we know could have come into being in the time that has passed since the Great Searing.'

An uncertain silence greeted this revelation.

'But the Great Searing is the beginning of all things.' Gulda's voice was uncharacteristically unsure. 'The Guardians themselves came from it, they made everything from it. They . . .' She faltered and stopped.

319

Andawyr slowly shook his head. 'No,' he said, very gently. 'Proofs are there for you to see. Bring your sharpest wits, your strongest fist. You may lay the odd one in the dust, but not all of them – mercy knows, we've tried hard enough ourselves. I'm forced to admit to myself now that too many lines of good reasoning and tested experiment go back through time and do not converge at the Great Searing. It was obviously the beginning of many things – Ethriss and the Guardians, Sumeral and some of His creatures, such life as we know. But it was not the beginning of *all* things. Not by tens and hundreds of millions of years. I think Ethriss sensed this when he gave us that injunction.'

There was another awkward silence, then Antyr spoke.

'In the most common of the Serenstad Creation Myths, the creator, the Weaver of the Great Dream, Mara Vestriss – your Ethriss, presumably – didn't *create* men, but *discovered* them when his son Marastrumel tried to tear apart the fabric of the Great Dream in a rage. The story says that Marastrumel couldn't damage the fabric because it was woven from a single thread that was of the nature of the timeless time beyond the Dream and was indivisible. But in the new pattern he made with his violence could be seen the world of men and many others beside – all bearing the mark of both Mara Vestriss and his son. And when Mara Vestriss saw this, he realized that he didn't know how such a thing could have come about. And, as he struggled with this, the question came to him, "How is it that out of the timeless time, that which is indivisible, I became?" And then he knew himself to be truly ignorant and he withdrew from the Great Dream, determined to find an answer to his ignorance before he would attempt to repair the damage his son had wrought.'

Antyr's voice had become that of a fireside storyteller as he spoke the final sentences, but there was no incongruity.

Andawyr blew out a long slow breath and stroked Dar-volci's head. 'I think your myth might have more wisdom in it than much of our learning. It's certainly not unreasonable to imagine that Ethriss asked himself such a question, nor surprising that he was unable to answer it. And given he was wise enough to know that children invariably surprise their

320

parents sooner or later, it's not unreasonable to imagine he'd look to them to answer it for him.'

Hawklan shifted restlessly. 'I can't see what this has to do with our present concerns, Andawyr, but it's remarkable stuff to be casually announcing on a quiet Orthlundyn evening. How is it we've had no wind of it before now?'

Andawyr made a vaguely apologetic gesture. 'Until quite recently it was just the backwash of unrelated ideas. Profound, fascinating, far-reaching, certainly, but not urgent.'

'And now?'

'And now, I don't know. Bear with me, please. As I said, there are so many things coming together, it's difficult to order them. But, for what it's worth, I think that Thyrn has touched on this time before the Great Searing. Or touched on some lingering remnant of it.' He paused and his eyes became distant. 'Endryk told us that the place to which both Vashnar and Thyrn were drawn was like the Thlosgaral – dead, and barren – a place that seems to draw the life out of people – a place where crystals can be found.' Hawklan leaned forward but Andawyr answered his question before he asked it. 'I could give you several long lectures about crystals,' he said. 'But then you wouldn't know much. Put simply, they can store and transform the Power – amplify it, absorb it. They can be very dangerous to anyone who can use the Power. That's why we sent Atelon and Dar-volci to find out where they were coming from when they suddenly appeared at the Gretmearc. We used to use them for all sorts of things – latterly mainly the Slips for moving about the Cadwanen quickly, if you recall, but . . .' He shook his head thoughtfully. 'They distort things – distance, even time. As we learned more about them we used them less and less. Now they're just part of the Cadwanen's defence system.'

Gulda grunted. 'Why would Ethriss create them if they were so dangerous?'

'I don't think he did,' Andawyr retorted. 'In fact, I'm inclined to agree with Atelon – they're made things.'

'Which means?'

'Which means that someone else made them. It's not possible they came about by some random natural process – their inner structures are far too complex, too ordered.'

'Just because you can't account for them doesn't mean that's the way of it, does it? How else would they come to be scattered all over the Thlosgaral?'

Gulda's question ended in a dying fall as she anticipated Andawyr's answer.

'I'd surmise that they were made by the people who came before the Great Searing and that they were part of whatever weapon or weapons actually caused it,' he said, quietly, but very steadily. He had the air of a man who had just attained a reluctant goal but was ready to move on.

'They could be used as weapons, these crystals?' Hawklan asked into the ensuing silence.

'Oh yes. Using them as weapons is easy. It was using them more creatively that always taxed us,' Andawyr replied. 'From what we already know, it needs no great feat of imagination to see great arrays of them linked to form weapons of truly appalling destructiveness.' He met Hawklan's gaze squarely. 'Or that could draw the life from – unravel the very essence of – an enemy. Reshape it, remake it. However Ethriss came by them, we should consider ourselves fortunate that Sumeral didn't, or this world would have been His long ago.'

Hawklan looked at him searchingly for a moment, then said, 'This is a great edifice to be building on the foundation laid by one young man.'

'It would be if it were,' Andawyr replied resignedly but without any resentment. 'But it's not. Now I look back on it, it's been a long time in the making, and it rests on far more than young Thyrn's testimony.' He became explanatory. 'What he's told us is more like the keystone to an arch. It gives the idea stability – holds it together.'

'Apart,' Gulda corrected absently. Andawyr looked at her and silently mouthed the word 'apart'. Then, unexpectedly, both of them burst out laughing. Gulda's laugh was rarely heard. It was that of a young woman. It twined around Andawyr's guffaw to make a sound that infected both Hawklan and Antyr, drawing them into it even though they scarcely knew what they were laughing at and despite the darkness of the concerns they were discussing.

'Good for some, picnicking in the balmy evening while

others are slaving over their work.'

It was Usche, moving towards them through the soft light. Behind her confident stride came the large and uneasy form of Ar-Billan. Andawyr extended a welcoming arm and signalled them to sit down. Usche's eyes were wide with excitement but, seeing Gulda and Hawklan, she hesitated. 'I'm not interrupting anything important, am I?' she asked.

'Quite possibly,' Andawyr replied, still laughing. 'But don't worry about it. What have you discovered that won't wait until the morning?' He glanced at the papers she was carrying. They were the ones he had given her earlier. 'Not given up so soon, have you? Or are you going to tell me you've resolved my paradoxes and confusions?'

'Well, in a manner of speaking, I think we have,' Usche replied, excited again.

'We?' Andawyr queried.

Usche indicated Ar-Billan who was sitting stiffly with his hands gripping his knees. Usche bent her head close to Andawyr's and lowered her voice. 'He's got his own way of doing things – a bit laboured, but very clear-thinking once he stops standing in his own light.'

Andawyr chuckled at her matronly manner. 'Show me what you've done, then.' He took the papers and waved them in her face with fatherly menace. 'I have to say that this took me some effort, to put it mildly . . .'

'I can see that, it's incredible work. I'd never have . . .'

'To put it mildly,' Andawyr repeated, with heavy emphasis, cutting across her enthusiasm. 'And I'd come to a complete dead end.'

'Yes and no,' Usche persisted, with a mixture of nervousness and pride. 'Yes, if you wanted complete rigour, though I've a suspicion that might be impossible in principle, but no, if you accept what we've been listening to these past days – clearly separate and distinct worlds apparently existing simultaneously, and *accessible*.' Abruptly aware that she was waving an emphasizing finger in her mentor's face, she faltered, then added with a slight stammer, 'Just as a working assumption, of course.' The hesitation, however, was only temporary and some of her excitement resurfaced almost immediately. 'The only

323

thing is, I'm not sure what the conclusion we've come to means. The reasoning's sound, I'm sure, but the result doesn't seem to make sense.'

'Your logical pathway has led you into a pit, has it, young woman?' Gulda said, watching the exchange keenly.

'I'm not sure *what* it's led me into, Memsa: that's why I'm here.'

Usche took the papers from Andawyr and riffled through them. 'Are you sure these inserted figures are correct? They're not what we normally use.'

'Oh yes, they're correct,' Andawyr confirmed, soberly. 'They've changed.'

'Changed? But . . .'

'Changed.' Andawyr's tone allowed no dispute. 'Excuse me for a moment,' he said to his companions. Then, gripping his nose with one hand he began thumbing his way through the papers with the other. The others watched and listened in some amusement as he emitted a variety of clucks, whistles, and tuneless hummings. After a while, however, he fell silent and his face became serious.

Reaching the end, he carefully stacked the papers and, placing them on his lap, laid his hand on them protectively. Usche looked at him anxiously. 'Have I done something silly?' she asked, unable to read his expression.

'You've done nothing silly,' Andawyr said. 'Nothing at all. This is fine work. I'd not thought to have seen a way through the tangle I'd created so soon, but you've cut through it neatly and elegantly.'

'Only one part of it,' Usche said, almost apologetic.

'It was the part that mattered,' Andawyr replied quietly.

Something in his voice made both Gulda and Hawklan look at him keenly.

'But the conclusion?' Usche asked. 'What does it mean?'

Andawyr looked upwards briefly. Then he stood up and, without speaking, walked away from the circle of watchers and into the castle's enveloping shadow.

Deep beneath the towers of Anderras Darion, in the Labyrinth that guarded the Armoury, something changed.

Chapter 26

'Antyr, wake up.'

Antyr rolled over in response to the voice and to the hand gently shaking him. With some difficulty he first forced his eyes open, then screwed them tight in an attempt to focus on the offending soul who was so relentlessly rousing him.

It was Andawyr.

Antyr levered himself up into a sitting position.

'Come on, hurry up, it's like chewing fog talking to you when you're in this condition.' Tarrian's maliciously hearty intrusion boomed into Antyr's mind, making him wince.

'Clear off, will you?' he growled peevishly. Andawyr started and stood back sharply, prompting Antyr into a hasty apology. 'Not you, him!' This declamation was accompanied by the throwing of a pillow towards the offending wolf. Tarrian stood motionless and watched disdainfully as it slithered along the floor past him.

'Should I leave you?' Andawyr fluttered, anxious not to become involved in a domestic quarrel.

'No, no,' Antyr reassured him. 'Of course not. It's just that Tarrian can't walk past a downed man without kicking him – or worse. He says it's his predatory instinct, I say it's his malevolent disposition.'

'Actually, it's marking out friendly territory,' Tarrian said with the patronizing tone of someone unjustly slurred. Antyr was aware of Grayle chuckling quietly in the background. 'We're going to eat. See you down there.'

'What? Down where?'

But the wolves were gone. Antyr looked at Andawyr who

was doing his best to understand the one side of this conversation he could hear. He was also unsuccessfully disguising a jigging impatience.

'Is something wrong?' Antyr asked, rubbing his face with both hands and yawning. 'You wandered off very mysteriously last night.'

Andawyr let a little of the jig out, shifting his weight from one foot to the other and back again. 'Oh. I'm sorry about that. I needed to think about what Usche and Ar-Billan had done – still do, actually – it's very . . .' He frowned as though he was being drawn back into some unwanted preoccupation, then he managed to wave the subject aside. 'We'll talk about that later. Right now there's something I'd like you to see. I can't think why it didn't come to me days ago.'

'What?'

'Oh, just an idea.'

By now becoming familiar with Andawyr's aptitude for forgetting conversational niceties when he was engrossed, Antyr motioned to him to open the shutters. As they unfurled to merge with the surrounding carvings, a dull light drifted into the room. Antyr stood up and gazed out of the window. A grey sky greeted him, scarcely more awake than he was.

He gave Andawyr a baleful look. 'It's only just past dawn, isn't it?' he said.

Andawyr joined him by the window, then unearthed a timepiece from somewhere in the depths of his robe. He consulted it, squinted at the sky, then replied, 'Yes,' quite simply.

Antyr blinked owlishly. 'This, whatever it is, that you want me to see, that should've occurred to you days ago – will it keep a little while? Say until I'm washed and dressed.' He patted his stomach and gave Andawyr a none too genial look. 'Perhaps even eaten a little?'

Andawyr looked puzzled and then a little guilty. He made one or two vague gestures of apology and acquiescence, concluding with, 'I'll . . . wait for you in the refectory downstairs.'

When Antyr eventually joined him in the almost empty refectory, Andawyr was poring over the papers that Usche had given him the previous night. In front of him was a bowl of untouched and dejected-looking cereal. Tarrian and Grayle were at his feet, both chewing noisily on large bones that they had gulled out of the cooks. Antyr was about to speak, then he changed his mind and went to collect food for himself. As he sat down opposite Andawyr and began eating, the Cadwanwr was muttering and whistling to himself. He was still seemingly oblivious of everything around him when Antyr had finished.

Antyr watched him for a little while in some disbelief, then, by way of experiment, said, 'Give that to Tarrian and Grayle if you're not going to eat it.'

Andawyr grunted and, without looking up from the papers, picked up the bowl of cereal and held it out underneath the table. The two wolves ate it greedily, though with sufficient care to avoid knocking the bowl out of his hand. Andawyr's concentration on his work was undiminished.

'Sumeral and the Uhriel are at the gate, asking for you,' Antyr said.

'Hm.'

'I said, Sumeral and the Uhriel are at the gate, asking for you,' Antyr repeated, softly rapping his knuckles on the table.

Andawyr frowned, then looked up and met Antyr's ironic gaze with one that took a disconcertingly long time to show any sign of recognition. When it finally did, it was followed by a sudden flurry of confused activity which included the question, 'Have you been here long?' Antyr replied by indicating his empty plate. At the same time Andawyr retrieved his own empty bowl. He stared at it with a puzzled expression.

'I'll get you another,' Antyr said, without explanation.

'I'm sorry about that,' Andawyr said, when the Dream Finder returned. He tapped the papers significantly but deliberately avoided looking at them.

'It's all right,' Antyr told him. 'Though, to be honest with you, despite my travels with Yatsu and Jaldaric, early morning isn't my . . . strongest . . . time – it's the nature of my job as much as anything. I don't wish to seem churlish, but unless it's something really urgent, like, say, the end of the world, I'd rather let the sun get well on its way before I greet it.'

Andawyr looked briefly contrite, then began bolting down

his food, rather as though it were a regrettable necessity.

'I'm afraid I tend to forget the time of day,' he admitted, speaking with his mouth full. 'One of the penalties of being incurably curious. And living underground much of the time.' Finishing, he smiled broadly, wiped his hands down his robe and stood up. 'Bit of a walk, I'm afraid,' he said extending an inviting arm towards the door.

Leaving the gradually filling refectory, he indicated an arched entrance on the far side of the hallway and Antyr found himself following him down a wide, spiral staircase. Tarrian and Grayle padded ahead of both of them. Though it was difficult to gauge accurately, Anderras Darion being built on wildly uneven terrain, Antyr judged that this would take them below ground. At the bottom of the stairs Andawyr settled to a comfortable pace along a deserted corridor.

'Where are we going?' Antyr finally asked.

'Down here,' Andawyr said unhelpfully, pushing open a large wooden door to reveal yet more stairs. These were set out in a series of short straight flights winding round a walled core. Antyr wondered idly whether this was solid or hollow and, if the latter, what might lie inside it. He ran his hand along the wall as he followed Andawyr's relentless descent, passing by open passageways and doors on almost every landing. Like everything else in Anderras Darion, the workmanship was superb. The joints in the masonry were tight and straight, and the blocks themselves were well dressed. He noted too that there was no hint of the dampness and the stale mustiness that should have been an inevitable feature of such a deep cellar. For they were, without doubt, some considerable way below ground now. It was another of the many small wonders that had gradually unfolded themselves as he had grown used to the castle. He remarked on it.

'Oh yes,' Andawyr said. 'Like the Cadwanen, there's more than just light carried to every cranny in Anderras Darion.' He patted the wall. 'And there's no denying that the people who built it were very capable – at least as good as any we have today.'

'It feels different from the rest of the castle, though.'

They were walking along a wide passageway. In common

with the stairs and passages they had used since leaving the refectory, it was well lit, but it was deserted.

'It's much older,' Andawyr said. 'There are some who say that parts of Anderras Darion existed before even the Orthlundyn princes came here, but . . .' He shrugged. 'Who's to say?'

It took Antyr a little time to identify something else that was puzzling him.

'There are no carvings,' he said abruptly.

Andawyr glanced around as if he had never noticed this before. 'No great surprise, I suppose,' he said. 'Considering where we are. The Orthlundyn aren't a particularly vainglorious people, but they do like their carvings to be seen, and precious few are going to be seen down here. Then again, I wouldn't pretend to understand them when it comes to carving. Maybe the light's not to their taste, or there might be something about the stone – they're extraordinarily fussy about so many things. To you and me, a rock's a rock, but that's just because we're rockblind, as they call it. To them, a single stone can warrant an entire saga. I've known Isloman search for months, even years sometimes, before he came across a piece that suited him for a particular idea he had in mind. Once . . .'

He stopped.

'Here we are.'

'Here' was a broad, stone-floored chamber. Simple and spare in design, it was obviously from a different era than the rest of the castle and it had a dull, forbidding look that the lighting did nothing to dispel. There was also an aura about it that made Antyr feel uneasy, an unease that was not helped by ragged and disordered piles of weapons stacked here and there against the walls. 'From the war,' Andawyr said, answering his unspoken question. 'A lot were put back in the Armoury but . . . it was difficult . . .' He seemed reluctant to continue and Antyr did not press him. His attention, in any event, had been drawn to the far end of the hall.

'Careful.' Tarrian's and Grayle's voices, unusually speaking together and both almost fearful, filled Antyr's head. He looked down to see the two wolves close beside him, ears flattened, tails down.

'What's the matter?' he asked, concerned.

Neither of them replied.

Not that a reply was necessary, for it needed no great sensitivity to feel the ominous presence of the rows of closely spaced columns that Antyr found his gaze now drawn to.

'That's the Labyrinth,' Andawyr said, answering another unasked question. 'It leads to the Armoury.'

Antyr stared in silence for some time at the columns and the darkening gloom that they disappeared into. As he did so, he began to feel that something was watching him in return.

'It's not remotely like anything else I've seen in the castle so far,' he said weakly. 'It's . . .' His voice faded.

'Frightening,' Andawyr said bluntly. Then he was walking towards it. Antyr followed him hesitantly. The two wolves remained where they were. Antyr felt them withdrawing all contact from him. As he drew nearer to the columns, it seemed to him that they were much larger than he had first thought – as if they had been further away than they first appeared. He tried to reassure himself that this was just another optical illusion, typical of many that were to be found in the ingenious carvings that decorated the castle, but it did not help – the effect was disorientating. Nor did it help that, while every other place he had been to in the castle was well lit, either by radiant-stone lanterns or mirror stones capturing some part of the landscape, there were apparently no lights within the Labyrinth. Worse, the light from the hall faltered and faded into nothingness after the first few columns – columns that, he saw now, were placed quite randomly.

Rather to Antyr's relief, Andawyr stopped. Antyr thought briefly of making some jocular remark to lighten the sense of oppression he could feel growing within him, but the waiting columns froze the words before they formed.

Then he realized that Andawyr was speaking. His voice sounded distant and faint.

'I'm sorry,' Antyr said, his own voice ringing raucous and harsh in his ears. 'I was just distracted.'

'It's all right,' Andawyr said. 'This place is disturbing, I know. It commands respect.'

It was an odd phrase to use about an architectural feature

but, looking at the columns, Antyr understood what it meant. Andawyr was continuing. 'I was saying that the Labyrinth guards the way to the Armoury – the place where weapons from the wars of the First Coming are stored and where Hawklan found the black sword. It's the only way in and the only way out. But I didn't bring you here to show you the Armoury. I wanted you to see the Labyrinth itself.' He raised a finger to forestall a question. 'Bear with me, please.'

He reached deep into a pocket and, after some stern-faced rooting, withdrew his hand to reveal a collection of oddments that included several small lengths of string, various crumpled pieces of paper, a rusty key, the remains of a pen, two or three fragments of wood and no small quantity of dust and stones. He selected a pebble, carefully replaced the remaining debris in his pocket, then threw the pebble gently past the first columns. Remembering his training in siege warfare during his obligatory service in Serenstad's army, Antyr watched the pebble intently, half expecting to see some powerfully sprung trap scythe out from one of the columns. But nothing happened except for an innocuous click as it landed and rolled a little way along the stone floor.

A click that echoed.

And echoed . . .

Over and over . . .

Antyr found himself craning forward as the sound did not fade away but began to multiply, resonating to and fro, growing in intensity from the hiss of wind-carried sand blown across a beach, to the rattle of jostling corn stalks, to the hammering of hailstones on a slate roof. Then, with appalling suddenness, it was a screaming cacophony that defied description. Antyr was uncertain afterwards whether he staggered back or whether Andawyr pulled him, but by the time he recovered his wits, he was much further away from the columns than he had been, and his hands were clamped tightly over his ears. The sound from the Labyrinth was fading as rapidly as it had grown but even as it died it rose and fell like the hiss of a predator frustrated of its prey.

'What . . . what was that?' Antyr stammered, wide-eyed.

'That was the Labyrinth,' Andawyr replied. 'It not only

leads to the Armoury, it guards it. It can take the least sound and double and redouble it until it becomes a crushing weapon. What we just heard was the merest echo of what you'd have heard had you been inside it.' He hesitated. 'It can do other things as well, almost none of which we understand.' It impressed Antyr that the Cadwanwr made no effort to conceal how shaken he was by what they had both just experienced, but the look Andawyr was now giving him was disconcerting. 'I think you may be more familiar with it than you realize.'

'What do you mean?' Antyr retorted. 'I've never been . . .'

But Andawyr was taking his arm and leading him back towards the columns. 'Come with me.'

Antyr resisted after a few paces, bringing the Cadwanwr to a clumsy halt. 'I'm not going in there,' he said categorically.

'Don't worry, there's a safe pathway, obviously. Right the way through it,' Andawyr replied. 'But I only want to go a little way into it – just a few paces. It should be more than enough.'

'Enough for what?'

'To test my idea.'

Antyr raised his eyebrows. 'You haven't told me what this idea is yet.'

Andawyr bent down to pick up something. It was the pebble that he had thrown into the Labyrinth. Something had thrown it back. He dropped it into his pocket without comment.

'For the simple reason that I'm going to need an honest response from you. One uncluttered by what you think might be expected of you,' he said.

Antyr turned to Tarrian and Grayle for support, but though the two wolves were watching the exchange closely, they were still wilfully avoiding contact with him. He swore at them mentally, then reluctantly responded to Andawyr's renewed urging.

'Stay close to me,' Andawyr said needlessly as he stepped between two of the columns. 'It's quite safe.'

Antyr took a deep breath and followed him cautiously.

As he stepped into the Labyrinth, it seemed to him that it

too was drawing in a breath. He eyed the nearest columns nervously as though, despite Andawyr's assurances, they might suddenly close in on him. Unexpectedly alarming was a sense of oppression from above. Looking up, Antyr found that he could not see the ceiling. In the entrance hall, the columns spanned starkly from floor to ceiling without base or capital, but here they faded into a dark haziness. For a moment, he thought that he caught sight of those columns around him tapering giddyingly high above him but the impression was gone almost immediately.

'Just a little further,' Andawyr said, his voice oddly resonant, as though the Labyrinth were testing it, savouring it. Antyr padded after him, placing his feet with exaggerated care to avoid making any noise that this place might seize upon.

Andawyr stopped and spoke very softly. 'This should be far enough,' he said. Antyr looked at him suspiciously. 'I want you to try something for me. I just want you to close your eyes and stand very still for a few moments.' Antyr's look became even more suspicious. 'Don't worry,' Andawyr said, taking his arm again. 'I'm not going anywhere and in any case you're truly in no danger while you're on the path. Please indulge me in this: I wouldn't have dragged you all the way down here for anything trivial.'

'What is it you're hoping to find?' Antyr asked nervously.

'I'm not hoping for anything,' Andawyr replied. 'I just want your honest response.'

Antyr gave a slight shrug and, feeling more than a little self-conscious, straightened up and closed his eyes.

'What have I to do now?' he asked.

'Nothing. Just be quiet and listen.'

As the faint echoes of Andawyr's voice faded, a silence folded around the motionless Dream Finder. Gradually, alone in his darkness, Antyr became aware of his breathing and of his heart beating.

What was he doing here? he mused. He had no reason to doubt Andawyr's protestation that he would not have brought him here for any trivial reason, but he would like to have known what was expected of him. Was he supposed to be listening for some sound unheard by others? Voices like

333

Tarrian's and Grayle's that, normally, only he could hear, or those of the Great Forest that apparently spoke to Farnor? His brow furrowed and he leaned forward, striving to hear something, but the effort made him feel faintly ridiculous and, after a moment, he gave up, letting out a noisy breath.

The sound drifted away and Antyr felt the Labyrinth taking it, twisting it, magnifying it, slowly filling the air around him with a myriad such sighs and transmuting them into other, stranger sounds – sounds that reached inside him, stirring up ancient, unspoken fears . . .

'This was where I came!'

The words burst out of him, sweeping aside his intention to stay as silent as possible in this place. Andawyr jumped and cried out as he found himself witness to this unexpected and loud relevation.

'You frightened me to death!' he snapped, slapping his chest.

As the two men stared at one another, their brief exchange rose up around them, then came babbling back out of the darkness as a clamorous wave of sound, in the middle of which Antyr thought he could hear taunting cries and cruel laughter. Briefly it reached a peak, then it fell away rapidly, sinking into a sulky grumbling. Though the sound had been little louder than their own voices and posed no threat to them, it was sufficient to remind both men where they were: Andawyr grabbed Antyr's hand and led him quickly out of the Labyrinth.

'This was where I came!' Antyr repeated breathlessly as they emerged. 'When I slipped away – passed through a Gateway – back at the Cadwanen.' He jabbed a finger towards the columns. 'There wasn't even a vestige of light, but it was here!'

Andawyr was looking both smug and excited.

'It came to me from nowhere, in the night.' He snapped his fingers. 'I remember thinking at the time you described it that there was something vaguely familiar about it but I didn't pursue it. And now . . .' He clapped his hands. 'We must find Gulda.'

'What does it mean?' Antyr asked as they left the hall and

began the ascent out of the depths of the castle.

'I've no idea,' Andawyr replied. 'But it's important.' He patted the pocket containing Usche's papers. 'It's another facet of events showing itself. Something else to help us penetrate the mystery of your strange abilities, something to help us get to grips with what's happening.'

'It's good, then?' Antyr said.

'It's progress,' Andawyr replied. 'Whether where it leads us is good or bad remains to be seen.'

It took them some time to find Gulda but they were eventually directed towards a room opening on to one of the smaller parks. As they neared the door, the sound of a keyboard instrument reached them. One of the aspects of Anderras Darion that particularly appealed to Antyr was the music that was frequently to be heard there. It was rarely possible to walk far without encountering the sound of voices or instruments or both drifting through its hallways.

Andawyr was about to knock on the door when Antyr stopped him. Putting a finger to his lips for silence the Dream Finder gently opened the door and motioned his companion inside, still urging silence. Gulda was at the far end of the room and, for a moment, his eyes dazzled by sunlight streaming in through the high windows, Antyr thought he was looking at a tall, handsome figure seated at the instrument. As he blinked, the impression passed, and he dismissed it as he moved quietly to a nearby chair.

Gulda sat motionless as she played and the music she was making demonstrated both a power and a delicacy that held Antyr spellbound. The piece finished with a bubbling scurry up the keyboard, a momentary silence, then a soft chord. Gulda looked down at the keyboard for a few seconds, then nodded to herself and turned to examine her uninvited audience. Antyr extended his hands and clapped them, almost inaudibly.

'Thank you,' he said.

Andawyr shuffled uncomfortably.

Gulda bowed, then looked straight into his eyes. 'Thank *you*, Dream Finder,' she replied, standing up and walking towards him. Her stick flicked towards Andawyr. 'Unfortunately, Andawyr, despite his many doubted talents, has little

335

ear for music. Can't tell a violin from a kicked cat. A strange deafness, really, music transcending so much, as it does.'

Andawyr contemplated a rebuttal of this charge but abandoned it.

'Antyr came to the Labyrinth when he passed through a Gateway at the Cadwanen,' he blurted out without any preamble.

Gulda's gaze turned back to Antyr who nodded his confirmation.

Shortly afterwards Antyr found himself standing in the hall before the Labyrinth again. With him were Andawyr and Gulda, together with Hawklan and a rather irritable Loman, these two having been swept up along the way by a silent but commanding Memsa.

'I've enough to do running the castle without messing about down here,' Loman protested, not for the first time, as Gulda halted them all before the Labyrinth.

Gulda apparently ignored him and spoke to Antyr. 'The Labyrinth is deeply strange,' she said. 'Strange even by the standards of the Cadwanen, Anderras Darion, the Pass of Elewart, the Thlosgaral. It's a darkness at the heart of this castle every bit the equal of the light that it brings to the world. No one knows who built it, or when, or why. No one knows if the princes of Orthlund built Anderras Darion above it, or whether Ethriss brought it here in some way. The Alphraan understand better than many but even they admit to knowing little – when they can be persuaded to talk about it at all – which is rarely.' She turned to Loman. 'It scars people. Touches deep within them and leaves scarcely felt but lingering wounds. That's why Loman doesn't want to be here. He was to supervise the bringing of weapons out of the Armoury during the war. Guiding party after party through that winding pathway. Its whisperings seep into his dreams from time to time even yet.'

Loman returned her gaze, his burly frame oddly helpless. She gripped his arm supportively. 'I know what this place means for you, Loman, and I wouldn't ask you to come here for nothing, you know that. There are forces moving that are far beyond our understanding, endless connections being made, joinings, patterns. I have to follow my nose.' She gave her nose a merciless tap with a long forefinger. 'It may be precious little, but you and Hawklan understand this place better than anyone alive. I wanted you both to be here – *in its presence* – while Antyr tells us again about what happened to him at the Cadwanen, when he passed through a Gateway.' She paused. 'Because when he did so, he found himself here – in the Labyrinth.'

'What!' Loman exclaimed. 'That's not possible.'

'Seemingly, it is,' Gulda retorted.

'I *was* here,' Antyr interjected. 'How I came here, I don't know. But having entered it just now, felt it, heard it, I've no doubts about it, even though it was pitch dark when I came here before.' He held out a small concession. 'If I wasn't here, then there's another place identical to it somewhere.'

Loman grimaced and turned from side to side as though looking for a way to escape, but Antyr's unassuming certainty held him there. 'I'm not impugning anyone's sincerity,' he said eventually. 'But this business of being in two places at once is giving me trouble. It makes no sense. I'm a simple smith. I bend and shape iron. The things I know are solid and here. They can't be here *and* there. They . . .'

He threw up his arms in frustration.

Gulda tapped her stick on the floor. 'You're as simple a smith as Hawklan's a simple healer,' she said. 'But your point's taken. Little of this makes sense. The only thing that stops any of us dismissing all these tales out of hand is the presence of too many reliable witnesses – too much hard information. Sumeral is working to return, beyond any doubt, and, whether they make sense or not, these things both *are* and are part of His struggle. We can't afford the luxury of not accepting them just because they offend our common sense.'

Loman turned to Andawyr and Hawklan but found no relief there.

'In the very smallest and the very largest of things, what we call common sense vanishes, Loman,' Andawyr said, almost apologetically. 'Impossible things become possible.' He fumbled unconsciously with the papers in his pocket and repeated softly, as though to himself, 'Impossible things become possible.'

'The Memsa leaves us no choice, Loman,' Hawklan said. 'She's right. You and I probably know more than anyone else about the Labyrinth. I know this place disturbs you. I can't say I enjoy it myself. But it holds no threat for us except what we choose to make of it. We can listen to what's being said, can't we?'

Loman growled and clutched at a final straw. 'Anyway, there's nowhere I know in the Labyrinth that's completely dark. This hall is always lit, as is the Armoury. It's dim in there, but there's enough light to see where you're going.'

'On the path,' Gulda said.

'Yes, obviously, on the path.'

'And off it?'

Loman hesitated. 'Off it, you die,' he said categorically. 'I doubt you'd make ten paces before you were down.' He almost snarled his final words. 'If your eyes were open, you'd see the light as you were dying.'

Gulda nodded. She held out her hands as though measuring something. 'How big is the Labyrinth?'

Loman mimicked the gesture unthinkingly and puffed out his cheeks, relieved to be dealing with a practical matter. 'I've no idea,' he concluded. 'There are precious few plans of any part of the castle and certainly none of this place. And I've never had any desire to measure it. In fact, it can't be measured from the inside and it's too far below ground to be measured from the outside. Why?'

'Just curious. It could be vast. Plenty of places where the light doesn't reach.'

'I suppose so, yes.'

Gulda turned back to Antyr. 'Anyway, let's . . .'

Her words were cut short by a sound coming from the Labyrinth.

A howling.

Chapter 27

A ll five started violently at the sound suddenly surging out of the darkness of the Labyrinth. Before any of them could speak, however, it was all around them, ringing and echoing about the hall.

'It's Tarrian and Grayle,' Antyr cried out, though he could scarcely hear his own voice. 'They must have wandered in there after we left.'

Panic seized him and instinctively he reached out to them. Almost immediately he touched Tarrian's consciousness, but even as he did, the wolf rebuffed him so strongly that, though the blow was only in his mind, the fear and the wildness in it sent him staggering backwards into Loman.

'Are you all right?' the smith shouted at him above the still-mounting noise.

Antyr's panic redoubled. 'They're in there! Get them out!' He tried to run towards the Labyrinth but, on seeing his intention, Loman's grip, at first sustaining, tightened and held him firm.

'If they're in there and off the path there's nothing you can do. It'll kill you too if you go after them.' Loman's voice cracked with dismay as he struggled to make himself heard, but his grip on Antyr did not falter.

Then there was movement amid the clamorous columns and, flanked by the grey frenzy of Tarrian and Grayle, a figure stumbled into the hall. He had a knife in his hand. Gulda's stick flicked out protectively with unexpected speed as Hawklan, the nearest to the man, took a rapid pace backwards. Loman released Antyr to move to help Hawklan but it was immediately apparent that the man was a threat to no one.

339

Indeed, he would have fallen headlong had not Hawklan stepped forward quickly and caught him. The knife clattered to the floor. Gulda's stick swept down and knocked it deftly towards Loman who stooped and picked it up with an agility that belied his bulk.

Tarrian and Grayle left the man and ran straight to Antyr who dropped to his knees to embrace them. Both animals were frantic with excitement.

The noise from the Labyrinth fell away abruptly into a low swooping moan punctuated by what sounded like distant cries and dull percussions. Not that anyone noticed, for they were all too occupied with the cavorting wolves and the mysterious arrival.

A black shape flapped into the hall, the lanterns flickering its shadow over the walls and ceiling to add to the confusion.

'Heard the noise, dear boys. What's happening?'

Gavor landed awkwardly by the now supine figure of the man as Hawklan was examining him. 'Oh dear. He doesn't look very well, does he?' he offered.

The man was wearing heavy boots, a jacket secured by a stout leather belt, and loose-fitting trousers. Though made from a heavy and obviously hard-wearing fabric his clothes were stained and torn and impregnated with dust that rose up in small dancing spirals each time Hawklan touched him. A sword and another knife hung from his belt. Hawklan removed it and handed it to Loman who inspected it curiously.

Of average height and build, there was nothing about the man to indicate who he might be, but his face was strained and drawn as though he had been starved or was being driven by some terrible inner demon.

'I think he's only unconscious,' Hawklan said. 'Exhausted.'

'I don't understand,' Loman said. 'Where could he have come from? His clothes and his weapons aren't Orthlundyn, or Fyordyn for that matter. And look at this.' He held out the knife he had retrieved. It was bloodstained. Hawklan grimaced but did not speak. 'And how could he have come out of the Labyrinth?' Loman went on, rubbing his hand tightly across his brow as though that might erase his confusion. He gave Antyr a questioning look but Tarrian and Grayle were still careering wildly around the Dream Finder.

'They're too excited,' Antyr said. 'I can't reach them when they're like this.'

'It doesn't matter at the moment,' Hawklan said, gathering up the man. 'Let's tend to this one first.' He paused and looked thoughtfully at the now silent Labyrinth. 'Loman, get the Goraidin together and arrange to have a permanent guard in this place. The Labyrinth has always had a way of springing surprises on us in difficult times and I'd like both swords and clear-eyed witnesses here after this.' He looked again into the gloom of the Labyrinth, then spoke quietly to Gulda. 'Memsa, would you try to seek out the Alphraan? See if they know anything of this?' Gulda nodded slowly, without speaking. 'Thank you,' Hawklan said. 'Gavor, go with her.'

By the time the stranger had been laid on a comfortable bed in a sunlit room overlooking the Orthlundyn countryside, Gulda was trudging purposefully into the mountains, Gavor circling high above her, and Yatsu and Jaldaric had lost the draw for first duty in the Labyrinth hall while Loman was pacifying the other Goraidin.

Having assured himself that although his patient was bruised, scratched and probably under-nourished, he was indeed only unconscious, Hawklan sat down beside him and prepared to wait. Nertha was sitting on the opposite side of the bed. Antyr had sought out Vredech and she had come with him. Intrigued by Hawklan's healing skills since she had first met him, she had watched him intently as he examined the man and had asked many questions. Andawyr and Dar-volci were by the window, the one leaning on the sill, the other stretched out luxuriously affecting a studied indifference to this strange happening. Vredech and Antyr were in an adjacent room with Tarrian and Grayle, talking urgently. The rumbling tones of their conversation drifted into the otherwise silent room.

After a little while, the man stirred and opened his eyes. They widened as he looked around: he cried out and made to sit up. Nertha laid a restraining hand on him.

'Don't be afraid,' she said. 'You're safe here.'

The man tried to push the hand aside. Hawklan moved to

341

intervene, but it was unnecessary. The man was no match for either Nertha's experience or her determination. Hawklan smiled as he caught the glint of resolute compassion in the physician's eyes. 'You're safe. And uninjured,' Nertha insisted with gentle forcefulness. 'My name's Nertha, this is Hawklan and that's Andawyr. The felci pretending to be asleep on the windowsill is Dar-volci. This place you're in, in case you don't know, is Anderras Darion and you just arrived in a most unusual fashion from what I hear. Lie still for a few minutes while you gather your wits. Is there anything you want immediately? Food, drink?'

The man glanced from Nertha to Hawklan and back, his eyes fearful and doubting.

'Do you want anything?' Nertha asked again.

'Water,' came the reply after another unsteady inspection of the room and its occupants.

'I'll get it,' Andawyr volunteered.

The man closed his eyes, then slowly opened them as if to reassure himself that what he was seeing was actually there. 'I'm all right,' he said after a while, slowly pushing himself upright. 'At least, I think I am.'

Andawyr returned with a glass of water which the man drank greedily before handing the glass back with a guilty, almost fearful look.

'There's plenty more,' Andawyr reassured him with a laugh.

The man was running his hands over himself as if testing the reality of what he was seeing. 'Has it all just been a dream?' he said to no one in particular. 'A nightmare?' He looked at the window, then hesitantly swung off the bed and walked over to it. 'The sun,' he said softly as he gazed out. 'It's back.' For a moment it seemed as though he were about to break down in tears. 'I never thought I'd see it again. This is a dream, isn't it?'

Hawklan and Nertha both frowned in response to his obvious pain but Andawyr's expression was one of bewilderment at what he was saying. The man turned sharply. 'Or am I dead? Did they catch me – kill me? They were close – very close. I felt them, right behind me. Is this some kind of

342

afterlife?' He put his hand to his head.

'You're not dreaming and you're certainly not dead,' Hawklan said. 'I think you'll find you've got as many cuts and bruises now as when you left wherever it was you left. And we've got as many questions to ask of you as you have of us. Nertha told you our names: what's yours?'

The man hesitated before replying, still very uncertain.

'I'm Gentren, Gentren Marson,' he said eventually. 'My father's Andeeren Marsyn. He's . . . he was . . . the Protector of the land of . . .' He faltered, then gave a short bitter laugh. 'Of nowhere now, not now there's nothing but desert, tortured land and tainted skies.' He turned back to the window. '*Where* is this place?'

'Anderras Darion. The land you see out there is Orthlund. And you came here by some means that we'd dearly like to know about. Can you tell us about it? And who they are, the people who were pursuing you?'

'The Riders, who else? The three Riders.' Gentren's voice was a mixture of surprise and irritation, as if he were dealing with foolish children, though it softened almost immediately as he continued looking through the window. 'I'd no idea there was anywhere like this still left. I thought we were the last.' He turned back to Hawklan. 'And I don't know how I came here. None of this makes any sense.'

Andawyr gave a wry shrug. 'That's becoming a very familiar remark,' he said, dropping into a chair and swinging his legs up on to the end of the bed. It was a deliberately casual movement that had the effect of easing much of the tension in the room. He motioned Gentren towards the bed. 'Sit down and relax. I think it would be a good idea if you told us about yourself. So far, we're as mystified by you as you are by us. Tell us about these Riders.'

Gentren looked at him suspiciously. 'How can you not have heard of them?' he said, his voice suddenly full of both anger and despair. 'They've swept across the entire world, destroyed almost every living thing, transformed land and sea into vast, dead obscenities, blotted out the sun, fouled the air itself. Hardly any of us are left – people, animals, birds – all dead – or dying.'

The power in his voice seemed to darken the room and it was a few moments before Hawklan said, very gently, 'There was a war here several years ago but nothing such as you describe. Nor has any remotely like it happened. Wherever you come from . . .' He hesitated. 'Doesn't seem to be any part of this world.'

Gentren looked at each of them in turn, then seemed to wilt. He took Andawyr's advice and sat down on the edge of the bed.

'Not part of this world,' he echoed to himself. He ran his hand idly over the embroidered sheets. 'Is it really possible?'

He looked at Hawklan. 'Before the Riders came, some of my father's advisers – his savants, his sages, his learned men, men relentless in the pursuit of the truth – spoke of such things. They conjectured that other worlds might exist at the same time and in the same place as ourselves.' He smiled bitterly. 'It was an interesting notion with apparently much to commend it in the way both of reasoned argument and observation, I believe, though it was all beyond me. And it wasn't particularly important, was it? An academic matter only. Sufficient in itself. An elegant idea, apparently – exciting, even. A newer understanding. Then some of them were suddenly concerned. They began telling a tale that might've come from times long gone when blind superstition had to suffice for knowledge. A disaster was coming. The end of the world, no less. A deep flaw had somehow been made in the heart of things long ago. An imbalance was there. The least of things in itself, at the very limits of what could be measured. But it had grown for generations and was growing ever faster. Now the consequences of it were no longer small. Something was coming together – a terrible conjunction was about to happen – a conjunction that would bring these many separate worlds together.' He threw up his hands. 'Or something like that. It was all theoretical enough to be dismissed as a bookish storm in a wine glass. Until it became real, that is.' His searching hands patted his midriff. 'Where's my sword?' he demanded sternly.

Hawklan reached out and took the belt and sword that were leaning against the wall. 'Here,' he said, putting them on the bed beside him. 'Though I doubt you'll be needing a sword here. Or this.' He handed him the bloodstained knife.

Gentren took it and stared at it. His face was unreadable. 'I attacked one of them with this,' he said, his voice full of vicious self-mockery. 'A dismal piece of iron. Against the power that *they* had. I suppose if I was insane enough to do that then I could still be mad, couldn't I?'

'You could be,' Hawklan agreed. 'But you neither look nor sound mad to me, and, in my experience, mad people rarely ask that question. Besides, it seems from what you've said so far that, figments of your imagination or not, we're preferable to the company you've just left. Finish your story before you ponder your sanity. What did your father do about this advice he was receiving?'

Gentren gave a slight shrug. 'What could he do? He was concerned. These men were capable and highly respected. But they offered him no advice about what he should do. Their researches told them nothing except that this . . . conjunction . . . was coming and coming soon and that it would bring great destruction – possibly the destruction of the entire world. Concerned or not, he was a practical man. How could he prepare for a disaster whose nature was completely unknown to him? There was nothing he could do but politely ignore them – hope that it was just an error in their theories – their measurements. It wasn't an unreasonable hope, they weren't unanimous in their thinking. And it was all so improbable, so fantastic – the end of the world – I ask you – it had to be nonsense, didn't it? Despite the credentials of his advisers it wasn't something a busy Protector could pay serious attention to, was it?' He fell silent.

'Then?' Hawklan prompted.

Gentren began to tremble. He wrapped his arms about himself in an unsuccessful attempt to stop it. 'Then, suddenly, they were there. No one knew how or when they came, still less from where. They were just there. Three Riders. No great armies – no worlds crashing into us, tearing the sky open, splitting the earth apart. Just three people on horseback! But what they could do – what they did! – was beyond belief. They rode effortlessly about our world, destroying all they

345

came near to with seemingly nothing more than a wave of the hand. Towns fell, cities fell – literally fell – flattened – razed. There were no sieges, no battles, no parleying, no demands, nothing. No one knew what they wanted. They just swept places and people aside with no more thought than a man might give to scalding out an ants' nest. Some people tried to fight, some sent heralds to speak to them, most just fled – the country, the sea, everywhere was alive with panic-stricken people. But all to no avail. Those that they saw, they slaughtered out of hand with the same ease and indifference that they used on buildings and city walls.'

He stopped, his face taut and his fists clenched. The images he had conjured hung in the stillness, the more terrible for his quiet telling.

'Then they stopped. We thought they'd wearied of their . . . work . . . or perhaps taken all they'd wanted. There was a strange quietness over everything, as though all of us who were left were holding our breath. I think it was shock – sheer disbelief – as much as anything. How was it possible that so much could have come about so quickly? How was it that so many peoples could be destroyed and cowed so easily? A civilization, aeons old, smashed as though it were no more than a flimsy toy in the hands of a reckless child. But whatever we were thinking, it didn't matter. The destruction they'd wrought before was nothing compared to what began next.' He turned towards the window. 'I don't know what it was they did but they started changing the land itself. Fleeing survivors told us of mountains rising up from nothing – blue and jagged – and of seas retreating. We might have disbelieved them but, even where we were, we could feel the ground shaking under our feet, faint but quite definite – and very frightening.' He shuddered violently, startling his listeners. 'Then a deep blue haze began to fill the sky. It dimmed the sun – threw everywhere into a ghastly half-night.' He closed his eyes. 'The air became acrid and foul – burning the throat. No rain came after that.' He looked at the glass that Andawyr was holding.

'If this is troubling you too much we can talk later,' Hawklan said, resting a hand on his arm.

346

'There's precious little left to tell,' Gentren replied. 'For a while they were occupied with whatever they were doing, then they were moving out again, destroying new land as relentlessly as ever. This time we tried to oppose them. My father had managed to rally some semblance of an army. But, as before, it was futile.' He flicked his hand in an airy gesture. 'They just swept that aside as they'd done everything else.' His mouth curled in anger. 'We were *less* than ants to them. We couldn't even bite them before we died.'

'And what happened to you?' Hawklan asked.

'What indeed?' Gentren said bitterly. 'In the end, I did what everyone else did. The only thing I could do. I ran.' He looked around the room.

'How did you come here, then?'

Gentren frowned. 'I told you, I don't know. They were getting nearer. Everyone I knew was gone – family, friends. I was fleeing into the hills with some vague idea of hiding somewhere – just hoping I wouldn't be found. I remember I hadn't enough nails to shoe my horse properly and it lost a shoe and brought me down. But I kept on running until I fell into a ditch.'

His manner became calmer but more intense.

'I must have fallen asleep. I remember dreaming – dreaming about a plough tearing open the ground – three huge horses pulling it – and seagulls screaming and flapping behind it – bickering and fighting the way they do. They were all around me. I was trying to beat them off when I awoke, staring up from the bottom of the ditch through the dead grasses and reeds at that awful tainted blue sky. But the gulls were still screaming. Except that the sounds they were making weren't sounds any gull could make – or any natural creature. It was dreadful. It reached right inside me, tore at me.' Gentren's eyes widened as he relived the scene. 'And suddenly I knew who was making it. It was them. Everything they were was in that noise.' His face contorted and his hand reached out, clawlike, as if to crush something. 'All of a sudden, every part of me was alive with anger – so powerful – I'd no control over it. They were *here*! These creatures who'd brought all this horror and destruction were here – probably only a few paces from where I was lying. Part of me wanted to leap out of the ditch and cut them down – slash and hack at them until no part of them would even be recognizable.' His hand tightened, then relaxed, and he gave a sour smile, full of self-contempt. 'I didn't, of course. I grabbed my knife . . .' He mimicked the action, then paused, looking at the knife in front of him. 'But just doing that – feeling that familiar handle in my hand – feeling reality – told me I wasn't going to do anything. The anger was still there – but I didn't want to die. So I just held my breath – lay still, very still – willing them to do away. But they didn't. They stayed there – screeching at one another – to and fro – endlessly.' He put his hands to his ears. 'Then one of them was right above me. His horse kicked in part of the edge of the ditch making me jump – I thought it was going to fall on me. I must have made a noise because the next thing, the horse was craning round, looking into the ditch. Except that it wasn't like any horse I'd ever seen before.'

'Long bony head, malevolent eyes, and a strange way of moving – like a snake.' The voice was Vredech's, standing in the doorway with Antyr.

'Yes,' Gentren exclaimed. 'How did you know?'

'Go on,' Hawklan pressed, frowning at Vredech's interruption.

'It saw me. Looked right at me.' Gentren took a deep breath. 'Then the rider was turning towards me. I've never been so afraid, ever. I had to get away. I don't know what possessed me. I jumped up, drove my knife into his leg, then ran!'

This time it was Andawyr who interrupted. 'You *stabbed* him?' he said, eyes wide with incredulity.

'Yes,' Gentren confirmed, as if surprised at Andawyr's surprise. The Cadwanwr gaped. 'I didn't think about it – I just did it.'

Hawklan motioned Gentren to continue. 'I can't remember much after that. I was running like I'd never run before. Dodging and weaving across the hillside. I could hear the Riders behind me, but I didn't look back. It wasn't me running, really. Something inside me had taken charge and was hurling me along. I did things I know I couldn't possibly do – jumping from rock to rock – crashing through undergrowth. I do remember their screams, though – they were different – more human, somehow. It didn't sound like any language I'd ever heard but I could understand it well enough – it was full of anger and hate. I knew they weren't going to reach out and kill me with that power they had, like they'd done to entire armies. I knew they were going to capture me. I could feel the pain of the one I'd injured.' He closed his eyes and took another deep breath. His brow furrowed with concentration. 'The rest is vague – just the sound of my heart and my breathing filling everywhere. I seem to remember turning towards a light. And I remember the tone of their screeching changed – it became desperate, frantic. Then, very suddenly, it was fading away – dwindling into the distance like an insect whine. And I was ... falling ... I think ... yes, falling – tumbling through something I can't begin to describe – strange lights – strange sounds, all around me – sounds that became a howling. I remember thinking "They've killed me. This is what dying is like." Yet I was wondering what the howling was. And I remember thinking how strange it was I should be curious at such a time. Then the howling seemed to be leading me – keeping me safe somehow. And I was on hard ground – running again – running blindly through a darkness filled with a terrible roaring – but the howling was still guiding and protecting me. And now I'm here – wherever here is, with its open and clear sky – and sunlight – talking to you – whoever you are, with your strange names and ... your kindness.' He laid down the knife and looked at Hawklan as if for a conclusive answer. 'Am I dead?' he asked plaintively. 'Or mad?'

'Neither,' Hawklan replied bluntly and without hesitation. 'There are far stranger things in this universe than death and madness. Far stranger.' He turned to Andawyr. 'More hard information for you?' he asked.

'Oh yes,' Andawyr replied grimly. 'Too hard for the kind of comfort I'd prefer. I'll tell the others straight away.' He spoke to Gentren. 'There's nothing I can say that will ease the pain you must have suffered. To be honest, I can't begin to imagine

349

how you feel after what's happened to your world – indeed, I don't want to imagine the kind of desolation you must feel. I'd like to tell you that you're safe here but that wouldn't be entirely true. We know – we think we know – the creatures you called the Riders. We've dealt with their kind before. We know they're striving to reach us in this world, presumably with the intention of doing to it what they did to yours. In some ways we're better placed than you were to deal with them, but I fear we're looking towards a desperate and bitter struggle – one we may well lose.' Hawklan's eyes moved uneasily from Andawyr to Gentren and he raised a hand to intervene in this harsh verdict. But Andawyr waved him aside and while the gesture was gentle his words were unyielding. 'Your world has gone, but you may perhaps have an opportunity for vengeance in this one, if you wish. We could use your help if you're prepared to give it.' Gentren stared at him in silence. He was trembling again. Andawyr's manner softened. 'I'm sorry,' he said. 'This is all too much, too quickly, isn't it? Don't worry, there's no immediate danger, for sure. Rest here as long as you wish.' He pointed towards the door. 'When you're ready – when you've satisfied yourself that Hawklan's right – you're neither dead nor mad – you can go anywhere you wish about this place – this land. Speak to whoever you wish, ask whatever questions you wish. Vredech and Antyr will go with you. It was Antyr's Companions who guided you through the Labyrinth.'

Nertha coughed conspicuously. 'And Nertha will go with you, too,' he added hastily.

'How do you know about the Riders?' Gentren asked, seizing his arm abruptly.

'Later,' Andawyr replied. 'There's a lot to tell. And there's a lot more we can still learn from you, I'm sure. Rest now.'

A little way to the east of Anderras Darion, in the mountains, a strange encounter was taking place.

Chapter 28

G ulda stood on a rocky outcrop and gazed down into a
broad, sweeping valley. She had spoken a simple message in a clear and ringing voice when she arrived.

'Alphraan, the Labyrinth awakes again. Help us.'

Now she waited, as motionless as the crags around her and
seemingly as endlessly patient. High above her, Gavor
swooped and dived and tumbled through the unseen cascading
pathways of the mountain air. Below her, the shadow of a
small cloud slid silently along the valley floor.

'You use the Power with great subtlety, my lady.'

The voice was behind her. There was surprise and admiration in it that touched on awe. It spoke again, no louder, but
with a quality that sent the words spiralling up towards Gavor.

'Your wings make a rare music, Sky Prince. Join us if you
would.'

Gavor dropped a little way like an untidy bundle before
stretching his wings and arcing into a wide, rushing spiral.

'Aah!' said the voice appreciatively.

Gulda turned.

A small, slightly built man was sitting on a rock a little
above her. Dressed in what appeared to be practical travelling
clothes, simple in design though of an unusual cut, he was
studying Gulda intently. She returned the compliment. He had
the immediate look of a frail old man though, on examination,
neither his face nor his manner gave any indication of his age.
Gulda's piercing, blue-eyed gaze was not one that many could
meet comfortably, but the man's eyes twinkled in the sunlight
and a white smile cracked his face. It was definitely not the
smile of an old man.

'Great subtlety,' he emphasized. His voice was high-pitched and musical. Abruptly he was apologetic. 'Do forgive me for staring,' he said. 'But I'm afraid I've always been drawn to taller women.'

Gulda's eyes narrowed.

The man frowned in self-reproach. 'I'm not doing this terribly well, am I?' he said, scrambling nimbly down from the rock. 'Life's been more crowded for me than usual lately but I'm still not all that used to dealing with people. Especially *remarkable* people like yourself.' He looked her up and down. 'I was told about you, but I found it difficult to believe. Even now I find it hard. Gauche or not, I *have* to ask. Why do you choose to be the way you are?'

'I am what I am.'

'Oh, come now. A bland truism? Indulge me with an open answer. After all, we're both old in the ways of the world, aren't we?'

'I don't know. Are you?'

The man smiled. 'You're teasing me, my lady. Which I probably deserve. But while I may not be a true Sound Carver, and your skill with the Power may be considerable, I can do no other than hear what you are beneath the fiction you adopt.'

Gulda raised a warning finger. 'Don't listen. Nothing is to be shaped from what you hear there. And it is my fiction, my wish. Just as yours is yours.' She added the last sternly.

The man bowed. Then, after some rooting through his pockets, he produced two small pieces of cloth which he proceeded to knead into rolls and insert in his ears. At the same time he affected a look of great contrition. His manner made Gulda laugh. Eyes widening in wonder, the man gazed around as though he was following the sound as it rose to join the wind-carried murmuring rising from the valley below. Suddenly, he was very close to her, looking up into her face.

'Rare music, your laughter, my lady. Rare indeed,' he said, his voice deeper and richer. 'And you *are* a very beautiful woman.' He was two paces away from her by the time her warning finger levelled itself at him again.

'Enough,' she said, though her voice lacked the edge that

352

such a command from her would normally have had. Gavor landed on her shoulder, ending the exchange. He looked at the man, his head cocked first on one side then the other. The man bowed to him. 'It's an honour to meet you also, Sky Prince,' he said.

Gavor tapped Gulda's shoulder with his wooden leg. 'I don't wish to seem churlish, dear boy,' he said. 'But who are you?'

'Just a traveller recently come home,' the man replied.

Gavor clucked wearily. 'One of the problems of dealing with humans is that they're so often not what they seem. I've never felt the need for it myself. It can make life so difficult. Let's just be our plain ordinary selves, I say.'

The man chuckled, a dancing joyous sound. 'I'd heard you had a fine sense of irony, Sky Prince. Someone who carried the spirit of Ethriss through the ages and became the friend of the man who opened Anderras Darion can hardly be said to be an ordinary bird, can he?'

'That's as may be, dear boy,' Gavor said with the air of someone rapidly changing the subject. 'It's a complicated tale. More to the point, you still haven't told us who *you* are. You're not Alphraan, that's for sure . . .'

'And I'm not human either,' the man interrupted in a mockingly injured tone. 'Not wholly, anyway. You were a tad free with your insults before.'

Gavor drew in a reproachful breath and was suddenly fulsome. 'My dear boy, I *do* apologize,' he exclaimed. 'That was quite unforgivable. Thinking about it, I suppose I should have realized. But it was an understandable mistake, I hope you'll agree. The two legs you see . . .'

'Who are you?' Gulda asked before Gavor could plunge into what was promising to be a lengthy justification for his gaffe.

'I'm . . . kin . . . to the Alphraan,' the man replied. 'But I've been away for a long time – listening to the world.'

Gulda raised an inquiring eyebrow. 'How long?'

'When I left, the Great Gate was still closed,' came the explanation.

'And what have you heard?'

'So many questions, my lady. I . . .'

'He is the Traveller.'

The voices rolled over his answer. They were all around, at once one and many, at once shouting from afar and whispering nearby. The word 'Traveller' was filled with many meanings. 'You honour us with your presence, my lady, Sky Prince. Since the opening of the Ways and the heartplace, the Song has grown and it has become ever more difficult for us to touch on human affairs. But we are always yours and as he speaks, so is our will.'

Gavor spread his wings, and Gulda said, very softly, 'It is good to hear you again, Alphraan. May your Song sound through the ages.'

The voices rose in a wordless paean of gratitude that faded imperceptibly to become part of the sounds of the mountains.

The Traveller spoke. 'We heard the voice of the Labyrinth, and when we listened we heard you seeking our help.' Just as the voices of the Alphraan had filled the Traveller's name with many meanings, so now, as he spoke the word 'Labyrinth' it carried with it complex resonances, dark and mysterious. Gulda and Gavor both found themselves shying away from the sound.

'And can you help us?'

'No.' The Traveller's voice was full of regret. 'Not as you wish. The Labyrinth . . .' Again the word was disturbing. '. . . Is as great a mystery to us as it is to you. If not greater.'

'Your kin controlled it at one point during the war – kept us from the Armoury at a time of need,' Gulda challenged.

'So I've heard. A mistake duly admitted and amends made for, I believe. But it was a deed that required no deep understanding or great skill on our part. We merely splashed water in your eyes but we knew – we know – little of the sea from whence it came. What has just happened is quite beyond us. Just as we have shaped the sounds of the world for longer than humanity has walked it, so the Labyrinth has stood from far before our own time. It is deeply strange. The many paths through it lead to many places . . . and many times.' He looked at Gavor. 'Paths that shift and change unseen like the paths you follow in the air, Sky Prince.'

'*Many* paths?' Gulda queried.

'Many,' the Traveller confirmed. 'Though for the most part they cannot be mapped and measured. It is in their nature that to touch them is to change them.'

'The path to the Armoury doesn't change, and that's been travelled often enough.'

'The path to the Armoury merely changes slowly, my lady. Like these mountains – mote by mote.' The Traveller scuffed his boot across the ground, raising a small cloud of dust and leaving a dark scar. 'Others change like the seasons, others like the weather, but most change like the trembling of a leaf in the wind.'

'How can we find these paths, then? How can we travel them?'

The Traveller gave Gulda a regretful look such as a teacher might give an intelligent child who has asked, 'Why is this flower?'

'No part of the Song tells that, my lady. And if the Song doesn't tell it, mere words could never span it.'

Gulda's brow furrowed and she tapped her stick on the rock. 'I value your honesty, Traveller, but we need less mystery and more cold-edged knowledge. We need to know where this stranger has come from, and how. I've yet to hear who he is but I'd be more than surprised if whatever drove him here was something other than the cause of our present concerns.'

'Where we can help, we will,' the Traveller said, his manner anxious. 'We will be with you in the trials that you fear are coming. Anderras Darion is second only to our heartplace for us and our debt to you for the Opening of the Ways cannot be measured. But the Labyrinth is the Labyrinth. It is a thing made by men, and only men will fathom it.'

'You just said it was older than any of us,' Gulda retorted, not without a hint of irritation.

The Traveller flinched away from her tone. 'Yes. It is. But I also told you it was deeply strange – a great mystery – and it *is* a thing made by men, for all that it's older than men. It rings with their ways. No other creature could have made it.' He reflected some of Gulda's manner back to her. 'No other creature would have wanted to.'

Gulda let out a noisy sigh. 'I'm sorry,' she said. 'I know we have both your heart and your will. It's just . . .'

'Difficult.'

'Difficult indeed.'

The brief tension between them was gone.

'And frightening,' Gulda said. 'Sumeral is whole once more, Traveller, and His Uhriel are born again. Stronger by far than they ever were and seemingly roaming unfettered in their own desolate world as they struggle to come here.'

'We feared so. An echo of His ancient tongue, brief and distant, rent the Great Song but days ago,' the Traveller replied, clenching his teeth as though he were in pain. 'Foul beyond any imagining. There is no true light without darkness, nor true harmony without dissonance, but . . .' He faltered, apparently unable to continue. Soft sounds rose up around the three figures. The Traveller seemed to draw sustenance from them. As he recovered, he shook his head slowly. 'I have seen signs of His will, still active, on my journeying. That's why I came home – or was drawn back. To think, to be with my kin, to see again the Great Gate and hear its song, to learn. I fear that many Ways are opening that should not. There is a great turbulence in the Labyrinth.'

Gulda did not press him. 'I'll confess, I'd hoped for more,' she said gently. 'I think we're going to need our every resource to deal with what's coming. But it's good to know all's well with you.' She looked at him earnestly. 'Speak to us as the spirit moves you, Traveller – wait on no asking – Anderras Darion is yours, as you know.'

The Traveller smiled sadly, then touched the rolls of cloth in his ears. 'Unfortunately, the castle's a little too noisy for me at times, but I understand. My kin still go there from time to time.' He waggled his fingers teasingly. 'Flickering shadows at the edge of your vision. We'll be with you more than ever now. Listening where you cannot hear.'

There was a finality in his tone. There was nothing more he could say.

Gavor launched himself from Gulda's shoulder, dropping down into the valley, then sweeping up again. 'Jolly good, dear boy,' he called out. 'Much appreciated. We'll keep an eye out for you.'

'Thank you, Traveller, Alphraan,' Gulda said as she too turned away. 'We'll carry your words to the others. It'll be a reassurance, at least, to know you're with us still, and your vigilance will be valued. Light be with you, Traveller.'

'And with you, my lady. And you, Sky Prince.'

As Gulda walked away, the Traveller clambered back on to the rock where he had been sitting. Coming eventually to a sharp turn in the path, Gulda turned to look back at him. He had not moved. She flicked her stick at the distant figure by way of a parting salute.

'Tell Thyrn you spoke to me.' The Traveller's voice sounded as though he were standing next to her. There was a regretful if not guilty note in it. 'I didn't like leaving him the way I did, but I . . . I was preoccupied. I needed to be back here. I made him safe, and I made sure his friends would find him.'

'I will,' Gulda replied.

The Traveller made to leave, then he paused. 'It was an ancient place,' he said hesitantly. 'Where Thyrn was heading. Ancient like the Labyrinth. But corrupt. An evil place.' Then he let out a soft sigh, as though a thought had just come to him.

'The pups,' he said.

'The pups?' Gulda echoed, taken aback a little by this abrupt change of subject.

'Tarrian, Grayle – the pups. They transcend many things. They travel the ways between the worlds – touching and not touching. And the paths of the Labyrinth are no less, I'd think. Speak to them. Speak to them. Their knowledge is great – and deep.'

He was gone.

His last words reverberated around Gulda as she stared at the place where he had been.

Gavor dropped down on to Gulda's shoulder. 'Well, well, what an unusual . . . person,' he said. 'Very pleasant. Nearly put my claw in it, though, didn't I? Calling him human. Still, he took it in good part – no harm done. And remarkably clear-sighted, wasn't he?' Gulda eyed him suspiciously as he paused significantly and craned round to look at her. 'Saw right through you, for example, didn't he – *my lady?*'

Gulda pursued her lips grimly, then set off at her usual stumping pace, causing Gavor to tumble off her shoulder with a squawk.

'Shut your beak, crow,' she snapped.

Gavor chuckled and flew off.

It was night when Gulda returned to Anderras Darion. She told Andawyr of her encounter with the Traveller and in turn was told what Gentren had related. She did not react when the ravagers of Gentren's world were described to her, other than to close her eyes momentarily and give the slightest of nods.

'Everyone knows of this?' she asked.

'Yes.'

'All of which leaves us where?'

'I don't know,' Andawyr admitted. 'I'm beginning to feel like a one-armed juggler on a tightrope.' He ran a hand through his disordered hair. 'For one thing, we'll have to tell everyone about the Uhriel now – and how powerful you believe they've become.'

'Been made,' Gulda corrected. 'Though it's interesting that this Gentren was able to stab one of them.'

Andawyr shrugged. 'Probably caught him by surprise. The old Uhriel lived amongst men for generations. They were well aware of the risks of assassination and protected themselves all the time. But these new – creations – having the power to do what they'd done would have precious little cause to fear for their own safety. I'd be loath to risk any venture that relied on their susceptibility to an arrow or a knife thrust.'

'Yes,' Gulda agreed. 'But, even so, it's still interesting. We, above all, should know that lesser failings have brought the strong down at the hands of the weak before now.' She became brisk, laying the notion aside. 'Is any of this coming together yet? Is a pattern emerging that we can use? We can't speculate for ever: we need to settle down to some serious planning very soon.'

Andawyr looked pained. 'Many things are coming together,

Memsa. Oslang's been a tower as usual – quiet and incon-spicuous, but ordering, organizing, making people recast old ideas, plunge into new ones, generally think as they've never thought before. Knowledge is coming to the fore that I'd hardly have dared speculate about scarcely ten days ago. It's as if the arrival of Antyr and the others has acted like a catalyst – or the few grains of dust that can make a solution suddenly crystallize.'

'But?' Gulda queried, fixing on the uneasiness in his tone.

'But we still don't know *what* is going to happen, or when, or where, or how. We seem to be in the same position as Gentren's father – forewarned but helpless, poor sod.'

'Not quite the same,' Gulda cautioned edgily.

'Near enough to make no difference.'

Gulda banged her stick violently on a nearby table, making Andawyr jump.

'Damn it, Andawyr,' she burst out angrily. 'You above all can't afford the luxury of thinking like that. Your wits, your instincts, your . . .' She gave a reluctantly conceding wave. '. . . Your arcane symbols on bits of paper, all tell you of events coming together at many levels – of a moment pending when all things may be finely balanced – when perhaps the fall of the least of Gavor's feathers might be enough to tilt us – everything – into destruction.' She smacked her forehead ferociously, her anger mounting. Andawyr quailed. 'There may be precious little difference between us and Andeeren Marsyn but such difference as there is is vital and we must cling to it.'

Andawyr stammered in the face of this unexpected onslaught. 'I'm sorry, Memsa,' he began. 'I . . .'

Gulda waved him silent and growled. Then she was silent herself for some time, the only sound in the room the steady tapping of her stick on the floor.

'No, *I*'m sorry,' she said eventually, her voice subdued. 'That was unwarranted, inexcusable. It's just that . . .' She dropped into a chair and slumped back, flicking the hood of her robe forward to hide her face. 'It's just that, like everyone else, I'd thought it was all over. After so long, wandering, learning, teaching, what I'd always feared – what Ethriss had feared – had come about. Somehow Sumeral had returned – the Second Coming was on us. But we defeated Him – or His own folly did – it doesn't matter which. He was gone – His mortal form was shattered, His will scattered and broken. As much by good fortune as good management, I'll admit, but He was gone nevertheless. The Fyordyn, the Riddinvolk, the Orthlundyn for mercy's sake, farmers and carvers for generations now – they came together – formed an army from almost nothing. The great Fyordyn lords – the natural leaders of such an army – willingly accepted the generalship of Loman – a smith! A shoer of horses – someone I taught to read and write when he was a snotty brat, miserable because he didn't seem to understand carving like his friends did. And look how he rose to events . . .'

'He did fight in the Morlider War,' Andawyr intruded feebly.

Gulda ignored him. 'All these . . . remarkable . . . things came about. *Everyone* rose to events – ability, heart, spirit, all determined not to bow before Him. Was it all for nothing? Did we completely misjudge the depths of His deviousness? Was it all just a step in some plan too vast for us to comprehend? A testing of our will, our strength? A testing of the worth of His old agents, His Uhriel? A mere exercise?'

Andawyr did not speak. Apart from the fact that Gulda's remarks were rhetorical, he was shaken by the very fact that she was speaking the way she was. It was in every way as uncharacteristic as her previous outburst. Though he would not have admitted it, he had come to think of Gulda, like Hawklan – mysterious though they both were – as fixed points in his world – anchors that helped hold him secure amid his own whirling concerns.

Silence returned to the room, Gulda's questions hanging in the air, Andawyr effectively dumbstruck.

'Well, well, well,' Gulda said eventually, tapping the arms of her chair. 'It must have been a long day. I haven't had thoughts like that . . .' She ran her hand along her stick. '. . . In a tree's age.' She sniffed and pushed her hood back. The sniff startled Andawyr and he was almost afraid to look at her for fear he would see tears shining in those searching eyes.

'It's understandable,' he said lamely, completely at a loss to offer any real comfort to this enigmatic figure.

Gulda sniffed again, this time with stern purposefulness. 'Keep your feet to the backside of your people, Andawyr,' she said. 'I sense time slipping away from us like water through cupped hands. It's time for some serious work. Time to brace ourselves for war.'

Chapter 29

Andawyr grimaced at the word 'war' but made no direct reference to it.

'I suppose we should tell our neighbours about this,' he said uncomfortably. 'The Muster and the Geadrol need to know. Shall I send riders to Urthryn and Queen Sylvriss? Tell them . . .'

'Tell them what?' Gulda interrupted sharply. 'They *would* be in the position of Andeeren Marsyn – their "sages" warning them of impending doom but giving them neither advice nor any indication what was going to happen.' She tapped her head. 'No, we must solve this here first. And quickly, I suspect. Besides, I doubt Sumeral will try to match us sword for sword again – He's lost twice doing that. And while we'd be sore pressed to raise another army, we could raise a damned sight better one than He could if He suddenly appeared amongst us. No, He's trying another way. After what you've told me about Gentren's world I'm more convinced than ever that now He knows the Guardians are gone He intends simply to exterminate us.'

She curled her lip and, for the briefest of moments, Andawyr felt that he was looking at the face of someone fully as terrible as their enemy. The feeling was gone almost before he could register it and Gulda was standing up. 'Get everyone together tomorrow.' She glanced out into the darkness and relented. 'No. Make it the day after tomorrow. If they're all working as well as you say another day could make a big difference. But what we'll have by then will have to suffice. Decisions have to be made.' She took half a step towards the door, then hesitated. 'Use the Labyrinth hall. It'll help focus our minds.'

It was not a popular venue, least of all for those who had to haul chairs and tables down into the depths of the castle. Extra lanterns were brought as well and, though they brightened the hall, their light still did not seem to penetrate far into the Labyrinth. Rather they heightened the gloomy menace it exuded.

The previous day had verged on the frantic, with Gulda wandering about, apparently casually dropping in on the groups and individuals who were poring over the information they had received and the ideas that were emerging. With the exception of Marna, however, she chased Antyr and the other new arrivals out into the Orthlundyn countryside in the company of Loman and Isloman.

'They've told us all they can for the moment. Let them get as much of this place in their bones as they can,' she said to Andawyr as they left. 'Who knows what darkness they might be going into?'

Marna, very much at her own insistence, and not without some reluctance on their part, was still being trained by the Goraidin. Yrain undertook most of the work and her confident opinion to Gulda was that 'She'll soon get it out of her system.' This prompted a dark smile, a grunt, and the rejoinder, 'Let me know when it's out of yours.'

The tables and chairs were laid out in a wide circle and there was an air of anxious anticipation about those gathering in the Labyrinth hall. Tarrian and Grayle sauntered in and out from time to time, sniffing at everyone and everything routinely before lying down immediately in front of the Labyrinth and going to sleep. Dar-volci joined them.

The last to arrive were an apologetic Yrain and a red-faced and perspiring Marna. They slipped in hastily as Andawyr was about to speak, their progress monitored beadily by Gulda.

Andawyr made no elaborate preamble.

'As you all know, some sixteen or so years ago we discovered that what many of us, to our shame, had thought of as almost a child's tale – a myth – had happened. Sumeral, the Great Corrupter, was amongst us again. How and from where He returned, how long He had been in Narsindal, we don't know even now, but fortune exposed Him and both fortune and courage destroyed Him. Nor do we know what His intentions were. We judged Him, as our forebears did at the time of His First Coming, by His deeds. He corrupted, He destroyed, He took power over others, and sought ever more. He did all those things that to us, as peoples needing our own freedom and respecting the freedom of others, were intolerable.'

He paused and his voice echoed back from the Labyrinth as a soft murmur.

'In many ways His Second Coming was the same as His First. As before, He levied both the Uhriel and a great army against us and, as before, we knew that both had to be defeated. The one by force of arms, the other by the use of the Power. The only real difference between these two conflicts was their scale. For those involved, the pain and the horror were the same, but this time, fortunately, circumstances did not permit Him to spread His influence too far out into the world.'

Andawyr looked at his audience as if steeling himself for what he had to say next.

'It would seem, however, that we were premature in assuming that the destruction of his mortal frame and Derras Ustramel was the destruction of whatever He really is and of His determination to return to this world.' He waved his arm to indicate Antyr and the other newcomers to the castle. 'The testimony we've received is unequivocal. Somewhere He is whole and struggling to return. Struggling desperately.' He fidgeted nervously with some papers on the table in front of him. 'Further signs have come from apparently quite separate matters we at the Cadwanol have been studying. Signs from the time of the Great Searing itself – if not before.' There was a soft hiss of surprise but Andawyr ignored it. 'It would appear that many things are being drawn together that should be ever apart. A crisis deep in the nature of existence itself is imminent – a crisis that we can't properly articulate but which must inevitably affect all of us.' He smiled ruefully. 'It may even be that Sumeral Himself is as much a victim of this as we are of His evil.'

365

'What!'

The exclamation came from several sources, despite the discipline that was normal at such gatherings. Andawyr made no rebuke. 'Don't worry, I'm not making excuses for Him. He's as wilfully conscious as we are and just as responsible for what He does.' He fiddled with the papers again, momentarily preoccupied. 'Given these many different signs, the only conclusion we can come to is that it's only a matter of time before He is with us again.' He glanced quickly around the circle. 'He and those He has taken to be His new Uhriel.' His hand hovered uncertainly by his side, ready to reach out to deal with any outcry at this revelation. Instead, there was little more than a shuffling silence.

Yatsu spoke into it, softly. 'These creatures that Vredech and Pinnatte met and which destroyed Gentren's world *are* Uhriel, then? He's found new souls to replace those that were destroyed?' His manner and emphasis told Andawyr that this was a conclusion that the Goraidin had reached in their own discussions. He made to speak, but it was Gulda who replied.

'Yes,' she said starkly. 'I recognized their ancient language in the din we heard when Vredech and Pinnatte came back from wherever they'd been. I didn't tell you about it because for those of you who'd known the Uhriel – and for other reasons – I thought it too fearful a prospect to be made known too quickly. I know it's not our way to withhold information like that and I may have been wrong, but in any event it's irrelevant now. And it's to your credit you've faced that possibility yourselves.'

'And these other reasons, Memsa,' Yatsu pressed, watching her closely. 'How fearful are they?'

Gulda hesitated for a moment as she returned his gaze. Then she told her listeners what she had told Hawklan and Andawyr as they had stood on the sunlit balcony after Vredech's and Pinnatte's disconcerting return from the blue world of the Uhriel. 'The language they now possess is the language of the Power itself. That they know it means that He has chosen to give them a knowledge of it which far outstrips that of their predecessors.'

'You mean they're even more powerful than Oklar and the

366

others?' Yrain exclaimed, her eyes wide. She was not alone in her reaction.

'Yes,' Gulda replied. 'As far beyond them as they were beyond us.'

'Gods protect us!'

Gulda tapped her stick on the floor sharply. The sound of it rolled back from the Labyrinth like a marshalling drum-roll.

'We're here to talk reality, not pray, girl,' she snapped, jerking Yrain and several others smartly upright. 'Sumeral's renewed existence, His determination to return here, the making of His new lieutenants and the Power they can use, can be taken as *fact*, my friends. What we're gathered here for now is to determine what we're going to do about it.'

The force of her personality spread a silence over the hall that was like a smothering emanation from the Labyrinth itself. When Yatsu spoke again, he seemed to be having to struggle against it. His voice sounded distant and strained.

'We've faced many terrible truths over the years, Memsa, and somehow we've been able to prevail. It's an article of faith with all of us that it's the safest – the wisest – thing to do. But it needs no great grasp of strategy and tactics to know that if what you've just said is true, then *nothing* will be able to stand against Him. Oklar cut a swathe through Vakloss with little more than a wave of his hand – he smashed buildings and killed hundreds. When the Lords' army moved against him, the orders uppermost in the minds of everyone there weren't those for waging the battle but those for scattering and regrouping if there was the least sign of him using the Power against them. If Hawklan's arrow hadn't bound him in some way the war would've been lost before it started.'

The mention of Hawklan's name turned many eyes towards the tall black-clad figure sitting next to Andawyr, Gavor perched on his shoulder.

Silence welled into the hall again.

Hawklan replied to Yatsu. 'It's not an article of faith, old friend,' he said. 'It's an article of truth, tried and tested more rigorously than any of the Cadwanol's theorems and theories. It's the only way for us. And it's the only way we'll find an answer to this threat.'

'But . . .'

'But yes, we're all sick at heart at the prospect.' Hawklan's voice was suddenly edged with pain and anger. 'Not to mention sick to the stomach. For all we defeated Him, for all the good that's come about since His return awakened our three countries, the war hovers over us like an accusing wraith. I doubt there's anyone who was touched by it who doesn't remember some part of it every day. But that's of no consequence, unfortunately. You know the rules, soldier. I heard Yrain spelling them out to Marna only the other day: "When you're knocked down, get up – or die: your choice." A simple training adage that applies to everything that's happening to us now.' He stood up and his voice became grim. 'Choosing to live on one's knees rather than dying on one's feet is also a choice for each of us when we're faced with aggression. But if we look at what Sumeral did in the past and what's happened to Gentren's world, then it seems the choice He intends to offer us now is to die on our knees or to die on our feet. The Memsa's reading of affairs – which I agree with – is that, knowing the Guardians are truly gone from this world and having been twice defeated by fighting as one of us, Sumeral has given His Uhriel the task of simply destroying us.'

'Why should He want to do this?' Marna asked abruptly, her flushed face fearful.

Hawklan echoed Andawyr. 'We don't know. We've never known. There are very human qualities in much that He does – hatred, vengefulness, malice, savagery – qualities we can understand – qualities we all possess. Perhaps when we know why we have such traits ourselves we'll understand why He has them also. Perhaps not. As for His intentions . . .' He stopped, and once again he was standing on the mist-shrouded causeway across Lake Kedrieth. He closed his eyes and took a deep breath to distance himself from this persistent image. 'The vision He showed me was of worlds of great beauty, worlds where all was perfection, where there wasn't the least flaw. "Thus shall Ethriss's folly be remade", He said.'

There was an unexpected response. Marna curled her

unsteady lip disparagingly. 'He sounds like a spoilt child,' she snarled.

Hawklan looked at her. 'Indeed He does,' he said, with a soft, ironic laugh. 'Though I doubt I'd have arrived at that conclusion myself in an age's thinking. And unfortunately He's a very large and powerful spoilt child. One, it would seem, more than capable of destroying an entire world.' He turned again to Yatsu. 'Which brings us back to your concerns.'

'All our concerns,' someone said, to a general murmur of agreement.

Yatsu spoke. 'From what's being said, His next Coming will be a conflict of the Power against the Power and He's preparing to use it to an extent far beyond the ability of the Cadwanol to oppose.' He tapped the table idly and looked down at his hands before continuing. 'I long ago accepted that I might well have to die on my feet, if need arose, but there's a feeling of futility about this which I find . . . distressing . . . to say the least.'

Hawklan looked round at the other Goraidin. Yatsu spoke for all of them and it was no whining plaint. For a moment he contemplated giving voice to rousing words to lift their spirits, but he knew that this would be an insult to them. He could almost hear the Labyrinth throwing such words back to him mockingly. He gave a conceding shrug.

'Me too,' he said simply. 'When I faced Oklar I was like Antyr, Farnor, Vredech, Pinnatte, Thyrn.' They were sitting together and he indicated each of them as he spoke. 'I held out Ethriss's black sword and something within it, or within me, protected me, though to this day I don't know what it was or how it happened. It's one of many memories that plague me almost every day and I've no desire to face the likes of him again – ever. What's happened to Gentren's world is chilling beyond description and anyone who knows what we know can't feel anything other than fear and a sense of futility.'

He looked around the circle of watching faces, pale and silent.

'Perhaps, before we go on, it would be advisable to talk about a choice we each have and that we haven't touched on

369

so far. In fact we *must* talk about it.' Hawklan paused thought-fully for a moment before continuing. 'Knowing what we know, and in the absence of another, less grim interpretation – which I think is unlikely – each of us must decide whether or not we wish to do anything at all.'

He sat down to a bewildered silence.

'What do you mean?' Yatsu stammered.

'What I said,' Hawklan replied quietly.

'Do *nothing*?'

'It's a choice.'

There was a rumble of dissent from the Goraidin and some of the others, but it was far from unanimous. Hawklan addressed Antyr and his companions.

'Each of you faced a terrible ordeal and discovered an unexpected strength – a frightening strength – in yourself. You came here for help and guidance only to learn that you might be about to face an ordeal far worse – that perhaps you're living through the last days of the entire world.' He pointed to the Goraidin. 'These people are soldiers. Fine soldiers, whose service to others few could equal, but it's in their bones to fight to the last when no other alternative exists. You, on the other hand, aren't. If you wish . . .' He broadened his state-ment with a wave of his hand to take in everyone there. 'If any of you wish to walk away from this – to make the most of what time may be left – then do it now. The only regret you need take is ours that we couldn't help you more.'

There was some uneasy coughing and shifting of chairs, but Antyr spoke almost immediately.

'We've discussed this already, Hawklan – at great length.' He looked around the hall and smiled nervously. 'The light that's shone into places around here seems to make that inevitable. But circumstances, fate, call it what you will, thrust each of us into the darkness and then brought us here. Whatever lives we had are gone and can't be recalled – indeed, none of us would truly wish them recalled.' He faltered. 'We're all terrified by what we've learned since we came here. We wish it would just go away. But we belong here, and this is where we want to be.'

Hawklan lowered his gaze, both humbled and heartened by

this declaration. But Antyr had not finished.

'And you, Hawklan. What choice will you make?'

'Greatest of my Uhriel.'

Jolted by Antyr's question, Hawklan's mind filled abruptly with Sumeral's words and the vision He had shown him. He cursed its treacherous lure. Who was he that Sumeral should seek to draw him to His side? Old questions flooded through him. How had he come to this time? Or how had Gavor, for that matter – unknowingly bearing some part of the spirit of Ethriss? Fragmented memories of his final, long-past battle were still with him – the remnant of his broken army surrounded – fighting back to back – the last of his companions falling – a hand on his shoulder – a hand he had taken to be Ethriss's but which he knew now could not have been.

'That hand was mine, Hawklan,' Sumeral had told him. *'Ethriss spared none of his creations. I saw your true worth and I took you to be mine when I should rise again.'*

Was he, after all, just another of Sumeral's creatures? An unwitting pawn in some terrible game?

As he looked at Antyr and his companions, what he had just said to them returned to him. Like them, he – or he and the black sword together – had a quality of which he knew nothing save that it could redirect events and was seemingly beyond his control. Yet *was* it beyond his control? Consciously it was, beyond any doubt, but perhaps its actions were determined by his other, more deliberate choices. Perhaps it was like fire or water, or the Power itself – neutral, indifferent, capable equally of sustaining or destroying at the choice of the user. Just as Antyr and the others, all improbable heroes, had chosen to stand against an evil, so their antagonists – the blind man, Rannick, Dowinne, Imorren, Vashnar – had chosen to embrace it. And the unknown skills of each had manifested themselves accordingly.

Why hadn't this simple revelation come to him before? He felt a lightness that he had not realized had been so long gone from him and he smiled to himself as Andawyr's oft-used remark whispered itself to him:

'Obvious' is such a dangerous word.

Yet he had abandoned the black sword.

His smile faded as he bowed to Antyr and flicked a thumb towards the Goraidin. 'I'm with them,' he said casually. 'Whether I like it or not – and I don't – I'm of some importance to Sumeral. I couldn't walk amongst my friends and neighbours knowing I'd not exhausted every opportunity to protect them, however inadequately.' He sat back in his chair and stretched. 'Besides, I feel that Sumeral owes me an accounting.' There was no strutting bombast in the remark, simply a hint of grim humour. 'Nevertheless, I'll speak to each of you individually. We may well not survive what's to come and some of you have made the wrong decision.'

There was a stir at this but Hawklan raised his hands to indicate that he did not wish to pursue the matter.

'Which still leaves us with the problem of what we're going to do,' Gulda said, noting this signal.

'Deal with Him before He comes here.'

It was Vredech. He hesitated for a moment as he suddenly became the focus of attention, but his years in the pulpit rescued him and, after a self-conscious cough, he straightened up and took command of his congregation.

'I am . . . I was . . . a preacher, not a soldier, but when I was struggling with the torments of my old friend, Cassraw, a military word came to me. It made some sense to me then and I think it's relevant now. The word was "bridgehead" – that first toehold in an enemy's terrain – that first armoured enclave which allows an army to flood across.' He laid a hand on Pinnatte's shoulder. 'We've seen Gentren's world – unless there are two such, in which case my thoughts are even more urgent. It beggars belief that three . . . people . . . could have made it thus, but I don't have your experience of the Power and I must accept what you say. However, we watched them searching for what I presume is a Gateway to this world, and they failed. Yengar and the others say they saw something similar as they were returning here with Farnor. That attempt too failed. Powerful these creatures may be, but they're not all-powerful by any means.' He was warming to his subject, his speech becoming more rhetorical, with strong emphasis and telling cadences. 'And where was their Master as they struggled? Not with them, for sure. For whatever reason, this struggle was theirs and theirs alone, and it defeated them. It would be naïve to imagine that this will remain the case but it's a weakness, without a doubt.' He made a sweeping gesture. 'We mustn't allow them to gain even the least bridgehead in this world. Whatever peculiar . . . abilities . . . we have between us, we should direct them towards perhaps finding these Gateways ourselves and, if possible, destroying them.'

He ended with a curt nod and to a stunned silence that slowly filled with approving murmurs and hesitant applause.

'Bravo,' Yatsu said quietly but appreciatively. He glanced at the other Goraidin. 'I think we should all have become preachers. We might've worked that out for ourselves.'

Hawklan nodded. 'Your logic's impeccable, Vredech. Unless anyone's anything further to add, I suggest we turn our minds now to how to achieve this.'

It proved to be a long and tiring time as everyone strove to find some order in the whirl of ideas that were being put forth. As Gulda had predicted, the ominous presence of the Labyrinth focused the minds of all there as, from time to time, in response to some outcry or sudden silence, sounds emerged from it like those of a dark and powerful creature twitching in its dreams.

Eventually fatigue began to take its toll and towards the middle of the afternoon, after a brief consultation with Gulda and a brisk allotting of tasks, Andawyr dismissed the gathering. If such a word could be used under such circumstances, it had been good, he told them. 'Sleep on what we've done, we'll talk again tomorrow.'

During the rest of the day, Hawklan did as he had promised and spoke to everyone individually. The following morning, two people were leaving.

Chapter 30

Hawklan eventually found Loman, sitting dark and lonely by his cold forge. He looked up as Hawklan entered.

'Was it all for nothing, Hawklan?' he asked, before the healer could greet him. 'All those men and women torn from their hearths and their loved ones. All that horror. All that gut-wrenching fear. All those bodies broken and lives casually snuffed out. Was it all for nothing?' The brutal suddenness of the question made Hawklan stop, leaving the door to the forge ajar. Loman closed his eyes and sat back so that a shadow hid his face. 'You know, I still wake up sometimes, shaking all over – can't stop myself.' He waited on no reassurance. 'I know what it is well enough. It's physical exhaustion shot through with stark terror. I've been at the heart of the battle again – that killing time before we found ourselves facing the Uhriel – my ears are ringing with the dreadful din of it all. Not dreaming, you understand, but there again – there – touching, feeling, everything as real as you are now. It's as if it's still happening and part of me – part of all of us – is trapped there forever.'

Hawklan found his bleak tone almost unbearable. He did not speak.

'And now we find that the cause of it all wasn't destroyed after all? That it was all just a . . . temporary setback for Him? That He's going to return – worse than ever?' He struck the wall a shuddering blow with the edge of his clenched fist, then leaned forward and put his head in his hands.

'I don't think I've anything more in me, Hawklan,' he said after a long silence. There was no hint of self-pity in his voice. 'I can't go through that again, or anything like it. I'm spent.

Doing it once was asking too much.'

'Yes, it was,' Hawklan said. 'But you don't need me to tell you it wasn't for nothing, or that there was nothing casual about the deaths of those who didn't return, do you?'

Loman levered himself upright and began wandering about his forge, touching things.

'No,' he replied grimly, as he needlessly arranged some tools hanging from a rack. 'We've all rehearsed our words – our excuses. No real choice – self-defence is an absolute right – evil prevails when good men lie abed – the consequences of not fighting would have been infinitely worse – our duty to those unborn. Not forgetting the soldier's eternal solace – we did what we did because we were there.'

'Reasons, not excuses.'

'Reasons, excuses – I don't know – I'm not sure I can tell the difference any more – if I ever could.'

'They *are* reasons, Loman,' Hawklan said. 'As valid now as they were before we fought and didn't have the benefit of knowing the outcome – when there was only darkness and uncertainty ahead. And when the words aren't enough we take what comfort we can from our actions. It's the nature of war to plunge us into the depths of what we can do and, in the end, maybe the only difference between us and Him is that we laid down our arms when it was over and reached out to make some semblance of a just peace.' He paused, watching his old friend intently. Then he pointed to the silent forge. 'But it's no small difference, is it? You've marred more than one piece of iron with a pinch too much of this or a pinch too much of that, haven't you?' He shrugged. 'The fact is we're all scarred in many ways. But then, I don't think there's a law somewhere that says doing the right thing has to be either easy or pleasant.'

Loman picked up a short-shafted hammer, spun it deftly, then laid it quietly on his anvil. 'Hardly a new debate, is it?' he said softly. His manner was resigned. 'I'm sorry, inflicting it on you again, but this business seems to have hit me harder than I thought. It's all come out of nowhere – and so quickly. I'm finding it hard to face up to. I can't do what I did before. I . . .'

Hawklan laid a hand on his shoulder. 'Whatever else happens, that won't be needed, I'm certain. There'll be burdens of a different kind, and different people to carry them. You carried far more than anyone else then. Nothing's expected of you now.'

Loman frowned. 'It's not enough,' he said desperately. 'I can't walk away, but I can't face it all again. What about you, Hawklan? How do you do it? How do you stay the way you are? You did no less than me, but you still seem to be able to stay calm in the face of what's happening – to think, to plan.'

Hawklan gave him an arch look. 'Don't confuse composure with equanimity,' he said with a grim smile. 'I did a *lot* less than you in the war. You led an army. I just sneaked round the back.' The touch of humour faded and a spasm of pain passed over his face. 'My burden, to this day, is the feeling deep down that perhaps if I hadn't been here the war wouldn't have happened.'

Loman looked at him, startled. 'No, no,' he said, suddenly anxious. 'Don't think that. More likely Sumeral's being here brought you.'

'I didn't say it made sense.'

Loman became the comforter. 'You've been listening to too many of Andawyr's wilder ramblings about cause and effect.'

'It could be Andawyr's ramblings that'll find a way for us to oppose Sumeral again.'

'You think that's possible?'

Hawklan hesitated. 'I don't know.'

Loman nodded slowly. He picked up a small figurine standing in tidy isolation amid the chaos of the battered table he referred to as his 'desk'. It was a likeness of his daughter, Tirilen, carved by Isloman. She was his only child from a long-dead wife. Like all Isloman's work it expressed far more than a likeness. Its face seemed to move as Loman turned it in the evening light. Tirilen had fallen in love with a Fyordyn High Guard – one of many who had fallen in love with her as she had nursed them after the battle in Narsindal. Now she was his wife and they lived in Fyorlund. Loman missed her flying blonde hair and provoking manner far more than he ever owned to – many did – but he was genuinely happy that she was happy. For a while after her return from her terrible work in the battlefield healing tents, though outwardly her old self, she was changed. Loman had sensed a deep hurt in her that neither he nor Hawklan could reach. It had only passed, or perhaps been transformed, as her new love had slowly grown. Gently he brushed some dust from the figure. Hawklan watched him.

'Go to her, Loman,' he said. 'Go and see your daughter and your grandchild.'

Loman was breathing heavily. 'It's what I want to do,' he said. 'But . . .' He fell silent.

Hawklan came close to him. 'When whatever's going to happen, happens, maybe we'll prevail, maybe we won't,' he said. 'But, as Yatsu said, one way or another, it'll probably be the Power against the Power, this time. Precious little for us to do with our kinds of fighting skills, I suspect.'

'Even so, I still don't know that I can just walk away,' Loman said.

'We're spectators, Loman. Something that's not easy for either of us. But all we can do is watch and hope – encourage and support those who're doing the real fighting. Go to your daughter. They're so clever, these women, making their babies. Go and bask in the light of the new life she's created and show it the joys of your own.' Loman returned the figurine to its small place of honour. Hawklan's voice fell. 'If the worst comes to the worst, where better could you be? And if we defeat Him, then the castle won't suffer too much for your being away for a while.'

Thus it was that Loman was standing by his horse on the dew-damped grass in front of Anderras Darion at dawn the next morning. He was joined by Endryk. Hawklan had made to speak to him also, but the Goraidin had spoken to him first.

'Go and find your family and your old friends, Endryk,' Dacu had told him. 'And take this letter of commendation to your Lord for the help you gave to Thyrn and his friends. It was bravely done. I'd have been honoured to fight by your side. Any of us would have been.'

To the High Guard, this praise was both considerable and unexpected and he coloured as he received it. His response, however, was the same as Loman's. 'I can't just walk away.'

'Take it as an order, then,' Dacu replied gently. 'Far more's owed to you than you owe. We should have taken more time to seek out those who wandered away, lost, after that last battle. It's a stain on us all and your returning will help ease more pains than just those of your family.'

The Goraidin each said their farewells to both Loman and Endryk but the most difficult parting was Endryk's from Thyrn. Despite his best efforts the young Caddoran was unable to suppress his tears as he embraced Endryk and uttered a hoarse 'Thank you.' Endryk, moved more than he had anticipated, returned his embrace but did not trust himself enough to speak.

Gulda took Loman's hand and squeezed it powerfully. 'Light be with you, young Loman. You were a handful but you've done well. I always thought you would in the end. Give my love to your child and hers.'

'I will, Memsa,' he replied, massaging his hand. 'And thank you. Send for me if I'm needed. Failing that, I'll be back – in a week or so.'

As the two men prepared to mount, Tarrian and Grayle emerged from somewhere and headed purposefully towards Endryk. He looked down at them uncertainly.

'Nals is well.'

Endryk started as the voice sounded in his mind and Tarrian had to repeat the message twice before Endryk realized what was happening. Nals had been a stray dog that had been with him for much of his time in Arvenstaat. He knelt down in front of the wolf, the damp grass staining his trousers.

'He says he was sorry to leave you at the border, but he knew you were going to be all right – you'd found your way,' Tarrian went on, adding, with heavy male confidentiality. 'And he'd caught wind of a bitch. Got quite a pack now. And slowing down a bit, by all accounts. He says thank you for your companionship, it was good running with you.'

It was a peculiar and unexpected relief to Endryk. The sight of his sole companion of many years standing on the river bank as he and Thyrn and the others had crossed it and ridden away northwards still came back occasionally to disturb him.

'Thank you,' he said. 'But how do you know all this?'

'It's a wolf thing, Endryk,' Tarrian replied, wilfully mysterious.

Then the two men were riding slowly down the winding road that led from the castle. The small group watched them until they were out of sight.

The atmosphere in the Labyrinth hall was nervous and fretful. There were more than a few bleary eyes present, many discussions having carried on late into the night and sleep, in any event, having been generally elusive.

As before, Andawyr went straight to their concerns. 'Given that no one has an alternative to Vredech's suggestion, we've at least two problems in carrying any conflict to the enemy. Firstly, we know little or nothing about the nature of these Gateways between the worlds, and, secondly, should we locate their world, we know from experience that striking down an Uhriel is going to be no easy task. However, to our advantage, and as Vredech reminded us yesterday, we know that the use of the Power they apparently have now doesn't seem to be helping them pass through the Gateways, while some amongst us slip through them with ease – incontinently, almost. And we know that, given surprise, they can be hurt.'

'That's as may be,' Yatsu said, indicating the other Goraidin. 'But we're having some difficulty with the practicalities of all this. When Antyr was . . . transported . . . to wherever it was he fought with Ivaroth and the blind man, all Jaldaric and I saw was his body being guarded by Tarrian and Grayle. When Vredech and Pinnatte found themselves in the Uhriel's world, they too were here, apparently asleep.' He raised his hand to forestall a reply. 'I'm not disputing what we've been told, but it defeats me how anyone can be in two places at once.' He made an abrupt and dismissive gesture. 'But leaving that aside for the moment, we still don't know where these Gateways are, what they're . . . made of . . . for want of a better word, or how we can pass through them in any predictable way which is what we'll need to do if we're going to resort to some kind of assassination mission.'

Unusually, Andawyr looked helpless. 'The Gateways are

just points of contact between our world and other worlds,' he said unhappily. 'Like an ordinary doorway they're . . . nothing . . . defined by what's around them.'

Yatsu's expression told him what he already knew – this didn't help.

Usche caught Andawyr's eye and he nodded to her.

'These Gateways shouldn't be as accessible as they are,' she said. 'The different worlds just shouldn't touch this frequently. The fact that they are is just another indication of what Andawyr spoke of yesterday – something seriously wrong at the deepest levels of what we think of as our reality – something that goes back to the Great Searing. A deep harm was done at that time. What we call Gateways are more akin to . . . cracks . . . slowly spreading through a building.'

She hesitated for a moment, suddenly intimidated both by what she was saying and the intensity with which her audience was listening. She almost flinched as Dacu raised his hand to speak.

'Accepting what you're saying – and I'd dearly like not to – where does Sumeral fit into it? Is He the cause of this . . . cracking . . . or is He just taking advantage of it?'

'The latter, we think, though, in truth, we don't even know what Sumeral really is – whether He's a cause or an effect – He could be a manifestation of the flaw itself, or he could be a consequence of it.' Usche was trembling. Andawyr motioned her to sit down.

'We've no absolute answers, Dacu,' he said. 'This is the most we know. You're hearing in minutes what's taken years of floundering endeavour – painstaking thought, experiment, analysis. I'll be frank with you: as I stumbled towards these ideas, I felt that the roots of everything I've ever known were being shaken. At one point I thought I was going mad. But the roots weren't being shaken, I was just beginning to learn how deeply and how far they really go. Ethriss told the Cadwanol to go beyond and we're pushing the limits of our knowledge so far and so fast now that it's giddying for me, let alone you.' His manner darkened. 'It's just as well we are, though. Without this knowledge we wouldn't even have seen these problems coming. As for what we can do, we're doing it – talking, listening, keeping our minds and imaginations open – bringing everything we have to this. Carry on, Usche.'

The young Cadwanwr had composed herself but she remained seated as she spoke.

'We've known for some time that what we thought was the beginning of all things, the Great Searing as we call it, wasn't,' she began carefully. 'Too many things around us are just too old. We think now that it was caused by a weapon – or weapons – and that it or they also caused this fatal flaw.' A murmur of disbelief greeted this but she pressed on. The Labyrinth carried an echo of her sing-song voice around the hall, giving emphasis to it. 'I understand your doubts. I'm Riddinvolk. Like the Fyordyn we've a strong military tradition – a remnant of the Wars of the First Coming. We all carry weapons and are prepared to protect ourselves and our neighbours if an enemy threatens. We live in peace because of it and that we're all here today is testimony to the rightness of it. But I find it difficult to imagine a weapon capable of affecting an entire world, and impossible to imagine a society that would use such a thing! Nevertheless, this seems to have been the case.'

Yrain was drumming her fingers on the table.

'Oklar set the entire battlefront ablaze in Narsindal,' Yengal reminded everyone by way of support for Usche.

She acknowledged the comment gratefully but shook her head. 'The weapon we're talking about was no simple battlefield device. Nor was it anything that simply destroyed, like sword or fire. It was something that reached down into the depths of what we – what all living things – are. It unmade the essence of every living thing it touched – transformed it into something that fed on itself – grew and spread . . .'

It was becoming too much for Yrain.

'This is nonsense!' she burst out scornfully. 'In a war, all that weapons transform living things into is dead things. And how can you possibly know what happened *before* the beginning of everything?'

Gulda leaned forward but Usche spoke first, bridling at Yrain's tone.

'The beginning of all things, as you call it, *wasn't* the

382

beginning of all things. That's a fact beyond any reasoned dispute – accept it! I've told you we don't know what it was but the idea that it was caused by a weapon fits most of the facts.' She pointed to Thyrn. 'We've also got Thyrn's Accounting and we've been through that over and over, studying every nuance of his Caddoran ability and what he overheard between Vashnar and the person – the entity – whatever it was – that appeared to him. It spoke of armies beyond imagining – *engines of war* beyond imagining – engines that would *unravel the very being* – the very essence – of an enemy.' She jabbed her finger into the table in emphasis. 'But it wasn't Sumeral nor anything of His. It was *surprised* to find itself where it was – and surprised to find its former enemies in the same condition. It spoke of something happening that shouldn't have happened – something that resulted in all being defeated – something . . .'

'I see a brightness moving across the land, across the oceans – moving through all that lived, moving scarcely at the pace of a walking man – but relentlessly growing, sustaining itself. And all fleeing its touch – believer and heretic alike. None escaped. And then there was only brightness – a reshaping, a remaking.' It was Thyrn, retelling, in the Caddoran way, the words he had overheard when he had touched Vashnar's mind. The voice was that of a powerful and coldly ruthless personality, but, as Usche had said, it was laced through with surprise and growing realization. For a moment the darkness of the Labyrinth seemed to swallow all hint of sound in the hall.

No one spoke.

Andawyr reached into his pocket and withdrew a crumpled kerchief. Carefully he laid it on the table and spread it out to reveal three green crystals.

'I'll answer your next question before you ask it, Yrain,' he said, looking at the still frowning Goraidin. 'Crystals such as these can be used to do many things with the Power: store it, amplify it, transform it. We used to use them a lot at the Cadwanen but we use them very sparingly now. Their origins are unknown but potentially they're very dangerous to anyone with the gift to use the Power. That's why Atelon and

Dar-volci went looking for the source of them when they began to appear at the Gretmearc. In our arrogance, we thought we possessed the only ones in existence and, insofar as we thought about it, we presumed that Ethriss had created them himself.' He paused uncomfortably. 'That's not as lame as it sounds because, although they're apparently mined in the Thlosgaral, there's no natural process we know of that could create them. Even as far as we've been able to examine them, their structure's far too complex and ordered. They're *made* things. How, we don't know. "Why" is what we're talking about now. It's certainly quite possible to envisage crystals being used to form a terrible weapon.'

He swept up the kerchief and the crystals and dropped them into a pocket.

'Atelon's told you about the Kyrosdyn who attacked him in Arash-Felloren. He used crystals to enhance his use of the Power and his indiscipline cost him his life. His life energy was drained from him.'

Andawyr leaned forward and held up a warning finger.

'One crystal, and a little misused knowledge, will do this. Two, suitably aligned, could do four times the hurt. Three could do eight times. And so on. The more we think about what they are and what they can do, the more we think about them scattered and buried in the Thlosgaral, the more we believe they played some part in what Thyrn just reminded us of – something we take to be a memory of the beginning of the Great Searing. As for a society that would make such a weapon, sadly, unlike Usche, I find that all too easy to imagine.' He gave her a mentor's reproachful look. 'She's young yet and history isn't one of her favourite subjects. When it becomes so she'll learn that it's full of tales of communities racking and destroying each other with that absolute lack of restraint that only righteousness can give. Antyr's told us of the recent war in his own land. Vredech's told us of his religion degenerating into darkness almost overnight. We've heard of Arvenstaat's corrupt and self-serving senators, and of the bleak hatred and cruelty of the Kyrosdyn. Even Fyorlund itself fell into civil war under Oklar's influence. All examples of the festering legacy of

Sumeral's First Coming. All telling us that there are no depths to which we're not capable of descending.' He patted the pocket containing the crystals. 'I don't know exactly how these could've been used to make such a weapon, but that's simply because I've not thought about it enough.' Andawyr spoke the last words with a savage emphasis. 'I'm more than prepared to believe that they *were* used thus and that, as a result, the damage they did became magnified beyond any controlling, and overwhelmed not only the warring parties but far beyond, until no part of the world was untouched.'

A tremulous moaning came from the Labyrinth.

Chapter 31

Dar-volci, Tarrian and Grayle had stationed themselves in front of the Labyrinth as they had the previous day. All three were suddenly alert as the moaning filled the hall, then, without any discernible signal passing between them, they were on their feet and running into the darkness. Gavor launched himself after them from Hawklan's shoulder but, as the animals disappeared, a stern command filled the mind of everyone present.

'Stay where you are, all of you.'

Gavor flapped urgently, then turned away from the Labyrinth and circled hesitantly a couple of times before returning to his familiar perch. Hawklan reached up and touched his beak but said nothing.

'It's all right,' Antyr was shouting above the confusion of startled cries and clattering chairs. 'It's all right. It's Tarrian. We must do as he says. He wouldn't have spoken to all of you like that unless it was important.'

'What's happened? Where've they gone?' Andawyr asked, grasping his arm urgently.

Antyr's authoritative manner vanished with a helpless shrug. 'I've no idea.' He touched his forehead. 'They're somewhere far away already – I can barely reach them.' He closed his eyes in concentration, only to open them wide almost immediately. 'And I'm hindering by trying. Wherever they all are, it's beyond anywhere I can go.'

Andawyr looked at him for a moment. Then, after a further anxious glance at the Labyrinth, he began ushering everyone back to their seats. The sound that had caused the animals' hasty departure had been overtopped by the commotion that

Tarrian's unexpected instruction had caused but, as the hall grew quieter, it returned, though softer now, like the echo of a winter wind, felt as much as heard as it roams the echoing corridors deep inside a long-deserted mansion. Some of the listeners shivered.

'We'd better carry on with what we were doing,' Andawyr said unhappily, obviously unsettled by what had happened.

'Which was what?' Yrain demanded, though less belligerently than before. 'Listening to stories about a time before the beginning of time, about weapons powerful enough to do . . .' She threw up both arms in a flamboyant gesture. 'Something . . . to the *entire* world. Weapons whose remains are still lying about the place for anyone to pick up and use.'

She slapped the table in frustration, then held out an unsteady and apologetic hand as if to defend herself from Gulda, though the old woman had not moved.

'I'm sorry,' she said. 'I know. My impatience. But none of this still makes any sense – or any sense that'll enable us to *do* something. Whatever may or may not have happened in the past, we've *present* problems that need to be dealt with.'

Andawyr noted the demeanour of the other Goraidin. Although they were uncomfortable with Yrain's forthright manner, he could tell they sympathized with what she was saying. As did he.

'No apologies are needed, Yrain,' he said, glancing over his shoulder at the dark columns of the Labyrinth. 'Conditions are far from ideal.'

When he turned back he looked round the whole group.

The Goraidin: Yatsu, Dacu, Yengar, Olvric, veterans from the Morlider War with their younger companions Jaldaric and Tirke and the two Orthlundyn Helyadin, Jenna and Yrain. All had either accompanied Hawklan on his grim trek to Derras Ustramel or faced the Uhriel and Sumeral's army. All were gentle and self-effacing, all were cruel and tested fighters. All deserved better than what they were now being asked to face.

The Cadwanwr: Oslang from his own generation and Atelon, both of whom had helped to hold the Uhriel at bay as Loman had led the army into battle. Atelon had been little more than a novice then, rather as Usche and Ar-Billan were now. As he looked in turn at them, Andawyr reminded himself not to be either surprised or intimidated by their youth. The one brash, the other endearingly clumsy, it was nevertheless they and their like who were pushing forward the limits of the Cadwanol's knowledge – endlessly thirsty for and fearless of new ideas. It grieved Andawyr that they might soon be facing the very forces whose earlier defeat had rekindled the Cadwanol's search for knowledge.

Then there were the newcomers. Antyr and Vredech, Dream Finders with their deeply strange ability to span the worlds. Farnor and Thyrn. What were they? Healers of some kind, Hawklan said. They couldn't use the Power, they weren't Dream Finders, yet . . . ? Pinnatte, victim of the Kyrosdyn's foul experiment, patently intelligent and worldly-wise but almost inarticulate – at least in this world. Gentren, full of anger and confusion as he struggled to come to terms with the destruction of everything he had ever known. Nertha and Marna, brave and capable women: Nertha, anchoring and steadying Vredech as he searched into the nature of what he was, and generally keeping a watchful physician's eye on Pinnatte and Gentren; Marna pursuing some inner need of her own.

Isloman was there, too. Andawyr always found the carver's hulking presence a comfort though he knew that the big man's acute sensitivity to what the Orthlundyn called the Song of the Rock had always made the Labyrinth a particularly disturbing place for him. Like Oslang and Atelon, Isloman listened more than he spoke.

And, of course, there were Gulda and Hawklan. Both enigmatic, but surely pivotal in what was happening.

'Such a wealth of experience and ability drawn together,' he said, almost to himself. 'Yet so much mystery, too. Perhaps we won't be able to make any clear decisions about what to do until something *does* happen.' He turned to the Goraidin affecting a lighter manner. 'But that's the essence of surviving combat, isn't it? Being unclouded by what's past and what's coming.'

Yatsu doused him brutally. 'Being unclouded in the violent moment is one thing. Approaching it in blind ignorance is another.' He relented a little. 'I suppose if we don't know what's going to be useful and what's not, we'll just have to learn everything we can. Personally, I'd still like to know how people can be both here and elsewhere. Not to mention the small problem of where Sumeral Himself is.'

The soughing coming from the Labyrinth filled the silence that followed. It brought an unease to the group. Andawyr signalled to Usche to continue.

She scowled at him, then looked at Yatsu and took on an air of unhappy resignation. She cleared her throat noisily. 'Bear with me, please,' she began. 'This isn't going to be easy.' She thought for a moment before continuing. Her manner was didactic. 'If we look deeply enough into . . . these walls, these tables, everything, even ourselves . . . we come eventually to a region of unimaginable smallness where all the common-sense rules we take for granted in our ordinary lives cease to apply. Doubt and uncertainty reign. Cause and effect, even time and distance themselves, begin to have little or no meaning. It's a disturbing place but it *is* and it has to be accepted. Its nature is open to debate – considerable debate – but its existence isn't. It's at this level that the Great Searing did its harm. It's where what we call the Power has its origins. It's also the place we share in common with the worlds that Antyr and his kind are able to visit. We *think* . . .' she laid a heavy emphasis on the word '. . . that Antyr and his kind can apparently be in two places at once rather in the way that a musical instrument sounds on its own when other instruments are played nearby – a sympathy, a resonance of some kind – but . . .' She shrugged.

There was an awkward and dissatisfied pause.

A hesitant voice intruded.

'In our minds.'

It was Antyr. 'In our minds,' he said again, more strongly. 'This is where the Dream Ways are, this is where we reach the Gateways.' He turned sharply to Andawyr. 'You control the Power with your mind, don't you? Consciously, deliberately?'

Andawyr blinked at the unexpected question before answering quizzically. 'Yes?'

'So your thoughts reach down into this place?'

390

Andawyr's brow furrowed and he touched his temple. 'The highways and byways of our minds branch and divide endlessly, becoming smaller and smaller. They certainly reach down to where the strange effects of this region can be felt. But, to be honest, we don't really know how thoughts come into being, and we certainly don't use the Power directly at this level, any more than we instruct our arms to move from there. It's done much . . . higher up . . . in our thinking. And it's something that requires an ability that's inborn – a physical attribute written somewhere in the tangled threads that measure the making of us. Like eye colour, only more subtle – perhaps like the skill with horses that the Riddinwr have, or a gift for music or carving.'

'And my own ability – Dream Finding,' Antyr pressed on. 'This too would require a physical attribute?'

'Almost certainly, from what you've told us,' Andawyr replied after a brief hesitation.

Antyr voiced his conclusion slowly. 'It seems to me that to address the Goraidin's concerns . . .' He tapped his temple as Andawyr had. 'This is where we should look. If, by virtue of what you are, your thoughts – your will – can reach down – however indirectly – and use the Power from this mysterious place, then we . . .' he indicated Vredech and himself '. . . by virtue of what *we* are should be able to reach it ourselves. I can't imagine that Dream Finders would have survived so long if they hadn't had some kind of control over this dangerous ability – if we'd been prone to tumble recklessly into other worlds.'

Andawyr breathed out noisily and ran his hands through his tousled hair. 'You could be right,' he said eventually. 'Of course, any such control might be no more than a reflex, just as your hand would snatch back from a flame.' He became practical. 'But it's worth pursuing. We can study more carefully your basic Dream Finding disciplines and compare them with our own meditation techniques. I don't know why I didn't think of it sooner. If we can bring your ability to move between worlds within the control of your thinking, then . . .'

Pinnatte was shaking Vredech's arm and whispering to him.

'What's the matter?' Andawyr asked.

Vredech nodded to Pinnatte. 'He's pointing out that he for one didn't *think* himself into that nightmare world. And neither did I, come to that. Still less did I conjure up that appalling caricature of Dowinne and those . . . others?'

Andawyr looked at them both thoughtfully.

'Since leaving your home you'd had no Dream Finding "incidents" until you met Pinnatte, had you?' he asked eventually.

'No. I didn't even know what Dream Finding was.'

'And now you know much more?'

'He's a good grasp of what's needed,' Antyr intruded. 'Especially considering how little time we've had.'

Andawyr nodded. 'Pinnatte's very unusual,' he said. 'The Kyrosdyn somehow made him capable of using the Power *and* travelling between the worlds – something we think shouldn't be possible any more than a lantern can be lit and not lit at the same time – it did him terrible harm, as we know. But though the ability seems to be gone now, there may be a faint residue of it left. Perhaps, as you slept, your uncontrolled Dream Finding ability touched Pinnatte's mind, and some strangeness in him drew you both through a Gateway.'

'But why to that awful place?' Vredech pressed.

Andawyr looked pained. 'Why indeed? Perhaps a more important question might be, what drew the Uhriel there in the first place?'

'Maybe, but could such a thing happen to *us* again?' Vredech's black-eyed gaze held Andawyr's. Nertha laid her hand on her husband's.

'Yes, but if it happens, it happens.' It was Antyr who delivered this unexpectedly brutal reply, though his voice was calm and steady. 'I think it's time for you and me to face something.' He paused. 'Like you, I came here in the hope that someone, somehow, would help me – explain what had happened to me – explain the changes we've all found in ourselves. Rather slowly, I'll admit, it's dawning on me that no one can really help me except myself. Laughable though it may seem, *we* are an elite here – the only ones with the ability to find the Uhriel and perhaps carry others to them who might be able to kill them. We've no alternative but to find out how to use it properly.'

'Laughable it is,' Vredech retorted caustically. 'Elite is the last word I'd apply to myself.'

Antyr indicated the Goraidin. 'You misunderstand – we all misunderstand. I've had the privilege of riding with these people. They, above all, will tell you how inadequate they feel before combat – how anxious to avoid it. They don't feel like elite soldiers – they feel like frightened men and women. Only their experience sustains them. So what experience do *we* have?' He became earnest. 'Despite my drunkenness, despite your and Pinnatte's ignorance, as Hawklan said yesterday, we all faced death and survived. As did Farnor and Thyrn in their own trials. We may not understand the gifts we have, but equally we don't understand the resources that come with them except that we were all stronger then than we knew. We're even stronger now. We can do this.'

'You're making very free with my husband's life,' Nertha said angrily.

Antyr winced away from her tone, then said quietly, 'I don't think any of us are free at the moment, Nertha.'

The remark seemed to stir Gavor who abruptly glided into the middle of the circle. Hawklan eyed him suspiciously. Gavor did not often participate in such discussions and his acid manner was the last thing that was needed now. Nevertheless, he had everyone's attention.

'Do excuse my interrupting,' he said. 'But on the matter of unseen resources – and your freedom here, for that matter – may I tell you something I learned from Ethriss?'

The hall was suddenly silent. Even the sound from the Labyrinth fell to a distant whisper. Gavor waited for no permission.

'When Ethriss made himself known to me, it was quite a surprise, as you'll imagine – wonderful, actually – he unfurled in my mind like a silver cloud. Still, that's by the by. More importantly, as I became aware of him, so many of my memories of how he'd come to be with me returned at the same time. I remembered me and my companions fighting Sumeral's foul sky creatures at the Last Battle of the First

Coming. I remembered seeing Ethriss fall to Sumeral's final cast and I remembered sweeping down and seizing his spirit as it soared high above the battlefield – I'd keener vision then. As I snatched him up, he said, "It's finished." "Where shall I take you?" I asked him – it's difficult to know what to say in such circumstances – I was very upset. "I need to think," he said. "I must go into the place that is no place – where Sumeral sent the Prince Hawklan and where I sent my black sword – between the worlds, between the moments, where all is chance." '

Gavor paused and tapped his wooden leg on the floor.

'Do you mean that Sumeral *did* send me here?' Hawklan asked urgently.

'Do let me finish, dear boy,' Gavor replied reproachfully, still tapping his leg. 'He gave me a gift even as he was speaking – you know what he was like. He made my leg whole again. I didn't even have an opportunity to thank him, when I was in the mountains here – in a blizzard – no idea where I was – still less, when – and precious little idea even who I was. I couldn't fly and, within minutes, I was caught in the trap that took my leg off again. The rest you all know, but . . .' He flapped his wings as if to release a long-held tension. 'After Sumeral had destroyed Himself and as Ethriss was fading from me, I caught his thoughts. He was full of confusion and doubt. Hawklan had come to this time, the black sword had, I had, bearing him, Sumeral had. Too much for chance, surely? But it was what happened to my leg that seemed to disturb him the most. What he had done for me – such a small thing for him – had been undone almost immediately. Was there an inevitability to everything? Was all effort in vain? Then, he thought, was this world not his creation after all? Had it, rather, created him? They were old, old, doubts. Then he seemed to understand something – very suddenly. "Nothing's inevitable, Sky Prince," he said. "Life battles too strongly against such constraints – even the ones I imposed – it doesn't know its own strength." And he was laughing – at himself – as he finally slipped away. It was a good sound, full of hope. "Others will shape this world further," he said – still laughing at his own foolishness.

"Others stronger. And freer than I, the god." '

As Gavor finished, the Labyrinth's whisper became a soft sighing. He coughed theatrically, then flapped onto the table in front of Hawklan who immediately repeated his question, though more gently.

'He said Sumeral sent me here?'

'I do wish you'd listen, dear boy,' Gavor replied wearily. 'He said Sumeral sent you between the worlds. But how we all came here, he didn't know. And if *he* didn't, I'm certain Sumeral didn't when He disposed of you. And that's probably what He did. I'd say He just didn't want your mangled remains found on the Battlefield. You'd greatly weakened His army, and He knew if you were found hacked to pieces He wouldn't be able to stand against Ethriss's rage. But if you were simply missing . . . that would make for fretfulness, not anger. He made the best of a bad tactical situation – dumped you and ran. Shrewd move, really. But heat of the moment – nothing planned.'

Hawklan's face became unreadable as he held out his hand and lifted Gavor back on to his shoulder.

'What do you make of all this, Hawklan?' Yatsu asked.

'Precious little,' Hawklan replied, shaking off his reverie. 'Everyone's said what had to be said – made some semblance of sense out of what's happening. But I don't know where I belong in it. I can't use the Power, I'm certainly no Dream Finder. As I said, I'm with you – just another soldier – and a patcher of cuts and gashes. A relic from another time.'

'No,' Andawyr said. 'You're close to the heart of this, I'm sure.'

'You can prove this, too?' Hawklan said, a gentle taunt in his voice.

'No, but I'm not afraid to trust my intuition when I reach the end of the reasoning. You and that sword are important, I'm certain.'

Antyr agreed, adding, 'As is the Labyrinth. I was drawn to both from the Cadwanen, if you recall.'

Hawklan grimaced. 'Yes, the Sword. It troubles me that, though I've no need of it, the memory of it's becoming increasingly obtrusive. I can't shake off a sense of loss or, worse, of folly, in letting it go so easily. And what I've just heard doesn't help. It fell between the worlds to land at my feet in a time of need and I just dropped it back again.'

'It fell between the worlds to land at your feet in the Armoury,' Gulda said. It was the first time she had spoken and all eyes turned towards her. She looked at the dark columns at the end of the hall. 'On the far side of the Labyrinth.'

Chapter 32

Hawklan looked at Gulda intently, then suddenly stood up and began walking towards the Labyrinth.

There was a momentary silence before Andawyr and several others were on their feet running after him. Andawyr caught his arm and almost stumbled as Hawklan came to an abrupt halt.

'You can't go in there,' the Cadwanwr exclaimed breathlessly as Hawklan righted him.

Hawklan raised a hand for silence.

'Listen,' he said softly.

The sound from the Labyrinth was shifting and changing constantly, albeit imperceptibly. Now it was a wind discoursing with the mountains, now wordless voices rising and falling, now a warning animal rumble, now the breathing of a watching colossus – a sound that made several of the spectators taken an involuntary step backwards. Then it was something indefinable – unnatural and disturbing.

'Where are Tarrian and Grayle now?' Hawklan asked Antyr half whispering.

'Gone from me,' the Dream Finder replied. His face was pained. 'There's only emptiness where they should be.'

'Alphraan, do you hear this?' Gulda said, her voice not loud but very clear.

The faintest of whisperings made its way through the Labyrinth's shifting sound.

'This song we do not know, my lady. It is ancient beyond any knowing. And it is wrong – it should not be. Look to yourselves, you are going beyond. What you feared is upon you. We cannot help. We are sorry. We . . .'

The final words dwindled into nothingness, but the fear and urgency that hung about them was both desperate and unmistakable. Immediately the Goraidin were forming a defensive line between the Labyrinth and the others.

'Those of you who aren't armed, make yourself so, quickly,' Yatsu said forcefully, indicating the stacks of weapons lining the walls.

'What's happening?' Nertha demanded. 'Who was that speaking?'

'The Alphraan,' Yatsu replied hastily as he snatched up a couple of sheathed knives. Deftly he tested their edges and then thrust them into Nertha's belt before she could protest.

'As for what's happening, I've no idea,' he said. 'But they're stout allies, they wouldn't warn us for nothing. And they sounded very afraid.' His cold and purposeful gaze held her. 'These are good blades, you're a physician, you know how to use them if you have to.' For an instant, Nertha was back at the rain-soaked summit of the Ervrin Mallos in Canol Madreth, gasping for air as she struggled to protect Vredech from the manic apparition that had once been Dowinne.

Yatsu gripped her arms to shake her but she pulled free. 'Sorry,' she gasped. 'I'm all right. I understand. Look to the others.'

'I think it'd be a good idea to leave,' Yatsu said to Andawyr. 'Something might have happened outside.'

Andawyr agreed. The tone of the Alphraan's warning had shaken him. Before he could speak, however, a cry drew all eyes away from the Labyrinth.

It was Ar-Billan. He was pointing to the far end of the hall – or what had been the far end. Now, where there had been a stone wall, a few piles of weapons and, not least, a doorway, there was only a greyness. Not the greyness of a mountain mist concealing something, but a cold emptiness.

'Keep away.'

Both Farnor and Thyrn spoke simultaneously.

'What is it?' Andawyr asked. A glance told him that the two young men were very afraid.

'A tear – a gap,' Farnor managed to say. He was stretching his hand towards it and was obviously in great distress. 'Too much,' he said, and slowly he sank to his knees. Someone caught Thyrn as he too collapsed. Nertha was with them immediately, urgent and practical.

'They're like Vredech and Pinnatte were,' she said after a rapid examination. 'As if they're asleep. Hawklan, help me.'

But Hawklan was looking again into the Labyrinth.

Andawyr, by contrast, was peering into the greyness. He could not tell whether it was near or far – it seemed to extend infinitely in every direction and its featurelessness was both disorientating and luring him. It took a deliberate effort of will to tear his gaze away and look at the hall. At first, the tables, scattered chairs and strewn documents looked dark and unreal, as though they were part of a soiled painting, but as his vision cleared he could see that the greyness was slowly spreading.

As was the fear amongst the group, trapped between this eerie phenomenon and the Labyrinth.

'In our minds.'

Andawyr felt someone shaking his arm. It was Antyr.

'In our minds.' The Dream Finder had to repeat himself several times before Andawyr registered what he was saying. He felt a surge of anger twisting up out of his fear.

'This is no hallucination,' he said furiously. He glanced quickly at the fallen forms of Thyrn and Farnor: Nertha was still examining them but she was radiating helplessness. 'It's real. It's the worlds coming together.' He slapped his forehead brutally. 'Not enough time – too stupid, too slow . . . to work it all out. I . . .'

'Calm yourself, old man, and listen.' Gulda's voice was strong and imperious. It jolted Andawyr and momentarily stilled the mounting commotion of the milling group. The greyness was arching over them. Antyr began to shout, for it seemed that everything was being drained from what was left of the hall.

'In our minds.'

His eyes were becoming like pits of night.

'Our minds reach into the very heart of this. They'll guide. Whatever happens, don't doubt its reality – trust yourselves – you're stronger than you know – we all are – our . . .'

His voice was lost.

Andawyr had a fleeting glimpse of Hawklan, his face riven with pain and doubt, turning and walking into the Labyrinth . . .

Then all was greyness . . .

The air was acrid and the sky was a blue that none of them had ever seen before – save one: Pinnatte.

He was the first to speak.

'Their place,' he hissed, crouching low as though to avoid being seen.

'Quiet!'

Yatsu's command was forceful but equally soft.

And unnecessary, at least for the Goraidin. Both training and experience had kept all of them silent and they were looking around urgently, assessing the terrain they found themselves in without question as to how they had come there. There had been no sense of change or movement. They had been in the Labyrinth hall, suddenly, terrifyingly, dissolving into greyness, then they were here. Despite a fear that was almost choking her, Marna felt a frisson of satisfaction that she too had managed not to cry out. Quickly she began copying her chosen mentors.

Gentren, however, was no Goraidin. 'Yes – my world,' he exclaimed, his voice alive with conflicting and painful emotions. He pointed to a nearby ditch. 'This is where I hid – where I stabbed one of them.' His voice fell as several hands motioned him to silence. Then his anger and distress became suffused with bewilderment.

'It's the same as when I left it,' he whispered, bending down and laying a hand on the coarse mountain grass as if to test what he was seeing. 'This was the last part of the world unchanged. Why haven't they destroyed it – made it the same as everywhere else?'

'Perhaps you did more harm than you thought when you stabbed one of them,' Jenna offered but Gentren did not reply.

'Don't doubt its reality,' Dacu said, echoing Antyr's words for everyone's benefit. He patted his chest and dug his toe into the ground, dislodging a small stone.

Yatsu was counting. The eight Goraidin were there plus Marna, Gentren and Pinnatte. Despite determined efforts to maintain an appearance of calm, all of them were visibly shaken.

'Where's Andawyr? And Antyr – all the others . . .?' someone asked.

Yatsu glanced around with everyone else, then frowned and shook his head. 'Whatever the Cadwanwr were expecting, this must be just a part of it.' He turned away briefly, then said, 'I suppose we'd better concentrate on our own survival before we start bothering about them – or about what's happened.'

They were on the lower slopes of a small mountain. A little way below them the land levelled out into undulating countryside, and though it was difficult to see either detail or for any distance in the strange blue twilight, there were no signs of anything moving. Yatsu pointed in the other direction, towards the shoulder of the slope they were standing on. 'Let's check the other side then see what we can do about making camp.'

'In the name of pity, what is this place?' Yrain's dismayed voice echoed all their thoughts as they reached the shoulder.

Where, before, the blue air had closed about and hidden the landscape, here it seemed to highlight and accentuate the terrain now spread in front of them. Two rows of towering mountains, sheer-sided and jagged, marched to the horizon, etched in blue-in-black shadows against the strained blue sky. It was similar to the scene that Vredech had described, except that here there was a far greater clarity of shape and a multiplicity of symmetries. And the plain between the two rows of mountains was different. Whereas Vredech had told of a disordered lattice of cracks and ravines, this was so smooth as to disturb the eye by its evenness.

'Their place, more than ever,' Pinnatte said.

Gentren's face contorted, then he covered it with his hands and dropped to his knees silently. Yatsu made to speak to him but changed his mind. What could be said to someone whose entire world had been transformed into this abomination? It was no small measure of the man that he had retained his sanity.

Yengar and Olvric gently helped him to his feet as Yatsu

401

turned them all away from the Uhriel's handiwork and motioned them back to where they had arrived.

'Practicalities, my friends, practicalities,' he said. 'Let's do what we're good at. Shelter, water and food, in that order. And, given that this *is* the Uhriel's world, we'd better make sure the shelter's well hidden.' He turned to Gentren who had recovered a little. 'I'll have to press you,' he said. 'You know this land: are there any towns or villages nearby – farms, anything?'

Gentren shook his head. 'The nearest town is a good half-day's ride away but it's deserted – if it's there.' He looked around in desperation. 'And the most you'll find are a few like me, wandering aimlessly.'

'It's probably not a good idea to go too far from here,' Dacu said. 'There must be a Gateway here somewhere that leads back to our world.'

'We don't even know if our world still exists,' Yatsu replied grimly. 'But you're right. Besides, I don't relish trekking over this terrain in this foul air. Let's find shelter.'

'From what?' Gentren asked. 'There'll be no wind, no sun, no rain to hide from. It'll stay like this until . . . until they decide to do whatever it is they're going to do.'

Yatsu scowled. 'We'll need a hiding place at least,' he said.

A few brief instructions split the group into three parties. Olvric and Yengar returned to the shoulder of the slope to keep watch. Jenna, Yrain and Marna together with Jaldaric and Tirke were sent out to forage for food and water, while the remainder went with Yatsu in search of a suitable site for a concealed camp.

It did not take them long to find a cave that would serve admirably as both a shelter and a hiding place, but that was the extent of their good fortune. Jenna and the others had only bad news when they returned.

'No sign of any animals or birds, most of the vegetation is dying, and the two stream beds we came across were bone dry,' Jenna announced bluntly.

'There's been no rain for a long time,' Gentren said.

For the first time since they had arrived, something like despair gripped the Goraidin.

402

'What's the matter?' Pinnatte asked anxiously.

'The matter is that without water we're all going to be dead within a few days,' Dacu said to him quietly. 'And none too pleasantly, at that.' Pinnatte licked his lips, then swallowed.

'That changes our priorities somewhat,' Yatsu said. He turned to Gentren. 'Are there any rivers around here, or lakes?' he asked. 'They won't all have dried up completely, surely?'

Before Gentren could reply, Yengar was with them. He spoke very quietly.

'Three riders coming – across the plain.'

Nertha forced her hand to stop fiddling with the sleeve of her husband's tunic. Then she forced her thoughts into words.

'He's alive,' she said, her voice unsteady despite her clenched teeth. 'They're all alive. They'll be somewhere else – doing something – fighting this.'

She knew that this was her head battling against the clamouring fears of her body, but she clung to it. It was the truth – it was something she had experienced before – her understanding of events needed to be no deeper. No matter what happened here, while these people were alive, events, somewhere, would be moving.

'And I'm alive,' she reminded herself, equally determinedly.

Antyr's words came back to her. 'You're stronger than you know.'

She didn't feel it, she thought, but that too was nothing new. As a physician, she had seen many things that had left her wrung with pity and desperate helplessness but she had coped – and learned. Whatever had happened had happened and she must do what she could, while she could.

Face taut with control, she returned to what she knew – methodically checking the life signs of first Thyrn, then Farnor . . .

Then Antyr and Vredech.

For they too had collapsed as the Labyrinth hall with everything and everyone in it had silently faded away, leaving her with the four unconscious men, alone in a grey and featureless world.

He was screaming.

That much he knew.

He was without form and all about him was chaos.

It danced and shuddered to the rhythm of his cries.

On and on.

Then another rhythm was struggling to impose itself.

'Vredech.'

Over and over it sounded until it began to dominate the shifting shapes and patterns and noises that were flowing through and around him.

He began to recognize it.

It was what he had been. Once, when . . .

When . . .?

Time was nothing here . . .

It changed. 'Don't be afraid,' it said, insistently. 'Don't be afraid.'

A familiarity seeped into it . . .

Antyr!

Vredech knew himself and his awareness wrapped itself about the intrusion like a drowning man about his rescuer.

But the Dream Finder's will sustained them both.

'We're entering a dream nexus,' he said. 'You've done this before, with me, remember?'

Memories of the training he had received from Antyr since his arrival at Anderras Darion were unfurling, steadying him. It had been limited but it had been enough for Vredech to recognize the truth of what he was being told. Nevertheless . . .

'That was with Tarrian and Grayle holding me. This is . . .'

'Different. Yes. But not so different. You can feel your body, can't you? With Nertha tending us.'

'Yes . . . but . . . everything's wrong. She's alone, and afraid . . . this is fearful, Antyr, for pity's sake help me. I . . .'

For a moment, his panic threatened to return and overwhelm both of them. But Antyr cruelly crushed it.

'No! Quieten yourself. I don't know what's happened any more than you do, but whatever's drawn us here has drawn us together and left Nertha guarding us. You know her worth better than I do, so cling to it – just as I'm clinging to the knowledge that wherever Tarrian and Grayle are they'll be seeking to protect us.'

'But without them . . .'

'Without them, we'll be guided by our deeper natures – our deepest natures. We are the elite, remember? We must trust ourselves.'

Ironically, it was the honest uncertainty in Antyr's repetition of his final injunction in the Labyrinth hall that helped Vredech finally take some semblance of command of himself. As he did so, a question came to him about the nexus that he and Antyr were caught in. As he touched Antyr's mind with it, he found it was already being asked.

'Who is the dreamer?'

The darkness rang and echoed with cries.

Andawyr rooted frantically through the junk in his pockets until he found the small radiant-stone lantern. He struck it and the cries changed in character, becoming the accompaniment to a confusion of dancing shadows.

Another lantern was struck.

'Where in the name of pity is this?'

Isloman's voice overtopped the noise. He was staring at the glistening walls of what appeared to be a large tunnel. His face looked haggard in the unsteady lantern light.

Other voices were asking other questions.

'What's happened?'

'Where are we?'

Andawyr held up his lantern to identify the speakers.

Oslang and Atelon were there, as well as Usche and Ar-Billan.

'No good place, for sure.' It was Isloman again.

The babble of questions grew louder.

'Quiet!' Andawyr shouted. 'Just be quiet for a moment. All of you. Let me think.'

'Where are the others?'

'I said, be quiet!'

The second command had the desired effect and a shuffling and uneasy silence descended on the group. Andawyr looked around both at his bewildered companions and at the strange place they found themselves in. He focused his lantern to a tight beam but it merely confirmed that they were in a tunnel before the darkness swallowed its light.

The silence he had demanded, however, brought him neither stillness of mind nor clarity. The unspoken questions written on every face were the same as his own.

What had happened? And where were the Goraidin and the others who had been in the Labyrinth hall?

The only answer he could find to the first question was that this was certainly not the culmination of the conjunction that had been foreseen. Whatever form that might take it was unlikely that any of them would survive it. But this must be an ominous presage of it. A tremor before an earthquake. Insofar as they had any grasp on events, how much longer would they have before they were torn away completely?

An unreasoned insight came to him.

'It's that damned Labyrinth,' he said angrily. 'Anderras Darion might be Ethriss's castle of light, but that place has always been a dark secret at the heart of it. If I were given to wagering I'd say it was the place where this all began. Part of a battle centre of some kind for the monstrous conflict that brought this about. Perhaps Ethriss was telling us something he himself was unaware of when he put the Armoury within it.'

'Or built the Labyrinth around it,' Oslang said.

Andawyr shrugged. 'It's all irrelevant, anyway,' he said, unconvincingly brisk. 'Whatever's happened I suppose we'd better try to find a way out of here.'

This appeal to common sense prompted another inspection of the tunnel. The walls were perfectly smooth and curved round in a high circle until they intersected the level floor which was as smooth as the walls and apparently of the same material. At its crown the tunnel was some four or five times the height of Isloman.

'I can't imagine how this has been built,' the carver said. 'No honest chisel's ever been near it – there's not a mark to be seen.' He looked pained as he ran his hand down the wall. 'This rock's been tortured, not worked,' he said softly.

'The floor slopes a little,' Usche said. She looked significantly at Andawyr. In common with most of the older Cadwanwr, Andawyr's years of living and working in the Cadwanen caves had given him a remarkable instinct for navigating below ground. An inclination of her head asked the question, 'Up or down?'

Andawyr, however, had nothing to offer. Too many questions were vying for attention for such subtleties to make themselves heard.

'Upwards is presumably out of here, but downwards may go to the heart of something,' he said eventually. 'Perhaps to whatever's brought us here.'

'It might be no more than chance that's done that,' Oslang said.

'Possibly,' Andawyr conceded. 'As the conjunction grows nearer, extreme probabilities will come to pass, including more of Usche's "cracks in the building". I presume we've just tumbled through one. But why us and not the others, I've no idea.' He thought for a moment. 'Somewhere there's consciousness at work here, reaching down into the depths.'

'Whose, for mercy's sake?' Oslang demanded impatiently. 'Mine? Yours? Sumeral's?'

'I don't know, damn it,' Andawyr retorted. 'Maybe all of us. But I keep hearing Antyr shouting as that greyness swept over us. We must trust ourselves: we're stronger than we know.' He took Oslang's arm and shook him. 'Whatever caused all this unravelled things to their very roots and whatever our thoughts are they both stem from and go to those roots – affected by and affecting what happens there. Antyr hasn't a fraction of our knowledge but he worked that out for himself.'

'Which leaves us where?' Oslang pressed.

'Here, wherever here is,' Andawyr replied, shaking him again. He looked at the others. 'Scared, but not scared witless yet. And while we're alive and in full possession of those wits, we'd better use them.' He clenched his teeth and hissed out, 'Just keeping the will to fight might be as important as the way we fight.' He pointed along the tunnel.

'I'm for going down. Let's see what's brought us here.'

407

Chapter 33

The journey to the Armoury, short though it was, was never easy. The path through the Labyrinth defied all marking and the echoing columns that lay beyond it both lured and deceived with a song that reached into the darkest reaches of the soul. The guiding of people through it to fetch weapons for the hastily levied Orthlundyn army during the war had cost more than a few of them nightmare-troubled sleep for many months afterwards.

Hawklan stumbled along it, not daring to turn for fear that the consuming greyness would be at his back. Driving him forward, too, was the fear that the greyness had been drawn here by him, that his friends had been swept into nothingness because of his presence.

Questions formed slowly in his tumbling thoughts. Was this the fearful conjunction that had been so exercising Andawyr and the Cadwanol – everything lost in a bleak and desolate emptiness?

And what was he doing, fleeing, deserting them? Had he himself been plunged into madness brought on by his own fears and doubts?

He forced himself to stop and lean on one of the columns. Its touch, real and solid, steadied him. As too did the weight of a silent Gavor on his shoulder. He risked a glimpse backwards. There were only the gloomy columns.

Whatever had happened, it wasn't the end – surely? – it couldn't be. While he was alive he must have a role to play . . .? But there was a ringing hollowness to this assurance. What could he do, a solitary figure scurrying through the darkness – or just hiding in it? Where was he going? The

Armoury? There was nowhere else to go – the path led only there and to leave the path was to die. But what did he hope to find there? The black sword? That had just been Gulda speculating. And even if by some bizarre happenstance it was there, what use would it be? There was no great army laying waste the villages and farms of Orthlund, or beating at the gates of Anderras Darion. Still less was there an army to lead out against them. There were forces moving now of which he had but the barest comprehension. True, there was a quality in the Sword that had struck Isloman and Loman, carver and smith, almost speechless as they had touched its carved hilt and black glinting blade. And, too, he knew that it – or he and it together – had a strength that he did not understand. How else could it have protected him from Oklar's wild unleashing of the Power? But it was not enough. Should he find it, what more would he be, without true knowledge, than a lost and solitary soldier leaning on his futile weapon at the edge of a conflict that was meaningless to him?

He set off again, no wiser and still afraid.

Then he noted something.

A deep silence.

He stopped.

Normally the Labyrinth was awash with strange noises that snuffled and scuttered at the edges of the path like invisible predators waiting to rend apart those unwary enough to misstep.

But now there was nothing.

It was as if the Labyrinth itself was holding its breath . . .

. . . As if it had caught the scent of an even fiercer predator drifting through the darkness.

Scarcely a dozen paces would take him to the hallway of the Armoury and the bright sunlit images of the Orthlundyn countryside carried there by Anderras Darion's intricate maze of mirror stones. From thence, through the now ever-open wicket door, he would enter the Armoury itself to be amongst the cornfield rows of points and edges glittering in that same sunlight.

If Orthlund was still there.

He dashed the thought aside and pressed on quickly,

counting his footsteps and striving to ignore the deafening silence.

But at the last turn, where light should have greeted and embraced him, there stood only columns, watching, waiting, in the Labyrinth's dull twilight.

He heard a rasping, terrified breath as his body responded to the sight. Gavor slapped his wings. Both sounds fell dead in the leaden air.

'I . . . I made no mistake, surely?' Hawklan stammered as the pounding of his heart threatened to overwhelm him.

'Not that I noticed, dear boy,' Gavor replied, equally unsteadily.

Despair came in the wake of the initial shock, washing over him in full flood now, black and choking. Andawyr had thought him near the heart of what was happening. So had many others, not least Sumeral Himself. But what was he now? A dismal fugitive lost in this dreadful place where the least sound could be woven into a shrieking that would leave a man mindless, or into an avalanche roaring that would break him as surely as falling rocks themselves.

He could not move.

He had made no error, he was sure. He couldn't have. His deeper nature held the Labyrinth in too great awe to allow any confusion of the mind to so mislead him.

'Change,' Gavor said.

Hawklan started at the sound.

'The Traveller said that to use the pathways of the Labyrinth is to change them.'

Hawklan grasped at Gavor's words.

'Not the path to the Armoury, though,' he said, struggling to recall Gulda's account of her meeting with the Traveller. 'At least, not perceptibly. What did he say? It changes like the mountains, mote by mote?'

'For all we know, the mountains have vanished like the Labyrinth hall,' Gavor retorted flatly. 'And he did say there was a great turbulence in the Labyrinth.'

Despite the implications of what Gavor was saying, Hawklan felt their exchange steadying him.

'There are other paths, he said.'

411

'He also said that most of them change like the trembling of a leaf in the wind.'

Hawklan looked again at where the entrance to the Armoury should have been.

Nothing.

Just the blank, ominous columns, their presence sensed as much as seen in the gloom that pervaded the Labyrinth. He knew that, whichever way he looked, this would be what greeted him. His despair returned, undiminished. He had faced dangers before, dangers that might have seen him killed and that he would only too willingly have avoided, but dangers that he was nevertheless prepared to accept by virtue of the role he had accepted – the role his skills best suited him for: healer, protector. But there was a futility here that bore down on him like the weight of the castle itself looming high above this grim place. Dying in the course of opposing a greater power was a bitter enough prospect, but to die here – to drown in his own screams – for nothing – while . . .

While what?

While the world and everything – everyone – in it plunged into some nameless cataclysm that perhaps some action on his part might have prevented. That was bitter beyond any swallowing.

He realized that he was clenching and unclenching his hand painfully. He could feel again the black sword slipping from his grip and tumbling into the darkness. His arm twitched as he tried to recover it.

Could so slight a thing – the loss of a single weapon, however fine – be so significant now?

Yes, his instinct told him, even though the links of cause and effect that would make it so were neither foreseeable then, nor calculable by hindsight now.

'I think we'd better do something, dear boy,' Gavor said, fidgeting nervously. 'We can't just stand here.'

Hawklan opened his hand and gently rubbed it with the other as if to reassure it that it bore no guilt in the loss of the sword. Values deeply imbued in him and rehearsed constantly since his coming to this time began to reassert themselves.

He was alive.

He might be dead very soon, but then he might not be, and to cloud the present certainty with a future uncertainty was not only to mar the present but might bring about that feared future.

'Yes,' he replied, straightening up and carefully turning round.

The scene was as he had expected. Identical in all directions.

Well, whatever had happened to the hall hadn't happened to the Labyrinth, he thought bleakly. And it was still silent.

Almost as though challenging it, Hawklan clapped his hands. The sound was dull and lifeless.

'Which way?' he asked.

Gavor inclined his head round to look at him. 'Dear boy, don't ask me. It was your idea to come in here. How am I supposed to know. There's not a breath of wind in here. There never is.'

With a final glance at where the Armoury should have been, Hawklan held out a hand, indicating the way back to the hall. 'This way?'

Gavor clucked to himself twice, then nodded.

As he set off, Hawklan found that his legs were shaking.

He moved cautiously, every sense alert for the lingering echo of a footfall that might presage a reawakening of the Labyrinth. So many fears tugged at him that for much of the time he was able to keep any one of them from rising to dominate. Nevertheless, when he reached the place where the hall should have been and found himself facing the same array of gloomy columns that lay before him in every other direction, he felt an unspoken hope dying. For a moment, panic screamed at him from the edges of his mind, but he held it at bay. It would remain close, though.

Gavor did not speak, but shifted his weight uneasily.

'Alphraan, do you hear me?' Hawklan said.

There was no reply.

'Not that I'm normally inclined to think about such things, but I'd have imagined a bolder end for myself than this,' Gavor said laconically.

'Yes,' Hawklan said. Gavor had been his companion since

his mysterious arrival in Orthlund and it was more consolation than he cared to voice to have him still there.

Then, out of the darkness, came a sound.

Yatsu and Dacu crawled to Olvric's side. He made no sound, but an inclination of his head drew them to a rock from the side of which they could look along the plain between the mountains without being seen. It took both of them a little time to adjust to the eerie perspective that the unchanging blueness brought to the plain, but gradually they made out the approaching riders.

As they watched, there was a brief flicker of light, thin and vertical, on another part of the plain.

'What was that?' Yatsu whispered.

'I don't know,' Olvric replied. 'I've seen a few of them, in different places. They're never there long enough to look at properly and there doesn't seem to be any pattern to them. If they're signal lights they're like none I've ever seen. Just a single flash, then gone.'

'There's another,' Dacu hissed, instinctively ducking back behind the rock.

'Never mind,' Yatsu said. 'We've enough to worry about without fretting over mysterious lights. How long before those three get here?'

'Impossible to say,' Dacu replied, squinting at the riders. 'There's nothing to gauge anything by.'

Yatsu scowled. 'If they're who we think they are, we can't possibly fight them. We'll have to hide – buy some time to find out more about this place.' No one argued. 'Keep watching,' he said to Olvric and Yengar.

He broke the news to the others bluntly. 'We'll have to assume they're the Uhriel. That means the only thing we can do is hide and hope they pass by.'

'They came straight to Vredech and me when we were here,' Pinnatte said. 'It was almost as if the mountains were telling them where we were.'

'That's a comfort,' Marna said caustically, but Yatsu motioned her to be quiet.

'It's relevant,' he said. 'Everything that happened to him is 'relevant.' He looked around. 'Maybe if this area hasn't been changed yet they won't be able to do that.'

'We could ambush them,' Marna suggested. 'Gentren injured one of them.'

Yatsu shook his head. 'Maybe, if we'd absolutely no other alternative, but until then we hide.' He did not totally dismiss the idea, however.

'Did you see any trees nearby?' he asked Yrain.

'There's woodland within an hour's walk.' Gentren said, before she could answer. 'But I don't know what state it's in.'

'Good. If we can, that's where we'll go afterwards. There'll be better shelter there, and more chance of finding food and something to drink. We can also make some bows and spears just in case we do have to ambush them. Not to mention a few snares.'

Yengar was with them again, his eyes wide.

'One of them's disappeared,' he said. Yatsu made him repeat the news.

'Just vanished into one of those lights,' Yengar amplified. 'One moment he was there, then he was gone.' He snapped his fingers softly.

Yatsu looked at Pinnatte who shrugged.

'None of them vanished when we were here, more's the pity,' he said sourly.

'What about the others?' Yatsu asked Yengar after a brief and bewildered pause.

'They just carried on. We heard a faint shrieking noise like Vredech told us about.' He grimaced. 'It's not a nice sound, even at a distance, but I suppose it confirms who they are.'

'One down, two to go,' Yrain said.

'No, it's eleven to go unless we keep our wits about us,' Yatsu retorted curtly. 'Don't forget, none of us would have dreamt of attacking one of the old Uhriel and if the Memsa's correct, which she usually is, these . . . creatures . . . are many times more powerful. Furthermore, I need hardly add, this is their world. We don't even know whether this vanishing is to our advantage or not, yet.' He looked across the blue-tainted countryside. 'It's very open. Precious little cover if we go as a group and not much more if we split up.'

415

'We should stay here if we can – near the Gateway – wherever it is,' Dacu said, reiterating his earlier concern.

Yatsu nodded. 'How far does this cave go back?'

'Not far,' Jaldaric said. 'Twenty, thirty paces and nowhere to hide except amongst the rocks on the ground.' He held out his hand. It was dirty. 'No water, I'm afraid, but there's a damp patch at the back,' he said, wiping the dirt from his hand across his face. 'At least we can make ourselves less conspicuous.'

Yatsu was grim as he returned to Olvric and Yengar. The two riders were conspicuously closer, though it was still not possible to judge how far away they were. Apart from two more brief flashes of light, nothing else had happened since the disappearance – other than the remaining riders' relentless progress.

'Time to hide,' Olvric said, very softly.

A hand signal dispatched the Goraidin into the cave, but Yatsu whispered stern instructions to the others. 'Do exactly as you're told. Keep your faces to the ground – they'll be visible in the dark if you look up. Don't move. Don't speak. If any fighting breaks out, keep out of it.' He nodded towards the cave. 'We know one another, and we know how to fight together. You'll certainly hinder us and you might well get cut down by accident. Do you understand?' Gentren and Pinnatte gave a reluctant 'Yes' in the face of this cold-eyed ultimatum but Marna was obviously considering defiance.

Yatsu's hands flicked out. One tapped her lightly on the cheek while the other took a knife from her belt. Even as she was flinching from the blow the knife was at her throat. 'That's an order, cadet,' he said, unexpectedly gently, as he returned her knife. 'Your courage isn't in doubt, but you're not good enough yet. Not for what might have to be done here.' Then, to all three. 'But if the worst comes to the worst, do what you have to do to survive.'

Inside the cave he checked everyone's positions and whispered a few instructions to the Goraidin before lowering himself into the deep shadow of the rock-strewn floor. Within moments, Yengar and Olvric, crouching low, slipped silently into the cave and vanished from sight.

This would be the testing time, Yatsu knew. Waiting always was. It was what the Goraidin were supremely good at but it tested the calibre as much as any combat. In silent stillness the mind wandered, making sounds and images out of nothing to torment and delude, while the body cried out for movement. And here, who could say what deep shock waves the terrifying disappearance of the Labyrinth hall and their mysterious trans-lation to this place might yet release? Even he was having difficulty setting aside the voice inside him clamouring that perhaps all he had ever known had been swept into oblivion and that he was going to die futilely, cursing an invincible enemy in the darkness on this benighted and ruined world.

Gradually, he became aware of a sound – distant, but high-pitched and flesh-crawling.

Nertha continued to quieten her frantic thoughts by methodi-cally checking the pulse and the breathing of each of the four unconscious men at regular intervals. She did this with delib-erate slowness, using her own pulse as a guide to the passage of time. This was easily done. While the pulses of her involuntary charges were normal, hers was fast and urgent. It needed no careful seeking with delicate fingers. It pounded hollowly in her chest and ears.

Who is the dreamer?

Awash in a swirling confusion of sounds, shapeless colours and a myriad elusive, evocative scents, the diamond-sharp awareness that was Antyr shied away from the question.

In its eddying wake he was suddenly whole and as real as the body that he could feel a fearful Nertha tending. By him was Vredech, present but not visible, as he would be to him.

'This is the Nexus,' he said. It was the place into which leaked fragments of all the dreams that the dreamer had ever created. But here, he was lost. Here, it was the spirits of Tarrian and Grayle who would carry him to where the Dreamer's need was. But Tarrian and Grayle were gone on a hunt of their own.

He wanted to reassure Vredech, but he could not. There were too many questions.

417

Had they both come here to fulfil a purpose determined by a knowledge hidden in the depths of their minds . . .?

Or had it been an instinctive response as the encroaching greyness had overwhelmed the Labyrinth hall? Sheer panic? Vredech would not have abandoned Nertha, surely, but . . .?

Or had they been drawn here by some other power?

And Vredech's awful question returned.

Who is the dreamer?

Who was the creator of the chaos dancing all about them?

Then, as was the way in moving from the Nexus to the dream, without any seeming change, they *were* the dreamer.

The five Cadwanwr and Isloman had been walking steadily for some time. There were no features within the tunnel from which they might learn anything about where they were or even gauge their progress – though, from time to time, Atelon marked the wall with a small chisel he had borrowed from Isloman.

The sound of their footsteps was oddly dull and the nervous jostling of the shadows cast by the solitary lantern they were using added to their already considerable unease. Though they were not reduced to whispering, such conversation as they had was both sparse and subdued.

'We can't carry on like this,' Usche complained at one point, prompting a sharp 'What else can we do?' from Andawyr.

She was on the verge of plucking up courage to complain again when Andawyr stopped and held up his hand, unnecessarily, for silence.

'I thought I heard something,' he said.

'Felt something, more like,' Oslang rejoined. 'Like someone using the Power, but quite a distance away.'

'Yes, you're right. Come on.' And, without any pause for debate, Andawyr was striding out.

'Do you think this is wise?' Oslang asked as he caught up with him.

'At the moment I'm trying *not* to think,' Andawyr replied. 'In the absence of any indication about where we are or what's happened there's not much point, is there? We'll have to settle for travelling by instinct.'

'There's a light ahead.' It was Isloman. He moved past Andawyr and covered the lantern with his big hand. The group bumped to an awkward halt as he peered intently into the darkness.

'Yes,' he decided. 'Definitely – light ahead.' He released the lantern.

'You and your Orthlundyn eyes,' Andawyr said, blinking. 'I can't see anything.'

Isloman did not reply but took the lead.

Very soon the tunnel walls were tinted with a dim blue haze that grew in intensity until the lantern was no longer needed.

'This place is very bad,' Isloman said, as much to himself as the others. 'The rock cries out.'

'And it stinks of the Power being misused,' Andawyr added, giving voice to what he could see the other Cadwanwr were feeling.

'It stinks of *considerable* Power being misused,' Oslang said emphatically. 'We must be careful.'

The source of the light came into view. It was an opening in the side of the tunnel, identical in shape and size to the tunnel itself. As the group stopped to one side of it, the blue light pouring through it gave a ghastly hue to their anxious faces.

Cautiously, Andawyr peered round the edge. Then, motioning the others to follow, he stepped into the opening. It proved to be not a branch tunnel but a doorway. A few paces brought them on to a wide balcony that ran round a vast circular chamber.

In the far wall was a row of what appeared to be windows and it was through these that the blue light which filled the chamber was coming. The walls rose up to disappear into a dark blue gloom. Atelon moved towards the edge of the balcony, then dropped on to his knees to look over it – it had no balustrade.

'It's a long way down,' he said, reaching back with one hand to warn the others against approaching too quickly.

There were two other balconies beneath them, apparently deserted. As was the floor of the chamber. This was decorated with a single star at its centre. It had a silver sheen that cut through the blue light, and fine rays shone from it, dividing the floor into equal segments. Some way from the centre, and also symmetrically spaced, secondary rays continued the pattern.

'A bad symbol,' Atelon said grimly.

Andawyr nodded. 'We might have expected it.' He indicated the windows on the far side. 'Let's see where we are.'

The windows proved to be nothing more than holes cut through the wall. They reached down to the floor of the balcony and had no glazing. Hugging the wall and holding on to Isloman, Andawyr stepped inside one and edged tentatively forward.

Where the view down into the well of the chamber had been disconcerting, the view through the window was terrifying. His hold on Isloman tightening so hard that the big carver grimaced, Andawyr found himself looking down the giddying perspective of a curved wall that was many times higher than the highest towers of Anderras Darion. Radiating from it ran great saw-toothed ridges, their peaks rising and falling in elaborate curves all the way to the horizon – and, presumably, beyond – like frozen waves. Away from the base of the building, and spaced between these at regular intervals, other similar ridges began, the whole giving the impression of patterns within patterns, great complexity built from simplicity. But there was an obsessive, diseased quality to the scene, heightened by the fact that everything was blue. *Even the air*, Andawyr thought, as he blinked into the disturbing distance.

Isloman's grip tightened on him suddenly as, too engrossed in the scene, he leaned forward and his toe eased over the edge of the wall. He acknowledged the carver's urging but did not move.

Where was this place? And how could such a landscape have come about?

Answers came immediately and without deliberation. Even without the symbol of the single silver star, this building, everything he could see, was obviously Sumeral's work. It must be Gentren's world – a world transformed by Sumeral's new-found Uhriel for who could say what purpose? But the Power that must have been used was beyond imagining. Not the entire resources of a hundred times the Cadwanol could undo such work. Andawyr's spirit suddenly quailed and a suffocating blackness rose up within him. There was nothing anyone could do against such an enemy. All his learning, all his experience was worthless. He felt an urge to pull himself free of Isloman's sustaining hold and hurl himself into this jagged blue nightmare – to end it all. His mind teetered and his world filled with the sound of his rasping, indecisive breathing.

He could do it. Isloman's grip was not so tight.

But it was there. Quietly purposeful. Jump he might, but trip he wouldn't.

The blackness shifted.

To go that way would not end it all, would it? Such an act would merely abandon his immediate charges to whatever lay in this place, burdened even more. Their shocked and accusing faces swam into his mind, especially those of Usche and Ar-Billan – in many ways the innocents of the group. And, too, it would abandon everything he had ever worked for and valued – and the work and sacrifice of countless others who had opposed Sumeral in His many different guises.

As suddenly as it had come the blackness vanished. The prospect ahead was no less daunting but he realized that he had accepted the Goraidin's way at its deepest level. He could do no less than direct his every skill towards defeating Sumeral, futile or not. He might well die in the process, but he would not die either willingly or quietly.

Antyr's words, shouted as the greyness had engulfed them all, came back to him.

'Our minds reach into the very heart of this.'

Antyr's intuition about the workings of the mind had led him to a place that the Cadwanol's sophisticated reasoning and experimenting had hardly dared point towards. And, too, he reproached himself, though his own work on the pending conjunction had foundered because the stern and ordered thinking that had foreseen it could not cope with the infinity of events that might occur in a single moment, that same thinking told him that the smallest of actions at that moment might shift the balance and determine the outcome – *the very smallest*.

Who could say which action would prove to be pivotal?

Pivotal.

The word took him back to the stream near the Cadwanen where he had lain, seeking inspiration in its sun-dancing ripples.

How long ago had that been . . .?

Two weeks? Three weeks? He could not remember exactly, but it seemed like a lifetime ago, so many things had happened so quickly.

As he knew they must.

They would happen even faster now.

'We're stronger than we know,' he said, echoing Antyr as he turned away from Gentren's ruined world and back to his friends.

'Let's see what we can find out about this place.'

Chapter 34

A brief search brought Isloman and the Cadwanwr to an opening that led on to a wide landing. Where they might have expected stairs, however, was a sloping ramp.

'Down?' Andawyr asked rhetorically as he set off purposefully.

The ramp sloped more steeply than the tunnel they had first found themselves in and it was uncomfortable walking. It spiralled steadily downwards, pervaded by a blue light that was sufficiently bright for them to see where they were going without the aid of a lantern. It prompted some comment but no one could find a source.

'It's the rock itself,' Isloman said, his voice strained. 'It's screaming. This is a dreadful, dreadful place.'

As Orthlund's First Carver, Isloman was unusually sensitive to qualities in rock that others were quite unaware of. Now his whole posture radiated distress.

'Whatever this place is, it isn't the work of master builders – it hasn't even been built,' he said. 'It's been twisted and torn from the virgin rock.'

Andawyr laid a comforting hand on his arm, but said nothing.

They passed openings that led on to the two lower balconies and a cursory inspection showed them to be similar to the one they had left. Eventually they came to the floor they had seen from high above. Andawyr held out a cautionary hand as they gathered in the broad doorway.

What had appeared to be a mosaic at its centre proved to be very different. The silver star was hovering some way above the floor, solid and many-faceted, with thorn-sharp points pricking the blue air. No support to it was immediately apparent. The rays that, from above, seemed to run from it were actually ridges rising from the floor, undulating up towards it.

'They're like those ... mountains ... outside,' Ar-Billan said. 'Same pattern.' He bent forward and looked at them intently. 'Probably the same proportions, by the look of it.'

He was about to step closer but Andawyr stopped him.

'You're right,' he said. 'But we must be careful. This is no decoration. Everything here will have a purpose, and a bad one at that.'

Looking anxiously from side to side he stepped into the chamber.

'It's strange,' he said, apparently satisfied that there was no immediate danger. 'This must all have been achieved by the use of the Power, but I can feel nothing of it.'

He looked around and scowled. Serried ranks of unkempt Cadwanwr scowled back at him, for the circular chamber was lined with tall, narrow mirrors. The result was a vast blue desert, littered with ridges and overlooked by row upon row of ill-omened stars. As the others joined Andawyr, so crowds appeared all around them.

Despite their predicament, Usche was wide-eyed. 'It's like being at the centre of infinity,' she said, spinning round and watching her myriad counterparts aping her.

Andawyr grunted and fiddled with his nose. 'I'm open to suggestions,' he said.

'Smash it. Smash it all.'

Isloman's harsh verdict drew all eyes to him.

'I meant, what's all this about?' Andawyr remonstrated.

'I know what you meant, but this isn't the time for debate,' Isloman retorted. 'We don't know how or why we came here – whether it's chance or some devilment on Sumeral's part – or whether we're all dreaming, for that matter – but there's nothing here I want to learn about any more than there's anything I'd want to learn from murdering children in their beds. Smash it.' He took his chisel back from Atelon and made to stand on one of the ridges, apparently with the intention of assaulting the baleful star.

'No!' Andawyr cried out urgently, seizing the big man's arm and pulling him back.

Isloman jerked his arm free angrily and seemed intent on arguing, but Andawyr did not give him the opportunity.

'I told you – none of this is decoration,' he said, seizing Isloman's arm again. He pointed at the star. 'That thing's the centre of something – a terrible focus for everything here. Who knows what touching it might do?' He looked questioningly at Oslang and Atelon.

Both of them looked unhappy about what he appeared to be asking.

'We'll have to, I suppose,' Oslang said. 'But be careful – *very* careful.'

Andawyr ushered everyone back into the doorway, then stood with Oslang and Atelon at either side of him.

'I'm just going to touch that thing with the Power,' he said. 'Very quickly. See if I can learn anything about it.' He turned to Usche and Ar-Billan. 'Whatever happens to me – or to all three of us – don't interfere. Do you understand?'

They both nodded.

Andawyr rubbed his hands together nervously, then wiped them down his rope. After a glance at his companions he closed his eyes and became very still. Instinctively, Isloman moved protectively in front of Usche and Ar-Billan.

There was no sound and, whatever Andawyr did, Isloman saw nothing of it. But suddenly he was catching the little man as he was thrown violently backwards. The force of the impact sent both of them sprawling. Isloman rolled over, clutching his stomach, obviously winded, but Andawyr lay still. Oslang and Atelon, visibly shaken, were by his side immediately but as Oslang bent over to examine him, he became aware of Ar-Billan nervously clutching at his robe.

Looking up, he saw that the chamber was no longer empty. Picking its way towards him over the jagged ridges with a repellent fastidiousness was a strange horse, bearing a helmed and armoured rider.

Hawklan froze at the sound. It was a faint clicking.

Was the Labyrinth awakening?

Was this the presage of a tumult that would rise and rise until it dashed him to his death?

The clicking grew louder. Hawklan could do no other than hold his breath, even though he knew that no sound was too slight for the Labyrinth to seize upon.

'Hello,' said a familiar voice in the darkness.

Hawklan, senses heightened by fear, started violently at the unexpected sound.

'Dar-volci,' he gasped out in a mixture of anger and relief.

'What are you doing here? What's happened?' asked the felci.

'Where are Tarrian and Grayle?' Hawklan asked in return.

'They've gone,' Dar-Volci replied. 'I was trying to find my way back to the hall.'

'Gone?'

'Gone. Just disappeared. They were running ahead of me, then everything went very peculiar and they weren't there. Rather churlish, I thought, leaving me without a word.'

The faint attempt at humour merely served to highlight a very uncharacteristic unease in the felci.

Hawklan crouched in front of him. 'What do you mean, everything went peculiar?'

'Just that,' came the unhelpful reply. 'And there I was, on my own. Now everything seems to be changing all the time.' He repeated his own question before Hawklan could press him further. 'Anyway, what are you doing here?'

Hawklan told him.

Dar-volci let out a series of anxious whistles. He began twisting round as though slowly chasing his own tail. 'All gone? Andawyr and the others – all gone? And the hall and the Armoury?'

Hawklan had never seen him so disturbed.

'And we're lost?'

'We're lost.'

Dar-volci stopped turning, chattered noisily to himself, then looked around.

'Not good,' he muttered. 'And this place is still changing.'

Hawklan followed his gaze but could neither see nor sense anything untoward.

'What do you mean?' he asked. 'I can't see anything.'

'Something's happening, dear boy,' Gavor said. 'I've felt it in my pinions ever since we came in here, but don't ask me what it is.'

Hawklan knew that his companions were telling him all they could.

'Very well,' he said to Dar-volci. 'Take us to where Tarrian and Grayle disappeared. Perhaps we'll find something there.'

'I can't,' the felci replied. 'I told you, everything's changing. It's almost as though the Labyrinth is only real where we can see it – or where you are,' he added as an afterthought.

Hawklan frowned. 'Go where your feet lead you, then,' he said as encouragingly as he could. 'We must keep searching. We can't do nothing.'

Dar-volci let out a final low whistle, then pattered off. Hawklan followed him.

They walked for a long time through the unchanging landscape of the Labyrinth. Although there was no hint of a return of its death-dealing sounds Hawklan became increasingly aware of a sense of oppressiveness as they moved on. Whether it was something outside himself or just mounting despair he could not have said, but it grew relentlessly. Increasingly he found himself taking deep breaths and looking warily at the columns as if at any moment they might move together and enclose him like an insect gripped in a spider's web.

'Stop a moment,' he gasped. He sat down and, leaning against one of the columns, closed his eyes. Gavor hopped down from his shoulder and stood next to Dar-volci. Both of them looked at him in silence.

In the deeper darkness behind his eyes, Hawklan struggled to set aside the fears and anxieties that were clamouring ever louder. The worst of these was that he was going to die in this desolate limbo, though this was heavily fringed about with a sense of guilt that in some way he was betraying his friends – they needed him, they needed what he could do.

But what *could* he do . . .?

Fight? Heal?

Yes: both. They were sides of the same coin. But what

could he fight here? And what could he heal?

He opened his eyes. Gavor and Dar-volci were still watching him patiently. This place was oppressive to him, but it must be truly dreadful for Gavor, he thought, a creature who soared joyously on the unseen, shifting pathways of the high mountain air. He reached out to the bird who clambered on to his hand.

'I was going to say we've been in worse places. But we haven't, have we?' he said.

'Afraid not, dear boy. Are you ready to move on?'

'Yes and no.'

Hawklan lifted the raven on to his shoulder then placed his hand against the column he had been leaning on as though it were an injured limb.

Turmoil filled him and he pulled his hand back quickly. How could that be? He was no carver. He had no sensitivity for cold stone. Isloman and the other Orthlundyn routinely twitted him about his rock-blindness.

He placed both hands against the column. The turmoil was there still – it had not been a trick of his imagination – but this time he did not pull away. It was no new sensation for him. It was the disturbance he felt in any wound – a struggle between forces of disorder and equilibrium – imbalance and balance.

What could it be that would make this dead stonework respond thus?

He remembered Usche and Andawyr. This conjunction that they feared stemmed from the place of infinite smallness where all things have a commonality – 'These walls, these tables, everything, even ourselves,' Usche had said.

Now he could feel it.

This he could fight – and heal.

He touched the disturbance as he would any other wound, instinct guiding him.

A tremor shook him. For an instant he thought that the Labyrinth was preparing to attack, but he thrust the fear from him and persisted with his healing touch.

An incongruous 'Ooh!' from both Gavor and Dar-volci made him turn.

The Labyrinth was lighter. His eyes were drawn upwards.

Where before the columns had faded into low darkness, they now reached up much further, giving him the impression that he was standing in a great forest. Gavor glided down onto the floor and flapped his wings noisily.

'Carry on,' Hawklan said to Dar-volci.

As they walked, Hawklan briefly touched some of the columns. It was no light-hearted healing, however. He knew that the pain he was feeling was beyond his curing. It was like walking alone across a battlefield strewn with mangled corpses and ringing with the terrible cries of the wounded. So, as on a battlefield, he did what he could, leaving the greater part of the field to the mercies of chance.

Nevertheless, it gave him strength.

Slowly, imperceptibly, the light around them changed and though the columns were too close to see any further ahead, they could see them rising higher and higher. Wherever they were, this was no construct in the bowels of Anderras Darion.

He avoided dwelling on the thought. He would have no answers, he knew, and nothing was to be served by it.

Usche had said that the place of infinite smallness was one where cause and effect, even time and distance, had little meaning.

'It's a disturbing place, but it *is* and it has to be accepted.'

And if the coming conjunction had brought this disturbing nature here, then so be it. Hawklan accepted. He would do what he could – he would trust his healing.

He glanced upwards, then screwed his eyes tight. As the columns tapered together, fading into the heights above, it seemed as though they were gently waving.

'Not a movement. Not a word,' Yatsu hissed as the high-pitched shrieking faded.

It came again at irregular intervals, rising and falling in some unfathomable exchange. It was an awful sound that spoke to its hearers at depths far below their conscious understanding. Reaching into Yatsu it fanned the embers of his despair, threatening to ignite them into a consuming incandescence. Only the cold discipline that cruel experience had given him prevented it. That, and the trembling he could feel in Pinnatte lying by his side.

'It's a noise,' he whispered to the others, breaking his own injunction. 'Like fingernails on glass, maybe, but still only a noise.'

Pinnatte's trembling continued.

The shrieking grew steadily louder and more intense until eventually it was reverberating all about the cave, seeming to come from every direction and surrounding the cowering group.

Then, abruptly, it stopped. The sudden silence was like an impact.

Pinnatte stiffened. He was no longer trembling.

'Something's different,' he whispered urgently. 'They're . . .'

Yatsu's hand shot out and covered his mouth.

Black against blue, the silhouettes of two riders appeared at the mouth of the cave. The heads of their steeds were swaying slowly, side to side, up and down, as they peered into the darkness.

'Did you think to come here unnoticed?'

The voice was hung about with the lingering echoes of the shrieking from which it seemed to have been woven. A mocking concern in it intensified its jarring dissonance.

No one moved.

The voice came again.

'You mar the cleansing of this place with your presence. Come into the light. If service to Him whose return is nigh can be found, you may preserve those transient, trembling shadows you call your lives.'

Abruptly and with unexpected swiftness, Pinnatte was on his feet and striding towards the entrance of the cave. Nimbly he avoided a frantic lunge by Yatsu who swore under his breath.

'Come with me, all of you,' Pinnatte said loudly.

As he stepped out into the blue light to confront the two riders, he turned and repeated the command authoritatively, added, 'These are two of the three who are to be judged. Hurry, the time is near.' Then he was addressing the riders. 'And did your companion expect to escape judgement by fleeing?'

Any possibility of either concealment or surprise having

been lost, Yatsu signalled to the others to follow the lead that Pinnatte was setting. He was still addressing the riders as they emerged hesitantly.

'Or did you think to blame him for *your* failure?' Pinnatte's voice was arrogant and taunting.

Yatsu's mind was racing. All that he had seen of Pinnatte was a tongue-tied and confused young man, apparently aware of what was happening around him but somehow locked away from it. He had learned from Atelon that he had been a successful thief in the harsh streets of Arash-Felloren before the Kyrosdyn had laid their hands on him, and he had learned from Vredech, and now from his own limited observation, that Pinnatte was a markedly different individual in this world. But what game was he playing? Some reckless bluff?

Gulda had said that Pinnatte and Vredech could have been drawn to this world because Pinnatte might still have some residue of the apparently impossible ability both to move between worlds and use the Power. Could it be that this was coming to the fore here?

Listen! Yatsu ordered himself. *Listen. Watch.*

The latter, however, was not easy. The two riders were a fearful sight. Sumeral's lieutenants, His Uhriel, made flesh again. Black-clad and livid in the blue light, sitting astride their evil-eyed and serpentine mounts that might once have been horses, they radiated a presence that defied description. Yatsu fidgeted casually, his hands and feet moving continually. The other Goraidin were doing the same. It was a device normally used to unsettle the concentration of a possible enemy, but here, Yatsu knew it was more to control the violent trembling that was shaking them all. His mouth was burningly dry.

A helm was removed to reveal a woman's face. Once it might have been, if not beautiful, then certainly striking, but now it was gaunt and drawn, with a sickly, pallid lustre. Lifeless eyes, black and watery, stared out of it. *Dowinne*, Yatsu presumed with a shiver he could barely restrain, Vredech's erstwhile nemesis. Her rasping voice cut through his tumbling thoughts.

'You would take His name in vain? Blessed be it. You

would utter such profanity on the very world that will open the Great Way and bring us to His heartworld?'

Her voice and the sinuous writhing of her mount turned Yatsu's stomach.

But was there a hint of doubt in that challenge?

'Something's different,' Pinnatte had said before Yatsu had stifled him.

An Uhriel could have shrivelled all of them with the least effort, but one had fled and this one was debating . . .

Pinnatte held out his hand, fingers extended, and made a slow, vertical, cutting action. At his fingertips a line of bright light appeared. It widened and Yatsu had a fleeting impression of a landscape within it, then Pinnatte clenched his fist and the light was gone.

A dreadful life came into Dowinne's blank eyes as she stared down at Pinnatte.

'You are the one who came with Vredech,' she hissed. 'And you fled with him. Who are you?'

'This is not how it should be,' her companion interrupted. 'Not now the fount of the Great Way is known to us. This is trickery by His enemies. We must destroy them. We must complete our work quickly or it will be less than perfect. The time is near.'

Though the voice was shrill and jarring, like Dowinne's, there was almost fear in it, and Marna started in recognition. She pushed her way through the Goraidin.

'Rannick?' she exclaimed.

The rider looked at her for a long time.

'More trickery,' he said slowly. 'You have the likeness of one I knew before I was born again. But that is not possible. You could not have come here.'

'It *is* me, Rannick,' Marna said, almost plaintively. 'What's happened to you? What've you become? What've you done here?'

The rider let out a piercing cry and tore off his helm. Marna found herself staring into rancid white eyes set in a face, pale and gaunt like Dowinne's, but drawn and desert-leached. White hair moved about his head as though stirred by a wind in another place.

432

Marna stepped back in horror and whispered again, 'Rannick, what in the name of pity's happened to you?'

The Uhriel leaned forward and stared at her.

'Whatever you are, you cannot be here. All lesser Ways lead only to the fount. Where is the Gateway you used?' Marna staggered as he shrieked at her, but Pinnatte stepped between them.

'It is not for you to question my servants,' he said, his voice unexpectedly powerful. 'It is for you to be judged and to accept sentence.'

He cut his hand downwards as he had before and a thin light hovered briefly in the blue air. 'Here is a Gateway, doubter.' Then he flicked his hand towards Rannick's mount, which shied and let out a strange mewling cry. 'And here is the Power.' He turned to Dowinne. 'I *am* the one who came with Vredech. The one you deemed flawed and imperfect. That was but to test your vision. *And it was lacking!*'

The last words were filled with such menace and vehemence that both riders edged backwards. Yatsu looked at Pinnatte, suddenly even more fearful. Some strange attribute, hidden in their own world, was obviously available to him here. But had some darker trait come with it – something that the Kyrosdyn had seen in him? Were they now facing not two Uhriel, but three?

Pinnatte's contorted features were not reassuring. His eyes were wide and staring, and his mouth was drawn back to reveal teeth clenched with either rage or effort. Abruptly he moved between the two Uhriel, thrust his hands upwards, then cut violently downwards.

Where, before, a thin line of light had appeared, now great swathes of brightness swept out, engulfing the two riders.

Chapter 35

Nertha was veering wildly between near-panic and manic confidence. The greyness all about her seemed to be seeping into her very soul and, though no reason informed her, she knew that if she faltered, gave way to the despair that was clamouring at her, it would sweep her into oblivion. Resolutely she kept her thoughts from considerations of what had happened and what might happen. She was a physician – a healer: she must tend her four charges, here, now. They were all that mattered.

All were breathing, all had steady pulses. While this was so, all would be well, she told herself, over and over, continuing her steady, sustaining ritual of checking them.

Then Antyr's pulse began to falter.

'As you see and feel, so shall we,' Antyr said, speaking the words from long habit rather than from any clear intention.

But, he realized immediately, it was no ordinary dreamer he was addressing, nor any ordinary dream that he and Vredech had entered. When he had confronted Ivaroth and the blind man a strength had come out of depths within him that he did not know existed. From those depths came now the terrible knowledge.

'This is the dream of the dead.'

It was Vredech who voiced it.

'The long-dead,' Antyr added.

Row upon row of figures extended in every direction to an unseen horizon. They were all staring in the same direction, their faces lit by a bright and unnatural light, though no source was apparent in the black and lifeless sky. Although no one of

435

them seemed to move, a slow rippling constantly disturbed the whole and a low moaning rose and fell. It might have been a winter wind blowing across an empty and snowbound land but Antyr knew that it was not. It was the plaint of this multitude.

'How have we come here?' Vredech's question mingled with the shifting sound.

'Perhaps we should ask why we've brought ourselves here,' Antyr replied. 'We are the dreamer, we are the dead. The dead should not dream like this – joined, sharing, lingering through time so long. We will become as them if we linger, too.'

Tarrian! Grayle!

Antyr roared the names of his Earth Holders in the silence of his mind but only the song of this place echoed back to him.

'Nertha's slipping from us.' Vredech was suddenly fearful.

'Cling to her,' Antyr said urgently. 'As you love her, cling to her, like a child to its mother. And call for Tarrian and Grayle – they'll be hunting for us. You must hold us both while I seek an answer.'

He was walking among the vast crowd.

Each one he looked at seemed to be the same, yet at the edges of his vision they were all different – men, women, many ages, many races – all locked in this suffocating dream.

What had brought them to this?

He remembered Thyrn's account of the Great Searing. A brightness moving across the land – reshaping, remaking.

And in that remaking had come the flaw that had set all this in train.

It came to him that some part of the will of these people had not been remade – some part persisted past what should have been death.

And it had called to him and Vredech at a depth beyond their hearing. Whatever else might be happening, there was a need here.

Yet what was it?

Antyr felt his thoughts mingling with the sighing song. Bewilderment, anger, cries for vengeance, many things were there, but somewhere, tantalizingly, a truer meaning lured him on.

Then there was stillness, and the meaning was there.

Darker than the black sky that overarched this moving throng of unmoving people.

This was not just the dream of the long dead, it was the deep dream of those now alive. A living remnant of the ancient times that had spawned the horror that had become the Great Searing – a sink of ignorance and fear that bound all of them to that terrible past . . .

And that might draw it back.

The sound was all about him, passing over and through him. There was no mistaking its truth.

But now it held him.

And fear began to pervade him.

The ancient song was engulfing him.

Breathing heavily and still holding his stomach from the impact of catching Andawyr, Isloman clambered to his feet and moved to place himself between the approaching rider and the fallen Cadwanwr. He had taken barely two steps, however, when he was pushed violently against the walls of the passage. Though not capable of using the Power himself he recognized it immediately and knew that nothing was to be gained by trying to oppose it. He relaxed and the force holding him left him instantly.

Andawyr was opening his eyes when the rider stopped in front of him. He stiffened as he saw the angular head of the horse-creature swaying above him, malevolent eyes and twitching nostrils searching him. For an instant there was stark fear in his face. He had seen its like before, ridden by Oklar.

Like his mount, the rider too was leaning forward and staring at him.

Another champion gave Andawyr a little more time to recover.

'Who are you?' Usche demanded angrily of the rider.

Oslang reached out to stop her but it was too late. The same force that had knocked Isloman down struck her also, though being much lighter than the big carver it almost lifted her off her feet. Isloman managed to catch her and prevent what would probably have been serious injury had she struck the wall. He thrust her behind him before she had time to protest.

Ar-Billan's jaw jutted and he made to move forward but Atelon jerked him back forcefully.

The rider spoke. His voice was cold and inhuman, but its inflection was all *too* human, laden as it was with viciousness and malice.

'You have defiled the most holy of His places. The place where the Great Way will open, to bring us to Him. Punishment for this will need great and special reflection. Who are you and how did you come here?'

Andawyr tried to push himself backwards with the intention of standing but the creature brought its head closer and uttered a low growl. Andawyr wrinkled his nose in disgust as its breath wafted over him. Then, after a thoughtful pause, he punched it squarely on the muzzle.

Everyone started, not least the animal, which jerked its head back and reared slightly. The rider had obvious difficulty in preventing it from lunging at the now standing Cadwanwr.

'You'll punish no one, you obscenity.' Andawyr's voice burst through the clatter of skittering hooves. 'You'll go the way all His servants go – to some dismal doom – lost and howling.'

A hissing came from the dark figure as he finally gained control over his mount but Andawyr did not allow him to speak.

'That we're here – in His most holy of places . . .' he spat contemptuously '. . . is a measure of how flawed His plans are – how inadequate His will.'

Oslang and Atelon, badly shaken by this raucous and uncharacteristic challenge, exchanged glances both bewildered and desperate.

The hissing faded into an insect whine and the rider inclined his head slightly. Slowly, he removed his helm to reveal the thin, haggard face of an old man. It was framed with lank, lifeless hair and, though the pervasive blue light could not disguise its unhealthy pallor, it was lit with an unnatural energy. The eyes Andawyr found himself looking into were white and cloudy as though vision had fled from

438

them at the sight of some terrible truth.

The rider, like his mount, was moving his head from side to side inquiringly. The movement, both birdlike and serpentine, was repellent.

Then Andawyr let out a sigh of recognition and understanding.

'I had wondered,' he said, more quietly. 'When I heard Antyr's tale, blind man. And it *is* you. The one who tried to blind Hawklan at the Gretmearc so long ago. Oklar's sorry vassal – his miserable apprentice.' He became dismissive. 'I'd thought you dead at his hand long ago – he'd little tolerance for failure.'

The rider's hands tightened about the reins, pulling the head of his mount down until it let out a screeching whimper. Usche moved out from behind Isloman, but his arm came out to stop her going any further.

'Better he had killed you,' Andawyr pressed. 'Than that you should've fallen to this depravity. It seems you learned nothing from what I showed you.'

The blind man bent low towards him, his head thrust forward by his mount's neck, his teeth bared in a fearful rictus and his blind eyes wide and staring. 'How did you come here?' he said again with a frightening softness, his bony hand reaching towards Andawyr, claw-like.

'Ask Him,' Andawyr replied scornfully, meeting the dead gaze unflinchingly. 'Are not all things here arranged by His will?'

'With each of your blasphemies, you draw out your future torments by aeons. You have no measure either of your insignificance or of what you bring upon yourself.'

'You're premature in imagining you have power over us, apprentice,' Andawyr said, still scornful. An airy gesture indicated Oslang and Atelon, both of whom were struggling to maintain outward equanimity and to grasp their leader's seemingly reckless intention in provoking this fearful creature. 'They bound your erstwhile master's companions to await their deaths. And I was there when he himself was killed. Taken down effortlessly by an inconsequential enemy more ancient than any of us. I see a similar fate awaiting you and for all your seeming power you are not the least shadow of him.' He opened his arms as though to embrace the great building towering above them into the blue haze. 'It may be that in His failing days He has cursed you with a knowledge of the Power far beyond anything your predecessors possessed but, corrupt though they were, they were shrewd and learned in the ways of men – subtle and cunning – keen judges of their enemy. You and your fellows are less than children beside them.' He sneered.

'What we have done to this world is scarcely the work of children, old man,' the blind man snarled, very human now. 'Such a garnering of the Power has never been known.'

'It is precisely the work of children,' Andawyr replied in like vein. 'Vicious, crude, and futile – truly the work of apprentices. And it is a measure of *your* insignificance and your folly that you hurried here so quickly at our call to face your own doom. Did you think we did not know your true worth?'

Andawyr looked up at the hovering star, sneered again, then swung his hands over his head in a wide arc and brought them together in front of him. As they met there was no sound, but a blinding white light flared between them. The Cadwanwr and Isloman instinctively turned away as it spread out in an expanding sphere, cutting through the blue air and dancing black shadows about the arching confines of the wide doorway and the passage beyond. As it struck the mirrored walls so a myriad other lights sprang into life, illuminating the infinite plain and recreating themselves endlessly into distances beyond knowing. A tumbling mass of rearing steeds unseated their riders and crashed over on top of them. A host of young women dodged the arms of their protectors and surged forward, knives in hands, to dispatch the animals as only those who loved them truly could.

'Whatever it was, it used to be a horse and it's better dead, believe me,' Usche protested as Isloman frantically dragged her out of the mêlée. The air was ringing with a high-pitched shrieking that struck to the heart of its hearers. Isloman looked to Andawyr in anticipation of an order to flee but the Cadwanwr had dragged Oslang and Atelon together and was shouting something at them desperately. Usche and Ar-Billan joined him also.

Then, dark and awful against the lights still silently darting and dancing across the blue distance, the blind man was rising from the tangle of the dead creature. Isloman had been present when Oklar had revealed himself and unleashed the Power against Hawklan. The black sword had saved Hawklan but a great swathe of destruction had been cut across Vakloss. Nothing the Power touched could stand against it. And this one was even more powerful.

This is how it ends, came the thought.

And, for a time that could not be measured, he felt himself held at the finest of balances.

Resignation flowed over him, soothing, calming – a destination had been reached, a journey over time: time to lie down, to rest, to let all travails go.

Yet the scents and sounds of everything around him were washing through him, overwhelming in their intensity. At their heart was a glowing totality – a lifetime – his lifetime – leavened by many struggles and full of the joy of being. And though is was his and his alone, it was also part of a greater whole that would be diminished by its loss.

It must not end thus.

The resignation slipped from him like a soiled cloak. He prepared to face the monster who had made this awful place.

But even as this decision formed about him, the five Cadwanwr were in front of him, facing the risen Uhriel. Andawyr, Oslang and Atelon to the fore, Usche and Ar-Billan a pace behind. Isloman hesitated. He knew that what Andawyr had just done was little more than a party piece for entertaining children. It was the least of any novice's tricks. For some reason, Andawyr had engineered this confrontation, knowing that neither he nor his companions could hope to oppose such a creature.

What was he doing?

The question paralysed Isloman. Would some reckless action on his part bring a subtler plan to grief?

There was a strange pause. Everywhere was silent and the blue air was full of the crackling tension of a pending storm.

It broke.

Though the Uhriel made no arcane gestures or incantations Isloman knew that he was assailing the Cadwanwr. His white eyes were manic in the blue gloom and the five figures seemed to shimmer as their hands came up as if to protect themselves from the heat of a suddenly opened furnace or the blast of a hail-loaded wind.

Isloman felt nothing. But he knew he was of no consequence in this conflict – an ant under the churning hooves of the cavalry, surviving through chance rather than intention.

Yet he could not stand idly by.

But he had to.

Then the Cadwanwr were failing. Unaware of the nature of the conflict Isloman might be but it needed no great perception to read their postures and their expressions. And if they fell, he would be carried with them.

Every part of him cried out in denial.

He would not perish in this awful place or at the hands of this monster without doing hurt to both of them for as long as he was able.

His eye rose to the hovering star. Isloman was a gentle man, a creator of beautiful things, but circumstance had plunged him into many conflicts and he had ridden with the Goraidin as one of them. He had learned that though there were many ways to destroy an enemy, in the end it was always best to strike to his centre – swift, straight and with *every resource* committed. And Andawyr had declared this star to the centre of something – a terrible focus. Who knew what would happen if it were destroyed?

Isloman looked at the faltering Cadwanwr, locked in their silent conflict with the blind man, motionless amid the ruin of his slaughtered mount.

His hand closed around the chisel in his belt. A good piece of iron, tempered and hardened by the deep skills of his brother and worn to his own ways of working. It had unlocked many a fine carving from the waiting rock. He tossed it lightly and felt all the memories in its familiar shape and weight. Then, with a sure and unclouded confidence like that of a child, his powerful frame hurled the chisel at the star.

Across the blue-mirrored plain, still flickering with the distant remnants of Andawyr's sunburst, innumerable missiles twisted and glittered. As many Uhriel burst into black movement and stretched up to catch them.

And failed.

The chisel made a sound more felt than heard as it struck the star, but the blind man let out a cry that sent Isloman and the Cadwanwr staggering backwards.

Isloman was the first to recover. He looked at the star. It was slowly twisting and turning as though it were struggling to be free from unseen bonds. A thin bright ray of light shining from it swept about the chamber. The Uhriel was staring at it, transfixed.

Andawyr grasped Isloman's hand and pulled himself up. There was both triumph and desperate fear in his face.

'He did it,' he gasped. 'He struck the star with the Power – released it. I knew he'd no control. Get us out of here.'

'What? Where to?' Isloman exclaimed. He was dragging Oslang to his feet.

'Anywhere!'

The others needed no bidding. Usche, Ar-Billan and Atelon were supporting one another and staggering towards the passage.

They had taken barely a step when the light from the star struck the mirrored wall and the vast blue plain was instantly enmeshed in a lattice of brightness. Before they could move further, the lattice had grown and become solid, and a glaring flood swept through and over them.

As he felt himself fading, Isloman, through tightly narrowed eyes, saw the star fragment. Hovering where it had been, a wavering shadow in the terrible light, was a sword.

Then he was nothing.

Hawklan looked away from the giddying heights swaying above him. Wherever they were and however they had come there this could no longer be the Labyrinth he had known. But what was it? Surely it should be a device of Ethriss's? But might it be one of Sumeral's? Or was it a manifestation of the conjunction? Or a creation of his own mind?

To centre himself amid these doubts he touched the nearest column. A whirling confusion of voices rang through him.

'You are he? The healer? As Farnor and Thyrn?'

The voice was both many and one and was hung about with deeply unsettling resonances. It was as though behind each word lay a long and complex debate.

'We will shelter you from the return of the Great Evil.'

'Who are you?'

There was a reply, but Hawklan could not understand it. Images, dark and deep, bright and sun-dancing, burgeoning-new and ancient beyond imagining filled him. Dominant amongst them was a broad thread of fear.

'You are the Great Forest,' Hawklan said, grasping at an inspiration.

'We are.' It was a statement, not a reply.

'How can you be here?'

'Here? We do not know "here", healer. We are.'

'How do you know me?'

'*You* are. You are Mover and Hearer. You are rare. Few are with us so in this place.' The fear returned, and urgency. 'The Great Evil comes again. For Farnor we will shelter that which is your essence, until He passes once more.'

A feeling of warmth and rest enfolded Hawklan.

'Oi!'

Dar-volci was shaking his leg violently. 'This is no time to be nodding off.' His voice was loud and brutal after the subtlety of the Forest's language, but it jolted Hawklan free. There was no malice in what he had been offered, he knew, but there was error. He remembered Farnor telling him of a glimpse he had once had of the Forest's knowledge of times long gone, of what had probably been the Great Searing, and the fears that lay deep-rooted in them about that terrible change.

The Forest should know the truth. Who could say what part its ancient will might play in the unfolding events?

As he looked up, the wavering columns seemed to be both cold stone and gnarled trunks. He had a momentary vision of Ethriss binding a wounded place with a strange knowledge that he had found and that he himself did not understand, a knowledge that he suspected perhaps was older than his own. Was this where his own doubts began? In the Great Forest? Hawklan let the thought pass and extended a placating hand to Dar-volci.

'Far worse than the Great Evil returns,' he said inwardly, to the Forest.

A deep silence filled him, listening.

'Your judgement – the judgement you most feared and that you revealed to Farnor – has been sound. That which ended the time before and remade all things was indeed deeply flawed. Now a wind is coming that may uproot and scatter us all beyond any knowing. All your wisdom and knowledge, all that you are, is needed to oppose it. And that of Farnor and Thyrn.'

The silence lingered for a moment. Then, timelessly, Hawklan felt a myriad sky-turning seasons pass through him as, with a fleeting hint of both gratitude and terror, the Forest went from him.

He did not move for some time.

'Are you all right, dear boy?'

Gavor's anxious tones brought him to himself again. 'It was the Forest,' he said, attempting no explanation. 'The Forest and the Labyrinth are joined. They've taken Farnor and Thyrn to shelter them. I told them the truth.'

Dar-volci and Gavor looked at him steadily, then both said, 'Funny things, trees.'

'Still, better they know than they don't,' Dar-volci added. 'You did right.'

Hawklan was less convinced. Andawyr had judged him to be somehow pivotal in the pending events but he had only a growing sense of inadequacy and ignorance. He looked around. As before, the columns seemed to be both stone shafts and tree trunks.

But now, in one direction, it was lighter. He pointed.

'That way.'

Pinnatte's eyes were full of pain and desperation. Within the wavering lights he had created could be seen two worlds. One, alive with mingling rivers of molten rock, its wound-red sky black-streaked with choking smoke and lit by a rain of blazing stones. The other, stark and dead – a bitter landscape, so cold that the wind itself was frozen and ancient mountains had been crushed and remade into buttressing heights and frozen cascades of glittering ice.

The two Uhriel, held by the lights in the space which was of no world, struggled frantically to escape, their steeds rearing and screaming.

The Goraidin moved forward hesitantly.

'Keep away from me,' Pinnatte gasped. 'Keep away from the Gateways. I thought I could send them through, but . . . I can't . . . I'm not strong enough, I . . .' Sweat was running down his face and he was swaying. He was obviously weakening.

'What can we do?' Yatsu shouted.

'Whatever you have to if they break free,' Pinnatte managed. 'You'll have little time. I can . . .'

Then he was sinking to his knees and the Uhriel were redoubling their efforts.

The Gateways closed.

Pinnatte slumped forward.

The Goraidin needed no discussion to determine their actions and only a brief flurry of hand signals presaged their plunging forward towards the suddenly released Uhriel.

Swift and cruel sword strokes cut the throats of the two foul mounts before their riders could fully control them, while others hacked and thrust at the two Uhriel as they fell amid a confusion of flailing legs and writhing bodies. Though it was not in the nature of any of the Goraidin to murder, the ability to kill quickly and efficiently was something they took a dark pride in – it was a necessary part of their profession. They brought it to bear now, four of them setting on each of the fallen Uhriel while Marna and Gentren stood back, looking to reach Pinnatte through the fray.

But it was to no avail.

Whatever armour it was that the Uhriel wore, it withstood such blows as struck it. But, more frightening by far, though many well-placed points struck through open joints and at exposed flesh, and though wounds gaped and what might have been blood poured out, the Uhriel did not fall.

Marna felt her mouth parch and the blood drain from her face as she watched both of them rising to their feet despite a hail of attacks that would have killed a score of men. A seemingly deliberate slowness of their movements added a further horror to the sight. Her stomach was hard with a cold terror as she saw them look around at their futile attackers. Attackers on the faces of whom Marna saw open fear.

Yet they pressed their savage attacks relentlessly.

Until the Uhriel drew their own swords.

Devices of strange vanity for such powerful creatures, they were long and bright, and they shimmered and sang like the Uhriel themselves as they cut through the blue light. Then the roles of the fighters were reversed as the two moved against the many. The swords, moving from hand to hand and swinging in wide and unexpectedly swift arcs, forced the Goraidin out into a defensive circle. Injured though they had been by the Goraidin's assault, any hurt done to the Uhriel had not been sufficient to still their intent. Bleeding and ghastly, they moved towards Pinnatte whom Marna and Gentren had finally managed to drag to comparative safety.

Marna looked at Pinnatte, now barely conscious, and understood.

'He's still binding them somehow!' she shouted. 'That's why they can't use the Power. Kill them! Kill them now, while you can! Quickly!'

She drew her own sword and stood in front of Pinnatte, as did Gentren. The air was ringing with the high screeching of the Uhriel and the dreadful sound of their whirling swords. Yrain attempted to parry a scything blow from Dowinne but the impact tore her blade from her grasp and sent it spinning high into the air. Only long-sharpened reflexes took her backwards quickly enough to avoid Dowinne's shrilling point. As it was, it slashed through the slack of her tunic. The gash became blue and crystalline. Yengar and Jaldaric lost their swords similarly whilst Tirke's was shattered and his arm numbed into uselessness. There was a momentary lull, then knives were drawn and the Goraidin were rushing into the backwash of the swinging swords to attack their foes. But, stripped through they might have been of the Power, the Uhriel were still oblivious of the wounds they were receiving and were also possessed of great physical strength. One by one, the Goraidin were hurled back across the rock terrain.

Then the Uhriel were at Pinnatte, the Goraidin exhausted and broken, scattered about them. Dowinne's sword swung in a broad, singing arc over them, while Rannick faced Gentren and Marna, his whitened eyes and blasted face alive with hatred.

Marna stared back at him with an expression that was little better, though she tried to look through what he had become to what he had been before they had both been drawn into this nightmare – vicious and cruel, but still human, still vulnerable. But there was nothing there, no weakness in him to wring out pity in her. Teeth bared like a cornered animal, she tightened her grip on her sword and held it high.

Rannick paused momentarily, his head inclined as though he were listening to something. Then, as she struck at him, his arm swung up dismissively and knocked her off her feet. She landed several paces away. Gentren replaced her, crouching low and as determined as he was terrified. He met the same fate.

Rannock looked down at Pinnatte for a moment, a dreadful smile lighting his dead face. He raised his sword.

'No!'

It was Olvric. The Goraidin, grim-faced and bloodstained and with a bone protruding from a useless arm, was levering himself up on his sword. Dowinne could have struck him, but she hesitated, as did Rannick. For a frozen moment, it seemed as if the ground beneath their feet was coming alive, as those Goraidin who were still conscious struggled to follow Olvric's lead.

Doomed they might be, but not defeated.

And in that moment none saw a brightness on the horizon.

A brightness that was not the sign of a coming dawn.

They saw it only as it swept over them.

Chapter 36

Desperately, Nertha bent close to Antyr, first listening for his breathing, then offering her cheek. But she could feel nothing. She checked his pulse. It was still there, more distant than weak. She had never felt anything like it before.

A bizarre mixture of fear and professional pride wrapped about one another and became a deep anger.

She swore. 'I will not lose you to this – whatever it is. I will *not* lose you!'

Her face grim with determination, she quickly checked the others. Lying on their sides like sleeping children, as she had placed them, they were unchanged. She lingered briefly, running a loving hand down her husband's cheek, then she rolled Antyr on to his back and, holding his nose and arching his neck, placed her mouth over his.

His chest rose as she blew, then sank as she stopped. Still she counted as she worked, periodically checking his pulse and the condition of the others. After a while, she began to intersperse her counting with profanity and an aching inner cry for help.

'*Tarrian, Grayle! Tarrian, Grayle!*'

'Tarrian, Grayle!' Antyr cried out. 'To me!'

But no sound came, other than the dreamsong of the dead in the living.

Vredech's voice reached through it, like a distant sound carried on the wind.

'No one can help us here, Antyr. This is *our* burden.'

Anger from the song leaked into Antyr. 'Your faith tells you this, Priest?' he cried.

449

The reply was unexpected.

'Yes. Faith in you, Dream Finder. That and the hold I have both on Nertha and on you . . . just.'

But . . .?'

'This is what I do here, Antyr, and what I will do, while I can.'

Antyr felt the song drifting over him again.

'But why am I here?' he managed.

'What are you?'

What am I?

Dream Finder. Adept. Warrior of the White Way.

Words. Only words. To hide as much as to reveal.

He was Antyr, son of Petran, flawed and frightened, blundering and ignorant in a place where no one should be. He was no different from the endless rows of figures stretching away from him in every direction, their faces lit by the unseen light that had unmade them and that had bound them to this time.

He did not know what to do.

But flawed and frightened as he was, blundering and ignorant as he was, he was also the Antyr who had faced Ivaroth in mortal combat and the terrible power of the blind man.

He could not do nothing.

He looked into the unseeing eyes of the nearest figure.

'Turn away from this fearful glare,' he said. 'You hold the living to your time. Your pain is the source of Sumeral's strength here. Release them, and be free. Turn to the light that reveals, turn to the truth.'

He placed his hand over the figure's face and, for a timeless moment, as with his Earth Holder, he was it and it was he, knowing all that he knew and was.

The figure closed its eyes.

He passed to the next.

And the next.

Faintly he could hear Vredech calling.

'I can't hold you, Antyr, I can't hold you.'

He moved on.

Antyr's heart stopped.

Nertha searched for its beat frantically. Her profanity

450

worsened. She tore open the neck of her tunic so that she could breathe more easily. Both sweat and tears ran down her face.

Fingers entwined, she began pressing Antyr's chest rhythmically. Counting, swearing, and calling openly now on Tarrian and Grayle.

Then they were there. Eyes like wild suns. Deep-throated growling like the sound of tumbling rocks and pitiless killing teeth bared white in the greyness.

Her every instinct told her to flee, but her will denied them. She met Tarrian's awful gaze with one of her own and bared her teeth into his slavering maw.

'This is my domain,' she snarled. 'Find them in yours. Find them both. Bring them back.'

Gavor flapped his wings.

The Labyrinth, its columns becoming ever more like roots and trunks, twisting and tangling up into unseen heights, was becoming steadily brighter. With the increasing light came also sound, and a breeze.

It was no pleasant zephyr, however. There was a harshness in it that made Hawklan turn his face away. Nor was the sound kinder. Shattering glass, wind-torn roots and yielding timbers, the screams of midnight prey and battle-wounded, all were there, and more.

Hawklan looked up.

Above him was a foaming vortex, dark and ominous, like the mingling of countless broken worlds. As he stared at it, he could not tell whether the columns of the Labyrinth reached up to it, or hung down from it like searching, twisting tentacles.

Then they were out of the Labyrinth. In front of them, the ground ended abruptly. Hawklan stepped forward carefully, to find himself at the edge of a plunging height. It dropped sheer, into a depth he dared not see. He took in a throat-closing breath and stepped back unsteadily.

Normally Dar-volci and Gavor relished taunting him for his fear of heights, but they were silent.

Looking about him, Hawklan saw that he was at the edge of a great pit.

At its centre was a vast tapering column and, to his right, was a slender bridge spanning across to it. At the end of the bridge stood a familiar figure.

He ran towards it.

Gulda pushed her hood back when he reached her. She held up a finger before he could speak.

'I've no answers, Hawklan,' she said, her bright eyes pained and her hand opening and closing about her stick. 'Many threads are coming together and I am drawn here by one of His weaving.' She looked at him significantly. 'As you know. I dare not trust myself to act, but you must. Trust yourself.'

'But . . .'

She stepped to one side and pointed her stick along what Hawklan had taken for a bridge. It was scarcely a pace wide. The breeze had become a wind and it was growing stronger.

'You have done well. Your transformation of the world where the Sword fell, imperfect though it was, has opened the Great Way and brought you to Me.'

'Our hurts are made whole by Your Praise, Great Lord. With our Power and Your wisdom we will release You and sweep Ethriss's folly away.'

Gory heads bowed and gashes leaking, the Uhriel were kneeling. Without looking up, the blind man held out his hands. Resting on them was the black sword.

A hand closed about its hilt.

'Your Power will indeed cleanse this place. I accept it. Accept now My wisdom.'

A single stroke severed all three heads.

'I can't walk along that,' Hawklan said, his eyes wide with fear.

Gulda did not answer but lowered her stick and resumed her silent vigil. There was neither reproach nor encouragement in her manner.

'Out of words, dear boy,' Gavor said. 'But I'll stay with you.'

'And me,' Dar-volci said.

It was difficult to hear them: the wind was growing stronger and the noise from above louder. Hawklan looked up again. The vortex was lower. It was a fearful sight, grim and vast. He glanced once more at the motionless figure of Gulda, head bowed now, then at the narrow pathway ahead of him.

At the far end, suffusing the top of the isolated column, was a bright light.

'Great mercy, I'm afraid,' he said, his voice trembling.

Then, with a deep breath, he walked onto the narrow span, the wind tugging and buffeting him. Gavor spread his wings and floated off Hawklan's shoulder as the healer pressed on uncertainly, shoulders high with tension. Hawklan struggled to keep his gaze fixed resolutely in the distance, but it was drawn inexorably downwards. His legs were shaking so violently that he could scarcely control them, but he was a long way from the beginning when he stopped.

The depths on either side tempted him.

'One step at a time,' Dar-volci said.

'I need to rest a moment,' Hawklan said, breathing heavily. 'This wind, this noise . . .'

He crouched to make himself less vulnerable to the tugging of the wind.

Then he was on all fours, scarcely able to move.

'I don't think you have a moment,' Dar-volci said, shaking him gently.

Hawklan looked up. A light was moving towards him along the bridge. For a moment his fear threatened to become outright panic but as it surged to a peak, so it was transformed into cold anger and battle-readiness. His legs were still trembling – his whole body was trembling – but the movement was familiar and he knew it for what it was: ancient reflexes releasing him to fight.

He stood up.

The light drew nearer.

Hawklan began walking towards it as steadily as he could. The wind was continuing to grow stronger and the noise from the turbulent sky louder. Violent, roiling and shot with lightnings and endlessly shifting colours, it was still descending. Whatever it was, there could be little doubt that nothing would survive its touch.

Wings reaching into the ways of the wind to keep his flight steady, Gavor suddenly soared above him, a black and sharp-edged silhouette stark and clear against the confusion.

Hawklan looked back along the bridge. Gulda was still there, though he could see her only indistinctly. He turned back to the approaching light.

It was nearer now.

And he felt again the presence he had felt as he had trekked across Narsindal to stand before the mist-shrouded castle of Derras Ustramel.

Sumeral had been given form again.

Hawklan moved forward. He was alone, unarmed, racked by the tearing wind and menaced by the siren call of the abyss beneath him, but he knew he must stand against this abomination. Futile it might seem but even as the thought came to him he could hear Andawyr proclaiming that he should not under-estimate the effects of the smallest action.

'You are smiling.'

The cold words formed within him as they had when he had heard them on the causeway across Lake Kedrieth.

Hawklan straightened and gazed into the light. It was barely five paces away from him. There was the hint of a figure at its heart. He did not reply.

'Ethriss's creations were ever flawed. Smiling in the face of their destruction.'

Still Hawklan did not speak.

'You have no questions? No plea to make – for his sorry world – for yourself? You, who could have been the greatest of My Uhriel – My chosen.'

Silence.

Hawklan opened his arms in a gesture that might have been acceptance or welcome. He looked up at the vortex.

'This is the dance of My new creation – the wiping away of all things so that perfection can be made.'

Hawklan shook his head. 'This will indeed sweep all things away – but it is not Your creation. The folly that brought it about created You also – the essence of all that is foul in humanity, unfettered and given form by cruel chance. This You must know, as Ethriss did. Prepare yourself for oblivion.'

He turned.

The bridge behind him was fading into greyness, but he felt no fear at the sight.

'There is nowhere for You in this time. Whatever bound You here – sustained You – is passing on, free now. The Guardians too passed on when they realized the truth of their nature: so now will You.'

The brightness faltered momentarily and though the howling of the wind and the rumbling of the vortex filled everywhere, Hawklan felt only a long silence.

'You would have been a fine servant, Hawklan. Your treachery and guile are worthy of My favour. But I have been bound here too long. I will honour you as I honoured My Uhriel. With the key that will unlock Ethriss's cursed Labyrinth.'

Hawklan stepped back and the point of the black sword passed in front of him as it cut a singing horizontal arc out of the brightness.

'That is my Sword,' he said. 'It comes from the heart of whatever brought this upon us. Made by Ethriss when his doubts began, in the faith that it would protect us.' He opened his arms again. 'If You would be free, give it to me and perhaps I will have the knowledge that can truly end this.'

Two further steps back saved him from the diagonal cuts that came by way of reply.

'It is my Sword,' he said again. 'You cannot use it. It will doom you.'

'Take My merciful thrust or avoid it again and step into the nothingness at your back.'

Hawklan turned his head slightly. At the edge of his vision was greyness. He could go no further.

He was aware of Dar-volci at his feet, of the vortex closer than ever, chaotic and wild, of the wind tugging at him and of Gavor struggling with it. And, not least, he was aware of the point of the black sword little more than a hand-span in front of his throat.

There was great clarity.

He was moving to one side of the blade as it was moving forward. His right hand was clutching the hilt of the Sword, while his left, opened wide, was extending into the brightness as he turned towards it.

Then it was gone, With a cry that pierced the roaring of the vortex, the figure was tumbling into the abyss, flaring like a falling star. As it guttered out, Hawklan was standing with his arms open, as though to embrace the whole world.

And clutching the black Sword.

That it *was* his he had no doubt. There was a completeness to him that he had not known since he had lost it. Yet no new knowledge came with it. Sumeral, the evil that had destroyed Gentren's world and plagued this one through aeons, was gone – but still destruction threatened.

He looked at Dar-volci and Gavor in desperation.

Gavor flapped in front of him, hovering briefly, before the wind tore him away.

'Strike to the centre, warrior,' he cried out.

Then Hawklan was running along the narrow bridge, the wind pounding him, grey emptiness at his back and the vortex ever closer above him, its roar rising in pitch until it became a screaming that threatened to rend him apart.

As he reached the place that had been the centre of the abyss, the turmoil began to worsen with each step he took until it was only his will that sustained him.

'I will not yield,' he shouted into the mayhem.

'*Nor need you, for you will be Mine soon enough.*'

Hawklan cried out as the cold voice filled him again.

In front of him were a myriad facets. In each could be seen the whirling vortex.

Save in one.

In that was only his own image, watching him with cold amusement.

'*Did you think I would be so foolish as to face My chosen with his own Sword? That was but My shadow you destroyed – a faltering echo in your world sent to bring you to Me with the Sword.*'

'To end you finally.'

'*No. To free Me.*'

Hawklan's grip tightened about the Sword grimly and he urged himself forward. But he could not move against the wind, so powerful had it become.

'No. It is beyond even you to take this last step. It tran-
scends the ability of any man. You are bound where you are by
what you are. Only the Sword and that part of you which is
truly Mine will be drawn to Me when the final joining comes.
And as it returns, so shall I be made truly whole, and so shall
I come in glory to the remaking of My heartworld.'

Despair racked Hawklan. He raised the Sword to strike but
all strength had left him. He was helpless. The vortex roared
triumphantly, bloody and dark, all about him.

'I will not yield,' he cried again, though he could not hear
his own voice and his heart was bursting.

Then, a whistling, high, loud and needle-clear, pierced the
clamour, and a pulsing, pounding rhythm shook it. Hawklan
recognized the call of Dar-volci and the urgent beating of
Gavor's wings. But they could do nothing now. He tried to set
the distracting sounds aside.

Then he listened to them.

And surrendered to them.

As he did so, the hunting spirits of Tarrian and Grayle,
feral, ancient and terrible, surged through him, releasing him,
carrying him to where he could not go alone.

The Sword severed the mocking image from top to bottom.

Chapter 37

L oman and Endryk were silent company for one another.
That they had the blessings of their friends, that they
were doing only what they could do, was poor consolation for
both of them.

That the day was fine and clear deepened their inner
darkness.

Something flickered.

They both started and their horses whinnied and skittered.

'Was that lightning?' Endryk asked, as he steadied his
horse.

They both gazed round at the clear blue sky.

Loman reined to a halt and raised his head as though he
were scenting something.

He grasped Endryk's arm and shook him roughly.

'It's over,' he exclaimed. 'It's over.'

Without pausing to debate the point, he turned his horse
about and began galloping back towards Anderras Darion.

Thyrn and Farnor opened their eyes.

All about them they could feel gashes and rents torn into
the reality of their world. But the wound that had overwhelmed them, that the Great Forest had reached out and
snatched them from, was gone.

Touched by the deep knowledge of the Great Forest, they
understood now their own quiet gifts. Reaching into the pain,
they healed, making good the hurts, sealing away for ever
those places that should not have been there.

The greyness faded from the Labyrinth hall, and all was as
it had been, save that all present were exhausted and drained,

and, in the case of the Goraidin, injured.

Nertha was embracing both her husband and Antyr, who was patting his chest ruefully. Tarrian and Grayle were shaking themselves and scratching.

Only Gulda was gone.

As was the Power.

Andawyr and Usche stood by the stream in front of Anderras Darion. It was early evening. Usche looked down at her hands.

'What shall we do, now we can't use the Power?' she asked.

'What we've always done,' Andawyr replied. 'Learn, teach. We must spread our learning further. Sumeral may be gone but we've learned from Antyr and the others that there's more than enough ignorance out there to feed our darker natures. He may not return, but the folly that made Him will always be there. There are plenty of places that need the light shining into them.'

'But without the Power . . .'

Andawyr dashed the objection aside casually, though there was a harsh edge to his voice.

'The likes of the Kyrosdyn don't have it either, girl. Be glad of that.' He softened, 'Besides, when did you last use it, other than in training?'

Usche shrugged, then shuddered. 'Except in that awful place, I don't know. You were always very sniffy about us using it for odd jobs.'

Andawyr made to put a comforting arm about her shoulders, then changed his mind and rubbed his nose.

'Yes, and rightly so too, it seems. It was a dangerous thing. Looking back, I can see we were riding an avalanche. It was an instability deep at the heart of things that made it possible and even if that hadn't threatened us, it gave us power that was beyond our ability to use responsibly.'

'I think you misjudge us.'

'Possibly, but I doubt it. Easy ways always seem to be treacherous. There's something about true learning, true progress, that demands effort – a painstaking turning of disorder into order – the common condition to the rare. On a good day, we move three steps forward and two back – five steps to make one. You know that.'

Andawyr looked up at the ramping towers and spires of the castle, then down at Pedhavin, thronged with people attending a festival of carvings.

'Look: stone upon stone, chisel stroke after chisel stroke. Thought upon thought. The effort lingers and informs those yet to come – tells them that, while our names and memories may be forgotten, we're the same as them and we offer them a foothold to climb even higher.'

'Climb to where?'

Andawyr laughed. 'Ah, you know that only children are supposed to ask questions like that, don't you? We'll find out when we get there.'

'Yes,' Usche said dubiously. 'You've told me often enough. We're just the universe's way of discovering itself. I suppose we'll understand when the last star blinks out.'

Andawyr clicked his tongue mockingly. 'You've been too long looking inwards, my dear. When we get back to the Cadwanen you must start looking outwards a little more – look carefully enough and you'll see a distinct hint of blue in the stars.'

He laughed again. It was a joyous sound in the soft evening.

Usche smiled and turned towards the setting sun. The Orthlundyn landscape was awash with its bright light. It turned the castle into a glittering beacon and, as it moved through the streets of Pedhavin, it drew applause and cries of approval and wonder as the many carvings responded to its subtle touch.

'Beautiful,' she said. 'It's beautiful.'

She sat down on the soft grass at the edge of the stream and let her hand play idly in the water.

And So . . .

Though what had happened became widely known and was much discussed and theorized about amongst the Cadwanwr and other inquirers, it never became a matter of legend and fireside telling. It was too strange. Sumeral and His army had been conspicuously and bravely defeated sixteen or so years before: that was enough for such tales.

Both the Cadwanol and Anderras Darion became centres of great learning, attracting scholars from many distant lands and sending forth its own. The Fyordyn, the Riddinvolk and the Orthlundyn continued in their ways, though, having heard about the homelands of Antyr and the others, they became even more appreciative of what they had. And protective. Their hearths remained ever open to strangers, though no house was without its Threshold Sword, sharp and bright, hanging behind the door.

Farnor and Thyrn, with the guidance of Hawklan and Nertha, became healers. They returned many times to their old homes. Antyr and Vredech too followed their strange profession, bringing help and solace to those whose troubles were not wholly of the body.

Tarrian and Grayle helped them, too. And roamed the mountains, singing to the Alphraan.

Gentren became a carver under Isloman's tutelage. He was ever genial, but his eyes were sometimes distant and haunted, and his work was often strange, desolate and disturbing.

Pinnatte spent his days studying in the library of Anderras Darion and working in the fields around Pedhavin. He was at peace with himself and though he remained hesitant in his speech it was no burden. When he spoke, people listened.

The Goraidin were all nursed back to health, though it was no light healing and all of them bore the scars of their terrible conflict. Marna became one of them and, with them, an instructor of those similarly inclined. They maintained a discreet and continual watch on the bounds of the three lands.

Dar-volci continued as Andawyr's nemesis, constantly reminding him of the felcis' responsibility for humanity.

Gavor remained Gavor.

Hawklan wandered, healing, teaching, laughing a lot, though some thought there was a loneliness in him.

He was lying idly in the shade of a broad-canopied tree one day when a shadow fell on his face. He looked up to see a tall figure silhouetted against the white-flecked sky. As he clambered to his feet, Gavor, perched on his toe, fell off amid a confusion of flapping wings and bad language.

The stranger was a tall woman with piercing blue eyes and hair as black as Gavor's plumage. She had a strong face and a commanding manner, and was beautiful.

Hawklan looked at her for a long time before he spoke.

'I didn't recognize you,' he said eventually. His voice was hoarse. 'I'd thought you gone — lost for ever.'

The woman smiled archly and put her arm through his. Leading him back to the road, she said, 'Since things have . . . changed . . . I'm not the woman I was, without a doubt, but I'm no slight thing to be lost so easily. And as age is setting in now — for both of us — I'm even less inclined to dither about what I want than I was before.' She tightened her grip on his arm. 'You'll be needing a companion in your wanderings, won't you?'

And companions they became. They both laughed a lot.

Gavor, ever the hedonist, was immensely amused and for a long time could only soar high into the blue sky and chuckle darkly, 'Dear boy, dear boy.'

After a while, their journeyings brought them back to

Anderras Darion where they married. In the Fyordyn tradition, the ceremony was held in the ninth hour.

★ ★ ★

'The time of Hawklan is so far in the future that it could be the distant past.'

NAMES AND PLACES

Ailad	See *Imorren*.
Alphraan	Sound Carvers. A race that lives beneath the mountains, generally shunning human contact. They have a deep knowledge of and strange skills in the use of sound.
Andawyr	Leader of the Cadwanol. Accompanied Hawklan on his journey to Derras Ustramel.
Andeeren Marsyn	Father of Gentren Marson.
Anderras Darion	Hawklan's castle. Originally built by the Orthlundyn at the time of the First Coming, it was transformed by Ethriss following the battle in which many of the Orthlundyn were lost.
Antyr	An Adept Dream Finder from Serenstad, one of the city-states ruled by Duke Ibris across the sea to the east of Riddin.
Arash-Felloren	Vast city south of Orthlund. Originally one of Sumeral's citadels.
Ar-Billan	A Cadwanwr.
Atelon	A Cadwanwr who befriended Pinnatte in Arash-Felloren. One of those who protected the army in Narsindal against the power of the Uhriel.
Arvenstaat	A land north of Gyronlandt. Home of Thyrn.
Blind Man	Demented acolyte of Oklar who wandered overland to come to Ivaroth's land.

Caddoran	Member of an Order of Messengers in Arvenstaat. Noted for their memory retention and mimicry skills. Probably once battlefield messengers.
Cadwanol	Order of learned men and women formed by Ethriss at the time of Sumeral's First Coming to help in opposing Him.
Cadwanwr	A member (Brother) of the Cadwanol.
Cadwanen	The caves housing the Cadwanol.
Canol Madreth	Small state in Gyronlandt, far to the south of Orthlund.
Cassraw	Preaching Brother in the church of Ishrythan. An untrained Dream Finder, he was touched by Sumeral who was attempting to return and began subverting the Church of Ishrythan into a dark fundamentalist sect. Married to Dowinne.
Companion	See *Dream Finder*.
Creost	See *Uhriel*.
Crystals	Mined in the Thlosgaral. Origin unknown. They are used to manipulate the Power.
Dacu	Goraidin. Accompanied Hawklan on his journey to Derras Ustramel.
Dar-Hastuin	See *Uhriel*.
Dar-volci	A felci. Accompanied Hawklan on his journey to Derras Ustramel.
Derras Ustramel	See *Sumeral*.
Dowinne	Cassraw's wife. Like him, she was touched by Sumeral as He attempted to return.
Dream Finder	An individual capable of entering the dreams of others. An Adept can move into the worlds that exist between the worlds.
Earth Holder	A Dream Finder's Companion, usually an animal. Guides and protects the Dream Finder in this world and the dreamways.
Eirthlund	Land to the west of Orthlund.

Enartion	See *Guardians*.
Endryk	Fyordyn High Guard who befriended Thyrn on his flight from Vashnar.
Ethriss	A Guardian. The First Comer from the Great Searing. Perceived as the creator of all living things. Slain by Sumeral at the end of the Last Battle of the First Coming.
Farnor Yarrance	Farmer's son. His parents were killed by Rannick. Fleeing to the Great Forest, he was befriended by the Valderen and learned that he was a Hearer.
Felci	Brown, sinuous, rock-dwelling creatures. They regard people as a lesser species that they have to keep an eye on. Full of mischief and laughter but extremely fierce fighters when needed.
First Coming	A prolonged and brutal time when Sumeral first sought to take possession of the world.
Fyorlund	Land south of Narsindal and north of Orthlund and Riddin. A benign monarchy/democracy ruled by Queen Sylvriss and the Geadrol, a conclave of Lords.
Gavor	A raven. Hawklan's companion.
Geadrol	The Fyordyn Council of Lords, the formal assembly of government. Painstaking, rational and ordered in character.
Gentren Marson	Survivor from a world destroyed by the Uhriel.
Ghreel	Landlord of The Wyndering.
Goraidin	A force of elite Fyordyn High Guards used for deep-penetration and reconnaissance work.
Grayle	Wolf, brother of Tarrian, Earth Holder to Antyr.

Great Forest	Properly the community of all trees but usually taken to mean their Most Ancient, who lie to the west of Eirthlund.
Great Searing	A time of great heat, or light, when it was thought that all things began.
Gretmearc	Large, self-sustaining market community in the north-west of Riddin.
Guardians	Shapers of the world who emerged from the Great Searing. Enartion with power over water, Theowart with power over earth, Sphaeera with power over the air, and Ethriss, the First Comer, the creator of all living things.
Gulda	See *Memsa Gulda*.
Hawklan	Once an Orthlundyn prince, translated from the time of the First Coming. Now a healer and warrior.
Hearer	Someone who can hear and speak to the Great Forest.
Helyadin	An Orthlundyn elite force similar to the Goraidin. Disbanded after the war.
Ibris (Duke)	See *Antyr*.
Imorren	Leader (Ailad) of the Kyrosdyn. An acolyte probably personally instructed by Sumeral.
Isloman	Orthlundyn. Older brother of Loman. Pedhavin's First Carver. Accompanied Hawklan on his journey to Derras Ustramel.
Ivaroth	Untrained Adept Dream Finder. Controlled by the Blind Man, he became a great tribal leader and attacked Duke Ibris's land.
Jaldaric	Goraidin. Son of Lord Eldric. Accompanied Hawklan on his journey to Derras Ustramel.
Jenna	Goraidin. Originally Helyadin. Accompanied Hawklan on his journey to Derras Ustramel.

Kristabell	A felci.
Kryosdyn	Notionally crystal workers but in reality students of the Power and its manipulation through the use of crystals.
Lake Kedrieth	See *Sumeral*.
Loman	Orthlundyn. Castellan of Anderras Darion. A smith. Younger brother to Isloman. Commanded the army that faced Sumeral's army in Narsindal.
Marken	A Valderen Hearer.
Marna	A friend of Farnor.
Memsa Gulda	Memsa Gulda.
Muster	The mounted gathering of the Riddinvolk.
Narsindal	Blighted land to the north of Fyorlund. Sumeral's fastness.
Nertha	Vredech's wife. A physician.
Nilsson	Leader of the fugitives from the war who occupied Farnor's valley.
Oklar	See *Uhriel*.
Olvric	Goraidin. Faced the Uhriel in the battle in Narsindal.
Orthlund	Land to the south of Fyorlund and west of Riddin. The Orthlundyn are the descendants of a great race that opposed Sumeral in the First Coming. Mainly farmers now, their obsession is stone carving, but their original character returned when Sumeral returned and they raised a powerful army.
Oslang	Under-leader of the Cadwanol. One of those who protected the army in Narsindal against the power of the Uhriel.
Pedhavin	Orthlundyn village beneath Anderras Darion.
Pinnatte	Street thief from Arash-Felloren. Used in an experiment by the Kyrosdyn to serve as a vessel for Sumeral.

Power	(Sometime, the Old Power.) Originally presumed to be a residual feature of the Great Searing but latterly seen as a phenomenon that underlies all things. Can be used with great skill by some, but improperly understood.
Rannick	Farm labourer. His innate ability to use the Power became corrupted when he made contact with a Sierwolf.
Rgoric	Late King of Fyorlund.
Riddin	Land to the south of Fyorlund and east of Orthlund. Its society is built around the Riddinvolk's love of horses.
Second Coming	The return of Sumeral, recounted in the Chronicles of Hawklan.
Serenstad	See *Antyr*.
Sierwolf	Ancient wolf-like animals created by Sumeral. Powerful and frightening, they feed off the fear of the victims they are destroying. Thought to be extinct but some survive in deep regions beneath the earth.
Sphaeera	See *Guardians*.
Sumeral	The Great Enemy of all the works of the Guardians. He came from the Great Searing after them, with other, lesser creatures at His heels. Variously known as The Enemy of Life, The Corrupter, The Timeless One. Apparently destroyed in the Last Battle of the First Coming, but emerged again to rebuild His fortress, Derras Ustramel in the middle of Lake Kedrieth in Narsindal. Destroyed again at the end of the Chronicles of Hawklan.
Sylvriss	Queen of Fyorlund, widow of Rgoric.
Tarrian	Wolf Brother of Grayle, Earth Holder to Antyr.
Theowart	See *Guardians*.

Thlosgaral	Barren, unstable desert region to the east of Arash-Felloren, the only known source of crystals.
Thyrn	Young Caddoran to Vashnar.
Tirke	Goraidin. Accompanied Hawklan on his journey to Derras Ustramel.
Traveller	Possibly part-human, part-Alphraan – helped Thyrn in his flight from Vashnar.
Uhriel	Sumeral's lieutenants. Mortal men corrupted by Him and vested with some part of His power at the time of the First Coming to oppose the Guardians. Creost, with power over water, Oklar, with power over earth, Dar-Hastuin with power over air.
Urthryn	Ffyrst of Riddin (first amongst equals), father to Sylvriss.
Usche	A Cadwanwr.
Valderen	Tree-dwelling people of the Great Forest. Sheltered and aided Farnor.
Vashnar	Chief Warden of Arvenstaat. Possessed by a power from an unknown time.
Vredech (Allyn)	Preaching Brother in the Church of Ishrythan in Canol Madreth. Married to Nertha. An untrained Dream Finder, he found himself locked in combat with his friend and fellow Preaching Brother, Cassraw.
Whistler	A figure who appeared to Vredech in his struggle with Cassraw.
Wyndering	A crossroads inn in the east of Arash-Felloren.
Yatsu	Goraidin. Accompanied Hawklan on his journey to Derras Ustramel.
Yengar	Goraidin. Faced the Uhriel in the battle in Narsindal.
Yrain	Goraidin. Originally Helyadin. Accompanied Hawklan on his journey to Derras Ustramel.